Dead Time

STEPHEN WHITE

DEAD TIME

DUTTON

DUTTON
Published by Penguin Group (USA) Inc.
375 Hudson Street, New York, New York 10014, U.S.A.
Penguin Group (Canada), 90 Eglinton Avenue East, Suite 700, Toronto, Ontario M4P 2Y3, Canada (a
division of Pearson Penguin Canada Inc.); Penguin Books Ltd, 80 Strand, London WC2R 0RL, England;
Penguin Ireland, 25 St Stephen's Green, Dublin 2, Ireland (a division of Penguin Books Ltd); Penguin
Group (Australia), 250 Camberwell Road, Camberwell, Victoria 3124, Australia (a division of Pearson
Australia Group Pty Ltd); Penguin Books India Pvt Ltd, 11 Community Centre, Panchsheel Park, New
Delhi – 110 017, India; Penguin Group (NZ), 67 Apollo Drive, Rosedale, North Shore 0632, New
Zealand (a division of Pearson New Zealand Ltd); Penguin Books (South Africa) (Pty) Ltd, 24 Sturdee
Avenue, Rosebank, Johannesburg 2196, South Africa

Penguin Books Ltd, Registered Offices: 80 Strand, London WC2R 0RL, England

Published by Dutton, a member of Penguin Group (USA) Inc.

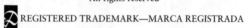

REGISTERED TRADEMARK—MARCA REGISTRADA

ISBN 978-0-525-95006-6

Printed in the United States of America
Set in Sabon
Designed by Leonard Telesca

PUBLISHER'S NOTE
This book is a work of fiction. Names, characters, places, and incidents either are the product of the
author's imagination or are used fictitiously, and any resemblance to actual persons, living or dead, business establishments, events, or locales is entirely coincidental.

to Brian Tart

Dead Time

Brothers and sisters I have none,
but this man's father is my father's son.

—Anonymous

One

The Canyon

She disappeared into a crack in the earth.

Locals had nicknamed the culprit the "polygamist high."

Even lifetime residents of the rim—people who bragged under their breath that they'd seen it all, twice—were complaining about the heat.

For the four days since a ridge of high pressure had stalled on a line that ended above the Utah–Arizona border just a little bit west of Colorado City and Hildale, the Grand Canyon had been cooking. With the atmospheric barrier in place, the natural inclination of the monsoonal flow to migrate up from the southern gulfs was bowing to the laws of physics and veering to the northwest.

The arid farmlands in California's Central Valley welcomed the bounty. But the coveted clouds and refreshing rain avoided western Arizona and the twin visitors' centers on the north and south rims of the Grand Canyon like relatives trying to steer clear of an alcoholic aunt during a family picnic.

Even the most silver-haired of the canyon old-timers stared at thermometers in awe. They'd tap at the instruments with their fingertips, as though they expected to jar loose the indicator arrows and change the readings that were causing them to blink and rub their dry eyes in disbelief.

The heat mocked them. Throaty sighs became their theme song.

Anything above 110 is pathetically hot. Near 120? At the rim of the Grand Canyon? Every day?

Thermal sedation.

What to do? Shake your head and pray the motion generates a breeze. Remind yourself that for your neighbor's kid in Baghdad, 118 is just an average summer day.

National Park staff had set up betting pools to predict the next time a daytime high would sink below 110 degrees and the next time that overnight lows would drop below the century mark.

The optimists were losing money.

Advice was free, and anyone planning a descent to the canyon floor and the banks of the Colorado River that August got plenty.

"Don't. Ain't worth it."

"Reschedule. Come back in October."

"You kidding me?"

There were empty beds at Phantom Ranch on the canyon floor. Hikers who were scheduled to go down to the river during the heat wave on the Bright Angel Trail—that's the one without fresh water available for hikers—were backing out. Most had been sitting on their treasured reservations—rustic cabin or dormitory beds, 4,000 feet below the rim, a pleasant walk from the Colorado River—for an entire year.

No one could remember the last time there had been so many cancellations.

On the Friday morning that marked six days in the grip of the obstinate high, a group of vacationers were leaving their cabin and preparing to climb to the north rim. One part of the group was a couple from Santa Monica in their midtwenties. The other part was comprised of four single friends—two women and a man who attended Occidental College in Los Angeles, and the guy's high school friend from their hometown in Orange County.

The two groups had hiked down to the river as strangers on successive days earlier in the week.

The couple's arrival in northern Arizona had coincided with the advent of the high pressure. The four singles hiked down from the rim to the floor a day later, during the first blush of the infernal heat. Once the six had arrived at the bottom of the canyon and discovered that because of a reservation mix-up they were sharing an eight-bunk cabin, they began connecting as friends. After a hot holiday spent swimming and hiking and swimming and eating and partying and swimming together, they were preparing to hike back to the rim together.

All were packed and fed and hydrated and as ready as they could be to hit the daunting North Kaibab Trail back out of the canyon the moment that breakfast was done and first light yawned that Friday morning. During the previous evening's supper they'd agreed to leave as early as possible in an attempt to minimize their exposure to the solar salamander that promised to broil them as soon as the sun arced overhead. Had there been sufficient moonlight that night—and had the lodge been willing to provide a middle-of-the-night meal—the hikers would have tried to get an even earlier start by initiating their traverse of the initial switchbacks off the canyon floor while daybreak was still a dream. And while temperatures in the canyon hovered near their overnight lows of one hundred degrees.

But the lunar phase wasn't cooperating. The moon hung in the black sky like a bent sliver of tarnished chrome, its form not even visible from the bottom of the canyon, its light inconsequential on the floor-to-rim trails.

A shirtless man approached the group of hikers as they made final equipment adjustments before their ascent. The intruder wasn't a big man—he was no more than five feet nine, but he had a chiseled chest, swimmer's shoulders, and the kind of abs that make other men's eyes still and their jaws tighten involuntarily, the kind of abs *that motivate the competition to do at least a couple of weeks' worth of crunches.*

The shirtless man wasn't a complete stranger—the group had met him the day before. He and the woman he was with had been part of the smaller-than-usual cluster of hikers that reached the canyon floor during the apogee of the previous day's vicious heat.

The new couple had exchanged brief pleasantries with some of the other campers before splitting off and pitching a tent in the campsite nearest the cabins. They didn't have cabin beds reserved and had chosen not to claim any of the bunks left vacant from no-shows caused by the heat wave.

The woman of the pair was friendly, even vivacious. She didn't seem depleted at all by the descent in the unforgiving heat. But the man she was with—the shirtless man—herded her away to seek shade, and he had chosen to keep to himself since arriving.

He seemed to want to be left alone.

The Grand Canyon could be a good place for that.

The shirtless man lifted his left hand in a sheepish, halfhearted greeting as he shuffled up to the group in the predawn, stopping a few feet outside their perimeter. Light from a solitary lantern washed across his torso. "Hey," he said. "Mornin'."

He had the group's attention. His voice had a pleasant timbre and soft edges. The men were focusing on him because he was a half-naked intruder walking into their midst from the darkness. The women were focusing, well, because of his chest and his shoulders. And those abs.

"The, uh, girl I was with yesterday? Remember her? We met . . . right? When we got down here? We talked to some of you? You guys seen her . . . around?"

The visitor's facial features were vaguely Asian. His dark hair was mussed and the lid of his left eye was dusted with pebbles of matter. He hadn't shaved for a few days, a fat sleep crease crossed one cheek like a scar from a knife fight, and he had a crusty booger curling like a tiny leech around the outer rim of his right nostril. His dusty jeans fit loosely at his waist and hung low on his hips, exposing the rise of his pelvic bones and an avenue of fine hair that trailed south from his navel. It wasn't at all clear that his ensemble included underwear.

Based on nothing but his appearance and his manner, he seemed like the kind of too-handsome guy who caught women's eyes during last call, the kind of guy those same women might regret waking up beside the morning after they'd ignored their girlfriends' pointed advice about it not really being a good idea to go someplace with "someone like him" for one more drink.

"Today?" said one of the male hikers in reply to the question. Jack was one of the students from Oxy College. "Have we seen her this morning? That's what you're asking?" He spoke because no one else had. Jack was polite. It was one of his many endearing traits. But he looked away from the man the instant he identified the dark curl on the stranger's nostril as snot, reflexively rubbing at the tip of his own nose as he bowed his head toward the sand. Jack had a thing about hygiene.

The shirtless man didn't respond right away. His eyes were moving from person to person in the group. His stare wasn't intended to be challenging—it was as though he was looking for something, some sign of recognition in someone's eyes.

"No. Nobody's been by this morning," Jack said, as though he were translating his friends' silence for the newcomer. Jack spoke into the dirt and sand, still unable to look back up at the man and the dried booger.

"Maybe last night. After bedtime, I guess. Since midnight or so," the shirtless man said with the shrug of a solitary shoulder. "I don't know. She got up in the middle of the night, said she had to pee. I went back to sleep. It's so damn hot. When I woke up a little while ago to get ready to climb back up"—he gestured toward the canyon

wall—"she wasn't around. I just walked down to the toilets by the river and . . . I hiked around a little down there looking for her, and . . ."

His words hung in the parched air. Almost everyone focused on the word "hiked" and glanced down toward the man's feet, at least for an instant. He was wearing a faded pair of once-but-no-longer red, beat-up, worn-heeled, drugstore flip-flops. His footwear argued that if he had hiked around near the river at all looking for the woman, he had hiked around only a little. The scorpion population alone rendered the Grand Canyon floor terrain ill-suited for protracted journeys in ninety-nine-cent flip-flops.

"She wasn't down there," the shirtless man continued. "I mean, I couldn't find her anywhere. Can't. I . . . um . . . was hoping she might've come over here at . . . some point. Looking for . . . I don't know. She's friendly, maybe to say hi, whatever. If you've seen her, you know?"

When no one responded to his meandering queries, he shrugged apologetically, as though his own suggestion about what might have happened to the girl since she'd wandered off to pee in the middle of the night didn't make sense, even to him.

"Don't think so," one of the women—Jules, half of the couple from Santa Monica—replied. "Anybody see her this morning? Hear anything?"

No one responded. She turned to her boyfriend, "Eric? You see her?"

Eric was stuffing his backpack. "No," he said.

"She and I were— We partied a little last night. Maybe too much," the shirtless man added, grinning at the memory in a way that caused his nose to move and the dried booger to crack. The lower part began hanging from his nostril by a snotty elasticized thread. He swiped at it as though it were a fly buzzing in front of his face—he knew something was there somewhere that shouldn't be, but he wasn't sure precisely where or what. "At least I did. You know how it goes sometimes?"

Jules said, "We partied a little bit last night too. We were back and forth to the river all night, kind of saying good-bye."

Eric, whose physique compared favorably to the shirtless man's, turned to Jules, his girlfriend. He whispered, "Do you know which girl he's talking about?"

Jules's ponytail of long blond hair picked up every ray of spare light in the dark canyon. Even in full sun, her hair was the kind of blond that evoked silver almost as much as it did gold. She furrowed her forehead. "You don't?" she asked.

He lowered his voice, and said, "Do you?"

She didn't whisper her reply. She said, "Curly brown hair. Pretty eyes. My height." She pressed her lips together for a moment before she repeated, "Very pretty eyes. Green, surrounded by . . . amber." She twirled a finger in front of her. "We said hi yesterday evening on the trail. Down there, on the way to the beach." She pointed toward one of the paths that led down toward the river from the cabins. "After dusk. We talked for a little while. Where we're from, what we did, that sort of thing. She seemed . . . nice. She has an accent. She said she's from, what, Latvia?"

"No . . . Estonia, I think," said Kanyn, one of the students from Oxy. "It's on the Baltic, near Russia, she said. I talked to her too, about the same time you did, Jules. She is friendly. Nice." She nodded. "And great eyes, definitely. Gorgeous." Kanyn couldn't look at the shirtless man either. The snot.

The shirtless man said, "Estonia, yeah. That's her. She is . . . friendly."

The group exchanged glances. Some surreptitious. Some not.

Two

His Ex, Merideth

If anyone else I knew from the old days in Boulder had died, Adrienne would have picked up the phone to let me know that something awful had happened.

She, not Alan—my ex-husband, Alan Gregory—had been the one who had called and ordered me to "Sit down, damn it," before she sobbed out the news of her husband Peter's murder so many years before.

Her harbinger duties weren't limited to death announcements. Adrienne called to inform me when Alan had a serious new sweetheart, and later on, that the sweetheart had become his wife.

Adrienne knew that I would want to know that the loving couple was pregnant, and later, that they had a healthy baby daughter they'd named Grace.

Adrienne would start each of the news-from-Colorado-involving-my-ex-husband conversations with something like, "Do you really want to know this, Merideth? I don't have to tell you. I don't. Say the word and I'll ask you about work, or the weather, or if you've found one decent man in New York City. We can talk about something girly. I can do girly. Not for long, but . . . Or I could bitch about something here. In Boulder, I mean. July? January? The damn chinooks? The Broncos? I don't like any of them."

I'd reply that of course I wanted to know what was going on in

Alan's life. Why wouldn't I? Then Adrienne would tell me whatever it was she had called to tell me and my heart would get plucked like one of the long strings on a harp.

Adrienne was my only enduring link to my Colorado past.

She and I had always been perplexed by some of the same things about Boulder. Neither of us had ever been able to understand the local populace's insistence about forgoing motors and using muscles—jogging, biking, cross-country skiing—to ascend the local mountains. Nor had either of us ever comprehended Boulderites' inclination to squander free weekends and precious holidays wandering off into the wilderness, pitching tents, squatting in the woods, and generally pretending they didn't have houses.

We were both baffled by women we knew in town who were more interested in a new backpack than they were in new earrings.

But beyond our addresses—we'd been across-the-lane neighbors—and our shared editorial critiques about the local mores, Adrienne and I had little in common.

Personality-wise she and I couldn't have been less alike.

Still, Adrienne and I *were*. We endured. Despite the differences, despite the distance, and despite the years, she and I continued to exist as something. Friends? Sure. Not buddies. Not . . . girlfriends. Not like my girlfriends here, in New York City or L.A.

Adrienne and I could never have gone shopping together. Not for fun. We'd never be eager to show each other the new shoes we just bought. I would never think to call her to go out to a bar for a recreational flirt with the latest crop of I-bankers from Morgan Stanley or Goldman Sachs. Never.

What kept us connected?

There was part of me that thought we had stayed in contact because we had the natural attraction that outsiders feel for each other. As neighbors in Boulder, we catalyzed each other like the components of epoxy. When we touched, we stuck.

In the mile-high air of Boulder, each of us had been an outsider.

She was the shoot-from-the-hip, New York–raised, Jewish urologist living in the always-hip, ever-progressive, but-be-careful-what-you-say Peoples' Republic of Boulder.

Me? I was a Left-Coast princess in a mountain paradise that, alas, did not appreciate royalty.

At least, non-Buddhist royalty.

Adrienne didn't call with the news of the latest death.

It was her diminutive body that had gone still.

It was her irreverent laugh that had been quieted.

No one from the old crowd bothered to assume her role. No one remembered that I'd been forgotten. No one thought to tell me that my old friend had died a wrong-place-at-the-wrong-time death from a senseless bombing outside a café in an Israeli Mediterranean resort town. I was left to learn about Adrienne's end while I was scanning the AP wire when I arrived at my office at the network where I worked in Midtown. I noticed a familiar name in a follow-up story about a recent bombing in Israel.

After reading the wire report of the new developments, and then rereading her name—I must have checked it five times—I cried alone at my desk in my office until my assistant asked me if I was all right. I wondered at the time if I had stopped weeping because my assistant had intruded upon my sorrow, or if I had stopped weeping because someone had finally noticed that I was so sad.

For other people it might have been a small distinction, but for me it was an important one. It was important, too, that I was asking myself the question at all, and that I was unsure about the answer. The very fact that I recognized there was a difference—between the desire to grieve privately and the desire to have my sorrow acknowledged publicly—was significant to me.

It's silly, but that I knew there was a difference was a sign of my growth.

I was changing.

Alan used to quote Confucius to me. He'd say, *"Confucius said the best time to plant a tree is ten years ago. The second best time is now."*

I'd wasted energy back then doubting whether the quote was really from Confucius. My growth had been a long time coming. Ten years sooner would have been a more ideal time for my development. Even five years sooner would have been good.

Since Alan hadn't called, I didn't know whether or not he expected I'd come from New York to attend Adrienne's funeral. Or if I'd show up at the reception. Or even whether he had given me a solitary thought since the bombing.

I wanted him to acknowledge that I had lost a friend, too.

An old colleague from Denver's NBC affiliate—it had been a CBS horn when I was there—had e-mailed me about the memorial service that was planned for Adrienne in Colorado. Her note said that her ex-husband—he was an oncologist in a big group in Denver's northern suburbs—had known Adrienne through the Boulder medical community. My old coworker knew that Adrienne and I had once been neighbors, and she thought I would like to know about the service.

The woman had been trying to get the hell out of the incestuous Denver news market since her divorce, and she was hoping that my gratitude might assist her in finagling a producing gig in New York or California.

Her ulterior motive didn't bother me. I knew what to expect from the business I was in. They call them networks for a reason.

Although I'd been back to Colorado—I adore Aspen and Vail, who doesn't—I hadn't set foot in Boulder between the two funerals, the earlier one for Peter, Adrienne's husband, and this one for Adrienne.

I take responsibility for my antipathy for the town. I'd never really made room in my heart for Boulder. I had expected Boulder to first make room for me.

The informal gathering after Adrienne's funeral was scheduled to be in the house where my ex-husband and I had lived during our brief marriage. The cottage—that was Alan's quaint counter-portrait when I described the house where he was living when we had first met as a "glorified shack"—had been built prior to the Depression as the caretaker's dwelling for a decent-size ranch. The frame home sat near the top of a western-facing slope in Spanish Hills on the eastern rim of the Boulder Valley. On a clear day—most of them were clear days, at least meteorologically—Alan and I could look out almost any window and see an expanse of the Rocky Mountains stretching from Pike's Peak north to Rocky Mountain National Park, and from the Front Range foothills immediately behind Boulder all the way west to the glaciers that frosted the Continental Divide.

I loved to stand beside our guests as they inhaled that vista for the first time.

Showing off our ramshackle house had never been an option.

Adrienne and her husband Peter had lived up the hill across the lane, only a few dozen yards away. Theirs was the big house, the one the founders of the ranch had built a hundred years before. It was the house I coveted.

I had always imagined that the architect had conceived a lovely turret for the southwest corner of the two-story farmhouse. A wrap-around covered porch would have been a perfect perch to take advantage of the expansive views toward Chautauqua and Eldorado. I suspected that the homesteaders had either lacked the vision or had been too modest to construct the signature element. The result of their timidity was that the prime corner of Adrienne's house was a blunt, windowless expanse of intersecting planes.

I picked up a car at DIA and drove straight from the airport to the gathering in Spanish Hills. So many people were already at the reception that cars—okay, it was Boulder, mostly SUVs—lined the familiar dirt lane halfway back to South Boulder Road. I had to park a few hundred yards away.

The hike to the dead end of the lane wasn't pleasant in heels.

Boulder or not, though, I wasn't about to attend a memorial service in anything else.

I spotted Alan and his black-lacquer-haired wife on opposite sides of their new great room seconds after I'd walked in the door. The renovations they'd done made the space feel familiar yet foreign. I thought they could have benefited from a more imaginative architect and a better designer.

Or maybe *any* designer. They actually had a pool table—with burgundy felt—in the center of the dining room.

I weaved through the crowd—the place was packed—toward the western-facing windows without turning my head even a few degrees. I didn't want to be sidetracked by anyone I knew before I made it to Alan. He was standing near the sliding door that led from the living room to the long deck on the mountain side of the house.

My ex was facing away from me, leaning forward slightly. He was involved in a conversation with a woman whom I thought I recognized but I couldn't place.

I paused behind him and waited for a few seconds. Alan had always had a thing for women's scents; I thought he might pick up mine. I hadn't changed perfumes since before we were married.

He didn't notice. I waited until a break in his conversation before I said, in a quiet voice, "Hey. It's Me."

Me.

Three

Her Ex, Alan

Jonas had been my son for mere days.

Jonas's father, Peter, had been murdered years before, when Jonas was a toddler. His mother, Adrienne, my dear buddy and neighbor, was so recently deceased that the depth of the loss I felt at her absence still crept nightly into my restless dreams.

Jonas had been by his mother's side in Israel when a terrorist's bomb exploded. He had witnessed her death and that of their Israeli cousin. Once they had finished healing, two shrapnel scars—one long straight one that ran almost the entire length of the bone on Jonas's left shin and another one shaped like the letter *L* on his left forearm—would be permanent reminders of what had happened to him that day.

Especially, what he'd lost.

In her will Adrienne had named my wife, Lauren, and me as Jonas's guardians. Adrienne's decision didn't digest easily for either her long-dead husband's family in Wyoming, or for her own distant family in New York, where Adrienne's only sibling lived with his wife and two sons. Her brother made it clear during a phone call on day three—days one and two, for me, were spent in shock as I flew to Tel Aviv to retrieve my traumatized stepson and his mother's remains from

Israel—that he considered the idea of his nephew becoming the child of "strangers" to be incomprehensible.

Lauren and I were the "strangers" that brother Martin was dismissing. The reality was that Jonas had lived yards across a dusty lane from us since the day he was born. Other than his parents, and maybe one or two luminescent pearls in a long string of forgettable nannies, he was closer to no one than he was to us.

Although we were anything but strangers to Jonas, we were strangers to Martin. And that, apparently, was what was most important to him as he maneuvered in the shadows cast by his sister's death. I forced myself to try to find some empathy for Martin's position. It wasn't hard to do.

Martin, however, made it hard to hang on to.

Adrienne had been estranged from her family, who had questioned every choice she'd made since she'd decided to attend medical school. When she had shown an inclination for biology in college, they had been hoping she would become a radiologist or a pharmaceutical researcher, certainly not a clinician. When she made it clear that she had a passion for patient care, they switched tracks and made it equally clear that they thought she should become a dermatologist. They had been appalled by her decision to become a urologist.

Adrienne's take was, "Bottom line? They don't like that I have a job that involves pricks. My mother won't tell her friends what I do. She thinks I'm one step removed from being Hand-Job Judy."

Although I'd been tempted at the time, I had never asked Adrienne about the eponymous "Hand-Job Judy." I really wished I had. That provocative omission was a poignant addition to the long list of conversations I would never have with her.

The familial disappointment didn't stop with career. Adrienne's family didn't like that Adrienne had fallen in love with, and then eloped with, a woodworker. A *carpenter*. They hated that she'd settled with him in the West in general, in Colorado specifically, and in Boulder in particular.

Over the years, Jonas's only contacts with his maternal uncle and his family had taken place during visits East with his mother. Adrienne considered the infrequent trips to New York to be obligatory vacations, which in her unique shorthand she labeled "oblications." Lauren and I kept an eye on the Boulder house while she was out of town. When the trips involved an oblication, the interludes were inevitably short and Adrienne always seemed relieved to return to her Spanish Hills home.

Martin flew west with his wife, a pleasant woman with lovely gray eyes and an unnervingly loud voice, to attend Adrienne's funeral services in Boulder, and to come to my home to the reception that followed.

I was trying to decide if that trip counted as a family visit. If Adrienne had been around I knew she would have said, "Hell, no." She would have considered her brother's pilgrimage the ultimate oblication.

Moments after meeting Martin, I had recognized that he was an impatient man, a compact car running on fuel with too much octane. Some part of his body was always moving. A foot tapping. His face grimacing. Fingertips rubbing together. Something. At first, my diagnostic curiosity was piqued, and I wondered if he had a mild form of Tourette's.

I soon decided he was merely annoyingly fidgety.

Less than twenty minutes into the reception after the funeral—the house was just beginning to fill with Adrienne's friends and loved ones—he insisted I join him on the west-facing deck outside the living room. He placed an unwelcome hand on my shoulder and said, "Al." The tone he employed was a faux-sincere that made me suspicious.

He explained that although he knew it was a "difficult time for everyone" and that he was sorry for all the inconvenience that Lauren and I had experienced—he, not I, should have been the one to go to Tel Aviv; of course, he still didn't know why he hadn't been called, but that was water under the bridge—he was prepared to "muddle" through the "legalities" of transferring Jonas's guardianship to him and his wife "right away, to minimize confusion, et cetera et cetera, for the boy."

He added that the estate would take care of the necessary legal expenses—I needn't worry about that.

I didn't know what to say. I fought the urge to tell him that of all the things I was worried about, paying lawyers hadn't made my top fifty.

My flabbergasted silence troubled Martin enough that he felt compelled to inject an additional explanation. "You know my sister," he said.

He hadn't said it kindly. Martin must have been assuming that he was conversing with an ally. *Could he be misreading me that badly?* I wondered. Grief does funny things.

I wasn't comfortable with the eye-roll that he used to accompany the statement about knowing his sister, nor the little nostril-snort that effectively completed it. I couldn't be certain what he meant with his comment about knowing Adrienne, but I suspected that when I did understand, I would conclude that it was demeaning to my stepson's mother's memory. I feared that it was, in four vague words, Jonas's uncle's way not only of trying to undo the wishes of my dear friend only minutes after her body was buried, but also his way of attempting to enroll me as a conspirator in whatever suspect endeavor he was contemplating next.

I took a quick step back so that his hand would fall from my shoulder. It worked. The hand tumbled to his side with a fat *thwop*, as though his arm had fallen asleep while it was up there.

"I did know your sister," I said. "Very well."

"Good then," he said. "We see eye to eye."

Like his sister, Martin was wide in the hips, and less than tall. He and I didn't see eye to eye literally. Figuratively? The odds were long, and getting longer by the minute.

"You know, Martin— Do you prefer Martin?"

"Marty is fine."

"Thank you. You know, Marty, I don't think we do," I said. "See eye to eye."

"About?" he said.

He was either honestly perplexed, which made him dim, or he was being disingenuous, which made him dangerous in one or two of a kaleidoscope of ways that I would have to sort through at a time when I was less distracted.

"Jonas," I replied. "My son."

My words were deliberately chosen. Marty smiled his reaction to them in a way that made me want to smack him. After a provocative pause he shook his head. Then he nodded his head.

Confusion? I wondered. Or, more accurately, I hoped.

He closed his eyes tightly and grimaced with his teeth exposed. It wasn't an attractive expression. With his eyes that way and his lips peeled back he looked like a rodent suffering from near-terminal constipation. When he reopened his eyes, things didn't improve much. He glanced my way again, but with a fresh look on his face. I interpreted it to be a melodramatic attempt to try to convey the sentiment that I should take whatever step I was contemplating taking next with a truckload of caution.

I did a reality check. I had to convince myself that this conversation was really occurring during Adrienne's memorial. My contemplative pause had the unintended consequence of softening Marty's tough-guy comportment, which made me begin to fear that he'd concluded his hushed warning had done the trick.

To be certain that I hadn't missed his meaning, he said, "I don't think you want to do this, Al. 'Go there' is what I think the kids say these days. I really, really don't. Blood is thicker than water."

I counted to ten. It didn't seem to help, so I did it again. My anger wasn't abating. I said, "I don't know what 'this' you're talking about, Marty. What my wife and I plan to do is to strive to honor your sister's wishes regarding her son, whom she loved in a way that was magical for us to watch. You and I have seen the same documents. In her will, Adrienne asks Lauren and me to raise Jonas. We intend to do that to the best of our abilities."

He lowered his gaze. When he looked back up he was facing away from me, contemplating the seemingly infinite swath of the Front Range. "You know she was . . . bisexual?" He swallowed the last word—the loaded word—as though it was a revelation not to be shared in polite company.

I raised my eyebrows involuntarily, not as a comment on Adrienne's sexuality—her sexual adventures, and occasional misadventures, were a far-from-secret part of the texture of the fabric of who she was—but rather as a reaction to her brother's condescending judgment about her. At that moment Marty and I were standing in a location with a fine view of Boulder, and I was inclined to give him credit for being sufficiently cosmopolitan that he would have at least an inkling that the rooms behind us were infiltrated by men and women whose sexual identities were not describable by limiting his choices to words that began with the prefix "hetero."

Marty caught my raised eyebrows but misinterpreted the gesture to be a sign of encouragement. He leaned forward a few inches and added, "More *l* than *s* if you know what I mean." He lifted a fist in front of his mouth and coughed.

"Excuse me?" I said, hoping I'd heard him wrong. And hoping that he really wasn't someone who used snorts and throat noises as punctuation.

The *l* was likely "lesbian." *The* s *is "straight"?* I thought. *That must be it.*

I wondered if I should tell Marty that Adrienne did not consider herself bisexual.

He said, "That's what I'm talking about. With Adrienne? At times, she could have a sweetheart—my kids adored her visits—but there're things that, well, you don't really want to know about her. My sister had her . . . call them blind spots. She didn't make the wisest choices. And she wasn't always a good . . . judge of what's best for the boy."

I despised that Marty was denigrating Adrienne's mothering, something he knew almost nothing about. I despised that he considered choosing Lauren and me as guardians to be one of Adrienne's unwise choices. I despised that he referred to Jonas as "the boy." I despised that he used "et cetera et cetera" in conversation.

I despised that he called me "Al." That one was petty, but there it was.

"Because of whom she slept with?" I said. I was going to say "loved" instead of "slept with" but feared the nuance would sail over his head like an errant Frisbee.

He exhaled. "Exactly."

He still thought I was agreeing with him about something.

"Marty, could we talk about this later, after things wind down here?" I said. "We have many guests. People who want to talk, need to talk, about Adrienne. This"—I turned toward the room full of her friends and loved ones—"is about your sister."

I made my living as a psychotherapist. Had Marty walked into my office as a prospective patient, within two minutes I would have recognized him as an annuity.

There was that much work to do. That many rocks to turn. That much resistance to which to apply the forces of psychotherapeutic hydraulics.

My professional radar had also pegged Marty's pathology as being of the personality-disorder variety. Unlike people with garden-variety neuroses who come in to see people like me because they are miserable, people with personality disorders often show up in the office of people like me not because they are miserable, but because the people around them are miserable.

I could well understand how people around Marty might be miserable.

Thank God it's not my job, I said to myself.

* * *

I stopped at the door from the deck to the house and opened my mouth with fresh determination to defend my dead friend. I managed, just barely, to control the outburst I was rehearsing in my head.

Before I was able to close the door behind me, he muttered, "We're not done, Al."

I had taken only two steps inside when an old friend of mine, a social worker, said hello. Her name was Cassandra Poteet. She was married to one of my favorite mental health colleagues in Boulder. I hadn't been aware that they knew Adrienne.

Cassandra revealed that a couple of her kids had been urology patients of Adrienne's. "Is Wallace here?" I asked, wondering about my professional friend.

She seemed at a loss for words, but finally said, "No, he . . . Wallace couldn't come." She lowered her voice. "He had some issues with Adrienne about Mason's . . . care. It's . . . awkward." Mason was one of their children.

Cassandra had said all that she wanted to say about the topic. We began to talk about Adrienne. Less than a minute into the conversation I heard a voice from behind me say, "Hey. It's me."

My mind translated the melody as familiar, even if the words didn't register as anything special. Intrigued by the refracted memory fragment, I said, "Would you please excuse me?" to Cassandra.

I turned to discover that I was looking into the eyes of my first wife, Merideth.

Me.

Her.

Whoa.

Four

The Canyon

Jack pulled his digital camera from his pack and powered it up.

Jules, the woman with the confident voice who'd remembered that the missing woman had curly brown hair and lovely eyes, noticed the stranger eyeing the camera. She said, "That's Jack. It's what he does. Ignore him, he'll stop soon."

Jack said, "Not much light. My last battery's almost dead."

Jules was a twenty-five-year-old litigator who had just signed on with a big firm in West L.A. She untied a red kerchief from around her neck and walked over to the shirtless man the way a mother with a washcloth approaches a young child with the detritus of breakfast stuck to his chin. Without asking if he minded being groomed by a stranger, she used the kerchief to flick the dried snot from his nose. She then used her fingers to push his hair back so that it didn't completely shadow his eyes.

She said, "That's better. Tell us your friend's name."

The shirtless man crinkled his nose and rubbed at his nostril. He was baffled as to why the woman had just wiped a bandanna across his face. And why that had made anything better. He had to force himself to refocus in order to ponder her question.

His apparent distraction and his hesitation in replying were not encouraging signs. Finally he said, "Jaana," as though he was pleased to have remembered the woman's name. "Two a's. Or three, I guess."

The shirtless man's demeanor about the woman's absence was so low-key and his concern about her whereabouts so off-key that the larger group was losing interest in his dilemma. Most had returned their attention to rechecking their equipment and supplies to finish preparations for their imminent ascent of the canyon wall.

"She your girlfriend?" Jules asked.

"We're . . . friends. We hang out. We see each other sometimes. I live in Vegas. She brought me down here."

The group digested the news.

"Coming on this . . . hike, trip . . . was her idea," the shirtless man said again. It was as though he was determined to hang any bad-judgment tag on Jaana's back. "I'm not much of an outdoorsman. Kind of sore this morning. You guys have blisters?" He bent his left leg, raising his foot. An angry red orb the size of a quarter was sprouting on his heel.

"I can give you something for that. What time did Jaana get up to pee?" Jules asked. "Do you remember?"

"I was asleep. I don't know."

"About . . . what time? Was it ten o'clock? One o'clock? Four o'clock?"

He shrugged. "I don't know."

"Early? Late?"

"Not too late."

"Lisa?" Jules said to one of the other women. "Were you able to sleep last night? You see anything?"

Lisa was one of the group of singles, the high school friend of Jack's. The heat had been troubling Lisa more than anyone else in the group. She hadn't been able to sleep for more than an hour or two at a stretch since she reached the canyon floor. She said, "Not much. I was up for a while, like always." She looked away before she said, "Other people were up too." She quickly scanned the group. "But I didn't see her."

The shirtless man fixated on the news that others were up. "Anybody see her after dark?"

Jules pressed Lisa. "You didn't see this girl? Jaana?"

Lisa hesitated for a moment. "No."

"You're sure?" Jules asked.

"No, Jules. Nothing."

Jules made eye contact with the other four in the group. "You guys?"

Head shakes. Shoulder shrugs.

The shirtless man said, "Okay."

Jules's boyfriend, Eric, paused from a long pull on a water bottle. He made an effort not to sound dismissive as he said, "I'm sure she's around someplace. She has to be. I mean, where the hell would she go?"

On a hot black night on the banks of the mighty Colorado River, at the bottom of the deepest gash on the continental surface of the planet, few people went wandering.

Without a raft or a kayak or a riverboard and a lot of safety equipment, where the hell would someone go? The only places to meander on foot are either up one of the trails that herringbone up one side of the canyon or the other, or down one of the convoluted footpaths that hug the river or curve off into its estuaries or dead-end in the infinite variety of water-carved slot canyons. In the dark, alone, without the aid of a good flashlight, every one of those hikes is reserved for the reckless, depressed, or self-destructive. Or drunk.

"She wasn't . . . upset, was she?" Eric added when no one responded to his earlier remark.

The shirtless man shook his head while he comported his face into a puzzled expression, as though he didn't really understand the question. He said, "No. She was pretty . . . happy." He smiled at some thought. "We had a good time last night. I did."

A woman who had been standing slightly away from the group, taking it all in, spoke up for the first time. Line the seven of them up—the six friends and the shirtless stranger—and ninety-nine out of a hundred people would select her as the youngest in the bunch.

And not just by months, but by a few years. Although she was nine-teen, she looked like a high school sophomore.

Or freshman.

She was part of the group of singles, a sophomore at Oxy. Her name was Carmel, pronounced like the town on the Monterey Peninsula.

She was wearing what the others in the group had come to think of as her Grand Canyon uniform: a tight tank top, shorts that barely covered her crotch—and didn't completely cover her ass—and a canvas hat with a brim the size of a parasol. The narrow backpack she was preparing to lift to her shoulders appeared taller than she was.

Her smile was almost constant. Her uncomplicated manner and natural beauty earned her a lot of attention in life. She was a girl men tried to separate from the pack when she was out at bars or clubs with her girlfriends.

She turned to the shirtless man and spoke, her voice carrying the kind of persistent hope that could be mistaken for innocence. "She's probably someplace waiting to watch the sun rise." She lifted her eyebrows and smiled again. "That's what I did the first night we were here when I couldn't sleep because it was so hot. I walked down to the river and I sat on a rock and I looked east and I waited. For daybreak. It was soooo peaceful. The waiting. The water rushing in the river. The air so still. And at sunrise, the very first light? It is just amazing down here early, just before dawn."

She glanced up toward the rim while she waited for the man to reply. When he didn't, she said, "You'll get to see for yourself in a little while. It's absolutely . . . I don't know. Illuminating." She laughed at herself. "That was dumb. Jeez. But I bet that's where your friend is right now. She's on a rock someplace, looking east, waiting for the first light. Letting the sound from the river clear her head. Cleanse her spirit. She'll be back with you soon, once she's done taking it in." She concluded with a fresh, teeth-baring smile aimed directly at the shirtless man. She knew from experience that her big eyes and kind smile were reassuring to people.

Her girlfriends had often warned her that she was guilty of mistaking men's interest for men's interest. Her friends' well-intended caution had never done the young woman any good. She'd been shocked by bad intentions more often than the cute blonde in teenage horror movies.

Carmel tugged on the strap hanging at her left hip and turned ninety degrees. "I can never, ever, ever, get it right. Is this thing straight, Jack?"

"Hello," replied Kanyn, her female friend from school. Kanyn was a lithe woman who wore her own heavy backpack as comfortably as she would wear a T-shirt to bed. "Jack doesn't know from straight."

Some of the group laughed. Some didn't. Jack laughed.

"Where exactly did . . . Where did you go that morning? To watch the sun rise, I mean?" the shirtless man asked Carmel. "I can go look there. For Jaana."

Carmel said, "Down past the beach." She pointed in the direction of the trail that led from the cabins past the campground, toward the river. "Not the part you see near the path, but downstream a little. Not too far. Past that first set of rocks. That rise? There's a trail. I know it just looks dark right now, but you'll see it. You know which one I'm talking about?"

The guy nodded. He said, "No, not really."

"You won't miss it— I mean, you can't get lost, it's a canyon, right? Head downstream, stay by the river, and don't climb. I just sat on a flat rock."

Jules chimed in with some questions for the shirtless man. "Your friend's things are still in your camp, right? She isn't someone who would try to climb out during the night? Or go in the river for anything? By herself, I mean . . . She wouldn't . . . ?"

Do something that stupid?

The shirtless man said, "Her stuff's here. Everything's there, her pack, her bag. Our water. She's the one who warned me about the river. She told me not to get fooled, that the river water is really cold.

"She has to go back up today. This morning. Like, now. This trip was just a . . . you know. Come down. One . . . night . . . here. And then . . . back up. You know."

Jules said, "And you two were . . . getting along okay?"

"No. Great. Just great."

Jack started making some adjustments to Carmel's pack. He lifted the weight higher on the provocative curve of her hips—the allure of that arc was one to which Jack was completely immune—and pulled at the shoulder straps to encourage the heft to stay where he wanted it to stay. He asked the man, "She works up at the rim? Your friend?"

The shirtless man nodded. "North rim. The cafeteria at the Visitor's Center? She's a cook. You may have seen her. Up there, I mean."

Eric wanted to get started up the trail. He was the oldest member of the group—a twenty-seven-year-old with a law degree who had just finished doing a fellowship at Stanford's Hoover Institute. If it turned out that a leader needed to emerge for any reason on the march up to the rim, he would be the one the others would look to. He took a long gaze at his watch, as if he were having difficulty making sense of the numbers, then gazed up toward the canyon walls.

A buttery aura had just begun to whisper dawn in the eastern sky, painting the ragged edge of the rim like a spill of diluted watercolor.

He said, "We're heading up the North Kaibab in a few minutes. When we get to the rim, we'll let somebody know that your friend may be late for her shift. Okay? It looks like you two are going to get a late start, and it's going to be slow going today. Make sure you take extra water because of the heat. And take care of that blister first." He tapped the crystal of his watch. "Come on, everybody, what do you say we go and deplete some glycogen?"

All the other hikers, with one exception, responded to Eric's call to get moving. The exception was Jules, his girlfriend.

She caught Kanyn's eyes for a split second. Thought she saw something there.

Five

His Ex

Alan didn't turn to face me right away.

He was talking with a woman I thought was familiar from the old days, but I couldn't place her. I did think she was a mental health type. She was tall and slender—to be candid, she was the kind of wan and skinny that makes sane people wonder about metabolic disorders—with frizzy hair that must have been a nightmare to manage. Her clothes looked, well, borrowed. None of the pieces she'd chosen were exactly somber, but she'd made enough of an effort at choosing mourning attire that the resulting combination didn't stray too far beyond the boundaries of grief's zip code. She should have known better than to have worn so much mascara to a funeral, though.

Talk about the tracks of her tears.

"Alan," I said. I wished he would have sensed that I was there.

He allowed the woman to finish a most-pedestrian thought about how much she would miss Adrienne's laugh—I'd always appreciated Alan's patience with people almost as much as I'd been frustrated by it—before he placed a hand on her wrist and said, "Cassandra? Would you excuse me for a moment?"

Cassandra? Did not ring a bell. I rarely forgot names and faces. Why couldn't I identify this woman? I watched Alan's shoulders broaden and his back expand as he filled his lungs with air. He was steeling himself for a fresh gale of grief.

I could see in Alan's eyes the moment he turned around that he hadn't suspected I'd be in town. But I couldn't see much else there. One of my persistent vulnerabilities in our relationship was my inability to read Alan's gaze. One of his persistent advantages in our relationship was having a gaze that was difficult for me to read.

"Merideth," he said. Then—after he'd expelled all that air from his lungs—"I'm so sorry."

That I'm here? That our friend is dead? That you didn't call to tell me what happened?

My narcissism no longer ambushed me. My troubles seeing beyond my immediate reach had been the source of some significant friction for Alan and me.

I should, of course, have seen the marital storm clouds forming. During the early flare of our mutual passion Alan had chosen the first two letters of my name—it's "Merideth," not the conventional *M-e-r-e-d-i-t-h*—as his endearment for me.

I would come home from work. He'd say, "Hi, Me."

I'd say, "Hey, you."

I had naïvely considered the banter to be clever romantic patois. I didn't realize until long after our separation that the sobriquet served as scarlet letters of my self-involvement, ones that I'd helped hang around my own neck.

In the last few years I had begun to come to terms with who I am, learning to treat my self-centered predisposition like an aggravating trait in a friend I otherwise adored. I no longer berated myself for my propensity toward self-involvement.

In other circumstances—other than me intruding on him during our friend's funeral—I imagined Alan would be genuinely pleased that my peripheral vision had improved. He could be magnanimous, but to a fault. Another complicated issue for us when we were married.

* * *

For a moment, I thought Alan was going to embrace me after he got over his shock. But he held back.

I lowered my voice. "I'm sorry too," I said. "I know you loved her."

When Alan failed to step in for an embrace I held out my left hand toward him, palm-down, as if offering to grasp his hand in a restrained gesture of compassion. The move was calculated. And no, it wasn't that I was worried that I wasn't at the top of his hug list that day. Most days, the man would hug anyone. I didn't want to move in because I wanted to give him a chance to spot my new engagement ring. I preferred not to have to tell him.

That was insight.

Insight is a lovely thing. Like the diamond adorning the fourth finger of my left hand, it is often useless. But lovely nonetheless.

I thought Alan would take my hand, but he didn't. His right hand and wrist were encased in a sky blue cast. He reached out for me instead. I shouldn't have been surprised—he usually did. Reach first, that is. We embraced, an act at once habitual and unsettling. Slipping into his grasp was as familiar as sliding into a hot bath. As his arms wrapped around me, and his fingers—at least those on his un-casted hand—pressed across my shoulder blades, I could feel his body shudder a little.

That brought back memories too.

He said, "It's such a tragedy. What happened in Israel. I miss her so much."

He hadn't noticed the ring. "I know," I said. "You have a cast on your arm."

"I broke my hand. It's nothing."

I wanted to tell him about the baby. And about the wedding.

My narcissism governess—she was a psychological fiction I'd created to assist with my ego-observation challenges—awoke from her slumber just in time to spare me from myself.

"Later would be better," the Bitch whispered in that gravelly, aggravating, know-it-all voice of hers.

* * *

The Upper West Side therapist that I'd started seeing a few months back—he was a young guy, only a couple of years out of his residency at Johns Hopkins—would be pleased that the governess had intervened at that moment. Creating the Bitch had been his prescription to help me internalize the monitoring of my self-centering tendencies.

Her role? She was my psychological dominatrix. She was the coach who knew the moves that helped me tame my too-buff sense of entitlement. She was the town crier for the somnolent burg of my superego.

She was helping me get ready to be a wife, and a mother.

Six

Her Ex

Merideth's arrival in my home for Adrienne's reception had ambushed me.

I hadn't thought to invite her. Or to send her a note about the funeral. I hadn't called about Adrienne's death.

My oversight lacked consideration. And it certainly lacked compassion. If my plate hadn't been so full of other things at the time I might have turned double-barrel shells of recrimination upon myself. But my plate was beyond full. I'd screwed up in so many crucial ways over the previous year that I shrugged off the sleight to Merideth. I had a plethora of worse sins on which to spend my store of mea culpas.

With Marty in the picture, the immediate future looked no less complicated than the recent past.

Merideth and I talked for a while before we moved on to other conversations.

I spotted Lauren diagonally across the crowded room. She was eyeing Merideth, who was in the midst of an animated discussion with Diane Estevez. Diane was my partner in clinical practice, and a dear friend whose tenure in my life exceeded that of both of my wives. Lauren, my current wife, had seen photographs of Merideth, my ex-wife. Lauren knew at whom she was staring.

It might have been prudent for me to turn away sooner. But I became mesmerized watching the drama. My wife shifted her gaze, searching, until she caught my eye. With a raised chin and a slight tilt of her head, she gestured for to me to follow her down the hallway toward our bedroom.

"Is that Merideth?" she asked when I was within whispering distance.

She knew it was Merideth. "Yes," I said.

"Did you know she was going to be here?"

Her question didn't feel accusatory. "No," I said. "I'm as surprised to see her as you are."

She searched my eyes for prevarication. Satisfied, she said, "Okay." She'd said it in a then-we'll-deal-with-it voice.

"You holding up?" I asked. I was asking her about her MS, and her energy.

She nodded.

Didn't mean much. I translated the nod to mean that she would make it through the reception. It might take her twenty-four hours to recover, but she would make it through.

"Seen the kids?" I said.

"They're downstairs with Mona. They're fine."

Mona had been Jonas's latest nanny. She was still on the payroll, helping us out.

Lauren said, "We should get back to our guests."

I touched her arm. "I think Marty is going to try to take Jonas from us," I said. "We need to watch what we say to him, and to Kim."

"He said that? That he's going to try to take Jonas?"

"Not in so many words," I said.

Her eyes got fierce. "Let him fucking try," she said.

She marched back to the reception.

Contemplating another loss was too much for her. It had been a tough spring for all of us.

* * *

Although I suspected that Merideth would linger until the very end of the event, she left the reception along with the second wave of departing guests. As she said good-bye to me on our small front porch she asked me if I had "just a moment." Before I had a chance to say I did, she took my casted hand and led me away from the house about ten yards until we were standing on the valley side of the garage, looking southwest toward the Flatirons and Eldorado Springs.

A breeze carried the buzz of traffic from the nearby turnpike. I gazed at Merideth. She was trying to squelch a smile. "Yes?" I said.

Her eyes lit up in a way that I had seen less and less as our marriage had disintegrated. "Today is about Adrienne," she said. "I know that. Before I leave, though, I want you to know that I'm pregnant," she said. "And engaged."

The "and engaged" tag came out in a more hurried fashion than I think she had intended. My eyes caught the glint of a diamond on her finger. The rock was the size of an extra-strength Tylenol. The ring and setting were either white gold or platinum. I was guessing platinum.

"Congratulations," I said. "Twice. It's nice to hear some good news, Merideth. That's wonderful."

"I've had three miscarriages already, so nothing's certain where my uterus is concerned."

Although no DNA laboratory had ever confirmed my role, it was likely that I'd had something to do with the conception phase of the first of Merideth's three miscarriages. The responsible, and irresponsible, coupling had occurred many years before, during the separation that preceded our divorce.

That particular lapse in judgment aside, I'd never questioned the appropriateness of the outcome. Of that particular pregnancy. Of the long story of my relationship with Merideth. Of our marriage. Certainly not of our divorce.

"You excited about the baby?" I asked. Merideth's enthusiasm about being a mother wasn't a given. Any maternal instincts had always been buried under a thick blanket of insulation woven from her professional ambition and what I perceived, fairly or not, as an inability to place anyone—like an infant—reliably ahead of herself in any important queue.

"I am, Alan," she said. "I'm ready to be a mom. I really want this baby. I've grown a lot."

She looked at my eyes for an indication of how dubious I might be of her self-assessment. I tried to make sure that there was nothing there for her to see. I wanted to believe her. "Well, I hope your luck has changed and that this pregnancy goes perfectly. I'm . . . truly happy for both of you. All of you."

She held up both hands, fingers crossed on each, doubling her plea for good fortune. "I'm at ten weeks now. I've never made it to ten weeks before. This one feels right. It's different. I don't know why, but biologically, it feels . . . more real, like it's truly part of me. I think this one will be my baby. I can't believe I'm going to be a mom."

She seemed genuinely pleased and excited at the prospect of becoming a mother. Although I wanted to trust in the transformation, I also knew that where Merideth was concerned my reading comprehension skills were not legendary. At least not legendarily good.

She dropped her hands so that her fingers were laced and cradled low across her abdomen. Her flat belly—Merideth was no stranger to vanity, and she had never been someone unwilling to pay the price in crunches and Pilates sessions that were necessary to keep her abs on an uninterrupted vertical plane—belied no contour indicative of pregnancy.

As the weeks, and her pregnancy, progressed, I thought Merideth would display the constitutional evidence of procreation reluctantly. When her belly did begin to bulge in a way she could no longer fashionably disguise, she would make certain that her maternal silhouette was presented to the world to its best advantage. The designer maternity salespeople at Bergdorf and Barneys and in the

boutiques on Madison Avenue would salivate when they spotted her
rounding belly preceding her in their doors.

"Who's the lucky father? And . . . future husband?"

"His name is Eric. Eric Leffler?" She paused, waiting for me to
nod or, even better, raise an eyebrow.

Merideth had expected me to recognize her fiancé's name.
She hesitated when it was apparent that Eric Leffler was unfamiliar
to me.

Based on history, I thought she would try to find some way to offer more clues. She did. "He made his name during the '04 election.
He was one of the youngest consultants in the party, but he called
the outcome of the House races better than anyone on either side.
And he was the contrarian of record in '06. We know how that
turned out."

I shrugged. I knew how the election turned out, and how little
had changed because of it. I didn't know much more. "I don't follow
that kind of thing. Sorry."

"His early work was on the myth of democratization. Now everybody wants to know what he's thinking about the Middle East."

I shrugged again. I still didn't think I knew who he was, but I was
weighing the wisdom of pretending that I did.

"He's on leave from Columbia. He's a fellow at the Freedom
Trust Endowment? A consultant? He's a regular on cable. That's
how we met."

I tried not to subject myself to the kinds of shows on which my
ex's fiancé was likely to appear. For me, watching partisans argue
had become a form of torture that should have been banned under
the Geneva Conventions. When the water-boarding sessions proved
futile at Guantánamo, I assumed the most hardened prisoners were
subjected to nonstop cable news.

The man had an impressive CV. Although I knew where Columbia was, I didn't think I'd heard of the Freedom Trust Endowment.
Given the context, I assumed it was a think tank of some kind. Given
the size of the diamond the man was able to afford to adorn my ex-

wife's finger, the man either made a pretty good living or came from money.

"Are you happy, Merideth?" I tried to ask the question in a way that might bring the conversation back from the coasts, back down below the stratosphere. The events of the previous few weeks, culminating in Adrienne's death, had left me in desperate need of gravity. I didn't have any energy to spare for celebrity guessing games with my ex.

"Eric's younger than me. Us." She laughed. "He helps me feel young. Yes, I *am* happy."

She stressed the verb form of *to be* in a way that I thought was overdetermined—rather than convincing me, the odd emphasis with which she colored the word ended up injecting some doubt into my appraisal of her actual contentedness. I cautioned myself that all the historical complications of my time together with Merideth might have been altering my perceptions. She and I had baggage.

I think she sensed my reaction, because she quickly changed the subject. "Diane told me that you're going to raise Jonas," she said. "I don't know Lauren, of course, but I certainly understand why Adrienne chose you."

"Thank you," I said. "Lauren is a terrific mom."

She lifted her wrist and glanced at her watch. The timepiece was on her left wrist, a reality that allowed her to display her engagement ring every time she felt the impulse to check the time. It felt unkind that I doubted that the watch placement was a coincidence.

"I'm sorry," she said. "But I have to get back to DIA. Security these days, you know? Stay in touch, okay?" She looked at me with a sincere face that I'd once fallen for every time. "You will?"

I wouldn't. Stay in touch. Neither would she. We'd been divorced a long time. We hadn't stayed in touch.

"Sure," I said. "Take care of that baby. Thanks for coming today. It would mean a lot to Adrienne."

I watched her rush down the lane. Pregnant and on three-inch heels, her balance never wavered.

In six or seven months, Lauren and I would get a birth announcement.

We would send something nice. Merideth would consider the gift quaint. The circle would close around Boulder again, at least for a while. My ex-wife would be outside the perimeter.

Seven

The Canyon

Jack noticed the mini-drama between Jules and her boyfriend, Eric, and Jules's glance at Kanyn. He wasn't sure what was going on.

"She have a last name? Your friend, Jaana?" Jack asked. Jack had finished helping Carmel and had lifted his heavy pack onto his shoulders, but he hadn't tightened the straps. He lowered the weight to the ground. He wasn't quite ready to abandon his agenda with the shirtless man.

Everyone paused a few beats to give the shirtless man a chance to assign Jaana a last name.

"Like I said, we're just friends," he said after a pregnant pause. "Got together a couple times. This is just a . . . "

"Lark," Jules said, glancing toward Lisa. She still hadn't retied the scarf around her neck. Nor had she slipped either of her arms through the shoulder straps of her Kelty.

"Yeah, I guess," the man said cautiously. It was as though his hungover brain couldn't find whatever neurochemical fuel it needed to permit it to remember exactly what "lark" meant.

Jack said, "If we see her, or if we see anything that might be, you know, important, on the way out, we'll give word to someone coming down when we pass on the trail. All right? That way you'll know if we see anything."

"Okay." The shirtless man was developing an affinity for the conversational rhythm. His eyes were locked on Jack's.

Jack said, "Want to know what I think?"

The man nodded.

"She probably got tired of sleeping on the sand and she grabbed an empty bunk in one of the cabins when she got up to pee. She's probably asleep right over there. Right now, as we speak. Recovering from your party last night." He pointed toward the nearby cluster of cabins. "I bet that's where she is."

"Maybe," the shirtless man said.

Jack waited until the shirtless man looked him in the eyes before he asked one last question. "What's your name?"

"I'm Nick," he said.

"I'm Jack. You got a phone number? I'll let you know . . . if we learn anything. You know, on our way up. Wait! That gives me an idea."

Jack pulled out his digital camera again. The group let out a collective groan. Jack had been pointing the camera at someone during their entire holiday. "I'll take a quick pic of you. If we see her, I'll show it to her, tell her you're looking for her."

He snapped a photo of the shirtless man from the waist up.

Jack checked the screen. From the waist to the neck Nick looked like he was posing for a swimsuit ad. From the neck up, he looked like he'd been caught in some state trooper's dash cam at three o'clock in the morning.

Jack was flirting. The women all recognized it. Eric missed it. He was guilty of assuming that the fact that Nick had somehow talked an attractive woman into a one-night assignation in the canyon meant that he was a dedicated heterosexual.

Jack wasn't assuming anything of the kind.

The women had been part of a late discussion a couple of nights before, liberally lubricated by tequila shots, when Jack revealed that he considered himself a gifted gay seer—he possessed a unique version of X-ray vision that gave him the special ability to see through closed closet doors. "Not gaydar," he'd told the girls. "I'm no better at that than anyone else." He adopted his best Sixth Sense *whisper*. "But I can see people hiding in closets."

Jack tucked away his camera and in seconds had a pencil and notepad ready for Nick's phone info.

Eric was tired of waiting for Nick to move on. He had wanted to begin the hike out by three in the morning to avoid the scorching heat near the rim after the sun was high in the sky, but Jules and Carmel were adamant about not hiking in the dark. He stepped forward and lifted Jules's pack, holding it up to her so that she could slip it on. His gesture was made more out of exasperation than kindness. She hesitated before she extended her left arm and lowered her shoulder.

"You didn't see her? Jaana?" Jules whispered to her boyfriend. "I couldn't hear what you said before."

"No," he said. "Let's go. We should be halfway up by now."

"Sure?"

"I said I didn't."

She cinched the backpack straps tight and buckled the belt while the other hikers began to march past Nick in single file on the way to the trailhead.

Jack repeated his assurance that she was probably asleep in another cabin. That Nick should go check.

Once the entire file had passed, the shirtless man stuck his hands into the pockets of his shabby jeans and shuffled off toward another cabin that was just beginning to show signs of morning life.

His plan was to ask those people if any of them had seen Jaana.

Eight

Her Ex

I didn't know what Jonas's uncle Marty was planning. But he had some leverage. Before her death, Adrienne had stacked the deck in his favor.

Although Adrienne had named Lauren and me as permanent custodians for her son, she had thrown a joker into our winning parental hand: She had sequestered most of the half of her substantial estate she hadn't bequeathed to charity into a trust for Jonas's welfare. According to the terms of the trust documents, Martin and I were the co-trustees of Jonas's funds. Adrienne had stipulated a few guidelines for us to follow, but by and large, Marty and I would have to agree on how to invest, and how to distribute, the assets of the trust until Jonas was twenty-seven years old.

Why twenty-seven? If I ever made it to heaven, I would ask Adrienne why twenty-seven, and to please tell me the story about Hand-Job Judy.

Having known her well, I allowed for the possibility that Adrienne's testamentary machinations weren't unwitting, but rather that she had named her nebbishy brother and her stubborn neighbor as co-trustees so that she would have some earthly entertainment in case heaven's diversions weren't captivating her on any given day.

Adrienne would have predicted that her brother and I wouldn't agree on how to manage Jonas's affairs. Hell, she would have known damn well that Marty and I wouldn't agree on what day of the week it was, let alone in what bank to put Jonas's trust checking account.

I could hear her laughing all the way from heaven.

Marty and his bravissimo but kind wife, Kim, stayed until the bitter end of the reception. My wife, Lauren, was fried from being on her feet for so long. It wasn't a surprise; history had taught us that her version of MS and long stretches of vertical activity weren't compatible partners. I told her I would finish cleaning up the house. She said good-bye to Marty and Kim, promised to keep an ear tuned for the kids, who were downstairs decompressing from the emotional day, and she retreated toward the bedroom to get horizontal.

She touched me on the neck, just below my ear. Her last whispered words to me: "Don't give an inch."

Marty found me moments after the last of the other guests had departed. He rubbed his hands together and said, "Ready? Let's talk business."

The man was a caricature. I was still trying to decide of what. I squelched a sigh and allowed myself to feel some hope that at least Marty no longer seemed interested in gossiping about his sister's sexual orientation.

The optimist in me considered that progress.

Marty gestured outside and told me not to worry, that Kim would "finish straightening up the kitchen." He herded me back out toward the deck that faced the Continental Divide—apparently that was our spot for man-to-man chats. Over my shoulder I said, "No need to bother, Kim. I'll take care of it later. I mean it, don't."

Marty said, "She doesn't mind."

Kim sighed. The volume of her sighing was as exaggerated as the volume of her speaking voice. Something told me that it was an adaptation to a marriage where her partner had trouble hearing anything at all.

Emily, our big Bouvier, rushed to get outside before the door closed. She was protective of me; I could tell that she didn't trust Marty. Emily had good instincts.

Marty's agenda items for our latest terrace tête-à-tête were, one, the sale of Adrienne's house and, two, Jonas's summer plans.

Until that moment, I hadn't given either topic a moment's consideration.

Over the next few weeks—during some tortuous phone calls between Colorado and New York—Marty and I reached an accommodation. He would postpone pressing for the sale of the house for six months if I would permit Jonas to fly east to New York to stay with him and his wife and their kids for three weeks during summer vacation.

Once Marty reluctantly accepted that our intransigence about the issue of Jonas's guardianship was not a ploy, he began insisting on a long summer visit. The negotiations started with a demand by Marty for Jonas to spend the entire summer in New York. I'd countered with one week. The three-week interval was our compromise.

Although three weeks felt like an eternity in Jonas time, I tried to feel good about the middle ground I'd maneuvered.

I chose a pitching change during the sixth inning of an early season Rockies game at Coors Field to present the three-week option to Jonas for his consideration. The Rocks were already five games back in the NL West. A righty and a lefty were warming up in the bullpen. After Jonas yelled his advice to the manager—Jonas wanted the southpaw in the game—my stepson had some advice for me, too.

Jonas had a primitive understanding of the position he was in— he was a chess enthusiast, knew the consequences of being down a piece, and knew well the role of pawns—but he wasn't eager to leave the anchor of his Spanish Hills homes, old and new, to spend an extended summer holiday with relatives who were almost total strangers to him. He suggested a modification to the plan—he asked me if I would go east along with him so that I could stay close by during his summer trip.

I thought it was an adaptive solution. I ran it by Lauren. She, too, was impressed with Jonas's idea. I had already decided that I would be taking at least a month's summer break from my practice. I needed some time away. I would use some of it to go east with Jonas. I would literally be close by if he needed me—and he and I would be able to spend a day together exploring New York City during each of the three weeks he was with his aunt and uncle's family in White Plains.

Lauren saw the new summer schedule as an opportunity too. She had just been informed that the local U.S. Attorney had decided not to prosecute her for a prescription drug importation fiasco she'd gotten messed up in earlier in the year. The day after I told her I was considering going to New York with Jonas, she began planning a long-postponed trip to the Netherlands to track down a daughter she'd given up for adoption as an infant many years before we met.

She considered the timing auspicious medically, as well.

Her neurologist had recently recommended a change in her MS medications. For many years she had been taking IM interferon injections to control the onset of new multiple sclerosis symptoms. Given her recent instability, her doctor wanted to switch her to Tysabri, the first of the monoclonal antibodies available for MS prophylaxis. As part of the transition protocol she would need to go off interferon prior to her first dose of Tysabri.

She would make the trip to Holland during the hiatus between the two medicines. A "double holiday," she called it.

Grace was torn about the change in plans. She'd been excited about spending the summer in Boulder with her new brother, but she was also thrilled that she was going to get the chance to go to Europe for a girls' adventure with her mother.

What neither Lauren nor I said to each other, however, was that we were both content to use the break from each other to continue to heal. It had been a difficult year for each of us personally. It had been a troublesome year for us as a couple.

Jonas's needs provided a perfect platform.

Mona, Jonas's nanny, eagerly volunteered to house-sit, keep an eye on Adrienne's vacant home, and watch our three dogs.

Our summer cards, it seemed, had been dealt.

Nine

The Canyon

In the predawn, the vertical rock wall seemed to reach from the center of the earth all the way to the dark sky. The group climbing out grew quieter as the incline grew steeper. They all knew that the day promised—cross-your-heart-and-hope-to-die kind of promised—to grow hotter as the pitch of the trail grew more acute and as the sun climbed higher.

After the first section of the North Kaibab Trail the group developed a determined rhythm. Jules's boyfriend, Eric, set an early pace that she thought was too aggressive. Lisa kept up with him. Jules, Jack, Kanyn, and Carmel fell back about fifty yards. The interval between the groups soon stretched to seventy-five.

Jack got the women laughing with a playful description of Shirtless Man's abs.

Jules had the long, easy stride of a natural athlete. The exertion of the climb didn't wind her as it did the others, though the dry air turned her voice husky. She said, "You can have his abs—but those pecs. I mean, come on. I can almost—almost—understand Jaana's decision to come down here with somebody she just met. Though he did seem one shot short of a cocktail."

"Be nice," Carmel said. "He got a little drunk, so what?"

Jack agreed. "Who cares, who cares, who . . . cares? I'm going to give the poor man the benefit of the doubt all day long . . . and if I get lucky someday, maybe all night long. You should cut him some slack too, ladies. You should! So the guy was a little hungover. Which one of us hasn't been there, waking up somewhere where nothing quite makes sense? Does it matter? And just forget all your slutty fantasies about him, because I have dibs on those pecs. And that butt. I'm the one who has his photo in my camera and his phone number in my pocket. That should tell you all something about his . . . true inclinations."

"Jack! He's not gay," said Jules. "Didn't you see him staring at Carmel's boobs?"

"Light from a dying star," Jack said dismissively. "Wagers? Anyone? I don't even care if it does turn out that the boy is from a tribe that hails from the dimmest part of the planet. As God is my witness, Jaana—wherever the hell you are—I understand you, girl. I would have come down here with that man for a night . . . or two."

"Jack!" Carmel scolded him.

Jack laughed. "I'm sorry, little mama. But I would have. Call me a slut, doesn't matter. That"—he sighed dramatically—"package doesn't come along every day. And sometimes on Christmas morning you care more about opening the package than you do about what you find inside. Am I right? Am I?"

"Amen," Jules said. "But once the holidays are over . . ."

"I know, I know. I'm not saying the boy has relationship legs. But I am saying he has a chest and an ass that you only see on statues. What does it matter to me? I'm planning my Christmas morning, not my Valentine's Day."

Jules asked, "Did you give him your number, Jack?"

"You kidding? He won't call me—he's not that far along in his personal awareness. But he'll remember me when I call him. That's how it works." Jack grinned.

The women laughed. They laughed more when it became clear that although any of them could've drawn a topo map of Shirtless Man's pecs, none of them could remember the color of Shirtless Man's eyes.

Jack knew. He pursed his lips together and raised his hand like the teacher's pet until the girls were looking at him. "Dark mostly, gray I think. But there's some teal on the edges," he said. "And some little periwinkle flares near his pupils."

Jules laughed so hard at Jack's description of the color of Shirtless Man's eyes that she shot some of the Gatorade she was drinking right out through her nose.

Kanyn had moved ahead. She was halfway between the two groups.

Twenty minutes later, as more of the day's light began to seep into the canyon, Carmel stopped near the end of a diagonal section and asked everyone to pause for a moment. They had reached the hairpin of a switchback a few hundred feet above the canyon floor. "Let's all take one long look for Jaana," she said. "See if she's . . . on a rock, or maybe sleeping. Maybe she went to meditate someplace and she fell asleep. We have a great vantage here." She raised her voice and called out to the three men marching ahead, "Stop for a second, everybody. Look for Jaana."

Eric called down to them from his position above them, past the hairpin. "Why? How the hell does a guy lose his girlfriend in a place like this?"

"Just stop for a second. Everybody, please," Carmel said. "What if Jaana's sick, or she's hurt? We can see more from up here than they can see down there. Maybe she's wearing something bright. Now that there is a little bit of light, we'll be able to see the color. It will stand out."

"Be brighter than her boyfriend," Eric chimed in.

Lisa laughed. No one else did.

"Please," said Carmel.

Eric ignored her. He didn't slow his pace up the trail.

"It could be somebody's life we're talking about," Carmel said.

Eric's voice was cold. "If we don't get out of here before the sun gets directly overhead, it could be all of our lives we're talking about.

She's not our problem. There're plenty of other people down there to help that idiot look for her. You think you see something from here, then what—you're going to run back down there only to find out she's hooking up with somebody in one of the other cabins? You'll have wasted a ton of energy and lost the best part of the day for making progress to get out of here."

Carmel was offended. "How could you say that? What if it were one of us who were lost? And what if one of us is the one who is supposed to find Jaana?"

" 'Supposed to find—' Never mind." Eric wasn't much of a fan of fate. He didn't respond any further.

The women on the lower section of trail continued to examine the canyon floor. So did Jack.

Lisa resumed the monotonous climb behind Eric.

Kanyn took a few tentative steps uphill.

Depth of field was especially difficult to discern in the shadows. The hikers scanned the landscape below. Checked the narrow swaths of beach. Surveyed the twine-colored trails that cut into the sandstone and led into the side gorges of the canyon.

Despite the fact that more than a hundred years had passed since John Wesley Powell's first Anglo expedition moved down the canyon, human forms remained alien in the landscape. In the area away from the civilization created around Phantom Ranch, spotting visitors on the canyon floor was as easy as finding astronauts on the moon.

At the campground between the ranch and the Colorado River, where Jaana should have woken up in a sleeping bag beside Nick, smoke snaked in a gentle ribbon from a stove. Someone would soon be starting coffee.

One after another each said, "Nothing."

Jack said, "I got a bad feeling about this."

Carmel removed her wide hat. She said, "Me too. Could she have fallen into the river? Is that possible?"

Eric and Lisa were directly above the others on a switchback. Lisa called down, "You guys should get moving. It's not getting any cooler."

Jules glared at her.

Jack said, "You know what? I'm going back down."

Jules hesitated. She looked up the hill at her boyfriend, then back down toward the river rushing through the canyon. Finally, she said, "I'm with you."

Carmel said, "I think Jaana needs my help too. I feel her calling."

The three turned downhill.

Kanyn watched them. She stood frozen on the trail for a moment as the once-cohesive group split, some climbing, some descending.

After another twenty seconds she took a step uphill.

For almost a minute Eric and Lisa continued their climb up the wall.

"Stop," Lisa said when she looked back. "Eric, hold on. Some of them are going down. Look."

Eric stopped. Kanyn had resumed her climb. The other two women and Jack were making a gravity-assisted descent back toward the canyon floor.

"Shit," Eric said. Jules was among the descending Samaritans.

"Let's hold on here a minute," Lisa said. "Let Kanyn catch up with us."

Eric stared down to the river for an extended period, then craned his neck back so that his eyes were pointed in the direction of the distant rim. It wouldn't be long before the rising sun would be high enough to clear the edge of the canyon and become visible in the eastern sky. Hot would soon get hotter. He imagined the heat radiating off the dark rocks higher in the canyon.

"I'm climbing out before I get fried by that damn sun. I don't care what the hell anybody else does."

Kanyn caught up with them in two minutes. No words were

exchanged before the three resumed their climb. Eric paused to allow the two women to pass him, taking up a position in the rear to contain the impulses of any more stragglers.

The column stopped when it reached the turn of the next hairpin. They hadn't stopped to look for Jaana, but rather to monitor the progress of the posse that had split off. The trio retracing their steps were approaching the network of trails on the canyon floor. Before long they would be approaching the oasis at Phantom Ranch.

Eric abruptly pulled off his sunglasses and screamed, "Jules! Jules! God damn it, Jules!"

His angry bellow sliced through the morning calm and the vehement echo followed instantly, bouncing fresh rage off the vertical faces of the gorge.

"You have the fucking car keys," he said. "God damn it."

He threw his hat down at his feet and kicked it. It levitated about eighteen inches before it floated down and tumbled over the edge of the narrow trail. It skipped and stopped and started again until it got caught on a rock outcropping about halfway between the switchbacks.

Ten

The three who continued the climb that morning were interviewed individually by the ranger coordinating the search at the North Rim. Eric was first. Then Lisa. Then Kanyn.

When did you last see the missing girl?
What was she wearing?
What, if anything, did she say?
Did you see her with her companion? Did they get along?
Did you speak with her at all about her plans to come back up to the rim?
What was her mood? Was she upset?
Did she say anything about the guy she was with? Were they getting along?
What did he say when he came up to your group this morning?
Did he seem drunk? Angry? Worried?
Did you see any blood on him?

Before they reached the rim, Kanyn dropped back on the trail so she could speak to Eric privately.

"Before? You said you didn't see her," Kanyn said. "The girl he was with. Why? I know you talked to her."

"When?"

"Last night. Just after dark. Between the campground and the river."

"*He asked if we saw her around bedtime. I didn't.*"

"*Still. You saw her.*"

"*We said hello on the trail. That's all.*"

"*You weren't on the trail when I saw you. You were back by the canyon wall. You were talking.*"

"*Were you alone?*" Eric asked her.

Kanyn hesitated. "*Yes.*"

"*Could you hear?*"

"*No.*"

"*You didn't see us. What you think you saw is not important,*" he said.

"*If they haven't found her, they're going to ask us questions when we get up to the top, Eric. What are you going to say? You want me to lie about it?*"

"*I didn't see that girl last night. That's what I'm going to say. If you say otherwise, I'll say you're mistaken.*"

"*Why?*"

"*There're some things it's better not to be involved in.*"

"*You can just pretend something didn't happen? How do you do that?*"

Eric didn't respond at first. "*I don't know what happened to her, Kanyn. I can't help them.*"

"*Do you think he had something to do with it? Nick? The shirtless guy?*"

"*Whatever happened, they'll figure it out. The Park Service people. They'll do what they do. Whether I saw her or not won't change anything. And whatever you think you saw, I'm pretty sure you're mistaken.*"

"*I hope he didn't do anything to her.*"

Eric said, "*They've probably already found her.*"

He picked up the pace. She matched him.

"*Do you want me to lie, Eric?*"

He took a few more steps before he replied. "*I'm going to tell them I didn't see her last night, Kanyn.*"

"Do you want me to lie?"

From above them, Lisa called out, "You guys are slowing down."

Kanyn let Eric pull ahead and catch up with Lisa.

Aloud, to herself, Kanyn said, "Well, I saw her."

Jack, Carmel, and Jules had dumped their packs at the ranch and were nearing the boat beach on the Colorado to assist with the informal search for Jaana.

Carmel pointed toward the canyon wall. "This is where we were last night. Did we see her?" Carmel asked. "Was that her with Eric? Was that Jaana?"

Jack said, "I don't know. I checked my camera this morning when we first got on the trail. Everything I took last night without the flash is just dark, dark, dark."

"Could it have been her?" Carmel asked. "Do you think?"

"Could have, I guess. But it could have been someone else. That's what I thought last night—that's what we all thought last night. I don't know about you guys, but I was a little buzzed by then."

"Lisa? Is that who you thought it was?" Carmel said. "She's been all over Eric."

Jules said, "We all thought it was Lisa. I'm not saying for sure that it was, or it wasn't. If it was, I think what we saw is between me and Eric."

"So you think it was Eric? For sure?"

"Mel, this is between him and me. Let us handle it."

"Jules, what do you—"

"I don't know, Mel. It was dark. I'm not even sure it was Eric. I'm certainly not going to pretend I can identify a woman I only just met if I can't even identify my own boyfriend."

Jack said, "It might not have been her, Mel. We don't know what we saw. At least I don't know what I saw. Not for sure."

"Can I see the pictures you took?" Carmel asked.

"*The batteries are dead. I can't take anything, I can't show you anything.*"

"*You don't think that was Eric we saw? I'm pretty sure—*"

"*I can only say what I think I saw, Mel,*" Jack said.

"*Jules, you're a lawyer. Do you think—*"

"*I don't know, Mel. I just don't know.*" She turned and smiled. "*Let's just find her. Then none of it matters.*"

Carmel said, "*Yes. Let's go find her. Right now.*" She hitched her pack higher on her hips and skipped twice down the trail.

Eleven

Her Ex

The cast came off my hand in late June.

A little more than a month later, Jonas and I were in New York.

He was—against his wishes, and against my better judgment—a thirty-minute train trip away from New York City, spending a few weeks with his aunt, uncle, and two cousins in White Plains. I agreed to stay close by. We would spend a day together each week doing something fun.

After checking to see what a hotel would cost for three weeks in New York City, I used Craigslist to find a sublet in Murray Hill, only a short walk to Grand Central. The woman renting her apartment to me insisted I pay for the full month she'd be gone.

My landlord was a woman about my age named Ottavia Barbarini.

Her apartment was a tiny—by Colorado standards—one bedroom, but it had a lovely view to the west. Ottavia explained how each year there were a glorious couple of weeks during which she could look down Thirty-ninth as the sun dropped straight between the long rows of buildings before splashing in slow motion into the Hudson.

"Summer or winter?" I asked her.

She recognized that, given the brief interval of my sublet, it was an important question. She laughed and said, "Sorry. You will miss it."

Based on my limited Craigslist experience I accepted Ottavia's biased appraisal that my new sublet was a steal, but I also allowed that New York rules applied—I was paying the equivalent of a hundred and fifty percent of my monthly Boulder mortgage payment for three weeks' use of about twenty percent of the square feet. I also knew I got the deal from Ottavia only because I was stupid enough to be looking to stay in Manhattan during a time when anyone who had the resources was doing his or her best to get out of the city to someplace where air actually moved, where breathing didn't require that lungs do double duty as dehumidifiers, and where the myriad odors assaulting their nostrils weren't stupefying in their complexity and general putridity.

Ottavia was charming and funny. She spoke beautiful English, but her Italian accent—she said it was Sicilian—was spicy. I had to concentrate to understand her.

She initially danced around my question about what she did for a living, but eventually revealed that she worked in a health ministry at the United Nations. She let me know she would be in the Canary Islands while I was in her apartment. She would be almost unreachable. "I have a mobile. I can get messages. I would rather not," she said.

My sublet fees were undoubtedly subsidizing her holiday.

After she showed me around the apartment, she revealed the rules of our apparently illicit arrangement. When she stopped suddenly and turned to face me in the hallway, I found myself only inches from her.

Her perfume was perfect. For five seconds I was incapable of noticing anything other than how good she smelled.

"Don't worry about the doormen," she said, interrupting my appraisal. She made a motion with her hands that I couldn't decipher. I guessed the gesture meant "They're cool." She instructed me that if the building super asked or if, God forbid, her landlord knocked at the door wondering what was going on, I was to tell them that I was her brother visiting from Champaign, Illinois. Under no circumstances was I to answer her telephone.

I said, "You have a brother in Champaign? At the university?" I was making conversation.

Her shoulders jumped along with her eyebrows. "I make one up. All my sublets are relatives from Champaign. Uncles, aunts, brothers." She smiled. "No one here knows Champaign. They think France, wine. What are they going to do?"

She meant her landlord, and her super.

"I don't speak Italian," I said. "Will that be a problem?"

She leaned toward me as if to share an intimacy. She was still smiling—her front teeth could have used a little straightening, her solitary physical flaw. "The war?" she said, comporting her face so that it held a bushel of dramatic confusion. I didn't bother to ask which war, suspecting that was the point.

"Say nothing more to them," she insisted, making a gesture with her left hand that I translated as dismissive. Of her landlord, not of me. "Not a word. Not necessary. My landlord is in the Hamptons. He won't come back to the city unless . . . Not necessary. No. I told them you were painfully shy. A serious . . . problem. You are on medicine."

"Medicine?" I smiled.

"Sì." She reached out and touched me above the elbow. She left her fingers there. I think she was pleased that she had sublet her apartment to a willing coconspirator. "You can move in two days if you would like. I leave tomorrow night. JFK. My holiday begins." She laughed.

Her laugh was like a song. I wrote her a big check.

She offered to buy me lunch to introduce me to the neighborhood. She looked at her watch and frowned. "But quick?" she said.

"You choose," I said.

"*Pesce?* Fish?"

"Great."

"Bene. There's a place in Grand Central."

After we ordered she took my Zagat guide from my hand and circled a few places she liked in Murray Hill, in the neighborhood near Grand Central all the way over to Times Square, and in the nearby Garment District. She told me which deli was good and where to buy groceries. When she asked me if I wanted any recommendations for clubs, I declined.

She found that amusing. I explained vaguely about Jonas in White Plains.

She glanced at my left hand. "You are married? Sì?"

"Yes."

"Your wife is . . . ?"

"Traveling. In Holland."

"Ah, sì . . . And . . . non. I understand. And with your time here when Jonas—sì?—is away, you . . . ?"

You understand what? I thought. "I hope to get to know the city better. Relax. Kill some time."

Ottavia made a perplexed face. "You want dead time?" she said, struggling with the idiom.

I was tempted to explain that her interpretation was more apt than she could imagine. Instead, I said, "Something like that."

"I am in town for one more night. Then I leave." She opened her hands as though she were releasing a dove. "You will be gone to Colorado—Boulder—before I get back."

She pronounced it *"bowl-dare."*

"Sì," I said, unconsciously adopting the rudiments of her vocabulary.

"This will be the only time we . . . meet."

She was describing an opportunity gained, not one lost. My next words could hardly have surprised me more. "I know almost no one in the city. Would you have dinner with me tonight, Ottavia?"

Were my superego doing any monitoring—like the rest of me, it appeared to be taking August off—it would have noted that I had spoken without consideration, because any consideration at all would have stopped me in my tracks.

Ottavia looked away. I thought for that instant that I might have misread her.

"We will go downtown," she said. "I know a place. Sicilian. More *pesce*. But for true."

Transit lessons over, lunch complete, we walked through the massive terminal out onto Forty-first. "Have fun here, Alan," she said. "In the city. My home. I will leave with a safe heart. I know now I can trust you. That's good." She placed a closed fist between her breasts before she added, "Ciao."

She took off down the sidewalk to get to a bus or a different sub-way line. She walked away in that determined, head-fixed, gaze-set, long-strided way that is peculiar to solitary women in big cities. Half a block away Ottavia turned back, caught my eye, and waved. I was surprised that she'd looked back. But mostly I was surprised by the fact that I was still looking at her when she did.

I'd been looking at her ass.

Her face lit up in a laugh before she resumed her march. I assumed that her amusement was at my New York virginity. And perhaps at my extramarital virginity. In a few more sec-onds she was gone from my view, lost in the sidewalk chorus of Midtown.

I pulled out my cell and checked the time. I'd see her again in less than six hours.

I was looking forward to it.

Holy shit, I thought.

* * *

For the rest of the afternoon I wandered between Fifth and Times Square. I joined in the madness while the skyscrapers emptied and the streets and sidewalks filled with people hurrying or exhaling at the end of their workdays.

My eye found lovers. Couples holding hands. People stealing kisses. People greeting before they ducked in someplace for a drink. Looks of love.

Were a patient describing the afternoon to me, I would tell him, "You see what you're prepared to see."

When I got back to my hotel room—I was staying at the Pod Hotel a dozen blocks away—I sat on the edge of the bed below the air-conditioning vent until my copious sweat dried. It took a while. I paced. Although I had splurged for a double, square footage was at a premium. I busted my shins into the desk chair before I gave up pacing and flopped on my back on the bed.

I called Ottavia to cancel our dinner plans. I told her that I had sudden family business; I had to go to White Plains to see my son.

Her voice told me that she didn't believe me, and that she was disappointed.

"I was looking forward to starting my holiday early," she said.

"I'm sorry," I said.

I expected she would say good-bye and hang up. She didn't. "Alan," she started. She held the silence for an interlude before she said, "I have a man I love in Taormina."

She allowed that truth to expand and fill the air before she hung up.

I couldn't decide why I had canceled. Or why I had lied. The only thing I knew for certain was why I had made the date in the first place. As darkness continued to fall, I knew that a night in the city with a lovely woman was just what I needed.

I also knew the woman should have been my wife.

I vowed to stay home, within the confines of my pod. I called Lauren.

In psychology, my reflex to reach out to Lauren is called "undo-ing." It's the trailing half of an ego defense that shrinks refer to as "doing/undoing." Undoing is the attempted psychological bleaching that we do to cleanse away the residue of some just-committed psychological sullying.

Planning to go out with Ottavia—and whatever might have come next—had been the "doing."

Twelve

By the time I had been in New York for nine days Jonas had joined me in the city twice. His visits gave me a chance to eyeball his coping, the license to play tourist—we'd actually made two separate visits to the Empire State Building, one daytime, one nighttime—and his companionship gave me a chance to learn with some relief that I enjoyed my new son's company when he and I were alone.

On the first day that Jonas was with me, I dropped my cell phone onto a sidewalk near the Museum of Natural History. My ancient clamshell bounced off the concrete and ricocheted off the rounded base of a newspaper stand before it skittered from the curb into the street. Within two seconds the front tire of a New York taxicab obliterated one of the world's oldest operating mobile devices.

Jonas was both horrified and amused. He insisted on rescuing the carcass from the street as though it were the remains of an injured pet. After performing a quick autopsy on the corpse, he held up a thumbnail-size piece of plastic. "Your SIM looks okay," he said.

I shrugged. I didn't know what that meant.

"That's good," he explained, recognizing my ignorance for what it was.

Our next stop was Times Square. I took him shopping for baseball jerseys for him and for his cousins. He took me shopping for a new phone. The kid's knowledge about mobile phones made my jaw drop. My old phone had been a technological antique, but it met my needs. Its primary virtue was its simplicity. It could do nothing more—or I'd never learned to coax it to do anything more—than make and receive phone calls. The new phone Jonas selected for me could probably cook a brisket if I would buy the groceries and hit the right buttons. He promised to teach me all of my new phone's features the next time we were together.

To cover myself in the interim I begged him to teach me how to make calls on the device, and maybe even answer them. We sat on a bench on the narrow island in the center of Times Square while he gave me my first lessons. The kid had the patience of a born teacher. It was a trait he had not inherited from his mother.

The lesson was one of those precious moments with kids that parents don't see coming. I didn't want it to end.

Although I was lonesome during the extended periods that Jonas was in White Plains, I recognized from my close call with Ottavia that I had demons to fight. Any shrink will tell you that the greatest time of danger for a suicidal patient is not during the depths of despair. Risk is at its peak during the brief window when the patient first begins to look a little brighter. I recognized the signs. I was beginning to feel brighter.

My personal danger had nothing to do with suicide. A different kind of self-destruction was on my mind. I recognized that Ottavia represented danger, but convinced myself I could dance around it. Companionship, at least not the kind I had fantasized about with my Manhattan landlady, was not a solution to what was ailing Lauren and me.

As an antidote I discovered to my relief that I was able to suck excess energy from the city like a parasite. In the short term at least, the incessant verve of Manhattan provided a contact high. I could see a time in the not-too-distant future that I might have to insulate myself from the peripheral mayhem and filter out the background noise of the city. But I wasn't there, yet. New York was what I needed.

Summer in the city? Part of the package. I coped by breathing through my mouth and learning to sweat.

If I'd been walking hungry and empty-handed into the empanadas place on Thirty-ninth when the new phone in my pocket chimed—Jonas's first task the next time I saw him was going to be to download me a less embarrassing ringtone—I probably would have let the call roll over to voice mail. But I was walking out of the restaurant, still hungry, with my take-out lunch already in hand. My plan was to eat my lunch in close proximity to the air conditioner in Ottavia's living room. I figured I could take care of the call on the walk back to my flat without postponing my meal.

Caller ID on my mobile read E LEFFLER. The name rang no bells. I flipped open the phone partly because I was curious to know who E Leffler was.

"Hello," I said, joining a dozen pedestrians on that block of Midtown with a mobile phone stuck to an ear. I had intentionally tried to sound neutral in my greeting, but I could tell that I'd tinged the "hello" with suspicion that the caller had reached me in error.

"Alan? It's Me," she said.

Me. Merideth.

"Merideth? Hi." *Leffler. Eric Leffler. Ah, yes.* Her fiancé, or by now, perhaps husband. The big-time consulting genius. Some hale fellow at the something foundation. A talking head for the network that wrote Merideth's paychecks.

I said, "How are you? How's that baby of yours doing?"

I did the gestational equation. Merideth had announced that she had been ten weeks pregnant when I saw her after Adrienne's funeral. She should have been twenty-two, twenty-three weeks along. I imagined her belly. Cantaloupe-to-volleyball round.

"Not so good," she said in reply to my question. Her voice was

DEAD TIME • 67

tentative. My marital history with her helped me recognize the sticky cadence—she was inserting staccato pauses during quick inhales while trying not to descend into whimpers.

"What are—"

"Listen," she said. "Okay? Just listen." She completed an audible cycle of inhale and exhale. "I'm calling because I need you to get in touch with somebody for me . . . somebody we knew back when . . . we were together. An old friend of ours, or yours."

"Merideth, I'm—"

"I'm not done," she said. "Please listen. I also need to know if Sam Purdy is still on suspension. For that thing . . . he did? Diane told me about it at Adrienne's funeral. I need to talk with him—or maybe you can talk to him for me—to see if he would be interested in doing a job for me. For us?"

Us? Me and Merideth? My pulse skipped at the idea that she and I had a job that needed doing.

Sam Purdy was a Boulder police detective, and a good friend. He was in the midst of a six-month suspension without pay from the department for misleading his superiors about a personal conflict he had on a case he had been investigating. The conflict? He'd been sleeping with the victim, who happened to be another cop.

Merideth grew tired of waiting for me to respond to her entreaty. She said, "It's something . . . private, or we'd hire someone here. Very . . . private. For me, and for Eric. Do you think Sam would . . . Could you talk to him maybe . . . ? As a favor for me . . . Please? I know you guys are . . ."

The part about calling Sam didn't trouble me—Sam may have been eager for some work—but my role in the equation that Merideth was scrawling on the board remained indecipherable, and my discomfort at getting a call from her hadn't abated. Whom did she want me to contact? I reviewed the roster of people in Boulder who had been our friends during our marriage.

Too long a list. I got nowhere.

I said, "Sam's still on leave. For another few months, I think. Merideth, what's wrong? What's going on? You're crying, or at least trying very hard not to."

With that, the effort to stem the tears ended. She sniffled for a few seconds before she blurted, "I lost the baby, Alan. Right after I was in Boulder. I can't lose another one. I just can't."

The lost baby? I made a guess. I said, "You had another miscarriage?"

I was baffled as to why she would need Sam Purdy's help if my conjecture were true. The I-can't-lose-another-one part? I had no idea.

"It was awful. The worst. They were all bad, but this one was . . . the worst. Only a few days after Adrienne's funeral. I'd almost completed a full trimester. I thought I was safe, you know. Home free? No warning. I had some funny pains that didn't seem serious, and then some cramps. Then"—she swallowed—"some spotting." The sticky cadence became more pronounced as she continued. "And then . . . one more goddamn D&C and . . . I swear I can't let it . . . Not now . . . Not again, no . . . No."

I felt sad for her. "I'm so sorry," I said. I remained perplexed. What did she mean by "another one"? And how could Sam be of any help with Merideth's reproductive problems? "Where does Sam fit in, Merideth? I don't understand."

"Okay . . . I didn't think you'd answer the phone. I thought you'd be with a patient and I'd just leave you a message." She blew her nose. "The surrogate has gone missing. Or we think she has. At least I do. She's hasn't been at her place here in like three days. She's not at . . . her apartment in L.A., where she lives, either. She's not answering her cell. It's not like her, not at all. She's a friendly person, outgoing, she's chatty, and she always returns my calls. Eric doesn't want to use anyone local to find her because . . . well, that's too long a story . . . I was hoping that maybe Sam, you know, could do something discreetly . . . Look around, maybe. Contact people who know her. Unofficially, I mean. We have some ideas, and we can pay him, Alan. That's not a problem. He just needs to talk with some people for us."

The surrogate? "The surrogate? You have a surrogate? For your baby? I don't get it. She's carrying . . . ?"

"Yes."

"And she's . . . missing, and you want Sam to find her?"

I was hoping for some elucidation, but she didn't offer any. "Have you called the police, Merideth?"

"It's not that simple."

I could have asked her why not. It didn't feel like the time. "Are you at work?" I asked.

She made a nasal sound that might have been another quick blow into a tissue. I interpreted it as assent. "L.A. or New York?" I said.

Merideth had worked in California for a long time before taking her current network weekly newsmagazine gig. Adrienne had told me that Merideth still spent a week or so every couple of months in L.A. She'd held on to her L.A. condo.

"New York."

"Can you take a short break?" I said.

After another moment spent trying to recompose herself, she managed to say, "I probably should, shouldn't I? That's a good idea, Alan. I'll go get some iced coffee or something. Thank you. Thanks."

"I mean right now, Merideth—can you take a break and meet me? I'm in the city. In New York. Not too far from you."

"What?"

The solitary word did dual duty—part wonder, part accusation.

"I'm offering to meet you. Pick a place close to your office. Give me twenty minutes, maybe half an hour. I'm down near Grand Central." I looked around for a street sign at the nearest intersection. "Madison, near Thirty-ninth."

"You're in the city?"

"Jonas. Adrienne's son. My— Our son. I'll explain when I see you."

She was silent. I began to steel myself for some repeat of the caution she'd offered when she was in Boulder about our "generosity" in agreeing to become Jonas's new parents. What I should have been steeling myself for was my ex-wife's susceptibility to narcissistic bruising.

Where Merideth was concerned, I was blessedly out of practice.

Her silence extended. I said, "He's spending a few weeks with his uncle—Adrienne's brother—in White Plains. I need to be close by. He's . . . vulnerable. It's been a tough stretch for him."

She moved her cell too close to her lips. The sound of her breathing hit my ear like a strong wind. "You're in town. And you didn't call?"

Here it comes. I could have said, "No, Merideth, I didn't call you." But it seemed superfluous and unkind. I took my own temperature—I felt no animosity toward her. Just compassion. I stayed silent.

"How long have you been in the city?" she asked.

She was handing me a saltbox while she exposed a fresh wound on her flesh. The familiar choreography between us, simple steps executed with perfection, brought back memories. Not good ones.

"Only a few days," I said, reducing my stay by a factor of three, reflexively buying into whatever guilt promotion she was shoving my way.

"Is he with you now? Jonas?"

"No. He's with his aunt and uncle today. Hey, I'm here, and I'm offering to meet you. Right now. You want to come down here? Would you like me to come there? We can talk. Would you like that?"

Thirteen

I should not have let her pick the spot.

I should have said, "I'll be at the Whole Foods in Columbus Circle in half an hour. We'll get a smoothie." Or, "How about Bryant Park? Why don't you come down here?" Merideth wouldn't need any help from me in finding Bryant Park—I was certain she finagled seats in the tents for a few of the runway shows during Fashion Week.

Hell, even a deli, or a coffee shop, or a bar at some Midtown hotel near her network studios would have made a fine spot to meet. But, no, I let her pick the spot.

The story of our marriage.

She chose Strawberry Fields.

By the time the cab turned into the southern end of Central Park I'd refocused on the fact that Merideth felt she had a real crisis on her hands.

The surrogate? Is missing? That's what she had said.

During our marriage we'd had a few tunes that we considered our songs. "Strawberry Fields Forever" was one. Merideth had arrived in our relationship with a pristine copy of the original 45 but lacked a turntable that would play it. It turned out that I possessed a turntable. At the time we thought the serendipity was evidence of how naturally we completed each other.

I considered the possibility that she had grown fond of the Lennon garden since she'd moved to New York City. Maybe it was a place that would provide solace to her at a moment of emotional upheaval. Perhaps she'd pulled me uptown thirty-something blocks instead of meeting me halfway for a damn good reason. Perhaps her choice wasn't about sending me a message.

And perhaps my next New York cabbie would have a name I could pronounce.

I knew that no matter how late I arrived I would get to Central Park before she did. It was a given. Merideth didn't wait, at least not for me, or for our friends.

I didn't bother to scan the paths or the benches for her when I arrived. She wouldn't be there. Merideth didn't show up like the rest of us. She made entrances. An entrance requires an audience. Protocol required that I had to take my seat, flip through *Playbill* a couple of times, roll it into a tube, and wait for the house lights to dim.

Central Park wasn't crowded. The day was too muggy and too hot for all but the most diehard strollers and tourists. I sat on a bench below a tree and tried to think cool thoughts. Almost fifteen minutes after our appointed rendezvous time I watched a black Town Car roll to a curb on the west side.

The orchestra in the pit in my head started playing "Penny Lane." The rear door of the Lincoln sufficed as the curtain. Merideth stepped from the backseat as though she'd practiced the choreography. There was not a single clumsy moment as she unfurled herself from the car. She paused two steps from the curb, unconsciously holding a pose as though she'd hit her mark.

She was wearing bronze metallic shades, an eggplant shirtdress that hung on her like jersey but shimmered in the summer light as though every tenth thread had been spun from gold, and heels that seemed impractical for a workday in the city. Her hair was pulled back into a taut ponytail. She carried a long, thin purse in her right hand that looked like it might have been designed to transport a demi-baguette or a large salami.

Merideth appeared confident and benevolent as she began striding into the garden. It was as though Central Park, or at least this section of it, were hers alone and that she felt a profound sense of civic pride for sharing it.

She also looked gorgeous, though her beauty didn't stir me as it once had. Neither my brain nor my groin registered any attraction to her. I felt only the twice-removed presence of watching a familiar actress stepping onstage.

I'd already attended too many of Merideth's performances to fail to predict what would be coming next. My ex-wife was a thespian who, regardless of role, always ended up playing some version of herself.

I suspected she spotted me after she exited the Town Car—the bench I was sitting on was directly in her line of sight—but it took her a few additional seconds to acknowledge my presence across the garden. When she waved it was as though she had just picked me out of a crowd. There was no crowd, of course, just me sitting alone on a bench in the shadow of an old tree.

I stood and returned her wave. She began walking toward me. About halfway to the bench she moved into a high-heeled jog. Near the end of her run her urgency exploded, and she lengthened her stride. Cynically, I wondered if she was trying to make certain that I got a great view of her lovely legs.

I was also thinking that I could have been watching the final few frames of a commercial for a new women's razor.

Fourteen

His Ex

It seems like it's always something. Home, work, Eric. Lately, Eric a lot. For a successful man, he needs a lot of reassurance. I didn't see that coming with him. He's shown he can hold his own on Sunday mornings with Russert, is quick enough to parry Carville's best, which isn't easy, and once even got Stephanopoulos to cower.

Women, especially attractive women, flummox him, which is endearing. And not. He's a decent companion at a formal dinner, but the truth is he requires too much handholding at cocktail parties. Kind of like Alan in that way.

I tell myself that maybe it's his age.

Whatever. It seemed like it was always something, with someone. You would think at work I could've walked from my office to the bathroom, from the bathroom to the elevator, and then get across the building lobby to the sidewalk in the middle of the afternoon without having to have three impromptu meetings about a segment that we weren't even planning to tape for another two weeks. None of the people who interrupted my march to the door learned anything they didn't already know.

While I made my escape from the building I had a choice of either looking like a diva—wearing sunglasses in the elevator is not my favorite look—or having to explain my red eyes to everyone I ran into on the way outside. I chose to play diva. I knew my reputation well enough to know that it was an act that required much less explanation. In my business vanity is a forgivable sin.

I'd wasted a few minutes at my desk freshening my makeup after I hung up with Alan. Just some eyeliner and blush. And lip gloss. I had already used a couple of minutes weighing whether to call for a network car to take me to Central Park for our rendezvous. My assistant thought I should just grab a cab uptown.

But with my recent luck, if I took a cab I'd end up in one that hadn't had the air conditioner turned on since Memorial Day. After the driver had spent half a shift behind the wheel in an oppressively hot taxi I knew damn well what he would smell like. I absolutely did not want to be all sweaty and aggravated when I finally got to the park.

Still, I hesitated about the car choice because I suspected that Alan would make some unnecessary assumptions if he saw me arrive in a Town Car.

Everything has meaning in his world.

Marry a shrink, and try to get away with being mindless. I dare you.

I had my assistant call for the car and reminded her to ask the driver to crank up the AC before I got downstairs. Hell, I've earned it. I effing have.

I didn't used to say "effing." That's an accommodation for Eric.

He effing doesn't like profanity.

Alan had been in New York for a few days and didn't call me. If I hadn't phoned him to ask for a favor, I wouldn't have known he was in town. Would it have killed him to call and ask how the pregnancy was going?

I'm not an idiot. Alan wasn't eager to see me.

If my shrink had asked, I probably would have given him a list of possible explanations why Alan hadn't called. But I was already convinced that Alan hadn't told me he was in town simply because he didn't want to see me.

The only thing I wouldn't have been certain of was the reason for his reticence.

Me? For the moment at least, I preferred to dwell on the fact that it was sweet of Alan to offer to meet me at all when he realized I was upset. Although my tears had always been hard for him to ignore, he didn't have to make the offer to see me. And he didn't have to agree to my suggestion of Strawberry Fields as a spot for our rendezvous.

He would not have missed the allusion. Alan, as husband or therapist, has always been big on allusion. So I knew he still cared.

And that is precisely why I suspected he hadn't called.

I shouldn't have started running when I saw him waiting on the far side of the garden, but I was thrilled that he was in the city and that he'd offered to change his plans and come and hold my hand. But I did start running, and once I'd started—although my new Jimmy Choos were perfect with my outfit, they were far from the right shoes for a jog, however abbreviated, in the park—I had no confidence that I'd be able to stop without catching a heel, or worse, ripping one of the woven gold ropes that had started slicing into the tops of my feet. I just kept running until I could use Alan as a safe way to control my momentum.

Fifteen

Our greeting was more awkward than I'd hoped. We sat.

Alan turned forty-five degrees on the bench so he could look at me. I slipped off one of my shoes and crossed my leg so I could massage the red rails that I'd carved into the top of my foot during my ill-considered sprint.

"After this last miscarriage, I said, 'That's it.' My body was telling me no. My brain was saying I couldn't do it again. As much as I want a baby, I . . . "

In the old days he would have taken over the massage. The man could give a hell of a foot massage. Not only as foreplay, either—he would rub my feet even if he knew there wasn't a prayer we'd have sex.

That time? No. No offer to take over the foot massage. I shifted my gaze toward him occasionally as I spoke. Alan was big on eye contact. I wanted to be certain he was paying attention. This was about my baby.

"Eric thought God was telling us something with the miscarriages. That He had other plans. Adoption. He wasn't sure. 'We'll know when we know,' he said."

I waited for a judgment from Alan. About Eric, and God. But Alan's expression didn't change. With Alan that didn't mean much—if he wanted his face to be a mask, it would be a mask.

The Eric/God thing was a discussion I didn't want to have

with Alan at that moment. I wasn't totally sure how I felt about it myself.

"We had fertilized eggs left over from the last conception. It had been an in-vitro, not . . . natural, you know—not intercourse. Most couples do. Have leftover eggs." I don't know why I said the part about intercourse. Alan knew about intercourse. He probably knew about leftover eggs, too. I was nervous. "Using a surrogate was Eric's idea. Indirectly."

Alan's eyebrows floated when I said that. Just a few millimeters, but still.

I went on. "He didn't actually suggest it. Not like that. He said that he had a friend who had done it. 'Used a surrogate?' I'd asked him. 'No,' he said. 'My friend was the . . . surrogate. For her half sister and her husband.' Turned out they'd used the surrogate's half sister's egg. And donated sperm.' "

Alan—finally—entered the conversation. "I did a psych eval for a surrogacy agency as part of an approval process." He paused before he added, "A lesbian couple."

"And?" I asked. *Point?*

"That's it. My only experience with surrogacy."

Typical Alan. Where his work was concerned, he wrote headlines. You never got the story. The opposite of my work. The opposite of me.

"A girlfriend had already asked me, 'Why waste them?' She meant the fertilized eggs. She said we could donate them to some other couple. Some, you know, infertile couple. But I couldn't give a stranger my fertilized egg. Nine months later they would have my baby. Can't do that. After Eric brought up what his friend had done, I started thinking if the problem is that I can't carry a baby to term, why not try a surrogate? If we used our own fertilized eggs, it would still be our baby. Biologically.

"I told Eric I wanted to do what his friend had done. He said he had to . . . give it some thought. That took a while, but he . . . came around eventually. I was surprised, to be honest. But he said it sounded fine to him, with some conditions."

I shouldn't have been embarrassed to tell Alan the whole story about Eric's process of coming to terms with the surrogacy, but I was. Eric didn't have to think about it as much as he had to pray about it. The surrogate thing. Eric was uncomfortable with the anatomy and biology of it all—his values are who he is—but the bigger question for him was whether we were interfering with God's plan.

I'd argued that for all we knew using a surrogate was God's plan. He didn't put us on this earth in the fifteenth century. He put us here in an era of reproductive options. Maybe He wanted us to choose this option.

It took Eric a week to get there. But, much to my delight, he got there.

For the year plus that I'd known Eric, I've been trying very hard to understand his relationship with God. He didn't seem any more religious than anyone else when we were first introduced, but as I got to know him better, and with every piece of bad news either of us got—and, yes, we've had our share—the ferocity of his faith redoubled.

My fragile faith wanes under the exact same forces. I don't understand that.

Eric's faith—I admit the secular molecules in me have trouble with the word—provides him great comfort. It certainly gives him strength. Although I can't understand it, and at times I'm dubious about it, mostly I'm grateful. Sometimes when I'm fighting my own demons and feeling alone, I envy him the solace he finds from his relationship with God.

I should say "gods." There are definitely distinctive gods in Eric's universe of faith. The capital-G God is a fearful, wrathful force for him. A heavens-quaking, earth-fracturing power.

But Eric's relationship with Jesus is different. Eric thinks of Jesus as a friend. If Jesus showed up at our door tomorrow morning, Eric would bring him in for waffles and then ask him to play tennis at the club.

But if God, the capital-G one, pounded on our door, I think Eric would cower beneath the piano and start repenting. He'd confess sins he didn't even commit. Probably contend I was a virgin and offer to sacrifice me on some altar.

I didn't know for certain if Eric addressed his prayers about the propriety of us using a surrogate to solve our conception woes to the capital-G God or to Jesus. Eric kept those kinds of details about his faith to himself. Were I to guess though, I would guess the surrogate question had earned the blessing of the Big Guy. That God seemed to get the serious stuff.

Jesus was there to provide comfort, support, and the kind of quiet guidance that allowed Eric to sleep after he heard the latest reports from Sudan or Iraq, the kind of solace that gets him through crosstown traffic or a slow elevator ride when he's running late for an appointment, the kind of patience that allows him to endure a fender-bender without wanting to tear the other guy's head off.

Eric didn't know that I was thinking of doing a piece on it. Mixed marriages. One half of the couple with casual religiosity. That would be me. And one half of the couple with the more dedicated, brand-name kind.

More and more it seemed, that would be Eric.

I thought I saw Alan nod as I was talking. Alan's nods weren't much. Sometimes you'd need a motion detector to be sure he'd actually shifted his head. I'd developed the right radar while we were together. I could tell.

I said, "A couple of years back I produced a piece about modern conception options. I had my assistant pull the file and I tracked down the lawyer we'd used as an expert for background on surrogacy. He . . . does these things. All the time. Eric and I made an appointment. The lawyer walked us through it. The practical side, the legal side. You'd be surprised, but there's not much law governing all this. No federal guidelines, and state statutes go from nonexistent to permissive to a few banning surrogacy entirely. He put us in touch with some surrogacy agencies."

I was getting close to babbling mode. I could feel it starting, but I couldn't stop it. "It's not that big a deal anymore. Surrogacy. Lots of women do it. Some A-listers, even." My girlfriends would have asked me to dish. The lawyer had told us about one actress who'd worn a maternity suit until her surrogate delivered the baby in another city.

But Alan didn't bite. I didn't expect him to. My ex could tell me who won the last ten Tours de France. He couldn't tell me anybody who'd made "Page Six" in the *Post* in the past year.

"Eric and I went to an agency, dangled our toes in the water, eventually interviewed some girls. Women. They were all right. Nice. Eric got discouraged, though, called them 'rent-a-wombs.' A couple of the women intrigued me—we did our due diligence on them, all the way through reading their psych evals. No real red flags emerged in their backgrounds, but neither of them felt right to Eric. He wanted to feel a connection. Does that make sense?"

I knew better than to ask Alan questions like that. He didn't have to say "Does it make sense to you?" His eyes would do that for him. So I refused to look at his eyes.

"One night at dinner at home—we were both in the city at the same time, which doesn't happen very often. I'd cooked." Alan's eyebrows jumped when I mentioned cooking. "I've learned how to make crêpes. We got this appliance, this thing. And I can roast a chicken. A good chicken, with a lemon inside. And herbs. I do twice-baked potatoes. With good cheese. I buy dessert. Anyway, during dinner, Eric said, 'What about Lisa? We could use Lisa.' Lisa was his friend, the one who'd been a surrogate."

* * *

My radar had noted something incoming when Eric said her name the first time. I'm not bashful. I asked Eric what kind of "friend" Lisa had been. Were we talking girlfriend? Lover? One-night stand? What? I needed to know. I'm not sure it would have mattered to me. Jealousy isn't my thing. If I was convinced they were over, I would have been okay with it. I waited for him to tell me more. The fact that he seemed reluctant to give me details didn't inspire my confidence.

"She was part of that Grand Canyon thing," Eric said finally.

"Ah," I'd said.

That Grand Canyon thing.

He had indeed told me about it. But he hadn't told me much.

The Grand Canyon thing was a fault buried deeply below the surface of our relationship. The romantic geologist in me knew it had significant potential energy.

At the moment Eric had first alluded to the Grand Canyon thing, I remembered thinking that I had always thought Alan, too, lived above a buried fault. I had never discovered what that was.

Not long after, Eric and I flew to California for a get-acquainted session with Lisa. We stayed at my condo in West Hollywood and met her at a restaurant on Melrose. Had a nice meal. When she left the table to go to the bathroom, I took both of Eric's hands and I kissed him. I said, "I think she's lovely, Eric. She could be the one."

I'd meant it too. If I had been hiring a nanny whom I thought would be at my child's side for the next ten years, I would have hired Lisa on the spot. She was that warm and that sincere and that maternal.

She was yang to my yin. Or maybe the other way around. Had I paid attention while I was in Boulder I would know which was which.

* * *

I was finishing up my explanation to Alan. "After the meeting with Lisa, I knew—I just knew—that she was the right one. Womb. Mother. Surrogate mother.

"Eric wanted to pray on it some more. He wanted to talk to some people at his church. Get 'guidance.' That's one of his things. He's big on getting 'guidance.'

"It took a couple more weeks for him to get comfortable with it. Eric had . . . moral issues . . . with the whole leftover-eggs question. From the in-vitro." I waited for Alan to nod. He did. "But then . . . Eric has this dramatic, romantic side, too . . . this grand-gesture gene that I adore . . . He does these . . . events sometimes.

"I came home from work and Eric greeted me at the door wearing these great silk pajama bottoms I'd gotten for him at Barneys and . . . no shirt. The lights were low in the apartment, perfect music was playing. He lifted me off the ground and carried me to the bedroom. It was full of candles—dozens and dozens of them—a bucket of ice with some vintage Dom, the bed was covered with gardenia petals and . . . "

That's where I stopped the story. Alan knew about my penchants for Dom Perignon, and for gardenias. That wasn't a problem. But Alan didn't need to know that Eric had a chest for the ages. If pecs were precious metal, Eric's were platinum. Alan didn't need to know that when my girlfriends saw Eric in the pool or at the beach I would hear about it for weeks. Literally, weeks. They would be drooling over his chest.

Those pecs.

Alan didn't need to know that Eric had lowered me to the floor and that he'd undressed me slowly in the dim light of the candles. That he'd lifted me, naked, again and carried me to a bath that was drawn and waiting for me.

Alan didn't need to know that Eric had washed every inch of me.

Alan didn't need to know that for the next few hours we squeezed every last drop of semen from Eric's balls and every last moan from my lungs.

Alan didn't need to know I'd come once for every finger on my left hand, save my thumb. Alan didn't need to know that I'd loved Eric more, and better, that night than I'd ever, ever loved Alan during our marriage.

Alan didn't need to know any of it, but still, I wanted to tell him. To make him jealous? No. But to let him see that I'd grown enough as a woman so that a good man could love me. I needed Alan to know that about me. I needed him to see that the scarlet letters *M-e* no longer had a place around my neck.

I felt worthy that night with Eric. Eric had wanted me to know that despite the fact that I knew I was incapable of the most natural of womanly acts—giving birth to a child—that to him I was flawless.

Eric's God had offered him some damn good guidance.

Effing good.

"The negotiations with Lisa almost broke down. She has a paycheck-to-paycheck life. We knew the going rate for surrogates. We wanted to pay her for carrying our baby. But she only wanted reimbursement for living expenses. I offered to use some of my contacts after the baby was born, introduce her to some people in L.A.—you know, if she wanted to get a foot in the door at one of the local stations. She wasn't interested. We finally got her to agree to allow us to pay off her student loans. She'd gone to Cal State. In Long Beach. The loan payoff was much less than we thought we should pay her, but . . . what were we going to do? We had a deal.

"Then came waiting for the medical and psych evals and a lawyer in California talking to our lawyer in Connecticut. The surrogacy agency here had to coordinate with the surrogacy agency there."

I checked Alan's face to make sure he was still with me. He was. I thought he seemed rapt.

"After the money, the most difficult part of the negotiation was about travel, and where Lisa would live while she was pregnant. She didn't want to leave L.A., of course. I didn't want her to be out of my sight, of course.

"We compromised. The agencies helped. She agreed to come east for the in-vitro procedure from my fertility people here and then stay until we were sure she was pregnant. And stable. Then she would go back home. Later on, I'd take a pregnancy leave from the network and fly out and stay at my place in L.A. for the final couple of months before Lisa's due date.

"She would be followed by an OB in Los Angeles, and deliver there, in L.A. At Cedars. In between? We agreed to some restrictions on travel, but what are you going to do? She has to have a life, right?"

Alan still seemed rapt. "The in-vitro procedure went great. Like magic"—I snapped my fingers—"smoother than mine. Dean— Dr. Dunfey, the fertility guy, he's terrific, and . . . well, he's gay. How weird is that? Do you find it odd? A gay fertility guy?"

Alan didn't respond. He apparently hadn't given the whole ob/gyn gender/sexual orientation question much thought. No surprise there, I suppose. Maybe I'd suggest it to one of the producers I know on *The View*. It would be an effing good topic for them. It would.

"Dean let me put candles in the procedure room during the implantation and dim all the lights except the one he was using. We had music playing. Eric was there. Not *there,* exactly, you know, but he sat beside Lisa and he even held her hand when the catheter was in. I thought it was sweet. Me? I was right *there. Exactly.* It was . . . this will sound weird—romantic for me. The karma was perfect. I needed it to be perfect. Just in case those baby cells picked up any vibes, I didn't want them to be able to tell that there was nothing sexual going on. I wanted it to feel romantic, to feel erotic. I wanted the implantation of the fertilized egg to have the same passion and . . . I don't know . . . to be just like if Eric and I . . . were doing it *knowing* that I was ovulating and we were about to make our baby. I wanted everything to be right from the start."

An in-line skater—a novice, obviously—almost killed herself just then. She came barreling down the path behind us and barely caught herself on the back of the bench.

Alan made a fuss to be sure she was okay. I waited until she left. "Where was I? I was visiting Lisa at this extended-stay hotel where she was staying uptown when she had her first positive pregnancy test—it was just one of those sticks you pee on. We'd walked over and picked it up at Duane Reade.

"She was glowing when it turned blue. I was glowing too. I could feel my skin flush. That's how right everything was. Dean confirmed the pregnancy the next day. For the first few weeks he kept telling us that it couldn't have been going better."

I had my antennae tuned for judgment, but Alan was wearing his therapist's mask. He has compassionate eyes. They've always sucked me in. I didn't want him to be judgmental about this. I let them suck me in again. I liked that I knew it was a choice on my part.

I began to feel my energy wane. I had shared all the good news.

Alan could tell that I was done with all the good news. He said, "And then?"

"Lisa had less than a week left in New York before she was going back to L.A. I was going to take her out to brunch last Sunday. I try to get together with her a lot. I like her. She doesn't know many people here. Eric's gone so much on business. But, yes, yes, I know, I want to make sure she's okay, too. And that she's being good.

"The contract specifies things she can't do—use caffeine, drink alcohol, extreme sports—but I do want to make absolutely sure she doesn't stop at Starbucks in the morning for a double shot or that she doesn't have just one cocktail at the end of the day with some new girlfriend. You know me. I'm the one who has two cell phones just in case one isn't getting a signal. Come on. This woman is carrying my baby. I have to see her. I have to be sure." I knew I wasn't revealing anything Alan didn't already know about me. I thought he'd be pleased at my insight about it all.

"Okay," he said. The word was one note shy of condescending. I wish I had that skill. The ability to couch my condescension. I don't.

Now I have the Bitch, though. That's almost as good.

"Her hotel, the one we got for her, is in Morningside Heights. That's not too far from here—it's near the other end of the park. But she wanted to go to someplace she'd read about downtown. I offered to pick her up, but she said she had errands to run and would meet me there. When she didn't show up at the restaurant, and then didn't answer her cell, I went to her place to make sure she was all right. And . . . she wasn't home."

"She said she had errands," he asked. "Why would she be home?"

"She also told me she would meet me for brunch."

"Maybe she forgot. Or something came up. People do miss . . . engagements, Meri."

"Cell phone? Text? E-mail? Phone call? She has all my numbers. I put them in her speed-dial myself. If she wanted to find me, she could have found me."

"That was Sunday. Today is Tuesday," he said. "What happened in between?"

Alan was telling me that he wasn't going to get infected with my hysteria based on less than forty-eight hours of silence from my surrogate.

Well, why the hell not?

The Bitch spoke up just then. My narcissism governess. She said, "Why the hell not, dear? Two reasons: Because he isn't married to you anymore, and because he doesn't have to."

The reality was that Eric wasn't ready to panic with me either. From my perspective, he was way too calm about Lisa's "absence." That's what he called it—as though her disappearing act was akin to missing a couple of days of school. He reminded me that the contract didn't compel her to stay in constant contact with us.

Doing nothing to find Lisa wasn't possible for me. It wasn't in my genes. If I had to search around in Lisa's background without Eric finding out about it, so be it. But first, I had to convince Alan to help. I needed him to call Sam Purdy for me.

Alan had come uptown to meet me in Strawberry Fields. He'd help.

Sixteen

Her Ex

It's not always the easiest thing in the world to get a straight story from Merideth. It certainly wasn't while we were married.

The current irony didn't escape me—revealing the chronology of a recent sequence of events should be the most natural thing in the world for a woman who makes a fine living producing stories for a national network weekly newsmagazine. In her job Merideth is responsible for directing a team that produces—conceptualizes, pitches, develops, researches, writes, and tapes—the long-form pieces that arc between commercials during a prime time hour. Her stories act as lenses focused on the issues—inane, mundane, and occasionally even profound—of our time. She's received enough broadcasting awards—including a couple of Peabodys—to fill the insecure cavities in the souls of most people. As well as anyone in her field, and better than ninety-plus percent of her peers, the woman can analyze news, tease out just the right narrative thread from nonlinear factual jumbles, cut through extraneous crap, cajole her recalcitrant talent to present things her way—which is usually the correct way—and end up telling her audience a hell of a story.

When I happened to watch a show that included a piece that Merideth had produced, I could invariably guess which story was hers. Her signature clarity, organization, and sense of drama were easy for me to spot. There was usually a price to be paid, however, in viewing

Merideth's work. If she were a screenwriter or a novelist, reviewers would accuse her of failing to develop her characters. But she was a news producer, not a screenwriter, and her occasional failing was not allowing the players in the stories she was telling to show themselves to full effect onscreen. Merideth needed to be the one to define the characters, to be the puppet master pulling the strings. Her chosen narrative thrust always took higher billing than the players.

But put Merideth in the story? Everything changed. Once she was in, it became a different story, and the telling became an entirely different process. She'd stumble out of the gate, her sharp analytical perspective would vaporize, her professional distance would disappear, and her narrative sixth sense would be nowhere to be found.

My simple question to her that day in Manhattan was: What happened between that Sunday when Lisa skipped brunch, and our Tuesday rendezvous in the afternoon heat in Strawberry Fields in Central Park?

After much longer than it should have taken I was able to cut through the stops and starts, the tangents and dead ends, and learn that Lisa—the surrogate with Merideth's and Eric's embryo nestled in her cushy uterus—had vanished.

None of her friends or family had seen or heard from her.

Merideth is nothing if not resourceful. Her ability to corral the most elusive get is legendary in the news and feature business. She finds the most cloistered, cajoles the most shy, and seduces the most press-phobic. She remembers names and faces the way dogs remember smells. Phone numbers stick in her memory as though they've been Velcroed there. In her producing life she knows exactly when to send flowers, and exactly when to send veiled blackmail. She's sucked up more old dirt than all the Hoovers—the vacuums and J. Edgar—combined.

But Lisa the surrogate had vanished so completely that Merideth couldn't find her. Or find even a clue that might lead to finding her.

By late afternoon on the Sunday that Lisa the surrogate stood up

Merideth the mother for brunch, Merideth had already assembled a roster of every name and phone number in the voluminous file that she had accumulated about Lisa when she was still a potential surrogate. By early that evening, Merideth had started methodically calling the names on that list.

I could put on a psychologist's mask when circumstances required, and I knew well that Merideth could wear a producer's mask with the same effortlessness. During those initial hours, when her concern would not yet have exploded into panic, and her panic would not yet have devolved into anticipatory grief, her phone calls wouldn't have alarmed the friends and family members she was calling. Merideth would be as smooth as silk as she asked, "Have you heard from Lisa lately?"

She would have called everyone she could think of.

Seventeen

His Ex

At my insistence, Eric made a call.

He had a friend who had a contact in the NYPD who said he could get a guy to check on Lisa at the extended-stay hotel we'd rented for her in Morningside Heights. My word that Lisa had disappeared off the face of the earth apparently wasn't enough to get the cop to visit her place and look around to see if there were any clues inside that might tell us where she had gone with my baby. In fact, before Eric's friend's contact would even consider going over there he had to get confirmation from her sister, who lived across the river in Tenafly, and her mother, who lived in Carlsbad, California, that Lisa's absence was truly worthy of his time.

The sister, Stefanie—everyone in the family called her Stevie, apparently—had agreed to drive over the bridge from New Jersey that evening to meet with me and with Eric's NYPD guy. I'd already talked to Stevie—she hadn't been able to reach Lisa either. She didn't, however, share my concern about Lisa's welfare.

Eric was away, of course. He was in the District, consulting with somebody. Over the last few months, while he was prepping to be chosen for his dream job, I swear I saw him only when he needed to drop off dirty suits and shirts and get fresh ones. Half the time when I asked whom he was working with, or what he was consulting about, he'd tell me he'd prefer if I didn't. Ask, that is.

"Given your job," he'd point out.

I'd told him from the beginning that his work was off the record for me. Permanently. He didn't care. I did understand his caution, but it felt like being involved in a relationship with a spook. Or with a psychologist.

Before Alan and I left Strawberry Fields—he declined the ride I offered him—I asked him if he'd meet me at Lisa's apartment that evening.

He said, "Why?"

I told him part of the truth. "Because you'll see something I won't see. You'll see something her sister won't see. You may well see something the cop won't see."

His eyes turned suspicious. I've learned that honesty has that effect on men sometimes.

I said, "I'm good at what I do, Alan. Damn it, you're good at what you do too. You know as well as I do that we look at the world differently. We look at people differently. When we were together, I wasn't convinced that was necessarily a good thing. With this? Looking for my baby? I think our views will complement each other's. I'd be very grateful if you would meet me."

"Address?" he said.

"Where are you staying? I'll send a car."

He said, "Give me a time, and the address, Merideth. I'll get there on my own."

I could tell that he was fighting a sigh.

Eighteen

Her Ex

Merideth and I met Stevie, Lisa's sister, on the sidewalk outside the extended-stay hotel where Lisa was temporarily living as Merideth's and Eric's guest. The hotel was in a bland brick building in Morningside Heights, beyond the northern edge of Central Park, not too far from Columbia University. The three of us made small talk while we waited for the detective to arrive. It was awkward.

Stevie had arrived before us and somehow finagled a key to Lisa's unit from the building manager. She was fidgety. Not pathologically so, like Jonas's Uncle Marty. But Stevie was taut, like an overstressed string on a violin. She carried the tension of someone who just realized she'd run out of nicotine gum.

Merideth had been expecting a uniformed cop. She got a detective. Merideth had been expecting a man. She got a woman. The woman was ten minutes late for the rendezvous. She pulled her sedan into a no-parking zone across the street from the building and sauntered over to join our little huddle. She pantomimed the tip of an imaginary cap and barked a bored "Evenin'," when she was still five feet away from us. Her cell rang before any of us had a chance to return the greeting. She glanced at the screen, turned her shoulder, and said, "What?"

We cooled our heels for another five minutes or so as the detective walked away from us to deal with her phone call. It was obviously a personal call, not work. She was not happy with the caller. When she rejoined us, we all introduced ourselves—she said her name was Dewster. If she said her first name, I missed it. She stared intently at each of us as we said our names. I thought she was reflexively finding a way to attach our names to our appearances in her memory so she could pick us out of a crowd, or a lineup, later on.

I'd seen my friend, Sam Purdy, do something similar. It was a cop thing.

She turned to Stevie. "Got a license?" she asked.

"What?" Stevie said. Stevie hadn't been confused by Dewster's question. She was offended by it.

Merideth turned her head away from Stevie's view and smiled. Merideth has her issues, but thin skin is not among them.

In a weary voice the detective said, "I need confirmation that the family is reasonably concerned about her before I can go in and do this. The welfare check? There're rules. Guidelines."

Stevie's lips were parted in disbelief at the inferred insult.

The detective was losing patience. She looked at her watch. "I can't just barge in . . . you know? Got to be a public-safety concern. The Constitution?"

Stevie sighed and dug in her purse for her wallet. She opened it and held the wallet out so that her license was visible. The detective glanced at it.

"Jersey?" she said. "And you're worried about your sister?"

Stevie rolled her eyes. At the "Jersey" part or the "worried about your sister" part, I couldn't tell.

"Let's do this," Detective Dewster said. She looked at her watch. "I got to be across town for dinner. Have to pick up my kids and get over to some soccer meeting near Jefferson Park. Always something."

The home away from home that Eric and Merideth were providing for Lisa had none of the charm of my Murray Hill sublet. Although her interim flat was about the same size as my Midtown apartment, mine reflected the character and quirkiness of another time, as well as the design sensibilities of my Italian landlord, while Lisa's corporate abode reflected some interior decorator's determination not to reflect anything at all. The carpet was the color of dirt. It had a nubby texture, the sheen of cheap panty hose, and a discernible pattern—diamonds, with a mud-colored dot dead-center—that I assumed was intended to disguise the wear-and-tear of previous tenants. The rest of the one-bedroom space was monotonous and intentionally nondenominational. From the front door everything appeared to be beige where it wasn't white.

We wandered Lisa's rooms in single file. The detective was first. I brought up the rear. Two things were clear: Lisa wasn't home. Neither were most of her things.

The living room was messy enough to raise eyebrows all around, but the place hadn't been tossed. Nor had it been the scene of any obvious physical struggle. The bedroom was neat. The unit's only bathroom looked like a hotel bathroom after the guests had left.

As I followed the rest of the column back toward the front door, I still wasn't sure why I had been invited, other than to hold Merideth's hand because her fiancé was out of town. She had maintained that I was supposed to be able to see something significant in the place. But within ten seconds of walking inside it was apparent to me that this suite wasn't Lisa's home, a place where I might have been able to make some psychologically relevant appraisal of her situation. This apartment was the extended-stay equivalent of a chain motel room, and I thought it was clear to us all that whatever meager personal belongings Lisa had brought with her as luggage had departed along with her.

It was also immediately apparent that Dewster, the detective friend-of-a-friend of Merideth's husband-to-be, wasn't getting any happier about the errand she'd been enlisted to run. Her walk-through of Lisa's place took mere moments. She reminded me of a potential buyer of a new home who had decided she wasn't interested the moment she entered the neighborhood, long before she reluctantly stepped inside the house itself. The only actual physical effort the detective put into the search—beyond walking around—was to pull back the shower curtain, open two closet doors, and drop to one knee to scan the space below the bed.

Once Dewster convinced herself that there was no one in the place who was either already dead or requiring law-enforcement or medical assistance, she said, "We're done." She gave Stevie her business card and told her if she learned something new that she should contact her directly and she would walk her through the process of starting the machinery for tracking down her wayward sibling.

"Wayward" was Dewster's word. She hadn't used it generously.

Stevie held the detective's business card the way a stranger might hold a dirty diaper handed to her by a harried mother.

Dewster stopped near the front door of the unit. Over her shoulder she said to Stevie, "This woman—your sister—left here voluntarily. Lights off, door locked. No forced entry. No sign of struggle. I assume she had a suitcase when she arrived. It's not here now. No purse. No phone. She packed up, and she left."

It wasn't news to Stevie, who looked annoyed. And disinterested.

Merideth said, "But—"

Dewster interrupted her. "It's hard to accept. For family, I mean. It is. But sometimes people walk away from their lives. You don't know why they do it, but they do. Happens more than you think. What next? Your sister will turn up after a while. Maybe tomorrow, maybe next week, she'll give someone a call. That's what usually happens. She's gone off somewhere, maybe she met some charming somebody and . . . When she shows up again she might be sorry. Or not. She might say she was 'sorting things out,' like that." Dewster managed a wry grin. "She might admit there was a guy. And that she misread him."

"That's it?" Merideth asked.

Dewster turned to Stevie again. "If she's anything like my relatives, you'll hear from her when she's out of money. My sister's first husband? Don't even get me started on that guy. The call we got was from someplace in Honduras. Ever try to wire money to Teguci-galpa?"

Dewster intended it as a joke. No one laughed.

Merideth's eyes grew wide. "But she has my baby."

The detective jerked her attention toward Merideth and said, "What did you say? There's a kid involved?" She turned her head and glared at Stevie. "Nobody said anything to me about a kid."

Stevie's mouth flattened. I thought she was fighting an inclination to smile. She pulled her purse strap higher on her thin shoulder and looked at Merideth. Stevie was happy to leave the explanation of the baby issue to others.

Merideth said nothing. It was clear that she didn't want to go there, not with this detective friend of a friend. Her fiancé probably didn't want her to go there. I imagined that he had specifically cautioned her about not going there.

"So, kid?" Dewster said. "Yes or no?"

Merideth shook her head. In a small voice she said, "I don't have . . . any children."

Dewster didn't press it. She wasn't eager to discover any complications that would extend her evening. She'd done her reluctant favor and made a negative welfare check. She was eager to move on to whatever came next on her to-do list. She left us, and the apartment, with a dispirited wave of her left hand.

She was already speed-dialing her mobile with the other.

Nineteen

During Detective Dewster's brief visit Stevie's mood completed a quick evolution from annoyed to irritated, as though she'd been expecting all along that the outcome would be something akin to what it had turned out to be. I was left with the impression that this wasn't the first time she had been recruited for a fool's errand involving her older sibling.

Stevie had been directly behind the detective while she did her cursory check of the premises, trailing her from the kitchen to the living room to the bedroom to the bathroom and back to the tiled area by the front door. As I chased behind them, I'd heard Stevie mutter, "Just typical," at least twice.

I turned to her after the detective had made her exit and shut the door. "What is typical, Stevie?" I asked. "I thought you said earlier that this was typical of Lisa."

"Did I?" She shook her head and again moved her purse strap higher on those skeletal shoulders.

The histrionics were amateur. *Does that act actually work with someone?* Her husband? It was hard to imagine. I certainly didn't feel any inclination to play along.

I said, "I'm pretty sure you did."

She spread her fingers, palms up. "Who knows?" She raised her eyebrows disingenuously for punctuation.

Her eyes told me that she recognized I wasn't planning to give her act a glowing review. Her demeanor changed. She stopped the dramatics. She no longer expected me to believe her. And she no longer pretended to care if I did.

Merideth had told me that Stevie was a quasi-respected fashion writer who freelanced "for some of the minor trades," was married, and had a two-year-old child. I didn't know Lisa's age, but I was guessing that Stevie was in the twenty-five-to-thirty range.

Most of the time, anyway. In those few moments after Detective Dewster's departure she was fourteen, max.

Siblings could have that effect. I wasn't holding the temporary regression against Stevie—I was merely factoring it into the equation of what to expect next.

"Has she done this before?" I asked.

"Done what?" Stevie said.

Her developmental age was descending like a rocket countdown. *Fourteen, thirteen . . . Okay, we'll play it your way, Stevie.* "Taken off . . . disappeared, without telling anyone? Gone days without answering her cell phone? Like that?"

"Days? Like, two? I wouldn't know."

Prior to making the "that's typical" utterances, Stevie's petulance had been muted. Not any longer. I retuned my antennae to include the wide range of potential petulance frequencies. I said, "You and Lisa aren't—"

"Close? No, you can tell?"

Her sarcasm was cloying. She spread it way too thick. She was like an elderly woman who applied too much perfume because she'd lost her sense of smell. I was beginning to feel as though I were locked in an elevator with that old woman.

Stevie shrugged again and looked around. "For all I know this is something . . . she could do all the time."

"Does what you see here surprise you?"

"We grew up in Southern California. Irvine? I left Orange County three months before my eighteenth birthday to go to NYU. I never went back. Lisa"—she sighed—"never left."

Stevie ended her brief soliloquy with a quick, audible inhale as though she wanted to underline her impression that the facts she was deigning to share should have spoken volumes and left my curiosity about her sister completely sated.

She hadn't answered my question, but it was something.

Were Merideth so inclined she could have warned Stevie about her experience with me and informed her that portion control rarely had the desired impact on my inquisitive appetite. If fact, it often had the opposite effect. Meri wasn't inclined.

I said nothing. I waited. Stevie filled the void, as I suspected she would.

"Lisa stayed—well, she moved to Hollywood—and . . . that's her life. She likes being in the orbit of important people. She was some sitcom actor's personal assistant for a while. Did the surrogacy thing for Susie, our half sister. Susie is a screenwriter. That was nice. I thought it might change Lisa. It didn't." She glanced at Merideth and shook her head. "Lisa and I go for months without talking sometimes. I call her occasionally—don't get me wrong. But I end up on voice mail nine times out of ten. I'm only here tonight because she"—Stevie looked at Merideth as though she thought she deserved an apology from her—"made it sound like some kind of huge emergency."

"And you don't think it is?" I asked. Without any conscious intent to do so I had switched to my office voice. When I was on my game, it was a tone that was as nonjudgmental as pudding.

Stevie cocked out one hip. "Does this look like some big nine-one-one to you? *CSI* couldn't find anything worth testing in here."

I wondered if Stevie had been hoping for some blood spatter.

Merideth wasn't ready to accept Stevie's cavalier assessment about Lisa's behavior. She said, "But your sister left some of her things. Look." She pointed at the mess around the sofa in the living room. A couple of paperback novels, half a dozen magazines—an odd mix of fashion, pop culture, and outdoors—an open spiral-bound book of Sudoku puzzles, and a couple of newspaper crosswords littered the area around the couch and coffee table. A significant number of dirty plates and glasses had accumulated. A pillow from the bedroom was propped on one end of the couch.

"See? And in the bathroom? There's shampoo, and conditioner in the shower. Real bottles. Some of her clothes are still in the closet. There's some underwear in the drawers. She didn't take everything. If she was moving out, she'd take everything."

Stevie fought off another shrug. She sighed instead. "Cheap stuff. Nothing here looks very valuable. She bought some new things, so she had to leave stuff behind. Wherever she went, she probably flew. Had to fit into a carry-on for the plane. Those big bottles wouldn't make it past security." Stevie did a three-sixty as she reexamined the room. "Looks to me like she got fed up with this place—though I can't imagine why, it's so stimulating—and she left."

Merideth exhaled loudly. I remembered the exasperated affectation well from our marriage. It was a sign of burgeoning frustration and usually preceded an eruption of some kind. I took two reflexive steps back and set my feet. I would let the two women go at it without getting in their way.

"'Fed up'?" Merideth asked with what I considered surprising restraint. "With whom?"

The exact same "fed up?" question had taken off in my head too, but the follow-up I conceived to tag along after it was "With what?" The difference—between "with whom?" and "with what?"—was a subtle one, but since my follow-up allowed for increased degrees of freedom, I thought the distinction was important.

I figured that Merideth had asked "With whom?" because she was assuming that she would be part of the answer and she was daring Stevie to take her on directly.

Stevie didn't bite. Was she experienced enough with people like Merideth that she knew better? Or did she know something specific about her sister that gave her some special insight?

I was leaning toward believing the latter. Without moving forward, I said, "Stevie, is there someone else—your mother, maybe, another sibling, a close friend—who could help us make a judgment about how concerned Merideth should be that she can't reach Lisa? That she's not answering her phone? Merideth and Eric have a lot at stake here."

Merideth tried some diplomacy. She said, "Please forgive if I'm a little overbearing. I'm concerned about her, Stevie. I am. This doesn't seem like Lisa to me."

"And you know Lisa that well?" Stevie said, a half smile on her face. I thought Stevie recognized that her sarcastic side had a tendency to go steroidal, and for that moment, at least, she was trying to rein in its excesses.

"I thought I did," Merideth said.

"If you know her that well, then why the hell would you give her your baby?" The unstated tag line was *"You fool."*

Merideth's mouth fell open about half an inch.

Stevie pulled her keys from her purse. She said, "I am going back to Tenafly. I have my own baby to worry about. And please don't bother my mother with any of this. She'll be of no help—Lisa doesn't stay in touch with her—and she doesn't need your intrusion. I'll handle her." She shook her head. "I can't believe I agreed to do this. God, I hope they've cleared that accident on the bridge."

She turned to leave so quickly that her hair whipped around her face. She had to spit it out of her mouth.

I was about to take a seat on the sofa, in the midst of Lisa's junk cyclone. "Stevie," I said, "is Lisa neat?"

She stopped, turned, and glared at me. "What?" she said.

Her question was tinged with confusion at why I'd asked, as though I'd interrupted her retreat from the room because I desperately needed to know if her sister liked chocolate milk.

I opened my hands, encouraging her to take in the scene around me. She reacted by opening her eyes wide. They flashed rage. If lightning had erupted from her nose at that moment, I wouldn't have been completely surprised.

I elaborated. "Is your sister a neat person? Compulsive, that kind of neat?"

Stevie pointed at the debris scattered around the sofa. "See that? And that. And that. That's Lisa. Right there. That kind of mess. I shared a room with her for half my childhood. Does that look neat to you?"

"Thank you," I said. "That's what I wanted to know."

"It's a metaphor for her life, by the way. I'm always cleaning up after her."

"Thank you," I repeated.

"Yeah," she said. "Whatever." Again she spun to leave. Again she turned back for a last word. This one, too, was directed at Merideth. "I am not filing any missing-persons report. Just so you know where I stand."

Merideth said, "Okay."

Stevie tossed the unit key onto the nearest table and tried to slam the door on her exit, but air pressure in the building absorbed the force. The intended dramatic gesture ended up having the impact of screaming into a pillow.

"Well," Merideth said after the door closed. "I don't know what I did to offend her." She shook her head as though she were eager to erase the spectacle from her memory.

I lifted the bound book of Sudoku puzzles and flipped some pages. Lisa was good at solving the number graphs—the book was almost completed. Someone had scrawled a couple of phone numbers on the back cover of the book, along with the word "pizza," the word HEAD in small caps, the capital letter *J*, the word "dessert," and the word YOUTUBE, again in small capital letters. "Pizza" was underlined twice. YOUTUBE once. "Dessert" and HEAD had earned no additional emphasis. Lisa had also doodled some geometric forms. I looked up. "Was that all news to you, Merideth? What Stevie said?"

She was holding a Chinese take-out menu. She looked perplexed. I knew the face she was making. Merideth hadn't been puzzled by Stevie's soliloquy. But she was feigning innocence about it. Someone who hadn't lived with Merideth for years might have failed to recognize the distinction.

I went on. "The family tension? Her sister's appraisal of her lifestyle? Did you and Eric know all that about Lisa?"

"No . . . Yes . . . Not exactly." She waved the menu and made a disapproving face. "We agreed no Chinese. MSG?" She sighed. "Eric and I did our due diligence, Alan. We did a background check. All the legal things. A credit check. Internet search. I did Lexis-Nexis. We talked at length to the previous . . . family that she was a surrogate for. We read the psych eval."

Oh boy.

"Did you interview any of her references? Talk to her family?"

"The other family, yes," Merideth said. "Susie? On the phone. We talked to her. She thought Lisa was great. Come on, Alan. Eric knew Lisa from before we met. They had mutual friends. Eric is . . . comfortable with her. The other family was thrilled with what Lisa had done. That was . . . good enough for me. Eric is a good judge of people."

Her tone was defensive. I didn't push her on the details—she was my ex-wife, not my patient. In whose womb she and Eric had chosen to stash their blastocyst was none of my business. I changed the subject. "Do you and Eric pay for maid service here?"

Another sigh. "Alan, where are you going with this?"

I gave Merideth full credit for trying to keep the condescension out of her voice even though she only half succeeded. "Humor me," I said.

"No. We asked her if she wanted maid service. She didn't. We only pay for cleaning at the end of her stay. You saw the washer and dryer. She can do her own sheets and towels. She doesn't cook. Why do you ask?"

"The bed's made," I said. "All of her mess is in the living room."

"So? Why is that important?"

Merideth was being dismissive at the same time that she was

growing more anxious. As much as she wanted my help with her missing surrogate problem, she wasn't totally prepared for me to actually discover something that she had missed in the quick examination of Lisa's temporary home.

"It may not be," I said. I stood and walked in the direction of the bedroom door. Merideth followed me. I gestured at the bed. "Most people leave stuff near their bed. Even in a hotel. A book. A magazine. A water glass. Something. Look, the TV remote is still sitting across the room."

I turned. Merideth was only a foot behind me. I could see that her eyes had begun to get moist. "Yeah?" she said. "So?"

The "so" was poignant.

"I don't think a messy person—Stevie was adamant that her sister's a slob—would make her bed like that. With hospital corners? Or straighten things up. Put away the remote across the room." I stepped forward and lifted the corner of the quilted bedcover. "See? And with the bedspread folded perfectly the way it is? That looks like it was done by a housekeeper, not by a slob."

Merideth said, "Are you suggesting she hasn't been sleeping here?"

"I don't know what I'm suggesting. You wanted me to notice what doesn't look right. This doesn't look right."

"Where would she have been sleeping?"

The important question, of course, was "With whom?" The "where" was relatively irrelevant.

Twenty

A Town Car was waiting in front of the building when I stepped outside. The driver had iPod buds in his ears, his eyes were closed, and his lips were singing silently along to some private concert. I was guessing hip-hop. He startled and jumped out the door when he saw me standing on the sidewalk. He said, "Dr. Gregory?"

Merideth was right behind me. I shook my head at her. She said, "The car is paid for, Alan. It will just go to waste if you don't use it."

Old shit. I was angry that she'd ordered the car despite my protests. I stepped forward and gave the driver ten dollars and told him no thanks. Merideth spoke to him for a moment before he pulled away.

"You don't have to be a jerk. I was trying to be nice." She walked away, down the block. She climbed into the driver's side of a dark gray Lexus.

I was being a jerk. My reaction to the car service was an end-of-the-marriage reflex that wouldn't die. I passed her as I walked down the sidewalk toward the intersection, where I hoped I could get a cab. She was checking her eyes in the vanity mirror. She knew I was on the sidewalk beside her, but she wouldn't acknowledge me. It all felt familiar.

I hurt for her. The visit to Lisa's rental hadn't provided any new avenues that were likely to help Merideth find her surrogate, or her baby. And the likely possibility that Lisa was sexually active during the pregnancy provided a new level of worry and concern that Merideth hadn't anticipated having to deal with.

I got a cab right away. After a block the driver caught my eye in the mirror and confirmed the address. His accent suggested he was from the Middle East.

I told him he had the address right. "Go by the park, please," I said. "Maybe down Central Park West?"

"I can go through on Eighty-sixth, you want. Then take Fifth. You cool enough? More air?" he asked.

I was shocked. New York cabbies can endure a tremendous amount of heat if their dollars are buying the fuel for the air conditioners.

"I'm cool," I said. "Thanks."

In the steamy car my proclamation sounded especially silly. The driver and I both laughed. The evening of riding in cabs was a Merideth inspired luxury. During my stay I'd been trying to limit myself to trains and feet. I hadn't yet figured out the New York buses.

The driver cut across Central Park by the reservoir. I watched the scenery go by while I pondered Merideth's situation.

Even though I thought her fears were premature and exaggerated, I understood Merideth's concern about Lisa's absence. In her shoes, I would have had the same fears. But I wasn't ready to buy into her alarm.

After witnessing Stevie's practiced tantrum about her sister, my inclination toward alarm was even more tempered. Stevie's description of an irresponsible streak in Lisa's character rang true, and if it was, it might be a sufficient explanation for her sister's relatively brief period of radio silence.

When I'd taken molecular biology in college, the professor had started the first class in the darkened lecture hall under an immense projected photograph. The picture—a close-up of the provocative hollow created by the cleft between a woman's uplifted breasts—was guaranteed to focus my attention, and that of all of my classmates. The professor allowed the image to dominate the room for a long interlude before she began her lecture.

"We will spend the next few weeks talking about cleavage," she said in a most professorial tone. "The other kind."

Where the other kind, the mitotic kind, of cleavage was concerned—as in so many things in life—Lauren and I had been among the fortunate few. When we chose to have a baby, we were able to get pregnant the way heterosexual couples have gotten pregnant for all but a few decades of the time humans have inhabited this planet.

We had sex.

Over the years we'd been aware of many friends who had not been so lucky on the other-kind-of-cleavage front. Getting haploids to do their things—a solitary sperm piercing the membrane of a healthy egg—and getting the resulting zygote to survive long enough to begin the process of cleavage is not always as uncomplicated as boy meets girl. The list of couples we knew whose reproductive efforts were successful only after determined intervention from medical specialists was a long one—probably longer than we suspected. Some of our frustrated friends had ultimately chosen to go the in-vitro route.

We knew other couples who had eventually decided to adopt, either locally or abroad. One couple we knew had given up and come to terms with being childless.

Whether it was due to age at marriage or environmental pollution or lifestyle or some esoteric factor that physicians had not yet considered, it was apparent that modern reproduction had become thorny in ways that science struggled to understand.

I was a clinician with a practice made up of a preponderance of women of childbearing age. I'd treated dozens of women over the years who fell into one of the above categories of procreative frustration. I'd done my best to help many women struggle with the emotional fallout of infertility. But other than the eval I'd done four or five years before at the request of an agency, I'd given remarkably little thought to the psychology behind the whole concept of surrogacy. It had never been on my personal radar.

Perhaps it was naïve of me, but I didn't consider surrogacy particularly controversial, at least not from a medical-ethical standpoint. It seemed to me that the decision to enter into a surrogacy arrangement involved consenting adults engaging in—after a healthy dollop of scientific intervention—the completely natural act of growing a baby inside a willing womb.

The psychological issues were much more complex.

The ethical minefield that Merideth had alluded to when we'd talked in Strawberry Fields—the question of what to do about all those excess fertilized eggs that are an inevitable by-product of the in-vitro process—was one of those divisive debates that thus far in my life hadn't slapped me in the face and demanded that I take a personal stand.

Are the fertilized eggs really just surplus biological material? Or are they children? Or are they, as some had begun arguing, tiny stem-cell factories waiting to be exploited for the greater good by science and medicine?

Once the creating couple, the parents, determined that it had no further use for the embryos, how should they be disposed of? Down the drain? Donation to science? Adoption by less fortunate couples?

I reached no conclusions before I had the driver drop me near Times Square.

I wasn't ready to go back to Ottavia's. I needed to renew my urban contact high before I hiked back to the sublet across town.

Twenty-one

I absorbed a good-size fix of whatever it was that Times Square had to offer before I returned to the apartment. I had to convince myself to check in with Merideth and ask what she thought about the night's developments. I came within a whisker of deciding that I didn't really have to make the call.

"It could have been worse, I guess," was Merideth's appraisal of the errand to Morningside Heights. "Lisa wasn't dead in the bathtub. But it could've been better, too. I hate, hate, hate the fact that Lisa might have a boyfriend. STDs, Alan? Come on, I don't have enough to worry about? And HIV? I do not even want to think about it."

"You don't know she's seeing anyone," I said. "She hasn't been out of touch for long, and it was just a thought I had when—"

"You were right. You were absolutely right. No one has been sleeping in that bed in her apartment. She has to be sleeping somewhere."

I said, "It's not the sleeping part that worries you."

"Damn right, it isn't."

I tried to point out the encouraging news. "Stevie's impressions of her sister suggest that Lisa being out of touch for a few days might not be that big a deal. I found her to be believable. Some sibling issues, sure. But believable. That's good, right?"

"Lisa being gone is a big deal for me."

"I know it is, Meri. I'm just trying to allow some room for

optimism. There are lots of benign explanations. She may be simply flaky. She may be having trouble with her phone. She may have . . . gone to Atlantic City, or maybe she met someone with a place at the beach and she's getting away from the heat."

Merideth replied, "You're telling me you think she likes slots, or she's hanging at the Jersey Shore, or that she forgot to charge her cell battery and hasn't figured out that it's dead?"

"I'm just saying that whatever is happening may not be . . . awful."

She exhaled. "Thank you," she said. I heard a tiny laugh. "So where was this Pollyannaish side of you when we were married?"

I wasn't about to go there. "You never told me who it is you want me to get in touch with in Boulder."

She hesitated before she said, "Sam?"

"No, besides Sam. You said something about an old friend of ours from when we were together. Someone who has a daughter."

"Eric doesn't want me to do it. He doesn't want me poking around in . . . what happened. If I do ask you to call Sam, you'll have to be real discreet."

"I'm more than happy not to do it at all. That will be totally discreet." I waited a couple of beats for her to give me the name of our old friend. I wanted to go to bed. "Okay, you'll tell me when you're ready. I need to get some sleep."

"Wait. Jesus H.— I'm ambivalent. Okay? Something bad happened during a camping trip in the Grand Canyon a few years ago, before Eric and I met. He won't talk about it."

So? I still wanted to go to bed. "What kind of bad?"

"Eric was there with a girlfriend. They met some other people and hung out together . . . doing whatever people do in places like that. What do I know about . . . camping, right?"

She knew nothing about camping. Cared even less. She could laugh at herself about it. That was new. And nice. I waited.

"Lisa was part of the other group. That's how she and Eric met. He hasn't told me much. But a girl . . . disappeared the last night they were down at the bottom. Is that what they call it? The bottom of the canyon? That doesn't sound right. Do you know, Alan? Come on, I don't want to sound like an idiot."

"I've heard it called the 'floor.' The canyon floor."

"Okay, the floor. I'll call it that. Lots of bad feelings developed about what happened after the girl disappeared. Friendships ended. It was a big deal. Lisa's the only one in the whole group that Eric's still in touch with."

"The girl who disappeared? Was that his girlfriend? Or part of the group they met?" I asked.

"A stranger. He had met her only once. She'd come down with a guy the afternoon before Eric's group climbed up. He barely knew her."

"I don't get the significance. But go on."

"We don't talk about this. It's sensitive for Eric."

I was exhausted. The conversation wasn't helping. Bad habits with my ex-wife kept surfacing like a beach ball I was trying to hold underwater. "Merideth, I know you. I know the way your mind works. I know you've already looked into this." She'd ordered a research assistant to put a file together. "Tell me what you found in your search."

She swallowed a sigh, displeased that I had that insight into her. "The girl disappeared in the middle of the night, the night before Eric's group left. She was with a guy she didn't know too well. The two of them were camping—real camping, in a tent. The guy said she got up to go use the bathroom. Or . . . go to the bathroom. There may have been an actual bathroom, or she may have been going to squat someplace. I don't know about those things. The guy she was with fell back asleep. When he woke up the next morning, she wasn't there. A search was started a few hours later. The Park Service got involved later on. Somebody found a bracelet that might have been hers. The next afternoon a flash flood hit the canyon, washed away any hope of finding more clues."

It was an interesting story, but the relevance continued to elude me. "What does all this it have to do with Eric and Lisa?"

"What to do next got contentious among the group. They were on the way out—you know, about to begin climbing—when they heard the girl was missing. Some of them wanted to stay and help get a search going. Eric wanted . . . to climb out right away. It was really hot. Dangerously hot—some big heat wave had hit Arizona. He had to get back to work, or something. I don't know. He couldn't wait, didn't see why he should. Felt she would show up any minute. He and Lisa and one other girl climbed out. That they didn't stay to help became a big deal for the others."

"Sounds like a difficult situation for everyone," I said, even though I was still unsure about the relevance. "What's the Boulder connection?"

"One of the girls in the group was from Boulder. She was going to college in L.A. at the time. Occidental? You know it? It's near Pasadena. She was with Lisa. They were both part of the group that Eric and his girlfriend met at the . . . on the floor.

"Back when we were considering Lisa as a surrogate, and he was telling me how he met her, Eric mentioned that one of the other girls on that trip was from Colorado. When he said the girl's last name, I connected the dots. Realized then that I thought she might be someone you and I knew. Or at least we knew her parents." She paused. "I probably met the girl back then, Alan. I didn't used to pay much attention to people's kids. I'm not proud of it, but it's true."

I was surprised that Merideth recognized the shallowness of the social water where she had waded much of the time we were married. I said, "Eric doesn't know what you know? He doesn't know about your Boulder connection to Lisa?"

"I never told him. This whole chapter of his life is off-limits."

She said the words definitively. It was her way of telling me not to ask her why she was keeping the information from Eric. I silently reminded myself none of it was my business. I asked, "Is Lisa still in touch with the girl from Boulder?" *And can we give her a name, Meri?*

"Eric doesn't know. He says that he and Lisa have never talked about the Grand Canyon. About what happened down there. The missing girl. What happened since. Nothing. It's some big taboo."

She didn't sound like she believed him. I added that impression to the ever-enlarging it's-none-of-my-business register. "What did happen down there?" I asked. "The missing girl, did they find her?"

"I told you all I know," Merideth said. "She disappeared overnight. They did a search. That flash flood hit. Came. Whatever flash floods do."

"She hasn't shown up anywhere?"

"Apparently not."

"Is she dead?"

"She may be dead. She may not be."

I chewed on the sparse details for a moment before I said, "Why don't you call the people we know in Boulder yourself? Why do you want me to do it?"

"They were your friends. Mental-health types."

Merideth had always divided our friends into subspecies. Mine were the mental-health types, hers were the TV-news people. I always thought the groupings sounded like competing clans of antagonists in some celluloid science-fiction fable I wouldn't want to sit through.

"Anyway," she said, "if I call and tell the girl that I'm Eric's fiancé, she'll assume I'm on his side. You might be able to come off as more neutral."

My neutrality didn't sound like a particularly desirable trait. It felt more like she was comparing me to Switzerland in 1941. She was also undervaluing her ability to seduce information from reluctant people. Merideth was a pro at it.

"There are sides in all this?" I asked.

"Yes," she said. "Those who climbed out early—Eric and Lisa and that other girl—are on one side, and those who stayed to help with the search are the other. His old girlfriend is part of the group that stayed." She sighed. "It's a long shot, Alan. I doubt the girl knows anything about Lisa. Maybe I should just forget it. But it's all I have."

"Meri, it's late. It's up to you. Are you going to tell me who she is or not?"

"The girl's name is Carmel. Like the town. *Car-mel* . . . Poteet," Merideth said. She had no doubt I would remember the family. Poteet is one of those surnames that is tough to forget.

I said, "Carmel is Wallace and Cassandra's middle kid. I haven't seen her in . . . well, years." I had no picture in my head of Carmel after age fourteen, or fifteen at the most. I remembered her most clearly as a preteen—a small, fun kid who was about half the size of her older brother, Mason.

Her father, Wallace Poteet, Ph.D., was among the first wave of psychotherapists to stake a private-practice claim in Boulder in the late sixties and begin mining the rich vein that was the town's insatiable appetite for mental-health services. He was also one of the only sources of referrals I had, besides my partner Diane Estevez, during my first year or so in private practice. It's safe to say were it not for Wallace's faith in me, and the work he sent my way, it was possible that my practice would not have survived its infancy.

Wallace was a mentor, a benefactor, and a friend. I owed him.

"I don't know where she is—if she's in L.A. or Colorado or . . . Do you still see them? Her parents, the Poteets?" Merideth said.

"I see Wallace at professional meetings, occasionally at parties. Cassandra was at the reception, Meri. I may have been talking with her when you came up to say hello."

I heard the lilt of recognition spike in Merideth's voice. She said, "Oh my God. She was Sandi, wasn't she? Not Cassandra. I knew I didn't forget that name."

"She's Cassandra now," I said.

"She's lost quite a bit of weight. Has she been ill?"

"She started running. Doing marathons. She's trying to qualify for Boston."

"She grew her hair out too. I never knew it was that . . . frizzy," Merideth said. "People change."

I thought she said it with a little wonder in her voice. "I think Carmel's still in L.A. Would you like me to call Wallace? Get in touch with her for you? Yes or no?"

"Let me sleep on it," she said.

"Sleep sounds good," I said.

Sweet Jesus.

Twenty-two

The man Merideth wanted me to enlist as an off-the-record private investigator was my closest friend of many years, a Boulder police detective named Sam Purdy. Our friendship had started in the months after my marriage to Merideth had ended, so he wasn't part of the divided spoils of the relationship.

That also meant that to get Sam's help, Merideth needed mine.

One of the many things Merideth did not know about my friendship with Sam was that he and I shared a recently minted confidence that was exerting gravity on our relationship in a way that was anything but subtle. From the moment that Sam shared what happened the night he had confronted a woman who was threatening our children the previous spring, we knew we were bound together by the woman's fate.

Our initial instinct was to create some distance. I stayed away from him to protect him from any stain of association with me. He stayed away from me to protect me from being darkened by the shadow of what he had done for us.

The ions had their charge. Resistance, not attraction.

I hadn't spoken with Sam in more than three months. The last time we'd been together had been at Adrienne's graveside service at Green Mountain in Boulder. I'd been at Jonas's side that day. Sam had arrived late and hovered at the periphery of the gathering. At the end of the service I gripped one of Jonas's hands as he used the other to toss a fistful of Colorado clay onto his mother's coffin. By the time I'd looked around for Sam, he was gone. He had not come by the house later for the reception.

I missed him.

I didn't know how Sam had been managing the suspension he'd received from his superiors. The boss cops knew nothing of the secret he and I shared. They were punishing him for a venial transgression that involved lust, bad judgment, and some secondary sins of omission he'd committed along the way.

After his disciplinary hearing I'd called Sam to see how he was doing. He didn't return my call. Money was always tight for Sam—Boulder isn't an easy place to live on cop's wages. I didn't know if he had the financial resources to go six months without pay—I suspected he did not—or whether he'd found another job to carry him through the interim.

I wondered too how he felt about breaking up with his longtime girlfriend, Carmen. The lust part of his transgression had broken the trust between them. I heard he'd flown out to where she lived in Orange County, California, to end it with her shortly after Adrienne's funeral.

I'd called him again a week or so after his suspension was handed down to offer him some money—a gift if he'd take it, a loan if he wouldn't. Once again he hadn't returned my call. I reached out to him one more time, a couple of weeks later, using a pay phone on Broadway only a few blocks from his North Boulder home. I knew he was there when I phoned; I'd just driven by his house and watched him reposition a sprinkler on his crappy front lawn.

He'd lost weight. The shorts he was wearing hung on his hip bones in a way that caused me to avert my eyes when I saw he was about to bend over to move the hose.

He didn't answer the phone that time either.

I wasn't able to get back to sleep after Merideth called to tell me she'd decided she did indeed want me to talk to Carmel Poteet. She had also asked me to get in touch with Sam.

I sat on the sofa and stared down 39th Street in the direction of the Hudson. The air conditioning in Ottavia's apartment seemed to have two speeds—too low or too high. I like to sleep in cold rooms; at night I chose too high. To ward off the manufactured chill I wrapped myself in the comforter from Ottavia's bed. It smelled of her.

I continued to like that smell.

New York didn't begin to get sleepy until after three.

I did the quick time-zone arithmetic and phoned Lauren and Grace in the Netherlands.

"Alan?" Lauren said. "Can't sleep?"

"Something like that. Woke up, wanted to hear your voice."

"That's sweet. Jonas is okay?" She was trying to keep alarm out of her voice.

"Fine. Good. You know, it's going better with him and his aunt and uncle than we could have hoped. I'm calling him more than he's calling me. I think my being in New York may prove to be unnecessary. His aunt Kim is a good person."

"Better safe than sorry," Lauren said.

We were using a lot of clichés and platitudes with each other, trying our best not to argue. It's hard to quarrel with moldy wisdom.

"Any progress for you?" I asked. Lauren was trying to track down the adoptive parents of the daughter she'd given up after getting pregnant while she was doing a year abroad in Amsterdam in college. She was hoping to arrange a first-ever meeting with her child, now a teenager.

"It's slow going," she said. "Lots of bureaucracy. Many things are easier in the Netherlands, but bureaucracy is the same everywhere. Even if I reach her family, they may refuse to let me see her, or she may choose not to meet me. It's hard, the waiting. We're trying to stay busy. Gracie and I are in line at the Anne Frank house right now. She is really excited to see it. We've been reading the diaries. Say hi?"

I said, "Of course."

Gracie was helium for my moods. She and I chatted until the line started moving and it was time for them to buy tickets. She said good-bye to me in Dutch.

That's what she told me she said anyway.

I made the first call for Merideth around eleven o'clock the next morning. Wallace Poteet and I spoke a few times a year, so my call wasn't a complete surprise. We spent a few minutes catching up. He asked how Jonas was doing, and what Grace's reaction was to having a new brother. I asked about his three kids.

His eldest, Mason, was a funeral director in Coral Gables. The youngest, Irene, was in her second year at Wake Forest. Carmel, the middle child, had finished school at Occidental and stayed in California. She was doing set design for a soap.

"I can't believe I have a kid in the business," Wallace said.

"Which business?" I asked. "Movies or funerals?"

He laughed. "Either. Both," he said. His tone changed. "You're calling for a reason, Alan. What's up?"

"You're good, Wallace."

"That and a dime," he said. He waited. A conversation with one shrink always involves some dead time. A conversation between two involves a lot of dead time.

"I'd like to talk to Carmel. I was hoping you could give me her number in L.A."

"Yeah? Why do you need to talk to my daughter? Wait, wait. Let me take my paternal temperature. Is this any of my business? One, two . . . Noooo, it's not. Definitely not. Is my daughter a grown-up? Yes, she is. So . . . sure. Give me a second to find the number. Cassandra keeps a list, or at least she used to. As I get older, I've become addicted to speed dial. Cara's five; that's her lucky number. Doesn't do you much good to know that, but . . . God, I'm hopeless." He laughed at himself.

Wallace's personal process was rarely disguised, and he was never apologetic about putting it out there. It was one of the things I found so attractive about him as a colleague, and a friend. I always knew where he stood. "I'm happy to tell you why I want to talk with her, Wallace. It's a favor I'm doing for Merideth."

The pause that followed was poignant. "Your . . . Merideth?"

"My . . . ex-Merideth, yes."

"If I can be candid, Alan, I'm surprised that Merideth remembers any of our kids. She didn't exactly pay a lot of attention to them when they were young."

From Wallace Poteet, that was as pointed as criticism got.

"Merideth would probably be the first to admit that now. She's grown up, I think. This favor . . . is about something that's happened in her life since she left Boulder. She's involved with someone who crossed paths with Carmel a few years back. They have a mutual friend, apparently. Merideth is trying to get in touch with that person, and hopes that Carmel can help. That's it."

My phone buzzed in my hand. I pulled it away from my face long enough to discover that another call was coming in. I had no faith in my ability to make call waiting work. I was hopeless. I let the call go.

Wallace said, "I found it. Here it is, Cara's number." He dictated ten digits. "That's her cell. She doesn't answer most of the time, but she's pretty good about returning calls in a day or two."

I was going to leave things there and wait until I had a chance to connect with Carmel. But I said, "Thanks. Wallace, do you by chance know anything about some Grand Canyon trip from a few years back—a trip to the canyon floor that Carmel took with friends when she was still at Oxy?"

It sounded as though Wallace dropped the phone. For about two seconds, I actually allowed myself the luxury of considering it a co-incidence. Once he had the receiver back near his face, his voice had a breathless quality. The illusion of happenstance evaporated. He said, "Did they find that girl? Is that what this is? Is she dead? She is, isn't she? They found her body. Criminy. Cara thought something had happened."

Words like "criminy" occasionally snuck into Wallace's vocabulary. I wondered if they were relics of his conservative Iowa upbringing. I'd have to ask him about it sometime. Some other time. I said, "I don't think—"

"Merideth is doing a story?" He had resignation in his voice—the resignation of someone who has just reluctantly accepted the reality of hearing very bad news. "That's why Merideth wants to talk with Cara? Tell me it's not . . . Oh, Lord in heaven. She does prime time now, doesn't she?"

Wallace did seem to know a little something about the whole Grand Canyon thing. I tried to ease his mind about Merideth's motives. "Wallace, no. No one found the missing girl that I'm aware of. And no, Merideth isn't planning a story. Quite the opposite. Her interest in speaking with . . . Cara—is that what you guys call her now?—and whatever happened at the Grand Canyon is a personal thing for Merideth. Not work. You apparently know much more about it than I do."

"Personal?"

"Merideth is engaged. Her fiancé was on the same trip. He was part of the group. I don't know how he fits in, but it's all become complicated for Merideth. She's hoping that Carmel can help her track down one of the other people in the group. This is a personal favor for Merideth. Nothing more."

I could hear Wallace inhale through pursed lips before he said, "Do you mind waiting a day or so to call her? I should probably discuss this with Cassandra first. She has better instincts about these things than I do. Cara's not as . . . strong as she appears sometimes. She has some . . . vulnerabilities. This Grand Canyon episode is one of them. It may end up that we decide to ask you to leave her out of this."

"Whatever you decide. I don't mean to cause any upset."

He sighed. "The fallout from that Grand Canyon trip . . . I thought it was over. Healed wounds? Ancient family history? That was wishful thinking, I guess. You know?" I did know about those things—buried things that refuse to stay buried. "Cassandra and I were hoping that she'd . . . recovered. Then a week ago she was in tears with her mom about it again. And now . . . you want to talk with her.

"Whatever happened on that trip was . . . difficult for Cara. That girl disappearing? She just vanished, Alan. That was bad enough, but the aftermath with her friends? It was so divisive. Cara was a wreck when she got back to L.A. Broke up with a boy she'd been serious about. She took a semester off at school. Went back into therapy."

"I'm sorry. I knew the girl went missing back then, but other than that I'm in the dark about what happened. I will certainly wait to hear back from you before I do anything else."

"You're sure this isn't about a story, right? Because if it is, the answer is a definite no—I would not want you to talk with Cara."

"Merideth is as reluctant to have any of this go public as you are."

"I appreciate hearing that. And yes—we mostly call her Cara. The family does, anyway. In Los Angeles she's Mel. She says Carmel is too . . . something. Provincial? Cassandra and I messed that up, I guess. Anyway, I'll give you a call after we talk."

"I'm in New York with Jonas, so call me on my cell. He's visiting his . . . aunt and uncle. I'm staying close by in case things go south."

"Got it. Your number's here on Cassandra's list. I'll be in touch. Good luck with Jonas. Our hearts go out to that kid. Anything we can do, you know . . . "

"Thanks, Wallace. One more thing, if you don't mind—who was the other person who brought up the Grand Canyon with Carmel recently?"

"It was someone else who was there, in the canyon. A guy, maybe. It upset Cara. He said something to Cassandra about a video, I think. Sorry."

Twenty-three

Merideth phoned me from a restaurant in Midtown that was a few blocks from Ottavia's apartment. She'd excused herself from a business lunch and was calling me from outside the bathroom.

"Meet me in fifteen minutes? I want to tell you what I'm thinking."

The tone of the summons felt familiar. I went anyway.

I spotted her on the sidewalk, walked up behind her. "Meredith," I said. I'd been outdoors for less than ten minutes, had walked only three blocks. I was sweating from pores I never used in Colorado, not even during a long summer bike ride.

I thought that even my ears were sweating.

Merideth pirouetted as though she'd known I was there and had been waiting for her cue. She air-kissed my left cheek. "I think she's dead," she whispered, declining to bother with a segue.

"Lisa?" I said. *Oh my God.*

"No. God, no. The girl from that camping trip. It has to have something to do with Lisa . . . leaving."

I took a half-step back. I asked, "Do you have a reason to think she's dead?"

Merideth tightened her jaw. "I'm not one of your patients."

I altered my voice, trying to find something less compassionate. "You're afraid the woman is dead?"

She nodded.

"Did you learn something new? Or is it . . . just a feeling?"

"It's just a feeling. But don't—"

"Assuming you're right"—experience had taught me that conversations went better with Merideth when I assumed she was right— "why would what happened back then have anything to do with Lisa—"

She said, "Eric and Lisa were there. That's all I have. That, and a bad feeling. I don't get it often, but when I do, I trust it. I got it about us at the end."

"Okay," I said. I would grant her the point. The set. Even the match, if it meant we didn't have to go back and relive our end.

She held her mobile aloft. "My car's on the other side of the block. It's penned in by traffic. Walk with me."

A traffic blockade could last a minute in Midtown, or it could last twenty. We walked. I told her about my conversation with Wallace.

She said, "You have to talk with Carmel." Her voice was composed. She was coming up with an action plan. "Convince Wallace. Or ignore Wallace. Just talk with her. Find out what happened back then. Find out what's happening now. See what you can learn about that girl. See if she can help me find Lisa."

"I won't speak with her against Wallace's wishes, Merideth."

"Then persuade him. You're good at it."

Compliment or accusation? I wondered. "I will do what I can," I said.

Did I mean it? The truth was I wanted to get Jonas and fly back to Colorado. I was ready to pretend that I had a viable practice, a stable family, and that my life had a satisfying, slightly boring routine.

I wanted to see the dogs. I wanted to be in Spanish Hills at dusk to watch the sun shred into gold and red embers that tinted the high clouds above the Divide.

"Did you call Sam Purdy for me?" she asked.

I wanted to see Sam, too. I missed him.

I considered lying to Merideth. But I wasn't eager to raise any suspicion with her that Sam and I were avoiding each other. She could be tenacious when she smelled conflict—at least conflict that didn't involve her. I didn't lie. I said, "I was hoping it wouldn't be necessary to bring him in. I thought I'd try Carmel first. I . . . I never expected this to get so complicated."

"It's necessary. Okay? Please give him a call."

"Why not hire a private detective, Merideth? A firm."

"I told you that I want somebody from out of town. Somebody discreet."

"Hire somebody from out of town. I think that anyone who's good will be discreet. That's what they do."

"I'm hiring somebody from out of town—Sam. What's going on with you, Alan? You have a problem with him?"

"No," I said. "But before I call him, I want to see what you have. Whatever is giving you the feeling the girl is dead. Nexis-Lexis. I don't care."

She sighed. "That's it? Then you'll call Sam?"

I immediately wondered what else I should have asked for. "Yes."

"I'll messenger it over."

We got to her Town Car, still stuck in traffic. A cement mixer was parked on one side, emptying its load. A double-parked FreshDirect truck, steam pouring from its engine, was on the other. I opened the back door of the car for her. I said, "I'll walk from here." As soon as I said it, I realized she hadn't planned to offer me a ride.

She began to climb onto the backseat. One foot inside the car, her hand on the top of the doorframe, she turned to me and whispered, "It's not just that I think she's dead. I'm afraid someone killed her."

I saw fear in her eyes. "The Grand Canyon girl? Or Lisa?" I said.

"The Grand Canyon girl."

"Do you know something, Meri?"

"It's just a feeling." Her eyes welled up. "I miss my baby. Is that silly?"

* * *

A messenger delivered a large sealed envelope from Merideth a few minutes after three. The doorman—during the day it was a hip, young Egyptian man named Haji who had a smile as invigorating as the Nile—signed for the package.

Haji had never said anything to me, but I suspected he was aware of the details of my arrangement with Ottavia. I thought that more than a few dollars—my dollars, ultimately—had changed hands. Haji was considerate to me. I figured he liked the money, and I was beginning to think that he liked the subterfuge, too.

I walked down the stairs to get the envelope. After a few days' practice, I could do the descent to the lobby rapidly—the motion akin to speed jump-roping while the floor fell out from under me. My quads were aching from the multiple climbs I'd undertaken since moving in, though, so I was taking a day off from doing ascents.

I thanked Haji for the package and waited for the elevator to take me back up to the flat. I'd never had a doorman before. I liked it.

The file that Merideth sent about the events in the Grand Canyon was sparse. She didn't know many details about what had happened, which surprised me; I had been assuming she knew much more than she was letting on. I reminded myself it was possible—knowing Merideth, even likely—that she hadn't sent me everything she had.

With the assistance of her network research staff she had compiled a series of succinct AP reports about the disappearance. Dateline: Grand Canyon National Park. They were written by an unnamed stringer, I guessed out of Vegas. The AP reports had been picked up by newspapers in Flagstaff, Phoenix, and Las Vegas. In addition, the file had printouts of brief Internet mentions of the events that had appeared on the Web sites of the NBC affiliate in Tucson and the ABC station in Phoenix.

The Phoenix station linked to some video of search preparations that had taken place up on the rim and of an interview with the U.S. Park Service ranger who was coordinating the search and rescue.

The station had apparently aired some coverage of the story at the time of the disappearance. Merideth's staffers had done synopses of the video clips. An update about the missing girl had consumed the entire single paragraph allotment for Arizona news by *USA Today* on the third day after her disappearance. Must have been a slow news day in the rest of Arizona.

Jaana Peet had grown up in a middle-class home just outside of Tallinn, Estonia. Her father was a baker. The local Estonian paper tracked the events in the Grand Canyon for about a week after she vanished. Merideth's crew had obtained English translations of the articles. They covered no new ground. One piece described the search. Another described the flash flood and the decision to call off the ground search.

In each piece, the geography where the local girl had vanished was described as "desolate."

The known facts were limited.

Jaana Peet was a twenty-one-year-old cook at the cafeteria in the lodge on the North Rim of the Grand Canyon. She had worked there just shy of half a year, since the previous February. She had originally arrived in the United States on a student visa, but hadn't been enrolled in classes anywhere since the fall semester of the previous year at the University of Nevada, Las Vegas, where she had been a communications major.

Photographs were of a lovely girl with a triangular face and huge, inquiring eyes.

Her companion on the hike to the Grand Canyon floor was Nicholas Paulson. In the news accounts, Paulson was initially described as a student at UNLV. Later reports listed him as being employed by a Las Vegas developer. The last report in Merideth's file identified him as the stepson of a prominent resort developer.

Jaana's coworkers at the lodge reported that her decision to go to the canyon floor on her day off was an impulsive one. She was excited that Nick was visiting her. She told her friends that she and

Nick would spend only one night in the campground. The next day, they planned to hike back out to the rim in time for her to make her late shift in the cafeteria.

Jaana's day off from her cooking job coincided with the tail end of one of the hottest weeks ever recorded at the Grand Canyon. Merideth's research file included nine articles that focused on the scorching heat that had consumed northern Arizona during the time just before and after Jaana's disappearance. The number of articles about the weather exceeded the number of articles about Jaana's disappearance. The heat wave had proven much more newsworthy than the search for the girl from Estonia.

Jaana had told friends that she wasn't worried about the heat. She didn't mind it.

People who had known Jaana on the rim—coworkers all, some also identified themselves as her friends—unanimously reported that she was an experienced hiker, that she had previously completed around ten round trips to the canyon floor, and that she wasn't someone who would be ambushed by the fact that the canyon was hot in August. She was neither an expert in the back-country nor a risk taker—she was unlikely to leave the well-marked rim-to-floor trails or to venture far off the paths that snaked away from the camping areas and ran along the river and into the nearby slot canyons.

A review of Grand Canyon National Park guest logs indicated that she had never previously signed up to take any route to or from the canyon floor other than the most common ones that leave the visitors' centers—either the Bright Angel or the North Kaibab.

Everyone interviewed maintained that Jaana would not have been unprepared for her hike. She would not have been careless around the river.

Upon his return to the North Rim, her companion, Nick Paulson, told the rangers that he was not an experienced hiker and would not have attempted the round-trip to the canyon floor had Jaana not assured him that he would have no trouble. He identified her as the leader of their expedition.

Multiple witnesses reported the couple's timely arrival at the canyon floor the day of their hike. A small group of people in a nearby campsite said that Nick and Jaana seemed to be pleasant, although Nick was depleted from the heat and the hike. He had developed bad blisters on one foot. Jaana prepared a simple supper at the end of the day. They drank a bottle of wine that she chilled in the river, and they quieted down for the night about the same time as everyone else in camp did.

The consensus among those who had spent any time with the couple was that Jaana was more gregarious and outgoing than Nick. She chatted with everyone she met.

Nick initially reported his companion missing to some other campers early the next morning. She wasn't in their camp when he awoke. He walked to the toilets near the the river looking for her so that they could begin preparations for their ascent back to the North Rim. When he didn't find her there, he backtracked toward Phantom Ranch where he found some other hikers preparing to climb out and explained that she had gotten up during the night and when he woke up he discovered that she hadn't returned to camp.

About an hour later a hastily assembled amateur search party began a search of the nearby campsites and cabins, and of the closest accessible beaches and trails. The group found no sign of Jaana. Over the course of the morning, the searchers gradually extended the perimeter of the target area.

Midmorning, the Park Service took over. Rangers organized additional volunteer searches that continued throughout the day on the canyon floor.

Midafternoon, one of the volunteers discovered a cheap woven bracelet that Nick thought may have belonged to Jaana. Friends later confirmed it was hers. The braid was found on a dusty trail about fifty feet from the banks of the Colorado River at the base of a waist-high boulder that had been rounded by a few eons of river flow. The spot was about a fifteen-minute walk from her campsite, between the boat beach and a nearby suspension bridge.

The first Park Service aerial searches began late that afternoon, by helicopter. Fixed-wing craft joined the search before dusk.

That first day, especially during the first few of hours after dawn, the alarm level about the girl's absence was low. Most of the people who were helping to look for Jaana expected her to wander back into camp at any moment.

Everyone was assuming she had gone off by herself to explore and perhaps had gotten injured. Some guessed she'd headed up the North Kaibab toward Ribbon Falls. Others thought she was on the River Trail on the other side of the Colorado. Most of the initial anxiety was that she might not have carried enough water with her on her morning hike.

The search continued without success for a second day.

Late the second afternoon, the grueling heat wave that had been smothering northern Arizona finally broke. Shortly after three o'clock the hot, still air was supplanted by gusty winds. Skies darkened to the south and to the west. Campers on the floor of the canyon heard a series of distant thunderclaps.

Visitors four thousand feet below the rim lacked the vantage to be able to see the approach of storm clouds, but a big, slow-moving thunderstorm had filled the void of the departing high pressure and stalled above the Bright Angel/Phantom Creek drainage. Rain began falling onto the drainage at the rate of more than an inch every twenty minutes. By shortly after six o'clock, rainwater overwhelmed the arroyos and natural channels, torrents of runoff poured from the slot canyons into the tributaries of the Colorado, and at 6:13 in the evening a ferocious wall of water exploded down Bright Angel Creek into the Colorado River.

The flash flood picked up rocks and debris at the confluence of the creek, near Phantom Ranch. Any hope of finding clues on the nearby trails or beaches vanished as the fast-moving flood jumped the banks of the Colorado and scoured the entire flood plain between the canyon walls.

The ground searches along the river were halted at the first indications of the approaching thunderstorm. Further efforts to locate Jaana were limited to helicopter and small airplane searches of the miles of the Colorado River that were downstream from where Jaana had disappeared.

By the morning of the next day, the third after her disappearance, official rescue efforts had ceased. Park personnel had moved into a "recovery" phase.

Signs were posted and all the registered river-runners on the Colorado were alerted to keep an eye out for Jaana's remains in the river, especially in eddies far downstream.

Over the course of those three quick days, the search for Jaana Peet had gone from casual to professional to despairing. The Park Service issued a press release on day four. Rangers considered it likely that Jaana Peet had drowned in the river and that her body had been carried downstream either before or during the flash flood. Although officials planned to remain vigilant, they couldn't estimate how long it might take to recover her body, or how far downstream her remains might have been carried.

One of the AP pieces in Merideth's research file quoted a Park Service ranger with almost twenty years of experience who said her body could be ten to twelve miles farther down the Colorado. A Grand Canyon river guide who had been running the river for a decade said forty or fifty miles wouldn't surprise him.

AP did a short follow-up story three weeks later. Jaana Peet remained missing. The article referenced a statement from the Park Service promising that personnel would continue to keep an eye out for her remains.

Nick Paulson spent only one additional night on the canyon floor. He accepted a ride out on a search helicopter about thirty hours after he had first reported Jaana missing. He had already been evacuated when the flash flood hit. At the request of the Park Service he spent one additional night at the lodge at the North Rim while he was being interviewed about Jaana's disappearance. He checked out of his room at almost the precise time that the thunderstorm was parked over the Bright Angel Creek Drainage. He drove back to Las Vegas in a Mustang convertible.

The contemporaneous follow-up accounts contained no additional information about Nick Paulson. Merideth's files showed no indication he had been interviewed by the press or by Park Service personnel after he returned to Las Vegas. One of Merideth's researchers tried to track down his current whereabouts. The researcher identified three possibilities, based on Paulson's age at the time of Jaana's disappearance. The AP news reports had pegged him as twenty-two at that time.

One Nicholas Paulson was in Boise, Idaho. He worked as a laborer for an oil company. One was literally a rocket scientist—he was employed by NASA, and was living in Huntsville, Alabama. The third was living in Las Vegas, where he was employed by a well-known resort development firm.

Twenty-four

Jonas and I talked daily while we were in New York. He would sit on the swing in his aunt and uncle's backyard and talk with me on his cell phone. I think the regular contact was reassuring to us both.

During a morning conversation the day after I received the research file from Merideth, he asked if we could cancel our weekend plans. He'd been invited to go to the shore with his cousins.

Jonas was a hard-core baseball fan. Though he was slender like his dad had been, he saw himself as a catcher. It was one of many revelations about him that had begun to pelt me within hours after he began to sleep in our house following his mom's death.

What else had I learned? Jonas adored astronomy and was able to get lost for hours charting the night sky. He was dying to go to a monster-truck show, was curious about drag racing, and liked early eighties music. He was embarrassed about his affection for SpongeBob.

His favorite baseball team was the Colorado Rockies, and to counterbalance the chronic despair that tagged along with that affection, he also had a backup thing for the Mets.

I had gone online and scored some pretty good seats for the Saturday Mets game at Shea.

I almost told Jonas I had tickets for a Mets game. Against the dreaded Braves. But I didn't tell him. That would have been selfish.

"You're sure?" I asked, as evenly as I could. Prior to beginning the extended visit with his relatives, I had prepared Jonas for the possibility that he might get some pressure from his aunt or uncle to minimize or cancel the time that he was scheduled to spend with me in the city. I had also assured Jonas that if it turned out he preferred to stay with his cousins rather than come into the city, that would be fine. I was in New York in case Jonas wanted contact. In case he needed me. It was up to him to decide if he wanted to take advantage of the safety valve I was providing—it wasn't a requirement.

I didn't expect him to cancel our visits. Adrienne had once told me that her niece and nephew were "dweebs." She'd allowed at the time—in a moment of familial rationalization—that she didn't consider it the kids' fault they were dweebs. Any dweebness was the nature/nurture responsibility of her dweeby brother, their father.

Jonas and I agreed on a code word he could use if he didn't feel free to tell me the truth about what was going on in White Plains. The code word he picked was "Callie." Callie was the name the breeders had given the Havanese puppy that Jonas's mother had bought for him before she died. All he had to do to alert me that he was under some kind of pressure from his aunt or uncle was to use her original name, Callie, in a conversation.

He didn't mention Callie while we talked about his trip to the beach. What he said was, "I really want to go to the shore. They have a boogie board."

He sounded excited. "Sounds great, Jonas. Should be fun. What beach?"

"I don't know."

"Is it close? Within driving distance?"

"I don't know."

Okay. "Is Kim around? I want to get some details. Wait—Jonas?"

"What?"

"Jonas, do you know how to swim?"

He laughed. It was a deep, belly laugh. Music. I could hear his mother's wit echoing from within him. "I'll race you sometime," he said.

"You're on."

"Thanks, Alan. Bye, Alan," Jonas said. "I'll find her." He yelled, "Aunt Kim! It's Alan. I can go!"

For the first month or so after his mother's death, he had stopped calling Lauren and me by our names, something he'd been doing since he had learned to talk. I didn't know what it meant that he had started again. It was one of those perplexing questions that one of my patients might ask me during a session. I was supposed to be the expert.

My patients always acted surprised when I said I didn't know.

Kim gave me all the details about the weekend. One of her girl-friend's families had a place in the Hamptons. "Not one of those places," she clarified. I assumed she meant it wasn't a palace. "That's where we'll be staying. Three families, a houseful of kids."

I liked Kim. I'd begun to suspect that I would find her kids likable too if I got to know them. But Marty? I thought he would end up being one of those acquired tastes that I never quite acquired. Like oysters. Or tinned anchovies.

I called the Netherlands. Lauren and I had a quiet talk that left me feeling nurtured and hopeful. She gave the phone to Grace, who was wonderfully chatty. She told me that they were still waiting to see if they were going to get a chance to meet her sister. She told me all about her visit to the Anne Frank house. When her attention began to wane, I asked if she liked Holland. "It's the best. I want to live someplace with canals, Daddy. Here's Mommy again."

Lauren sounded tired. I inquired about her health, and learned she was "okay."

"Are you hopeful about seeing . . . your daughter?" I asked after it was clear our health-status duet was done.

"Just a second," she said. I imagined her taking a few steps away from Grace to get some privacy. "I don't think her adoptive family is exactly happy we're here. I'm hopeful about things one day, other days I think they're just waiting for us to get tired of all the delays and go home. How's Jonas?"

I explained about the canceled game at Shea.

"That's good, right?" she asked. "That Jonas is comfortable there? That he wants to be there?"

"Yeah. That's good. I still don't trust Marty. But I'm liking Kim more every time I talk with her."

A few moments later, seconds after we had ended the call, I realized that I had still not told Lauren that I had been in touch with Merideth in New York. I convinced myself that it was because the contact was, in the grand scheme, unimportant. Telling her I'd seen my ex would only raise the contact to a level of importance it didn't deserve.

Had I been one of my own patients, as a therapist I would have reflected aloud that were rationalization an art, that particular effort deserved to be hanging at MoMA.

Twenty-five

I gave Haji the Mets tickets and spent a quiet weekend walking the city, visiting neighborhoods that I hadn't visited before. NoLIta was my new favorite. Harlem was a close second—I was having some remorse about not choosing one of the sublets there. The summer exodus of residents from the city had reduced weekend traffic on the city's sidewalks. I promised myself I would revisit my new favorites on a day when the streets were teeming.

Although I had left messages both at his home and on his cell phone, Sam Purdy didn't return my latest call until Sunday afternoon.

When he finally got back to me—I hadn't been certain he would—I was sitting in the shade outside a coffeehouse in what I thought was the Meatpacking District, drinking iced chai. The day was hot, but the humidity was tolerable, at least for the moment. I was guessing I had about ten more minutes before the movement of the sun across the southern arc of the sky would make a mockery of my shady spot and compel me to retreat. The other two outdoor tables enjoyed more protected shade than mine did, but the occupants appeared to have long-term plans for their real estate.

Caller ID read PAY PHONE. The subterfuge of using public phones was a habit that Sam and I developed during our crime spree, one that was apparently dying hard for him. We had started out in our mutual lawbreaking with misdemeanors. The call camouflage was continuing, I suspected, because we had graduated to felonies.

"Sam," I said.

"Hey," he said. "Sorry I didn't get back to you sooner. I've been on the road with Simon." Simon was Sam's son.

Sam was hoping I'd endorse the fiction that the reason he hadn't returned my call was because he wasn't able to drive and talk on the phone simultaneously. I granted him the invention. It's what friends do.

"Just got back from driving him to Minnesota." Sam held the long o sound of the penultimate syllable for two extra beats. One of the two additional beats was residue of his northern Minnesota heritage, the other was an intentional exaggeration of his accent for my benefit. "He's going to spend a few weeks out there with all his grandparents and cousins. See some family, do some fishing. Canoeing, too."

When Sam said "canoeing," it came out "c'n-oo-in." The word didn't even resemble a gerund. "Kid needs to get up close and personal with some real mosquitoes. Not the wimpy things that show up around here in July and August."

Sam and his ex were both from Minnesota—Sam from the far north, the Iron Range. They knew from lakes and fishing and canoeing—okay, c'n-oo-in—and they knew from mosquitoes masquerading as hummingbirds.

"Simon's good, Sam?"

Simon was good. His dream to spend the summer at a hockey camp in Vancouver that cost more per month than the sticker price of his father's first car was one of the casualties of Sam's job suspension. The trip north to hang with relatives in Minnesota was Simon's consolation prize.

Sam had no way to know that I was in New York with Jonas. I doubted that he knew about Lauren's Dutch child or that Lauren and Grace were on a quixotic adventure to connect with unlikely extended family in Amsterdam.

In so many ways, Amsterdam was not Sam's kind of city. I did think that if I could drag him through town with blinders on—literal blinders, so he would fail to notice the coffee shops and the red-light district—I could get him addicted to *rijsttafel* after one or two courses.

I brought him up to speed on my family's goings-on, my trip to New York to be close to Jonas, and the girls' jaunt to Europe. It took a few minutes. He digested the revelations about Lauren's past in stride. Where sexual indiscretion was concerned, Sam felt he was the blackest pot on the hearth, and he was not about to disparage anyone else's charred kettle.

As we talked, the sun's rays marched relentlessly across the table-top, threatening to consume me in their fire.

Our conversation was the kind of chat that good friends have. Sam and I were conspiring to ignore the relationship elephant in the room. The elephant was the fact that in the wake of an ultimate act of friendship the previous spring, we had been having great difficulty acting like friends.

Processing relationship dynamics with Sam had never been an easy thing for me—he was a reluctant participant in any activity that approached the intentionally introspective. I wasn't about to risk ruining the first few minutes of our only conversation in a long time by insisting that he confront the distance that had infiltrated our friendship.

"You holding up?" I asked him when an opportunity appeared to refocus the conversation on him. Sam's six-month unpaid suspension was a little more than half over. He had failed to notify his police superiors that he had been sexually involved with the victim of a hit-and-run case he had been investigating. That the victim was another police officer had complicated things for Sam considerably. As did the fact that he had a girlfriend at the time.

In reply to my direct question, he maintained that he was doing, "Good. Good." The second "good" pretty much erased any inclination I might have had to accept the fragile sincerity of the first. I asked how his trip to California to break up with Carmen—the aforementioned girlfriend—had gone.

"How the fu—" he sputtered before he said, "Come on, how do you think?"

He didn't want an answer. That's probably why I gave him one. "I would imagine it was difficult, and painful."

He laughed. "This is the point when I'm supposed to tell you how much I've missed you, right? That it's so much fun being buddies with a shrink?"

"Thanks."

"Don't mention it." He gave me a chance to defy him. I didn't. To reward my restraint, he said, "Wise."

"I've missed you, Sam."

He allowed me a moment to get ready for what he was going to say next. "We need to be careful, Alan. There are people in the department who see the convenience of what happened . . . on that ranch in Frederick. Someone could still put the pieces together."

I didn't plan to argue that point with him. Frederick, Colorado, was the site of the violent death of a woman who had it in for our families, Sam's and mine. Her death had not been serendipity—it had been preemptive self-defense on our part. Mostly Sam's. On the way to that secret finale, Sam and I had created fresh enemies in Boulder law enforcement—people who would take great satisfaction tying us to the woman's death, one the medical examiner had, for the present, called a suicide.

I said, "We can't pretend we're not friends, Sam. That looks suspicious too."

"We need to be wise."

"Okay," I said. "Merideth called a few days ago, Sam. She—"

"You told Merideth you're in New York?" He almost coughed out the words. That's how surprised he was.

Sam wasn't much for gossip, but he could recognize the raw materials when they were strewn out in front of him. He also knew me well enough to know that getting in touch with Merideth was so far down my usual to-do list that it would be difficult for someone to spot without binoculars. "No, I didn't. But she called me, I answered, and she knows I'm here. She was in tears."

"You went to her rescue?"

He said it in a way that made me want to tell him, "It's not like that." But I knew if I argued it wasn't like that, it would sound like it was like that.

I said, "She wants to know if you're interested in some work."

The relentless assault of the sun had consumed the tabletop and begun inching up my thighs. My chair was pushed back against the brick wall. If I didn't stand up, the sun's heat would soon poach my testicles in scrotal sweat. I stuck a couple of bucks under my glass and conceded my territory.

I began to cross the street because most of the shade was on the other side. Sam was silent while I was on the move, apparently considering something.

"You still there? I lose you?" I asked. I had completed half my jaywalk, pausing so an off-duty cab could speed by.

"What kind of work? I don't do security."

Security? That caused me to wonder what Sam had been up to during his suspension from the police department. "Looking into an old . . . case she's interested in. Talking to some people. Things you do every day. Things you're good at."

"Detective stuff?"

"I guess."

"I'm not a P.I."

"She's looking for something more . . . informal. That's my sense, anyway."

"Money is kind of tight," he mused.

Sam was convincing himself of something. I offered him an alternative. "I can help with money, Sam."

He ignored me. He asked, "Is this for her TV job? She's looking for a consultant? Like for a story?"

From his inflection I couldn't tell if Sam thought whether working as a consultant for a national TV news producer would be intriguing or inane. But it was clear that I had not been creative enough to recognize how easily Merideth and Sam were going to finesse the details of the arrangement she was contemplating—specifically, how they would get around the whole P.I. licensing problem that looked so imposing to me.

Sam spied the opening in the fabric of the ethical/legal fence immediately.

If Sam was interested in the work she was proposing, and if Merideth continued to think he was the best person to help her, I didn't want to screw things up between them. I decided to get out of the middle. I said, "I think I'll let you get in touch and you guys can decide what your role would be."

"What do you know already, Alan? I can tell you know stuff. You're dying to tell me something."

I sat down on the first step of a concrete stoop that was directly across the street from a nineteenth-century building covered with a visual cacophony of graffiti. The narrow building—remnants of a pulley system protruding below an ornate cornice convinced me that it had once been a warehouse—was wallpapered with volunteer art. Not one of its surfaces, vertical or horizontal, was spared decoration. Graphic things. Geometric things. Serene things. Obscene things. Some of it was . . . trash. Random trash, angry trash. But some of it was good. Captivating.

A sign announcing imminent redevelopment hung over a second-story window. The sign had not been painted over.

The adjacent buildings were all graffiti-free. It was as though the taggers and the neighborhood property owners had agreed that only the old warehouse would be defaced.

While I appreciated the artistic panoply, I gave Sam an outline of what I'd learned about the Grand Canyon thing. About Jaana and Eric, and about Carmel.

"Huh," he said, not exactly tipping his hand.

"Do you know her parents, Sam? The Poteets? Wallace and Cassandra?"

"He's a shrink? I wouldn't know him unless I met him with you. Maybe I arrested him once. Where do they live?"

"Shanahan Ridge. Not too far below NCAR." I said N-CAR, not N-C-A-R. Sam knew I was talking about the National Center for Atmospheric Research in Boulder. I. M. Pei had designed the complex to evoke an Anasazi ruin. NCAR sits on a high plateau above the southwest tip of Boulder on what is probably the finest single piece of real estate in the county, maybe even the finest parcel in the whole eastern side of the state.

Sam said, "I can't tell from your story—did you end up talking to their daughter? What? Carmel?"

"Yeah, it's Carmel. Cara. But no, I haven't spoken with her, and I'm not sure I'll get the chance." I explained the situation with Wallace and Cassandra, and their concern about revisiting the Grand Canyon trip with their daughter.

"There's no crime here, right? You're not leaving something out of the story? This isn't police work? I can't . . . do that."

"I've only seen media reports Merideth provided from the time the woman disappeared, Sam. There's no mention of a crime in any of them. Everything I've read makes what happened sound like a disappearance, maybe an accident."

"No body?"

"Nobody?" I asked, confused.

"Not 'nobody.' No corpus. That kind of 'no body.'"

"Not that, either. Not according to what I've seen."

A kid whizzed around the corner on a motorized scooter and stopped fifteen feet past the stoop. The minuscule motor on the scooter was belching blue smoke and whining like a baby with colic. The kid—I guessed he was twelve or thirteen—had stopped in the direct glare of the sun and seemed immune to its power to melt flesh. He kept glancing my way as he tinkered with the motor. I thought he was stalling while he decided whether the reason I was hanging in his neighborhood was something that merited his attention.

Sam said, "Sure, why the hell not? I'll give Merideth a call. See what she has in mind. With Simon gone I can use the distraction. Got her number?"

I gave him Merideth's mobile number. I added, "She can be difficult."

"I think I can handle it. I'm not calling her for her company. "

"She's changed, Sam. Grown up." I recognized my ambivalence—I'd gone from warning Sam about my ex one minute, to defending her the next. There wasn't a particularly compelling rationale for either inclination.

"Doesn't matter a whit to me," he said. "I hardly knew the woman before she was new and improved."

Jonas's uncle Marty called my mobile less than an hour later as I was climbing out of the subway station on my way to Murray Hill. I had to scamper up the long flight of stairs to get a strong enough signal to use my phone. My heart was racing. Not from the exertion of the climb, but because the call was so unexpected.

Marty hadn't called me once since I'd arrived in New York.

Tell me Jonas is okay. Tell me! "Marty. You there? Can you hear me?"

"Alan. Yeah, yeah. Fine."

"What's up? Is Jonas okay?"

"Jonas? Great. Listen . . . um. We should talk. I'll be taking the train into the city tomorrow for a meeting. How about we grab a bagel someplace near Grand Central?"

Twenty-six

I hadn't been aware of being homesick, so I was surprised at how thrilled I was to be back in Boulder.

When I walked in the door of my house after my extended sojourn in New York the three dogs greeted me like a returning hero—for about ten minutes. At that point they realized that it was I who had deserted them. They cut the celebratory dance short and began to mope, the two larger dogs choosing places to sleep so that their butts, and not their eyes, were turned in my direction.

I knew from experience that the older two, the Bouvier and the miniature poodle, would come around again by their next meal. With the puppy, though—the new Havanese that Adrienne had given Jonas—I didn't know what to expect. After the joy of my arrival home had subsided, she'd departed the herd and disappeared toward the master bedroom. For a few minutes I listened for sounds of mischief coming from that direction, but discerned nothing worrisome. I figured she had sacked out on the bed.

Puppies sleep a lot. Although it had been a few years since we'd had one, that's what I remembered.

My bagels-and-coffee breakfast meeting with Marty in Manhattan had been followed later the same day by dinner with Marty's family in White Plains. Jonas was there with his cousins, whom he seemed to adore. Kim was a fine cook. I could tell she had gone to a lot of trouble preparing the meal.

I'd taken the train to White Plains from Grand Central. Kim met me at the station in a Honda minivan that was, I couldn't think of a better word, trashed. Toys, balls, snack residue, clothes—lots of clothes—shoes, old newspapers, homework papers, school books, an ironic copy of *Real Simple*.

Kim seemed oblivious to the fact that she was driving Pigpen's car around town.

I pushed just enough stuff off the passenger seat to make room to sit. An accumulation of brown goo on the seat-belt latch worried me more than a little.

Before dinner, Jonas and I took a long walk so that I would have a chance to convince myself that his heart wasn't torn about what he had decided he wanted to do.

At a chaotic bagel bar in Manhattan that morning Marty had told me that Jonas had concluded that he was okay in White Plains by himself for the remainder of his stay, and that he didn't think he wanted to visit me in the city again.

To give Marty credit—not my natural inclination—he had not been gloating while we had bialys and coffee in the city. Still, I told Marty I wanted to hear the news from Jonas.

Marty invited me to dinner so I would have an opportunity to do just that.

Five minutes into my walk with Jonas he told me I could go home to Boulder.

The sentiment felt real. "You're cool here?" I said. "You don't think you want to come to the city again?"

"I like it here. I can see you back home," he said. "I'm having a good time."

He wasn't looking at me when he spoke.

Jonas was kicking a rock about the size of a golf ball. Each swat carried it forward five or six feet. Just before he told me he'd see me in Boulder, he kicked it two or three times, skipping it forward more than ten feet each time.

I felt a compelling need to see his eyes. He wasn't giving me a chance. I waited a few moments before I asked, "How are you sleeping?"

He knew what I was asking. From the day I brought him home to Spanish Hills from Tel Aviv, Jonas had grown progressively anxious as bedtime neared. It could take him hours to fall asleep.

"Okay," he said. "The same, maybe."

"Still trouble falling asleep?"

He looked up at me and nodded.

"Anything I can do to help?"

"Don't think so."

I'd already made a judgment that, despite Kim's cooking, Jonas's appetite hadn't improved. He was as thin as I'd ever seen him.

The fact that he seemed to be getting along well with his cousins was, in contrast, a great piece of news, the first real sign that the initial bruises from his trauma might be beginning to change colors.

"I want to be clear. You're telling me that you don't want to come to the city anymore?"

"Yeah."

"And you want me to go back home, Jonas? To Boulder?"

He kicked the rock again. I realized at that moment that my stepson appeared to be left-footed. I'd had no idea. He was right-handed. I had so much catching up to do.

Including some reading on mixed dominance.

"I think so," he said finally. "Yeah. You can go back to Colorado."

It was a gutsy move for the kid in so many ways. Since his mother's death I had been his security blanket, and he was sending me away. He was either oblivious to my feelings about his decision, which was good, or confident enough in my relationship with him that he felt he could risk my reaction, which was better. I hoped it was the latter.

I tried to make my next words tender. "If I do go to Boulder, I'll come back out and get you whenever you want. And I'll be here for

sure when your visit is over. We can fly back to Colorado together,"
I said. I wanted Jonas to understand that he could change the day-
to-day rules of our relationship if he needed to, but that any short-
term evolution he threw at me wouldn't change my commitment
to him.

"Maybe . . . I was, you know . . ." He kicked the rock and
skipped quickly ahead to catch up with it. I lengthened my stride a
little so I could keep up. He went on, "Maybe I can . . . I was just
thinking . . . I could fly back . . . by myself. I'm old enough, I think.
Aunt Kim will make sure I get on the right plane." He swung his leg
extra hard and whacked the stone a good fifty feet down the lane.

No skipping that time. He ran after it in full sprint.

The kid had speed. Who knew? You could have used a calendar
to time his mother in the hundred-meter dash. Peter, Jonas's birth
father, had been nimble. Jonas must have gotten his dad's quickness.

"Maybe you can," I said to his back. "Should we wait and see . . .
how you feel about it a couple more days? There's no hurry."

He pulled to a stop when he reached the stone, turned toward
me, bit his lower lip, and looked at my eyes. "Yeah. Let's." He waited
for me to reach him.

I said, "You like your cousins, don't you?"

He smiled and nodded.

I got chills. *Hey, Adrienne. Maybe they aren't dweebs. Who'd
have thunk it?*

On the train back into the city later that night I considered many
things. I wondered whether I should have acquiesced to Marty's insistence that Jonas make an extended visit east that first summer, so
soon after his mother's death. I wondered whether Jonas's newfound
attachment to his mother's extended family was artificial or real. I
wondered, too, whether, despite Jonas's wishes, I should stay in the
city.

Just in case things turned to shit.

And of course I wondered whether Marty would be calling me in some number of days to once again suggest that he and I talk. The next time would be to tell me that Jonas had decided not to return to Boulder at all.

If the last thing happened—if Marty tried to hijack my son—I would have to answer to Adrienne. She would be sitting in her heavenly perch witnessing what was happening down on earth. She wouldn't be pleased. I imagined that she would display her dissatisfaction by crossing over to the celestial dark side. She would track down whomever up there was in charge of the launching and targeting of meteorites, and she would order one with sharp edges sent my way.

I give you one thing to do, Bubela. One thing—look after my kid. And what do you do? After three months, you lose him to my schmuck brother. Oy.

I decided that fifteen minutes of alone time was a lot for a hypomanic puppy. Despite the quiet, I had a nagging concern that the Havanese wasn't merely napping someplace she didn't belong—like on my pillow—but that she was up to something nefarious. I walked down the hall to the bedroom.

The dog, it turned out, had not been sleeping. She had been quite busy.

Shredding. As far as I could tell, she had sliced up much of the June issue of *The Atlantic*. It had been on my side of the bed. While the dog had been on Lauren's side of the bed, she had been even more industrious. She had completely destroyed the blueprints of the floor plans for Jonas's remodeled room in the basement, as well as the glossy covers, front and back, of three design magazines that Lauren had been using for inspiration for the transformation.

I have had dogs for most of my life. I had never seen anything that even approximated the quality of the destructive work this ten-pound bundle of silky white and black hair had accomplished in less than a quarter hour of determined razoring. She hadn't ripped the papers apart, leaving big chunks here and there—something Emily used to do during her destructive puppy phase. Nor had the puppy taken the magazines or documents in her mouth and shaken them as though she were trying to throttle a chipmunk, leaving the paper in crumpled, saliva-drenched clumps.

She had methodically shredded them into small pieces as though she were intent on mimicking the work of a crosscut shredder. The bits that remained, less than a centimeter square, were not strewn about. She'd left them approximately where she'd shredded them. The activity was not about random destruction, it seemed to be about enjoyment of the shredding.

I stood at the foot of the bed in awe of her work.

She was proud of it too. Her tail, curled above her ass like a long mink apostrophe, was flying to and fro. Her little butt danced back and forth in counterpoint.

Twenty-seven

His Ex

Stevie refused to help me search for her sister.

Eric, too, remained unconvinced that Lisa's absence constituted a crisis. "She needs a little time. She'll be in touch," he told me. "Don't worry so much."

"But—" I'd say, before he'd interrupt me right back.

"She doesn't want our baby. She can have one of her own whenever she wants."

Then where the hell is she?

Besides being a teacher, Eric was a policy consultant. He counseled big businesses and famous politicians and governments of all stripes. He rarely told me what he told any of them. But me? For me he usually counseled patience. At face value, in these circumstances, it was a reasonable position. But when I pressed the fact that Lisa was carrying our child in her womb, her failure to stay in touch with us for even a few days seemed like the most unreasonable act imaginable.

Being patient did not seem reasonable. Barely even possible.

I tried to counter my natural impulse, which was to demand that Eric see things from my perspective, instead endeavoring with all my might to allow him to enjoy the prime spot at the front of our nascent family's very short line. He was reminding me every day—twice some days—that he was *this* close to getting the position he coveted in advance of the next campaign. Patience, patience.

For Eric, going public with the fact that we had hired a surrogate who had disappeared with our rapidly growing embryo in her womb might change the political and institutional perception of him in ways that he could not anticipate, and certainly ways that he could not control. He had been manufacturing a carefully crafted image. From his point of view, any controversial behavior in his personal life could only bring him the exact wrong kind of attention.

That would be notoriety.

Prominent people in politics and in big corporations don't embrace consultants who are forced to check baggage. People hire consultants who travel light. The smaller the carry-on, in fact, the better.

Eric was presenting position papers, returning phone calls to important people no one could know he was talking with, doing late-night meetings in hotels where other important people where staying. He was lining up support. Mostly, from my perspective, he was gone. Traveling. Unspoken between us was the reality that he didn't need the distraction of participating in an unnecessary search for his child's surrogate mother.

Eric had many colleagues and many friends—some were as religious as him, though many were not—who maintained that the only acceptable way to bear children was the way that couples had borne offspring through the millennia. One man, one woman, one marriage, and a fruitful copulation.

One womb. Only one womb.

If those circumstances, those biomechanics, and those natural limitations didn't serve to bless the couple with a baby, so be it. Adoption was the only permissible alternative. Any intervention that required the borrowing—or, God forbid, the perceived renting—of another woman's womb would be frowned upon.

Eric didn't want to be public with our conception plan because he didn't want to become the public face of surrogacy. If I gave him the podium, he would argue to me that we couldn't afford for him to become the public face of surrogacy.

I suspected that his wish that I not dig around in whatever had happened in the Grand Canyon was because of similar concerns. Public scrutiny of the facts of what happened in the Grand Canyon that day might bring Eric notoriety. He did not want notoriety.

If things had gone well, this would have been my second trimester, the quiet time during my pregnancy. His perspective was that now that we were using a surrogate, the whole thing should have been even quieter. The subtext? *Take care of this, Merideth.*

That's the way I feared Eric looked at it. My fault, anatomically. My problem, administratively.

He promised me he needed only a week or so to wrap things up with the people he needed to impress. Then the position would be his.

I didn't tell him that I had gone ahead and hired Sam. I figured the fight we would have about it would be a distraction for him.

He kept telling me he didn't need distractions.

Twenty-eight

Her Ex

I'd been back in Boulder for less than a day when Wallace got in touch with me again. The screen on my cell phone read POTEET.

His call distracted me from the intensity with which I was missing my family. And Adrienne.

During the first few weeks after her funeral, Jonas's grief at his mother's death was palpable. I'd tried to set aside my own sadness. But with my wife and daughter in Europe, and Jonas in New York, the eastern rim of the Boulder Valley had a huge hole where Adrienne's beating heart had been. I felt her absence from Spanish Hills like an increase in atmospheric pressure. Nothing was as light as it had been. The sky seemed smaller.

"Hi, Wallace," I said. I'd had no idea how long Wallace's deliberations were going to take. I was convinced that he and Cassandra would reach a decision that it wouldn't be in Cara's best interest to talk with me about the Grand Canyon thing.

I expected Wallace and I would talk vaguely about the power of old wounds. I would accept Wallace's determination with neither argument nor disappointment. Merideth, with whatever help Sam could provide, would muddle through her dilemma and solve the old Grand Canyon mystery on her own. Or she wouldn't.

"Listen," he said in a voice that cut off the small talk the way a sharp knife takes the top off a banana. "I need a favor. A big . . . favor."

I moved to let him off the hook. "There's not even a need to ask. If you don't want me to bother Cara about this . . . consider it done. I wouldn't even think of—"

"Give me a second here. The favor is that we *want* you to talk with her."

"What?"

"I'm concerned about my daughter. I wasn't even certain I was going to tell Cara that you wanted to talk with her about the Grand Canyon . . . experience. Maybe I should have trusted my instincts— she didn't react well when I brought it up. Regardless, the bottom line is that she won't talk to us about this. After a lot of back and forth, she agreed that she would talk to you."

Me? "Why?"

With strained levity he said, "I threatened to come out and stalk her if she didn't."

"What kind of concerned are you, Wallace?"

He pondered the question for a decent interval before he said, "About her well-being, Alan. Her withdrawal from us, from the family, truly worries me."

I was surprised. "Any history I should know about?"

"You didn't know her well when she was younger, but she's always been a high-strung kid, Alan. She didn't get the same mellow gene that her brother and sister have. Cara saw Frannie Rein for a while in high school—being fourteen wasn't easy for her. Frannie helped. But then Cara seemed to have a setback after the episode in the Grand Canyon. Withdrawal, depression. Drama."

Frannie Rein was a local psychiatrist. Frannie was good, an especially sensitive therapist with adolescents. But the fact that Wallace and Cassandra had chosen a psychiatrist—and not a psychologist or a social worker—for their daughter's therapy raised another question in my mind. I asked it aloud: "Was she on meds when she was seeing Frannie?"

The name of the drug would have told me important things about Frannie's diagnosis.

Wallace said, "No."

Considering the circumstances and the nature of the favor he was asking, his reply was not only too cryptic but also too parsimonious for my taste. "What about now?"

"Not that I know of. But . . . that doesn't mean she isn't. She's not a kid anymore. She's an adult." After a moment, he added, "They grow up."

The last words were wistful, but I also heard them as a caution from Wallace to a friend with younger children. I said, "And Cara agreed to talk with me, knowing that I . . . wanted to ask her about whatever happened at the Grand Canyon?"

"She asked me what you knew. How you knew. Whom you've talked to. I think it's only because you already know something that she agreed to talk with you at all."

"What did you tell her I knew, Wallace?"

"That I didn't think you knew much. My gut says she's afraid you already know something she doesn't want anyone to know. Whatever happened down there is a big secret, Alan."

Ten minutes later I had agreed to talk to Cara, if she indeed proved as willing a participant as her father thought she would be. A big part of the protracted conversation with Wallace involved a topic that was unavoidable for psychotherapists in complicated help-giving situations that involved family members or close friends.

Would I be talking to Cara as a psychologist or as a concerned family friend?

Although Wallace knew that the question would ultimately be resolved by Cara, and by me, he made it quite clear that he was asking for my involvement as a family friend. The distinction was crucial. If I were functioning as a family friend, I would be free to share my impressions with Wallace and Cassandra. Were I involved as a therapist—even if only long enough to convince Cara to find another therapist, one without a conflict of interest—my discussions with her would be confidential.

Since I had no way of knowing what Cara had in mind, the only commitment I made to Wallace was that I would contact Cara as a concerned friend. Anything that happened subsequently would be at her request, and by mutual agreement.

The last few minutes of the phone conversation with Wallace had to do with the "big" part of the "big, big favor."

He wanted me to go to L.A. to talk with his daughter. "She won't leave work. She can't. She has to be on the set every day."

"Weekend?" I asked.

"She won't come here," he said. "Not right now. She's made that clear."

"She won't?" I said, hoping to learn more.

"I know I'm asking a lot. You can probably tell from my voice that this feels urgent, Alan. Will you be able to get away from New York for a couple of days? Cassandra and I will pay for everything, of course." He wasn't trying to feign any nonchalance about the gravity of the situation. He wanted me to go talk to his daughter immediately. While I was fumbling to formulate a reply, he asked, "How soon are you and Jonas coming back to Boulder?"

"I'm in Boulder right now," I said. I then offered a capsule explanation of the recent progression of events with Jonas in New York.

"Risky," Wallace said, "for both of you." He had immediately recognized the psychological vulnerabilities that were implicit in the recent choices Jonas and I had made in regard to White Plains and Uncle Marty.

"Yeah, it is risky. I didn't feel the other options were any more attractive."

After about five seconds of dead air, he said, "You can make time, then? To go to California?"

I could hear the desperation in his voice. Wallace, too, was selecting his stores from a limited pantry.

We both knew I wouldn't turn him down.

Twenty-nine

Sam had never been to the Grand Canyon. After discussing what Merideth wanted, and reading the file she'd accumulated, he had told her that the Grand Canyon was where he wanted to begin his inquiry.

Merideth had offered to fly him to Vegas or Flagstaff and rent him a car for the comparatively short drive to the nearby Visitor's Center, but Sam was a man enamored of long road trips. He wanted to make the drive in his ancient Jeep Cherokee.

We were having a beer at what had become our regular fair-weather spot in Boulder—the roof of the West End Tavern, not too far from his North Boulder house and not too far from my office downtown. New construction had spoiled the view from the roof, but we still gravitated up there.

He said, "I like the road."

"It's summer, Sam. We're talking desert. Hot."

"But they say it's a dry heat," he added with a smidgeon of sarcasm. After draining his beer, he added, "So you finally tell wife two you've been in touch with wife one?"

"Merideth was first. Doesn't make her number one."

"Whatever. Did you tell her?"

"Yes." I'd told Lauren during the same conversation I told her I was returning to Boulder from New York. She had seemed neither upset nor especially curious about the Merideth episode. I had been relieved.

For the next few seconds I stared at the foam floating on top of my beer. Then I raised my eyes to the dusk pastels dissipating in the evening sky. Talking about first wives wasn't a favorite topic for either of us. I hoped Sam would see the wisdom in changing the subject.

I hoped for an end to global warming, too.

Sam allowed about thirty seconds to pass before he went editorial on me. "Conversation went well, I guess," he said. "The one with Lauren."

I laughed a little. "Went fine. Great. Better than this one is going. She knows when to leave well enough alone." I changed the subject, finished explaining the favor I was doing for Wallace and Cassandra in California.

"This isn't another favor for Merideth?" Sam asked. "You're sure about that?"

"Yes," I lied. "I wouldn't be going out there if Wallace hadn't begged me to go. He's worried about his daughter. "

Sam nodded in a way that was intended to be unconvincing. "When do you leave for L.A.?" he asked.

"Couple days. What about you? When are you going to the Grand Canyon?"

"Tomorrow morning."

"You think the answer Merideth wants is in Arizona?" I asked.

"Not really. But I told her she had to hire a real P.I. to do the missing-persons part of the puzzle. Staking out the surrogate's apartment in L.A.? Tracking her cell-phone usage, her credit cards, seeing if she just got a speeding ticket in Tallahassee? That shit—that's how she'll end up finding Lisa. I don't have an investigator's license. And I don't want one. I like the puzzle more than the chase. I like identifying perps more than I like tracking them down. This mystery starts that night in the Grand Canyon.

"Anyway, I should get going—I'm heading out early, before dawn. Want to be clear of the metro area before all the idiots wake up."

"You'll end up in the Springs just in time for rush hour down there."

Sam was feeling philosophical. "Life isn't perfect, Alan. You avoid one thing, something else gets you. Fate abhors planning. Do too much and you become an easy target for the gods."

I had been convinced for almost a year that what fate abhors is contentedness. But I kept remembering contented times, and didn't know what to do with the contrary evidence. "A target for what?" I asked.

"More fate." He attempted to finish his beer for the second time, returning his glass to the table with some force as a sign of his disappointment that the glass was already empty. "That's it for me. I want to be all chipper in the morning."

I had slept in my own bed for a total of three nights before I boarded the flight from DIA to LAX. Mona was back with the dogs.

The rental car that Hertz assigned to me in Los Angeles was a hybrid Camry. The sedan was significantly greener than the summer air that day in the L.A. basin, which I imagined was the point.

Over the previous couple of days Wallace had given me some background on his daughter's life in L.A. via e-mails and two additional phone calls. Cara was sharing half of a duplex in Mt. Washington with a couple of other people who were "in the business." He e-mailed me a map and directions to her house. I never actually spoke with Cara by phone during the planning stage for my visit; Wallace played intermediary in making all the arrangements with her. Wallace maintained that was the way Cara wanted it. I gave him the benefit of the doubt and assumed it was true.

Once I'd made the airline reservations I let Wallace know what day I was going and when I'd get to LAX. Within a few minutes he e-mailed me back to let me know that Cara was expecting me to stop by her place midafternoon.

My plan for my meeting with Cara was simple. I would wing it. While she and I talked I would assess what was going on with her and—ideally—be on my way back to Denver the next day, at the latest. If I could catch the last flight out of LAX to Denver the same day I flew in, I would do that.

The trip from the airport through downtown—Wallace's map routed me from the 405 to the 10 to the 110—was auspicious. Traffic was horrendous, but I didn't get lost, which may have been a first for me as an adult in Los Angeles. Although I'd grown up only an hour north of the basin, most of L.A. was unfamiliar to me.

Though the name of the place rang a bell, I didn't think I had ever before had a reason to go to the Mt. Washington neighborhood. I might have ended up there once during an unintentional detour with a friend's family when I was around ten. We'd been trying, unsuccessfully, to find our way to the Coliseum for an SC football game.

Mt. Washington was north and—although my L.A. geography was challenged, I thought—slightly east of downtown L.A., on a rise above the basin. Cara lived in half of a pre–World War I, Mission-style duplex. The charming old structure sat about ten steps up from the street. The decrepit tiled stairs that led up from the sidewalk cut though a glacier of eroding ice plant. The progenitor shoots had probably been planted around the same time Lindbergh crossed the Atlantic.

The duplex was in the middle of a block that intermittent re-development had left as a disjointed mishmash of homes. Oversize contemporary renovations loomed over neglected but charming eight-hundred-square-foot Craftsman bungalows. Yards full of lush landscaping were segregated from expanses of dead lawns, dry weeds, or packed dirt by new walls of stone or wrought iron, or by nothing more than dilapidated strips of half-century-old chain-link fencing. Rows of fan palms fronted a few of the oldest bungalows. Canopies of jacarandas shaded the more refined sections of the street.

Developmentus interruptus. With time, it tended to be a self-correcting disease.

A narrow courtyard packed with overgrown shrubbery and dark shadows divided the two units of Cara's duplex. The halves met up in the back to complete the shape of the building into a *U*. Well-tended birds of paradise in big, heavy urns flanked the substantial oak door on Cara's side of the building.

The unit on the other half of the *U* had no urns and no flowers gracing its door. On that side of the duplex all the curtains were drawn and newspapers and flyers were yellowing on the tiled landing.

I couldn't find a bell, so I rapped on Cara's door with my knuckles.

The brass mail slot by the door had an envelope sticking out, waiting to be collected by the letter carrier. The return address was Cara's, but the name on the envelope was Kanyn Gray. Wallace had said his daughter had roommates. I guessed that Kanyn was one.

I turned and looked beyond an intervening ridge. The view toward the central business district of L.A. from the front of the home was splendid, or at least my imagination allowed that it would have been splendid on one of those crystal days when L.A.'s air is as clear as tropical water.

That day wasn't one of those. The skyscrapers downtown—much more numerous than I remembered—loomed like raised fingers in the haze. I tried to decide if the color of the air that day was closer to gray or closer to brown. A woman answered the door before I reached a conclusion.

Kanyn, I wondered? *Cara?*

The woman wasn't at all cautious about opening her front door to a stranger. Whether that said more about the neighborhood or more about her I wasn't in a position to know. She flung the door open wide and stood silhouetted against an orange wall, her feet set wide apart. Behind her, flaking shellac marred the finish of the old mahogany door of a coat closet. The wood on the door was stained, or had aged, until it was almost black. The door had a cut-glass knob and wasn't closed all the way.

Above the woman's head a fat crack in the plaster fractured the cove that transitioned from the wall to the ceiling. The crack, I guessed, was why the closet door wasn't closed all the way. *Earthquake,* I thought, reminding myself I was in Southern California. *Old earthquake,* I thought, reassuring myself that my personal seismic risk that day was probably manageable.

I refocused. I didn't think the woman at the door was Cara. Although they were about the same age, she was taller than I remembered Cara being. I had not given the first moment of our meeting much thought, but I realized that I had expected that I would recognize my friend's daughter from her Colorado early adolescence.

After a prolonged interlude of silence—I was the one who should have spoken first, of course, but didn't—the woman said, "Hi. Can I . . . I don't know, help you with something?"

Friendly? Close. A little bemused, maybe. Nicer than I would have been had our roles been reversed. By the time she finally spoke, the duplex's architecture had started fading into the background for me. I realized that I might have begun staring. At the woman, not at the orange wall, the glass doorknob, or the cracked cove molding.

She wasn't beautiful, not in any glamorous, stereotypical L.A. manner. But she was intriguing. The proportions of her features were off, but not in an unpleasant way. Her face was a little too narrow, her eyes too far apart. Asymmetric cascades of faint freckles spilled down her cheeks like sand-colored pebbles on a beach.

She was cute.

"I'm looking for . . . I'm sorry," I said. I glanced down for a second to search for some composure, exhaled, and then I looked back at the woman again. "I'm looking for Carmel Poteet. I might be here a little earlier than she thought I'd be, but she's . . . expecting me."

She was wearing two snug, casual tops. The layer below was pale yellow with narrower straps than the pink layer above it. Either one alone would have been revealing. Together the two managed to be modest and not-at-all modest at the same time. Her jeans were the kind of tight that always seems to inspire my prurient curiosity about the getting-them-over-the-hips part of dressing.

She slid her fingers into the back pockets and allowed her shoulders to drop. The proportions of her body, I decided—thighs to hips to waist to chest to shoulders—were just fine.

I realized I was having an Ottavia moment. Not good.

"Mel's not here," she said. She narrowed her eyes and cocked out a hip. "Are you sure she's expecting you? She's good about appointments and things. Much better than me." She rolled her eyes in self-deprecation. One side of her mouth curled into a grin.

She wore no makeup, or she wore it so well that I couldn't tell. Her hair was short and styled carelessly. The color was in the middle ground between blond and not. It was a shade that had to be natural; it was hard to imagine someone seeking it from a bottle.

"Yes, yes," I said, after forcing myself to recall her question. "I am. I actually flew in to town to see her . . . today. Just now."

She opened her eyes wide. I noted that her irises were the same color as that day's L.A. haze. Not quite brown, not quite gray. The hue worked better—much better—for eyes than it did for atmosphere.

"She didn't say anything." She shrugged. "Sorry."

I hoped I might be invited inside to wait. I wasn't. "Okay, well. I guess I'll wait for her in the car. I have her mobile number. Maybe I can give her a call. Is she at work? I don't want to interrupt her if—"

The woman's expression told me that she wasn't about to tell me whether or not her roommate was at work.

"Right," I said. "I'm sorry to have bothered you. Thanks for your help." I began to turn.

"What's your name?" the woman said. "In case I talk to her."

I said, "Alan . . . Gregory."

"You flew in from . . . ?"

"Colorado. Boulder."

She nodded. If the question had been a quiz, I had passed.

"I've known Carmel for a long time," I said. "Since she was—"

She laughed softly as she stopped me with a headshake that was brisk enough to cause her hair to move. "Don't say 'little.' Okay? She's sensitive about it. Her size."

"A kid," I said.

"Better."

The woman stepped forward and pulled the door closed behind her. For a few seconds she stood on the compact tiled landing between the urns, her arms folded across her chest. I was startled when she reached past me. With a sudden motion she deadheaded a dated blossom off the bird-of-paradise. She twisted the flower off the stem hard, as though she were decapitating a chicken.

Her shoulder brushed against my arm as she pulled back. "Sorry," she said. "Sometimes the urge just . . . strikes."

"Oh," I managed.

"I love these," she said, gesturing at the flowers. "When I get a house, I want to have an entire hillside of them."

"We don't have them in Colorado."

"Mel misses Boulder," she said. "She talks about it a lot. Is it as pretty there as she says?"

She was standing no more than a foot from me, holding the faded bloom in front of her with both hands as though it were a wedding bouquet.

"It's pretty," I said. "But there are lots of varieties of pretty."

Carmel's roommate stepped away from me and sat on the top of the stairs that led from the cracked sidewalk. She'd picked the side of the step that was bordered by a rickety wrought-iron handrail, which left enough room for me to sit beside her. She was continuing to hold the dead flower in her hands.

I would have tossed it into the black hole of degrading ice plant.

Sunlight was fighting to find a way to sneak through the chemicals and moisture in the air. In the distance—above the flatlands that spread between downtown and the Pacific Ocean—I watched two breaks form in the low ceiling. Bright shafts opened, scalding the ground with light. The brilliance shifted, fragmenting the sun's rays. The shafts drifted closed. In seconds, they re-formed somewhere else.

I sat beside her.

She said, "I don't think I could live that far from the ocean."

"I know what you mean," I said.

"You an old . . . boyfriend?" she asked without looking my way.

"Me? No," I said, probably a little too incredulously.

"What, then?"

She sounded sincere. Although I was tempted to answer, I found a gram of discretion somewhere. "I think it's better if I leave it up to Carmel to tell you that."

"Nobody calls her that, you know. Carmel. Too . . . I don't know, precious."

"I haven't seen her in a long time. The last time was . . . in Boulder. I've known her since—"

"You said that already."

"I did. You're right."

After about fifteen seconds, she said, "It's my job. I'm a script supervisor."

"I don't . . . know what that is."

She adopted a husky, faux–Old West voice—she did it well—and said, "You're not from around these parts, are you, Cowboy?"

I didn't respond. I always embarrassed myself when I tried to do accents.

"I keep track of what's on film. Continuity. Chart deviations from the script. Keep everybody on the same page, literally. Keep the editor from trying to kill the director. I have to pay close attention to what everyone says on set. It becomes a habit."

It made perfect sense that there was such a job, but until that moment I'd been unaware of its existence. Often I can guess whether someone likes his or her work from the way they describe it, but I couldn't tell how Carmel's roommate would answer the question had I posed it to her. I did. "Do you like it? What you do?"

She eyed me. I thought she was assaying my sincerity. She said, "Not really. But it brings me a little closer to what I want. On a good day, if I hit it off with the assistant director or the DP, I pick their brains, learn things. That's good."

"DP?"

"Sorry. Director of photography."

"A step toward . . . ? What is it that you want?"

"To direct," she said. "I've done some shorts that have been . . . that are good. A friend has offered me AD—assistant director—on an indie thing he's doing. He almost has financing." She grinned self-consciously. "But he's almost had financing for a year."

Dreams, I thought. *I remember those.*

She said, "My roommates didn't expect me home today—maybe that's why Mel didn't tell me you were coming by. We were supposed to be on location today in Redondo. We had talent problems."

She emphasized "talent." I made a guess. "An actor didn't show up?" I liked hearing her talk, hoped she would continue. The alternative was sitting in the Camry and listening to the radio.

"Drunk from last night. Producer's pissed."

"Movie?" I asked.

"TV series."

"Which one?"

She told me. I hadn't heard of it.

"We debuted last spring, after sweeps. Did okay for a few episodes. Ratings softened, the show runner got squirrelly. I'm just praying"—she pushed her palms together like a chaste schoolgirl—"we get to finish our twenty-two. I can use the work."

She was still holding the core of the faded flower in her hands. She had pulled off most of the dead petals. What remained was hard bud.

I didn't know what a twenty-two was. Or a show runner. I could have asked. Instead I gestured toward the other half of the duplex and said, "Your next-door neighbor is kind of . . . reclusive? Is that a good word for it?"

She laughed. "The Addams Family? Mel met them when she first moved in. Two women, I guess. They're in the business. Since I've been here, they've been on some location shoot in, I don't know, the Czech Republic? Prague? Is that right? I've never seen those curtains open. Ever. Kanyn knows them best. She says they're all right. Their place gives me the creeps." She was twirling what was left of the flower in her hand.

I said, "You picked the orange for the wall inside the front door, didn't you?"

She looked at me sideways with softness in her eyes that I hadn't seen before. "How did you know that?" she asked.

"Same shade as the bird-of-paradise flowers. At least the ones that aren't . . . dead." I gestured toward her lap and the deconstructed bud. "I don't think it's a color most people would choose."

She smiled that lopsided smile again. We made eye contact for a second before she looked away. "I don't think Mel's working today. She could be out doing errands or something. That's possible. But I would guess she's at her . . . uh, boyfriend's place. When she's not here or at the studio, that's usually where she is."

"Her boyfriend lives nearby?"

"No," she said. "Tarzana."

I knew Tarzana. I knew it as a freeway sign on the . . . My memory of Tarzana was of dusky green hills climbing up from the side of the freeway. Dense trees. As a child I'd always assumed that rich friends of Edgar Rice Burroughs lived there. His sprawling ranch and estate had once taken up much of the land where the current town sits. It had been named to honor the author's iconic work.

"It's in the Valley," she said.

The flavor of voice she chose made the San Fernando Valley sound like a forsaken pace. Across a great desert or a wide sea. The fiction was seductive. Her seasoning kicked me into *Chinatown* thoughts. A desolate reservoir. Orange groves split by dusty lanes. Jack Nicholson's bloody nose.

My childhood experiences offered two other occasional vantages of the Valley.

One view was from a hard green seat on a hot yellow bus on school field trips to the La Brea Tar Pits or to some museum or factory in L.A. We'd see the Valley from the slow lane of the Ventura Freeway. The other was the view from the front seat of my father's convertible as we sped through the Valley on our way to rare Dodger games in Chavez Ravine, or during visits to an old college friend of his whom my mother didn't like.

My father's friend was divorced and gregarious. He lived on a big piece of rolling scrub land in Hidden Hills, near Calabasas on the far west end of the Valley. Although his house was much less elaborate than his neighbors' homes, it was a much nicer house than ours. My father's friend—my father instructed me to call him Mr. Thompson, even though Mr. Thompson told me he'd break my arm if I didn't call him Bud—had a swimming pool shaped like a deformed peanut. He owned horses. He would set me up to ride in circles around his corral while he and my father sat in the shade of a deformed oak, drank stubby brown bottles of Mexican beer, and ate carnitas and tortillas prepared by the woman who cleaned his house. My father and Bud laughed a lot. They sprinkled cuss words into their conversation like seasoning on a steak.

I thought Bud's daughter was hot. She thought I was first cousin to the crap she scraped off her horse's shoes. She rode sometimes during our visits, but she never stayed in the corral. I would watch her mount her huge white horse and urge him into a canter, not taking my eyes from her until she disappeared down the trail that snaked into the chaparral-dotted hills.

The riding ring was for wimps like me. I rode in circles.

Even as an adolescent, I recognized the power of the metaphor.

Each time we visited Hidden Hills I prayed—I literally prayed—

that I would arrive to find Bud's daughter sunbathing by the pool. My fantasy had her in a red bikini.

God apparently had more pressing prayers to answer than those related to my juvenile lust, though I couldn't imagine what could possibly be more important.

I was trying to convince myself that despite the tragedy that had changed my family when I was a fourteen-year-old in Thousand Oaks, north of the Valley, my California history didn't have to be toxic, and that it was okay for me to admit to this stranger where I had grown up.

Before I had a chance to come out of my fog, Cara's roommate explained the geography. "Tarzana's on the other side of the mountains. You can take the 405 or the 101." She hooked a thumb over her right shoulder. "These are the Hollywood Hills. The Valley is on the other side of the Santa Monica Mountains, farther up the coast. Inland from Malibu. You've never been to the Valley?"

"Have I missed something special?" I said. She found that funny. I said, "I grew up in Thousand Oaks, but I haven't been to the Valley in"—I thought about it—"twenty years. Has much changed?"

"Not really. I grew up in Orange County. Same story. More people."

I pulled out my phone to check the time. Cara was late. I didn't want to leave, but I didn't have a reason to stay. "I should let you go," I said. She stood.

Thirty

I walked most of the way down the steps toward my Camry before I stopped. I looked back up. I said, "I'm Alan, by the way."

"You said that already."

She was letting me know that my script was redundant. I took another step down the stairs, turned again. "You have a name?"

She paused long enough that I wasn't sure she was going to tell me. She tossed the flower bud into the ice plant. Finally, she said, "Amy."

Amy was the name of the girl from Hidden Hills. The one I never saw sunbathing by the pool. "Thanks for your help, Amy. Can I give you my number? If you hear from Cara?"

She narrowed her eyes. "Sure."

I thought she might make her own mobile phone materialize from somewhere. My younger patients did that whenever I imparted data they considered worthy of their recall. Data didn't exist for them until punched into their phones.

Amy didn't move a muscle. A breeze pushed a wisp of hair from her forehead. A quick shaft of sunlight poked through the haze, and for a protracted moment we were both in sunshine. I started to fumble for my sunglasses, but the solar spotlight flashed off as suddenly as it had emerged.

I asked, "You want to write it down?"

"I'll remember."

I gave her the number. Her lips moved as she committed it to memory, or perhaps as she allowed neurological gravity to roll it to the curb, like mental rubbish.

"Colorado is 303?" she said.

"It is."

"Good luck with Mel, Alan. Whatever errand you're on sounds . . . complicated."

I made it all the way to the car before Amy spoke again. "When you see her? You should call her Mel. You won't sound so old-friend-of-her-father-ish, you know?"

"Thanks." I decided to ask one more question. "Has she seemed depressed to you? Upset?"

Amy's expression suggested she was giving my question some thought.

"Girls are moody, Alan. Hollywood girls are moodier than most. Mel's . . . okay. She has issues. We all have issues."

"Yeah?" I hoped she'd tell me about their issues.

"Compared to Kanyn? Mel's a picture of mental health."

"In what way?"

"Kanyn's a doll, but she is the strangest person I've ever lived with. And that includes my family."

"Really?"

"Mel gets down, has crying jags. Kanyn? She falls off cliffs. One minute she's fine, the next . . . ? Mel has stayed up all night with her, afraid she'll slit her wrists or stick her head in the oven."

"It's that sudden?" I said. I climbed a few stairs.

"Yes," she said. She lowered her voice. "She pulls her hair out when she's alone, too. Not on her head. Her pubes. One at a time. I walked into her room once and saw a little pile of them on her night-stand. She told me what they were, said she'd been doing it since freshman year in high school." She looked away for a moment. "I shouldn't have told you that." She bit her lower lip. "That was stupid."

I said, "It's called trichotillomania."

"What?"

"The hair-pulling. It's called trichotillomania. It's a psychological . . . condition."

She looked at me as though I'd just made a gerbil appear from her ear. "How do you know that?"

"I'm a psychologist," I said.

"Spell it," she said.

I did. Her lips barely moved as she silently repeated the progression of letters. It was like watching a ventriloquist at work.

I said, "Nice meeting you, Amy."

I returned to the car and drove away. The Camry's instrument displays were telling me things about the status of its batteries that I didn't comprehend.

I had questions.

I wondered what the hell was going on with Kanyn. Trichotillomania—compulsive or impulsive hair-pulling—could present as an isolated symptom, but it could also be a complication for someone with the kind of severe dysthymia that Amy was describing about Kanyn. The pubic specificity was a variant I'd read about that I hadn't run across before clinically. I suspected Kanyn pulled other hairs too, not just her pubes.

If Cara was as good about keeping appointments as Amy suggested she was, why had she blown me off? Had Wallace gotten confused about the time? Or the date?

I considered contacting Wallace first to confirm I understood the plans, but after a moment's reflection I decided that leaving him in place as the intermediary between his daughter and me wasn't working well. I also figured that Wallace would either be annoyed at Cara for spacing out our meeting, or worried about her well-being for the same reason. I didn't see anything to be gained from aggravating what was already a difficult situation for father and daughter.

I drove for a while, crossing under the Pasadena Freeway at a location that didn't have any ramps. I knew I was lost. I pulled over to the side of the road and parked the car. I stared at the Hertz map long enough to know it wouldn't be of any help.

I tried Cara's mobile. After a few rings it kicked me to voice mail. The recorded greeting was pleasant and precise. I wouldn't have pegged the voice as belonging to her, though. People change. I said, "Cara? Alan Gregory. We must have had some confusion about the time of our meeting. I'm just leaving your place in Mt. Washington. Please give me a call so we can find another time."

I hit the speed dial for Jonas's cell. He didn't answer. The call rolled over to voice mail. I left him a message that I loved him and would call him back.

It was too late to call Lauren.

I considered my options. I could check into a motel somewhere in West L.A. and wait for Cara's return phone call. Or I could drive toward Tarzana and hope that Cara returned my call before I got there. It made no difference to me if we had our meeting in the Valley or in Mt. Washington or someplace in between.

I didn't feel like sitting in a motel for the rest of the day. Going to the Valley had meaning for me. Not going to the Valley had even more meaning for me. I decided to go to the Valley. The Camry had an electronic GPS mapping device. I powered it up, punched in TAR-ZANA CA, and waited a few seconds for the machine's digital wisdom. A pleasant, confident, executive-assistant-type female voice suggested I embark on what seemed to me like an unnecessarily convoluted route to take me to an onramp to the 101 north—the necessary first step on my journey to the Valley.

A convoluted route was better than my alternative, which basically would have involved driving aimlessly around whatever neighborhood I'd entered after venturing from Mr. Washington. I followed her spoken directions until I spotted the promised sign for the entrance ramp to the Hollywood Freeway North, the 101.

That early success left me feeling optimistic about my decision to go the Valley.

Then I reached the top of the ramp.

I hadn't counted on rush hour.

On the way to Tarzana I had plenty of time to contemplate the ways L.A. had changed in the years since I had left Southern California behind.

More cars. Lots more cars.

I panicked for a couple of miles—since my average speed was less than fifteen miles an hour, my attack was almost ten minutes—as I approached the intersection of the Hollywood Freeway and the Ventura Freeway. The two freeways, both familiar from my youth, had the same number—the 101—but for some reason I couldn't recall they had different names. It was a logistical conundrum that hadn't been at all important to me when I was not yet driving.

I settled in. The air in the Valley was cleaner than the air in the downtown basin had been—clear enough that I could see the silhouettes of the mountains rimming the Valley, the San Gabriel Mountains to the north, the Santa Monica Mountains to the south. The sun was starting its late-afternoon descent at almost twelve o'clock.

From my vantage in the center lane on the Ventura Freeway, it appeared that most of what existed in between the two sets of mountains was little changed over the decades since I'd last been to the Valley. The buildings adjacent to the freeway were taller. The malls seemed bigger and more numerous, and many surface parking lots seemed to have been replaced by multistory garages. Much of what had been developed had been redeveloped.

I recalled Bud's daughter in Hidden Hills. The first Amy. I got lost in a memory of the impossible posture she managed while mounted on her horse's back, her white-blond hair tickling the top of her perfect ass.

The congestion on the freeway morphed as I cleared Sherman Oaks. The change, unfortunately, was that it got worse. Instead of crawling along at a snail's pace, my fellow drivers and I were stopping for long periods of time and then driving for a hundred yards or so before stopping again. Some of the stops were fifteen seconds. Some of them were a couple of minutes. I never spotted anything that provided a clue as to why we were slowing or why we were going. I spent the dead time listening to songs from my youth on an oldies station and studying the paper Hertz map. I was certain that a good half dozen of the major roads I spotted on the map hadn't even existed when I left Southern California.

A sign indicated the approach of the interchange with the 405—the San Diego Freeway. I was just east of Tarzana.

My phone rang. I glanced down. CARMEL POTEET read the screen.

Thirty-one

"Cara, hi."

Shit, I should have called you Mel.

"Dr. Gregory, I'm— I know I was supposed to meet you today but . . ." She sighed. "Jack was supposed to be here last night, but he didn't show up. Nobody knows where he is. . . . I've been upset. I didn't want to be by myself, so I— I am so sorry. I just . . . forgot. I am so, so sorry."

Something that psychotherapists—and 911 dispatchers—learn early in their careers is that upset people often omit crucial context in their descriptions of precipitating events. To wit: Cara hadn't said who Jack was. Her boyfriend? Her cat?

"Call me Alan. It's okay," I said. "Is Jack your boyfriend?"

"What? No, no. Jack is an . . . old friend. Somebody I've known for a long time. I'm with my boyfriend now. In Tarzana."

"I'm sorry about Jack. Can I be of any help? I'm in the Valley, not too far from you, I think. I can be there in . . ." I was close enough to the former Edgar Rice Burroughs estate that I could see the hazy outlines of the Tarzana hills in the distance.

At highway speeds I'd arrive in Tarzana in a few minutes. At rush hour? I didn't know. I said, "Twenty minutes? Max."

She replied without hesitation. "No, thank you, no. I'm not . . . alone. I'm okay. I just don't think I'm ready to talk to you about . . . You know, not today. I'm sorry. I'm really sorry. Whatever's going on with Jack is really . . ."

Her voice drifted away. I thought I heard her say something to someone else, but the sound was muffled, as though she'd covered the microphone.

"It's fine. I understand," I said. "Should I call you in the morning? See how you're doing? Would that be okay?"

"Sure."

"Ten o'clock?"

"Eleven? I should be back over the hill by then."

"I'll call after eleven. Maybe we can have lunch."

She didn't reply right away. Then she said, "Maybe."

"You sure you're all right, Cara?"

"Yes."

"You would tell me if you weren't?"

It was a shrink question. Growing up with two shrink parents, she probably recognized it as familiar. She said, "Of course."

"Good luck with your friend," I said. But she'd already hung up.

I didn't quite make it to Tarzana. I used an off-ramp and seconds later an on-ramp to reverse direction on the Ventura Freeway. I was pointed back into the snare of the interchange, this time with the descending sun in my mirrors instead of my eyes. I briefly considered opting for a respite from the traffic by choosing a motel room in the Valley—every possible chain lodging option seemed to be available alongside the 101. But since Cara and I would be meeting sometime the next day on the other side of the Hollywood Hills, I decided to endure the congestion a little longer and spend the night closer to Los Angeles proper.

I had another option. Before I'd left Boulder, Merideth had sent me an e-mail with the address of her L.A. condo. She told me I was free to use it while I was in town to talk with Carmel. I knew my ex well enough to be certain her offer wasn't an act of magnanimity. Merideth was hoping that I would display my gratitude by telling her whatever I learned in Los Angeles that might relate to her missing surrogate.

I'd e-mailed her back my thanks, but let her know that I thought I'd just get a motel room. She immediately called my cell. The moment I answered the phone, she said, "It's your money. The doorman has your name. Show him your driver's license and he'll give you a key. Jesus effing—" She hung up before she finished the profanity.

She had pronounced Jesus, *hay-zeus*.

"You drove to the Valley?"

The latest incredulous question tossed my way was from Cara's bird-of-paradise roommate, the other Amy. I had just completed the transition to the Hollywood Freeway when she called.

"I did. Cara told you?"

"Mel, remember? You two are going to get together tomorrow?"

"That's the plan. A wasted trip to the Valley. Do you know her friend Jack?"

Five seconds of silence. "I think she's mentioned him. Why?"

I didn't want to betray Cara's confidence. "Long story. I don't know much."

"You don't lie very well. I'll ask Kanyn. She'll know."

The trichotillomania roommate. "I will take the not-lying part as a compliment."

"How bad is traffic? Where are you?"

"I just got back on the Hollywood Freeway. It's like—" I had an image of the sludge that would be in my circulatory system if I ate an entire cheesecake. I kept the visual to myself. "People really do this every day?"

"Every day. So was this trip to the Valley some Thomas Wolfe kind of quest?" she asked. "You have . . . going-home issues?"

I had no plan to answer the question, but I liked that she'd asked it. "Will you call me after you talk to Kanyn? I'd like to know what you find out."

"Take me to dinner. I'll tell you then."

Okay. "Fine," I said.

She said, "That was a lovely invitation," she said. "How could a girl say no?"

"Good," I said.

She laughed. "Where are you staying? What part of town? Or have you decided to commute from the Valley?"

I appreciated her humor. But replying that I was staying at "the Holiday Inn Express on Santa Monica Boulevard" sounded particularly lame. I said, "I'm staying at a friend's place—it's off Beverly in West L.A." That would be Merideth's flat. "Can you recommend a place to eat that's not, I don't know . . ."

"In the Valley?" she said.

"Yes."

"Perfect," she said. I thought her reply sounded like a non sequitur, or maybe some SoCal synonym for the ubiquitous British "brilliant." "Kanyn is the host at—"

Amy completed her thought with the name of a restaurant. To my ear, the sounds—I thought I had counted three syllables—tumbled together in a melodic riff that ended up not seeming like any recognizable word or series of words. I thought the first sound was a vowel, but said quickly, as Amy had done, the name was so foreign that the combined syllables failed to register anywhere in my language cortex. I couldn't have repeated the notes if someone had put a gun to my temple.

She went on. "It's not far from your friend's place. It's always impossible there, but Kanyn'll get us in. We may have to sit at the bar. Meet you at eight o'clock?"

"Great. Where is it? Cross streets?"

"Melrose? Third? Sorry, I'm good with scripts, but not so much with streets. I'll text you a map."

I hesitated a split second before I said, "Okay."

Amy tried to keep the condescension out of her voice. "Your phone can handle it?"

"I have a brand-new phone. It's working on an algorithm for world peace." Even though the manual for the phone was in Boulder, I was sure I could figure out how to open a map. My phone and I were friends.

Okay, we were casual acquaintances. I could make calls and check my voice mail. Jonas had demonstrated how to play short videos. If I could replicate that lesson, I could certainly coax it to show me a simple map. Right? The problem was in the replicating.

"See you at eight," she said.

She killed the connection. I realized that I had just made plans to have dinner with a single woman. Some might call that a date.

I had begun rationalizing alternative explanations for my plans before I closed my phone. The reflex would have been disturbing had I paid any attention to it.

I desperately wanted a shower. I'd had the foresight to stash the number of the Holiday Inn Express on Santa Monica Boulevard into my phone memory before I left Boulder. I found the number, highlighted it, and hit Send.

I was pretty impressed with myself.

"Not to-night," said the woman at the motel after I asked to make a reservation for "this evening." English was not her native tongue. Someplace in Asia had been first. I guessed Korea, but I wouldn't have bet anything of value on my guess.

"You're all booked?" I asked.

"No vacant-cy. Sorry. Not to-morrow, too. No."

Although her English was light years ahead of my Korean, continuing the conversation didn't offer much promise. I thanked her, hung up.

It was six o'clock. I was cresting the Hollywood Hills in the company of a huge posse of impatient, strangely somnolent strangers.

I didn't have a clue how long it would take for traffic to resume flowing normally or for me to get to the part of L.A. where I was going from whatever part of Hollywood I was currently quasi-parked in. I switched from one technological marvel at which I wasn't adept—my phone—and moved on to another. I took advantage of a

long phase of traffic-stalsis to ask my trusty GPS device to guide me
to Merideth's pied-à-terre.

I was telling myself that I would have told Merideth what I
learned from Cara about the Grand Canyon thing anyway.

The professional-sounding woman who was the voice of the device—I had anthropomorphized her by then—had the answer for me
in seconds, as though she had been sitting, somewhere, waiting for
me to pose my dilemma. *"Turn right in . . ."*

Amy was, I thought, a couple of years older than Mel. They were
both considerably younger than me. Other than an occasional therapy patient, it was a generation with which I had little contact. I
wanted to hear what Amy thought about Lisa's recent choices. Surrogacy, disappearing.

As a rationalization for us having dinner with her, I thought it
was elegant.

I got to Merideth's building at 7:10.

The doorman was a burly Hispanic man named Hector Herrera.
A discreet ON DUTY sign propped on the marble counter provided his
name. He didn't hover near the door like Haji, eager to open doors
for pedestrians or hail cabs—instead he was comfortably seated on a
stool, reading a copy of *Wired*. Hector had thick black hair and wore
a charcoal pin-striped suit that fit his square body as though he had
a bespoke tailor on retainer. I introduced myself and explained that
Merideth was letting me use her place. He stole a quick glance over
my shoulder out the front door. He didn't say anything, but my impression was that he wasn't awed by the Camry that I'd left in the
building's drive.

I thought about telling him it was a hybrid. Didn't.

Hector was efficient. He disappeared with my license into an office for about thirty seconds before he returned with a key and an
electronic fob for the building's security system. "Twelve-oh-six," he
said. His voice was a lovely tenor that carried a shallow, south-of-

the-border accent as an afterthought, almost a spice. "Ms. Gregory says hello, and reminds you that you know the alarm code."

I made the mistake of saying, "I do?"

"Yes, sir." Hector's eyes locked on mine and restrained me like a pair of handcuffs. "You do."

"Good, then," I said.

Hector didn't smile, but I thought he was at least mildly amused by my reaction to his tough-guy act. The clock behind the counter told me it was nearly 7:20.

"Hector," I asked, after I'd taken a couple of steps toward the elevator, "how long will it take me to get to a restaurant on Melrose, or maybe Third?"

"They run parallel, sir. But not long."

"Ten minutes enough?"

"In West L.A.? Yes, sir. Plenty."

"Any freeways involved?"

That question earned me a grin. "Not unless you get lost."

"Thank you."

"No problem, Dr. Gregory."

Dr. Gregory. Merideth had told Hector I was a doctor. He probably thought I was a vascular surgeon or something, which was why he couldn't figure out why I was driving a Camry. Merideth wouldn't reveal that I was a mere Ph.D. until after she was confident that my reflection had stopped shining on her.

Thirty-two

When Merideth and I were married, we didn't have an alarm in our Spanish Hills home in Boulder. If we'd had one, I would have tried that code first.

What were my other code-guess options? When she and I had traveled together as a couple, we used our birthday months in combination on hotel-room-safe keypads. That was a possible solution, I supposed.

Merideth, damn it, I said to myself. She'd roped me into a juvenile guessing game. I speed-dialed her mobile from the elevator lobby on the twelfth floor.

It was late in New York. She answered after two rings. "Hi," she said.

"What's the code, Meri? I'm in a hurry."

"You don't remember?"

She was cooing. As evenly as I could, I said, "I don't have time for a game right now. I need to get a shower so I can get to a meeting."

"It's a great shower."

"I'm glad to hear that."

"A dinner meeting?"

Still cooing. "Merideth, the code? Please. This may end up being helpful. Do you want me to try to be helpful or not?"

"Eight oh three oh."

8030.

Oh. All of Boulder's zip codes—when I'd moved to town there were only three—started with 8030. Merideth and I had never used those four digits as a code. Ever. For anything. I was sure about that.

"You never liked Boulder. How would I have guessed that code?"

"That's the thing with codes and passwords. You pick things that people would never guess, right?"

"So why did you tell Hector that—"

"I wanted you to call. Is that so awful?"

"Hector could have told you I was there."

"He did, Alan. Twice."

The cooing had ended. Maybe she actually had a reason to talk with me. "Is something new, Meri? Did you find Lisa?"

Her voice softened. "No, nothing."

"Sam learn anything?"

"He doesn't answer his phone and he's not conscientious about returning calls."

"True on both counts. Sorry. I tried to warn you."

"You didn't try very hard."

"You wouldn't have listened. I tried to convince you not to hire him. He'll get where he's going, but he'll frustrate you along the way."

"I thought you were being difficult when you said that. So where are you eating in West Hollywood? Mozza?"

I didn't reply. I still didn't know the name of the restaurant where I was meeting Amy, but I was reluctant to admit that to Merideth. It could have been Matzoh—Amy might have chosen a Jewish restaurant. But I had convinced myself she had picked a place with three unidentified syllables. Matzoh was one syllable short. I hadn't received the promised map on my phone, or if I had received it, I didn't know how to know I'd received it.

"Really?" Merideth said, assuming she had guessed correctly. "You can do the whole Batali thing in Manhattan when you come back for Jonas. Try someplace else. I'll make a call for you. You want to go to izakaya, or maybe A.O.C.? It's casual, but I like A.O.C." She paused. "Let me call for you. Please?"

"Thank you for the code, Meri, and thank you for letting me stay at your place. I'll let you know what I learn. I promise."

"You're not going to Mozza, are you? Where are you eating tonight? Tell me."

My brain pecked at the scattered clues. She'd said Batali. That meant the restaurant in her question was likely Mozza, and Italian, not Matzoh, and Jewish. "Olive Garden," I said. "I'm going to the Olive Garden."

"On Melrose?"

"Bye, Meri."

I heard her say, "Wait," just as I was closing my phone.

The 8030 code worked like a charm on the keypad. The first thing I noticed inside? Our old marital Tabriz anchored her modern furniture to the glossy walnut floor of her living room.

I loved the view that emerged when I finally located the button on the wall that elevated the huge panels of solar shades that covered the tall windows of her flat.

I loved the gazillion heads that massaged me in her gargantuan shower.

I found myself disconcerted by the smells in her home. All the subtle scents were of her. And, in an odd reflection of memory, of us.

I hadn't quite regained my balance by the time I was back in the Camry on the way to the restaurant at 7:45.

After giving it some thought during my shower, I decided A.O.C. might be the place where I was meeting Amy for dinner. Hector provided directions on my way out the door. No one had to know that I wasn't able to get my phone to regurgitate the map Amy had sent while I was in the shower.

* * *

With the help of the GPS lady—we were getting tight; I'd named her Chloe—I arrived at the restaurant a few minutes before our scheduled rendezvous. I read the menu to kill some time. It looked fine. Small plates. Wine. After a few weeks of travel I was no longer fazed that chicken cost twice as much on the coasts as it did in between.

I ambled around the block. I had no trouble keeping pace with a couple of lowriders crawling along in the right lane on Fairfax. They made me smile.

To my utter surprise I was discovering that I liked L.A. Despite the miscommunications and the traffic and the foul air I liked how I was feeling since I'd arrived in Southern California. I'd expected L.A. to drain everything dynamic from me that NYC had invigorated. It wasn't happening.

I finished circling back to the restaurant, waiting for Amy with my back against the wall. I spotted her half a block away. She was pausing at the curb for the light to change so that she could cross West Third. I still thought she was cute.

A crush of people engulfed us inside the door of the restaurant. Amy slithered through the crowd. I followed, tethered to her by our fingertips. At the front desk, she reached across me and touched the hostess on the arm. I guessed that was her other roommate. Kanyn was tall and blond with the brand of blatant beauty that I find incongruously off-putting. Her perfect eyebrows framed green eyes that seemed lit from within. Amy took my hand in hers and we followed Kanyn toward the dining room.

I couldn't help myself—as we walked, I checked the back of the hostess's scalp for bald patches that would be telltale signs of trichotillomania, or for an odd hairstyle intended to disguise the presence of decultivated terrain. I didn't see either.

Amy introduced me to Kanyn as we sat down. "Hi," Kanyn said. "It's crazy. It's always cra-azy," Kanyn said. "I'll catch up with you guys later." She smiled at me. She had a huge, inviting mouth and exposed all her teeth when she smiled. "Nice to meet you, Aaron," she said.

During our brief encounter Kanyn was animated and energetic. Clinically, that she didn't seem depressed told me nothing.

"I used to live near here," Amy said after we settled at our cramped deuce near the bar. Our neighboring diners were eating in such close proximity that I could've stolen the olives and salumi from their plates without fully extending my arms. I was hungry enough that I was tempted. "That was . . . two sets of roommates ago."

" 'Near' seems to be a relative term in L.A.," I said. "Seems to mean fewer than three freeways."

"Only a dozen blocks or so," she said.

"How long have you lived with Cara and— Sorry, with Mel and Kanyn?"

"Let's see . . . five months. Mel and Kanyn are old friends from college. I'm the . . . interloper. I met Mel on a set last winter. They had just moved into the duplex and were looking for another roommate. My previous roommate was getting married, so . . ."

A waitress came by. Amy ordered a glass of wine I'd never heard of. When the waitress turned to me, I said I'd have the same.

"Do you know what you just ordered?" Amy asked.

"No."

"What's that about?" she wondered, sitting back against the black chair. She was wearing a silky top in a shade of red that popped against the seat. She was continuing with the modest/not-at-all-modest fashion theme of the afternoon.

"New things. Restaurants with initials. New people."

"Moi?"

"I'm hoping you might have some insight for me."

"That's why you're taking me to dinner? Because you want my . . . insight about something?"

Her eyes weren't on mine when she asked the last question. I thought she had developed an interest in my left hand. Specifically, the fourth finger. My wedding ring.

"Not completely," I said.

She looked back up. "I thought insight was . . . your province. You're the psychologist."

"Turns out that sometimes ignorance is my province. This might be one of those."

The wine arrived. It was a white, slightly sweet. Fine. "You were going to tell me about Jack?" I said. "Carmel told me on the phone that she was in the Valley because Jack hadn't showed up when she expected him to. He is apparently an old friend"—I raised my eyebrows to express my lack of assurance about what I was telling her—"of hers. Mel was upset about it, wanted to be with her boyfriend."

"Jack is probably Kanyn's friend too. They know a lot of the same people. I only saw Kanyn for a minute before she had to come here. She seemed upset about something, but that's not unusual for Kanyn. Maybe it was the thing with Jack."

I decided to try to connect some dots. "Do you know anything about the Grand Canyon? Some trip Mel took . . . a few years ago? When she was in college. A girl disappeared?"

Amy's face told me she didn't know—her "No" was redundant. "I can ask Kanyn when she comes over. If it was a big thing, she'll know about it."

My phone vibrated in my pocket. I did the time-zone arithmetic between California and Holland and decided that it was unlikely that the call was from Lauren. It was more likely that it was from Merideth, determined to discover where I was having dinner. I ignored the call.

Amy went on. "Is that what . . . this is all about? Mel's dad's concern? You coming to L.A.? Some old camping trip?"

"I wish I knew. Can I tell you what I know? See if you have some thoughts?"

"Sure. But why me? I don't know anything about it."

"Why not you? You're a contemporary of Mel's. Maybe you'll have some insight—"

"There's that word again."

"Wisdom, then—is that better?—into how she might look at things."

"I always have opinions. Wisdom? That's a longer shot."

"I'll accept your opinions and hope for some wisdom. Is that fair?"

I'd convinced myself that if I made dinner into a fact-finding mission and didn't try to get Amy talking about herself, then I wouldn't flirt, and this wouldn't be a date.

But then again, earlier that day I'd convinced myself that an avatar was living in the dashboard of my rented Camry.

By the time I'd finished explaining what was going on with Merideth and Eric and Lisa and Stevie, our food had started to arrive in a series of small portions that landed like sets of waves. Amy had moved on to an Oregon pinot noir. I hadn't.

Amy's first question to me about the situation was, "And this is why you're in Los Angeles?"

"I think." To fill in some background, I offered an abbreviated version of the Adrienne and Jonas and Marty story, and the day trip with Merideth to Strawberry Fields. My agreement to help Merideth. Wallace's concern about his daughter. When I was done I asked, "Any thoughts about Lisa's disappearing act?"

She ignored my question. "Where is the rest of your family? Your wife and daughter? While you and Jonas were in New York? While you are here?"

"Lauren and Grace are in Amsterdam. That's another . . . very long story."

She nodded as though she understood something. She kept her eyes on mine. She sipped her wine patiently. I realized that she was waiting for me to tell her the long story.

I didn't want to.

She said, "Why do you care what I think? About the surrogate?"

"I don't know. Lisa—isn't that much older than you. I was wondering if there is some . . . generational influence at work in all this that I'm not aware of."

"Generational?"

"Different worldview. I'm continually surprised at how much changes."

"Interesting," she said. "I'm constantly surprised at how much doesn't. Music changes. Movies change. People? Not so much."

She put down her glass and picked up her fork. After a few seconds she set the silverware back down and lifted her wineglass again. She cradled it in both hands and leaned toward me. Her elbows were on the edge of the table, her face not far from mine. "You're what, ten, twelve years older than me?"

"Around there, I guess." I'd been thinking fifteen.

"Is that a generation?"

Good question. "Maybe."

"I was raised to keep my promises," she said. "To fulfill my responsibilities. I don't think those are generational-specific values. Not among my friends."

I felt chastened. "You're right. Absolutely. They're not. I don't know what I was thinking. I apologize."

She sat back again. "I wouldn't have made the decisions Lisa made. To be a surrogate? I couldn't do that. I admire her generosity, but . . . it's not something I could ever do. But if I were carrying someone else's baby, I would feel an absolute responsibility to let them know where I was at all times. Loaning your womb to someone? That's an incredible gift. But it's also a pretty sacred trust. Goes both ways, of course, but . . . unless Lisa is a callous person—which is hard to believe about a surrogate—if I were in your ex-wife's shoes, I would be much more worried than angry. I can't imagine not staying in touch with the baby's parents, so I'm assuming that if Lisa's not in touch, she's not able to be in touch."

"Thank you," I said. "I wasn't looking at things through a clear lens. I should've been able to get there on my own."

I thought she was done with the topic. I was wrong. "Being a surrogate would be way too much of an anchor for me. I haven't had a relationship that lasted nine months since high school. I have to follow the work. Especially if I want to direct. Vancouver. London. New York. Wherever."

"Relationships are—"

"For later," she said.

"Now?"

She sat back. "I hook up when I feel a need."

The brash intimacy surprised me. "That's enough for you?" I said.

"Enough what? Sex?" She shrugged. "Depends on the frequency. Enough romance?" She sighed. "Can't afford it. I won't sleep with guys who make my heart go flip-flop. Way too complicated. Enough companionship? Girlfriends and gay guys are easier for that. Usually better, too."

"You never want . . . more?"

"I always want more. Of everything." She looked at my ring again. "You do too." She waited a few seconds for me to untie my tongue. "Everything in its time. Sometimes it's lonely. I get over it," she said. "We all make choices."

Kanyn delivered a couple of guys who were a little older than me to the table beside ours. They kissed before they sat down. Kanyn turned to Amy. "Working through the backlog. You two need anything?"

Amy said, "You and Mel have a friend named Jack?"

Kanyn's face became a mask. "What did you hear?" she said.

I could see in Amy's eyes that she recognized the peculiarity of Kanyn's reply. "Nothing," she said. "Mel . . . went to the Valley. She's worried about Jack."

Kanyn forced a smile. "I'll call him. See what's going on. Gotta go."

* * *

We finished our meals in silence. We both declined the waitress's offer of dessert. I paid the tab when Amy excused herself to go the bathroom.

Kanyn wasn't at the front desk when we left. On the sidewalk outside Amy asked, "Is tonight about your ex-wife and this Lisa? Or is it about your current wife and me?"

"Maybe I was . . . I don't know . . . You asked. I said yes."

She froze me with her eyes. "I think you're attracted to me," Amy said. "Maybe we should talk a little about our first date."

"Our first date?"

"The one we just had, Alan."

I somehow forgot how easy it was to breathe.

She leaned in close. Her face was inches from mine. "See how it happens?"

"What?

"We're this close to hooking up, Alan." She held up her hand and extended her fingers. The space between her fingertips was much narrower than the gap between my lips.

Thirty-three

His Ex

I called in sick to work. I haven't called in sick to work in five years.

I always hated it when he got constipated. I'm talking about Alan, when we were married. And the constipation in question had absolutely nothing to do with his bowels.

I played it cute on the phone with him about staying at my condo, not desperate. I teased him. I didn't complain, I didn't push. Mostly, I didn't whine. But I felt desperate.

I did all the things that used to work with him when we were together, but I still couldn't even get him to tell me where the hell he was going to dinner.

Or more to the point, with whom.

Fifteen minutes after he hung up on me to go off to his dinner meeting I realized—Jesus *Effing*—that I was *still* waiting for him to call me back and get reasonable. Want to know why I left him? Put that near the top of the list—too many hours wasted waiting for him to be reasonable.

Thirty-four

Her Ex

The call during dinner hadn't been from Merideth. My cell's missed-call log registered the origin of the incoming call simply as PURDY. That would be Sam. He hadn't left a message. Sam seemed to have given up caring about people tracking our telephone habits. That was progress.

I was sitting on the balcony of Merideth's condo, facing vaguely west, as I tried to decide whether I wanted to return the call. I'd grabbed a bottle of water from the almost-barren refrigerator. To my left an insistent string of landing lights from descending planes—they dotted the sky at intervals like illuminated pearls—marked out the approach from the desert toward the runways at LAX. I followed the lights of one plane until it landed, allowed some room up the coast for the expanse of Marina Del Rey, and guessed that my seat on Merideth's balcony was facing almost directly toward Santa Monica.

I couldn't see the beach. Couldn't even discern a clear line where the lights of Santa Monica ended and the opaque Pacific began.

I returned Sam's call.

He said, "Hi. How's L.A.?"

"A little hazy. Not too hot. How about the Grand Canyon?"

"Definitely too hot. Short visit. I may need to fix the AC in the Cherokee. Ended up going to Vegas. Talked to a guy."

Sam was feeling cryptic. Experience told me this would be a short call. I said, "That's where you are now?"

"No, I'm halfway to L.A. Got some news. Want to hear it?"

"I'd love to hear what you thought of Las Vegas."

He ignored me. "I'd never given much thought to the Grand Canyon before I got there. I figured it was the result of some grand cataclysmic event. The earthquake of all earthquakes. The fault of all faults. A geologic Super Bowl, that kind of thing. But it was just erosion. Water on stone for a gazillion years. Life going by, drop by drop. Rain. Floods. Lots of floods. But no major drama. Hard to imagine when you're standing there on the rim looking down at the biggest damn gash in the entire planet, but . . . it was all just erosion."

I wondered where he was going. "Yeah?"

"You and me? I think we've developed a tendency lately to look for drama. That's what I'm saying."

"This is a metaphor?" I said. "We should be looking for erosion?"

"Be open-minded. You're supposed to be open-minded. You want my news?"

"Please."

"Nothing earthshaking from the Grand Canyon"—he laughed at his own pun—"but there's a lot to the investigation of that girl's disappearance that never made it into any of the newspapers," he said.

"Tell me," I said. I found myself settling in, awaiting Sam's story the way that I liked to sink into the sofa on Friday night with Lauren as we got ready for a long-anticipated DVD.

Sam had spent less than a full day at the North Rim.

He had a way with people. Although he was big enough and tough enough to be physically intimidating when he felt it was in his best interest, he was also capable of using his solid prairie roots and intuition about people to charm strangers.

"Aren't that many people who have gone permanently missing at the Grand Canyon," he said as prelude. "That was another revelation. That, and the erosion thing. You see the canyon from the rim, it looks like the kind of place that swallows people the way Canada eats hockey fans. I thought there'd be a thousand stories about folks vaporizing down there. But everybody who works for the Park Service can tell you the names and histories of the few people who vanished down there and have stayed vanished. Say that missing girl's name to any of the park rangers, they know what happened, and most of 'em have theories about how it all came down."

Within an hour of reaching the North Rim, Sam befriended a National Park Service ranger named Ramona Marks. She was a woman about his age who had unofficially inherited the task of wet-nursing the mystery of what happened to Jaana after she vanished. Whenever a hiker or a rafter or another ranger discovered a suspicious personal artifact downstream of Jaana's last known campsite, Ranger Ramona—that's what Sam was calling her during our conversation—was the Park Service officer who checked the latest find against an inventory she kept close at hand of what it was known that Jaana had been wearing or carrying the night she vanished.

Sam described Ranger Ramona as being "tall like Lucy"—his partner on the Boulder police force—but having "a stronger frame." I didn't know exactly what that meant, but that he described her at all got my attention.

Ranger Ramona had eagerly retrieved the thick investigatory file about Jaana's disappearance for Sam and sat beside him as she walked him through the records that documented all that had been done initially by the Park Service to find the woman after it was determined she was missing. Sam noted a couple of peculiarities. First, at a time when law enforcement was going digital, almost all the initial reports were handwritten. Second, Sam spotted a marked change in enthusiasm and resources for the search after the second day. He mentioned his appraisals to Ranger Ramona.

"First one? Ranger running the search didn't like computers. Handwrote whatever he could. Used to bitch that he came to work at the canyon because he didn't like technology." To explain the second, Ramona pulled out topo maps of the section of the canyon near where Jaana was last seen and explained to Sam about slot canyons and natural drainages, about nonabsorbent soils, about the end of the heat wave, and the return of the monsoons. Most important, she explained about the stalled thunderstorm and flash flood that had hit the Bright Angel Creek drainage thirty-six hours after Jaana had been reported missing. She described to Sam what flash floods looked like on the canyon floor, showed him photographs of the damage they do.

Ramona made it clear to Sam that if Jaana or her body had ended up in the river the night she disappeared—even if she were initially in an eddy—she was probably dead by dawn. If it turned out she was injured or incapacitated on dry land at any elevation that was close to the river that night, and if she was still there when the flash flood hit thirty-six hours later, the water that flowed out of Bright Angel Creek and the nearby slot canyons—along with the mud and rocks and crap captured by the torrential flow when it reached the Colorado River—would have carried Jaana's body miles and miles downstream.

From the moment the flash flood roared from the Bright Angel Creek drainage, she explained, there was no point in continuing to focus a ground search on the riverbed adjacent to the Colorado River where Jaana was last seen alive.

"What do you think happened?" Sam had asked Ranger Ramona. "You know the canyon. You're interested in what happened to the girl. You're smart. You obviously know the case. I'm thinking you have a theory."

Sam told me that he thought Ramona's reply was reluctant, which piqued his interest. "One of three things happened to Jaana Peet that night," she said. "She had an unfortunate accident—maybe she was careless, maybe she was stupid, maybe she was just unlucky—and she ended up in the river or down some cliff, and we've never found any sign of her body. Or . . . somebody hurt her and she ended up in the river or down some cliff, and we've never found any sign of her body. Or . . . she climbed out of the canyon by herself in the dark, which is why we've never found any sign of her body."

"That's it?" Sam had asked.

"She's not still down there, living in a cave—not anywhere near that campsite anyway, if that's what you're wondering. You been down to the canyon floor? To the river?"

"No. Like to. But I haven't."

"I'll take you down on my next day off."

"Wish I could, Ramona. Don't have time this trip. I'm on the clock. For that producer?"

"Rain check?"

"Rain check."

"It's not too hospitable down there, Sam. Magical, yes. Life-changing. Magnetic. Otherworldly. Erotic, even. But it's not too hospitable. Especially in the summer. She went missing just about this time of year. But it was hotter. Twenty-five degrees hotter than it is today. A legendary heat wave. Near one-twenty for highs during the days. People still talk about that week every time we get a little bit warm up here."

I stopped Sam at that point in his story. "The Ranger described the Grand Canyon as 'erotic'?"

"Got a problem with that?" he asked me.

He was daring me to have a problem with that. "No," I said.

Sam had pressed the ranger about her theory. "From your list of possibilities of what happened that night, you ever settle on a personal favorite, Ramona?" Sam asked. "Something that feels okay to you? Satisfying. Lets you sleep when you put your head on the pillow at night?"

"What's most likely is what I said first. People underestimate this canyon and this river in ways that never cease to amaze. They walk right up to a big warning sign that says don't do this, they take two more steps, and then they do it. They track down a ranger for advice about how much water to carry if they're taking such and such a trail down from the rim, and then they carry half as much. They listen to all our advice that says only well-equipped hikers who are highly experienced in the back country should take this trail to the floor or try that route to the river, and they head right off and buy a pair of brand-new hiking boots, put on some shorts and a T-shirt, get a daypack, stick a couple of liters of Gatorade, some gorp, and a granola bar in it, and off they go.

"This is not forgiving terrain. The weather can change in a heartbeat. A little mistake about where you stand to get a better view or how far you step off the trail to see exactly where you're heading next—I'm talking one extra step in some places, Sam—a rock gives way, gravity intervenes, and seconds later you're a thousand feet or four thousand feet farther down the canyon than you had planned. Before your brain even has a chance to recognize that you screwed up big-time, you're dead, half the bones in your body busted into kindling.

"It's true up here on the rim. Hell, I could walk you to places right close to here where people just fell off the edge of the damn canyon while they were taking snapshots to put on their refrigerators. It's true when you're halfway down the North Kaibab—and that's one of the easier trails to the floor. People think a maintained trail means a safe trail. Not true. And that river? Might as well be a people-trap."

"The rim part I understand. The weather part I understand. The canyon trail part I understand," Sam told her. "But the river part? I don't get that. Why's the river so dangerous? Other places, people fall in rivers all the time. I'm from Minnesota, we have rivers. People fall in. They fall in drunk, even. Most of them . . . live. If it's not winter."

Sam said that at that point Ranger Ramona went into a well-worn rap: "Since they built the dam fifty years ago—the Glen Canyon Dam—the Colorado is no longer a natural river. They release water from Lake Powell to keep the river flowing. What they let out of the lake is pulled from the deepest water that backs up against the dam. Deep water is cold water, even in the desert. So the Colorado runs cold here, year round. The outside temperature on the banks of the Colorado might be near a hundred twenty degrees, like it was the year Jaana vanished. The water in the creeks that feed from the side canyons might be pleasant. But that's all natural flow. Most of what's in this whole section of the Colorado is getting dumped out of Lake Powell at a pretty constant fifty-eight degrees.

"And that water is moving. The drop in altitude through the Grand Canyon is sharp. In rivers, gravity rules—the bigger the drop, the faster the water. Look outside." She pointed out the window.

"The Grand Canyon is all about geology. Rocks. Over time, a lot of those rocks you see on the canyon walls are going to end up in the river. In the sections where there's a sudden drop in elevation, there's going to be fast water, and where there are rocks or narrows in the canyon, or both, there're going to be rapids. The section of the Colorado that rumbles through the Grand Canyon is not made for bathers. Get in over your knees, slip just a tiny bit, or drift a few feet out of an eddy where you think you're safe—or worse, get pulled into the edge of a rapid—bing, the river knocks you over, starts pulling you downstream. Bang, you hit your head. Boom, you're dying before you know your hair's wet.

"No life jacket on? Fortunate enough not to hit your head? Some are strong enough or lucky enough to swim out of a fast-moving river. Most drown. Still lucky, don't drown? Hypothermia will get you. Fifty-eight degrees is cold, Sam. It's a hundred degrees outside and still you freeze to death. Doesn't matter what way she does it— head injury, exhaustion, or hypothermia—if the river wants to get you, you end up got. Dead.

"A couple guys wrote a book about all the ways that people have died in the Grand Canyon since John Wesley Powell's expedition first floated down the Colorado. One of the authors was a ranger, like me. It's an interesting read. You can get a copy at the gift shop, you want.

"A good number of the people who died here, died from nothing more than bad luck. A rock'll break free and tumble down a slope and it'll fall on someone's head. A thunderstorm'll blow up out of sight of the canyon floor and the first lightning strike of the afternoon will hit a guy who's doing everything else right. And there've always been flash floods. Don't forget those. The canyon exists partly because of a billion years of flash floods. Flash floods have gotten plenty of folks.

"But mostly the book tells story after story about people forgetting common sense, not preparing for the weather, ignoring warnings, overestimating themselves, or underestimating the canyon or the river. Sometimes all of the above in the same afternoon. Rangers see it on every shift."

Sam had been a cop long enough to know about all the ways that arrogance and hubris can be fatal. "But it isn't an accident that you think happened to Jaana? Is it?"

"Read that book. When the canyon kills people or the river kills people, stupidity is usually an accomplice. That's what most likely happened to Jaana."

"If I arrested people based on who was most likely to commit a crime, I'd be arresting a lot of innocent people. You seem reluctant to share your appraisal," Sam told Ramona.

She said, "Okay, this is opinion. I've read the file, that's it. You understand? I inherited a file, and I'm curious about solving the puzzle. Got it?"

Sam told Ranger Ramona he understood.

He told me that they both knew the caveats were crap. Ramona had a theory.

"What do I think? Someday I'll come in to work and some hiker or some river guide will call in and tell us they found a jawbone or a femur forty miles downstream. It'll be hers. Jaana's. That'll be the end of the story. It'll turn out the river got her in one of the ways the river gets people. How did she end up in the river? Probably never know."

"Forty miles?"

"Twenty. Maybe fifty. Or sixty. River is like a damn conveyor belt."

"I think I understand what you're saying," Sam said. "About what's most likely. But I still think you have an opinion about what did happen."

Sam said that Ranger Ramona stared at him for a good half minute before she said, "The guy she was with that day? I don't like him."

Sam flipped pages in the front of the file. Found the photograph of the man Jaana had been camping with in the first section. "This guy? Nicholas Paulson?" he asked.

"That guy. Nicholas Paulson."

"Tell me about him over supper?" Sam said.

"I'd like that," Ramona said.

Sam took Ranger Ramona to supper.

Jaana's date the night she had disappeared—the young guy from Vegas with a Mustang convertible—was the initial topic of conversation.

Ranger Ramona wasn't enamored with him. Sam asked if she'd ever met him. She had not. Her predecessor had interviewed all the witnesses to Jaana's disappearance.

"I've met plenty of guys like him in Vegas, though. I can cull one out of any herd of rich boys."

"Yeah?" Sam said, hoping for elucidation. He got it.

"A Daddy's-money boy. Pretty. Privileged. No sense of responsibility. Bad things are what happen to other people. That kind of attitude."

"Vegas money?" Sam asked.

"Developer. Resorts. Casinos. Bellagio? Mirage, maybe? I don't remember what they were building back then. Big bucks. He'd picked Jaana up at some club along with one of her girlfriends.

That's how they met. She'd go to Vegas and party with him and his friends on her days off. You can read it. It's in the file."

"She'd been seeing him in Las Vegas?" Sam had asked.

"Few times, he said. Going down to the river was her idea. He says he'd never been. Had only ever seen the canyon from a helicopter."

"You said you don't like him? As a suspect? Or as a man?"

"Guy didn't care she was gone. Seemed inconvenienced that he had to stick around for the investigation. She was disposable to him."

"He have a motive?"

"That's the thing," she said. "It doesn't make sense. If he wanted to get rid of Jaana, all he had to do was not put her name on the list at whatever club he was partying at on the Strip."

Thirty-five

Sam wasn't one prone to storytelling tangents, especially personal ones, so I shut up and listened when he departed his Grand Canyon story and began telling me that Ranger Ramona reminded him of his ex-wife, Sherry, when they were young—mostly in good ways. The Park Service ranger, he said, was soft and warm and touched him a lot during the meal. She had a hair-trigger laugh and dancing eyes that made him think she was paying attention when he was talking.

As surprised as I was by Sam's spontaneous digression about his personal impressions of the female ranger, I was even more surprised when he went off on a long, unexpected muse about Ranger Ramona's romantic disposition.

"She has this thing about unreliable lovers," he said. " 'Unreliable lovers'—that's what she calls 'em. It's well thought out—it's like she's developed a theory about it. We were all done with supper and we were each having a piece of lemon meringue pie—she's not the dieter type, dessert was her idea, she said the pie would be good, and it was good—and she looks up at me and says that when I first introduced myself to her that afternoon, her first impression of me was that I would probably be an interesting but unreliable lover."

"She did?" I said. "Just like that?"

"Out of the damn blue. I don't recall what we were talking about when that came out, but it wasn't about sex. I would recall if it was. I tend to remember my conversations about sex. They're not frequent."

"What if it wasn't out of the blue? What if she thought that Jaana's date was an unreliable lover? That's why it was on her mind."

"Possible," Sam said. "Sometimes you're smarter than I suspect, Alan."

"Thanks. I think."

"Up until this past spring, Ranger Ramona had been seeing a guy from Turkey who owns a restaurant in Flagstaff—an Applebee's, I think she said. Maybe it's a Chili's. I don't know. She said he was an unreliable lover. I got the impression she's concluded that it's a Turkish thing, that all Turks—at least the men—are unreliable lovers. But it was clear that it's not a trait she considers exclusive to the Turks."

"That's what I hear too," I said, intending the comment to be nothing more than a conversation lubricant. I was curious to know more specifically what Ranger Ramona meant by "unreliable." Was she talking fidelity? Or something more immediately related to the carnal act? Something that modern blue pharmaceuticals promised to cure if the unreliable man could overcome his phobia of priapism. I harbored a concern that if I asked for clarification, I would interfere with Sam's spirited homily about his evening out and about his impressions of Ranger Ramona's investigatory and romantic biases.

I did know that prior to the previous spring, when Sam and I had descended together into our joint hell, trying to protect our families from a man determined to eke vengeance from us where we were most vulnerable, there was no way the conversation we were having could have occurred. While he told me the unlikely story of his time with Ranger Ramona, I realized that it was possible that our friendship might be evolving in ways that would give me comfort.

I came to a quick conclusion that the current intimacy between us was only possible because he had come to view me as being his equal in terms of being flawed. He would get no argument from me. I suspected he knew that.

"There are lots of ways to interpret that," I said. "Unreliable lovers."

"Don't shrink out on me, Alan."

"What?" I said, fearing I'd gone too far.

"People are complicated," Sam said. "But most of the time they're complicated in uncomplicated ways. For even more uncomplicated reasons."

While I weighed Sam's wisdom—my initial impression was that there was some truth there—I swallowed my lingering curiosity about the meaning of the ranger's use of "unreliable" and washed it down with some of the bottled water I'd pulled from the refrigerator.

It wasn't my evening beverage of choice. During my earlier inventory of the condo's meager kitchen stores I had spotted a bottle of designer vodka in the freezer. I was tempted to wander back inside from the balcony and pour myself a few inches while I talked with Sam.

I hadn't done that in a while. Quaffed vodka alone at night. At first, "a while" had been a week. Recently, "a while" had developed into something I could measure in months. Low-single-digit months, but months nonetheless. For me that was progress. Before the progress, I'd had a longer stretch of months when I'd drunk alone frequently. Even daily. Not drinking vodka alone was another way I was doing better.

Sam continued his story about dinner with Ranger Ramona. "Why do women want to sleep with me?" he said, jolting me out of my introspection. "I don't get it. I'm not out looking. And I got no illusions here—I'm not the most handsome guy. If women actually choose me out of the lineup of available men, jeez, what does that say about how the world must look to them? Dear Lord."

I knew men who would ask the first question that Sam asked—the "Why do women want to sleep with me?" question—in a manner that could be described only as boastful. But braggadocio wasn't one of Sam's vanities. I waited a judicious amount of time for him to continue the line of thought on his own, suspecting that his query to me was rhetorical and that any answer I floated would end up being the equivalent of using my fingernails to clean a viper's fangs.

During the ensuing silence my attention drifted to the whine of a siren approaching from the north. I tracked it as it neared Merideth's building and then disappeared toward the south. The sound came close, but I never spotted the lights of the emergency vehicle.

Sam said, "I'm waiting."

"You actually want an answer?"

"You're the relationship genius. It'd be easier if they didn't. Want me. If women saw me as a . . . schlub. I don't see myself as the guy women want to sleep with."

Me? A relationship genius? Given the status of the romantic relationships in my life, I suspected that Sam was indulging in a little irony. I could have called him on it, but instead rode his momentum. "Maybe that's why they do, Sam. Because you don't seem to be asking."

He harrumphed. I didn't know too many people who actually harrumphed. Sam was one of the few. I feared he'd taken my reply to his question as a platitude and that I'd lost him.

He scoffed. "Even if that's true, so what? Bullshit. Women choose me. It's baffling, but it doesn't give me a free pass. In the end, I choose them, too. Me."

"Was Ranger Ramona right?" My question earned me some silence. I made the mistake of assuming that Sam had not understood my question, so I expounded. "With her impression? Are you an unreliable lover?"

"Did you really fucking just ask me that?" Sam said.

"Yeah," I said, wishing I hadn't just asked him that.

"How about we leave it that she didn't get a chance to find out about my reliability, romantic or otherwise. Have you been paying any attention to my life lately, Alan? My marriage? My suspension? Losing Carmen? I swear it's like my dick has become a weapon of mass destruction. I'm doing everything I can to keep the damn thing in the bunker."

"How's that going for you, Sam?"

I was surprised that he answered. "Ranger Ramona was tempting, Alan. But I've been celibate since Carmen and I split. Plan to stay that way until I figure things out."

I thought he sounded like me counting the nights since I'd drunk alone.

"Anyway," Sam said, "Ranger Ramona likes to talk politics."

Sam liked to talk politics too. He had a fantastical version of Ronald Reagan's tenure in office that he trotted out with some frequency. I said, "Ramona's flavor is not your flavor, I take it."

"She tried to convince me that George Bush's last act as president will be to pardon the entire executive branch above a certain pay grade."

Sam's appraisal of Ramona's prediction was only a few degrees short of mocking, as though she had revealed that it was her belief that it had been a cadre of wizards who had dug the Grand Canyon.

"What do you think?" I asked Sam, although I had a pretty good idea already, based on a contentious discussion we'd had about Scooter Libby's pardon.

"I think you and I are better off talking about sex, Alan."

Thirty-six

Sam did veer off the sex-talk highway, but he didn't go far. Kind of a frontage road.

He allowed that he thought women—Ranger Ramona was a prime example—were becoming as romantically cynical as men. They had grown wary of love, and were choosing sex from the menu of substitutes.

I was about to tell him about my recent experiences with Ottavia and Amy. But I didn't get a chance. Sam's romantically cynical side road turned out to be nothing more than a cul-de-sac. He quickly moved back to cop talk. Sam said he wasn't convinced that Ranger Ramona's finger-pointing at Nick Paulson was any more than a hunch.

"Cops," he explained, "don't like other cops' hunches. We only like our own."

After his supper with Ranger Ramona had concluded—and after Sam came to a decision that, unlike Ramona, he wasn't looking to extend the evening's social activities beyond dinner and dessert—she set him up in a gloomy conference room in the ranger station and told him he could read the case file all night if that's what "rocked his boat." Just in case her meaning was not abundantly clear, she tagged on a coda that if he was still around in the morning, she would be more than happy to buy him a hot breakfast while she answered any fresh questions that he might develop from his perusal of the case file. If he liked the pie with supper, she promised, he'd love the sticky buns at breakfast.

Sam swore to me that the last comment had been innocent.

He did want to read Jaana's file, and accepted that part of the offer. He told Ranger Ramona that they'd have to see about breakfast.

She said good night and left him in the conference room.

Ranger Ramona's next move ambushed Sam. She returned to the conference room less than an hour after she had left. She sat down next to him, reached over, and closed the file he was reading. She then suggested that were he so inclined, he could do other things until morning. "Unreliable lover or not," she said.

When he opened his mouth to reply, she touched a fingertip to his lips and stuffed a hand-drawn map to her place into his shirt pocket. She removed her finger at the same moment that she leaned in and gave him a soft kiss. She left the room without waiting for an RSVP.

Sam admitted that he had been tempted—her politics aside, he'd already allowed that Ramona was his type—but that he ultimately decided it was a bad idea. He added that he thought she'd expected the rejection from him, which I thought was a peculiar insight for Sam, considering his recent history with women.

He departed the empty conference room at two fifteen the next morning with a topo map of the park, a couple of pages of notes he'd taken, and a string of questions in his head about what had actually happened to Jaana the night she had disappeared.

Sam told me he left a note for Ranger Ramona detailing his new questions. He had thought long and hard about whether to leave her his cell phone number. Ultimately, he did.

His questions? He wanted to know if the park's visitor logs showed Nick Paulson returning to the canyon floor around the time the hiking boots were found. Sam's second question also had to do with footwear—it was about a solitary lime-green sneaker.

* * *

Sam drove away from the Visitor's Center at the rim of the Grand Canyon alone and in the dark. He pointed his Cherokee into the high desert. He drove until he arrived in St. George, Utah, just before dawn, picked a motel that wasn't part of a chain, and requested a room as far away from Interstate 15 as possible. That's where he slept for six hours before finishing the long drive to Las Vegas to talk to Nick Paulson in person.

"I spent a good chunk of the drive across southern Utah considering a pair of lime-green, high-top Converse All-Stars," he said.

"You did?" I replied. Sam had a roundabout way of getting to the point sometimes. This was looking like one of those.

"Witnesses—other people down at the river that day—said that once she'd set up camp, Jaana switched from hiking boots to a pair of high-top sneaks. Lime-green ones. Lesson there, Alan—wear lime-green shoes, people will remember your footwear."

I assumed there was a point. "Yeah," I said, hoping the point would develop without any prodding by me.

Sam spotted the subtext in my reply. "Patience, Alan. Jesus. A single left shoe—a size-eight lime-green Converse All-Stars high-top—was found eleven miles downstream on October 31 of the year Jaana disappeared."

"Halloween."

"That part's a coincidence," Sam said, displaying irritation that I'd interrupted him with the detail. "I'm pretty sure."

"Sorry."

"The guy who was initially in charge of the investigation, a National Park Service ranger named Lincoln Oden, thought at the time that the single sneaker was a pretty strong piece of evidence that Jaana's body had indeed ended up in the river the night she went missing. Natural river currents, he theorized, and the flash flood that followed her disappearance, would have carried her and her sneaker downriver.

"In the short note he added to the file after the recovery of the shoe the ranger predicted that hikers or river guides would soon be discovering parts of her skeletal remains."

I said, "That didn't happen?"

"It did not."

"You don't agree with the ranger's conclusion?" I wasn't smart enough to guess why Sam didn't agree, but I knew him well enough to read his skepticism with some precision. "Or you don't think it was Jaana's sneaker?"

"I think it was Jaana's sneaker. What I'm having trouble with is the inventory that was done of the rest of her stuff after she went missing. In the file there's a list of all the things that they found at her campsite, things she packed down with her from the rim earlier that day. Pack, sleeping bag, pad, food, water bottles . . . Nothing out of the ordinary, typical stuff for that kind of trip. Something you would expect to be there wasn't there, though."

"You going to tell me?"

"Her hiking boots," he said.

I didn't see the relevance. I said, "So?"

"Where were they? She didn't wear those lime-green sneaks on the hike down. The guy she was with said he was sure she was wearing boots. People at the rim who knew her all said in their statements that she was experienced, had done the rim-to-river hike before. Nobody with experience would do that descent in sneakers."

"I'm sure it was chaotic in the campsite after she disappeared, Sam. The boots must have gotten misplaced somehow during the search. Or maybe another hiker stole them."

"That's the ranger's theory too. It's in his report. He thought somebody ripped 'em off." Sam wasn't done. I waited. "A week after that single sneaker showed up downstream—it was early November by then—somebody spotted her hiking boots under some brush not fifty yards from where her campsite had been. Pair of size-eight Solomons, if you're wondering. Good boots. The woman who spotted them picked them up before any photos were taken, so it's impossible to know for sure whether they just happened to end up under that brush or whether somebody stuck them there. You know, intentionally."

"What are you thinking, Sam?"

"Let's just say I'm thinking."

I gave him a moment to go on before I said, "Can I change the subject?"

"You usually don't ask."

"Is Vegas your kind of town?"

"Spent an hour walking the Strip. I expected tawdry, but the place is harmless glitter, at least on the surface. A terrible town to be a cop, though—all that money's got to be a magnet for mayhem. Everything bad on earth has to be for sale there.

"I knew I would see dirt in every crack if I looked down for even a second. I didn't look down. Hey, not my problem, right? Wasted time trying to find a five-buck blackjack table. Ended up at a ten-buck table at the Venetian."

"And?"

"Started with a hundred. Got up a hundred. Lost the second hundred. Then I lost the first hundred and half of a another hundred I didn't plan to lose."

"How long did that take?"

"Twenty minutes. That's when I dropped in on Nick Paulson. He's the guy I wanted to meet."

Jaana's hiking companion. "Yeah? And?"

"Big fancy office. All glass walls inside. Stupid design. I could watch his secretary walk back to tell him I was there. I could watch his eyes get big. Watch him look at me and shake his head.

"She came out and told me to make an appointment. I didn't move. Couch was comfy. Magazines were recent. I asked her if she knows anything about Jaana's disappearance in the Grand Canyon. She goes and tells him what I said. I thought he might call security on me, but he knew exactly how to get rid of me. He called me in. We talked."

"Anything?"

"He thought I was there following up for somebody else. See? Feel the circle closing? He said he'd already explained everything he knew a couple, three days before. I told him if he repeated his speech, I'd be out of his hair before he could finish his next Red Bull."

"Who was the somebody else?" I asked.

"Another one of the hikers. Guy named Jack Fargo."

Shit, I thought. I said, "Carmel has a friend named Jack. He didn't show up last night when she expected him to. She was upset. I wonder if it's the same guy."

"Didn't show up?"

I told him what I knew.

He chided me. "That's it? That's all you got? The guy's missing since yesterday. You didn't go online to check it out? Find out if anything happened to him?"

"I thought he was just a friend of Carmel's, Sam. I didn't even have a last name until you just told me. I still don't know it's the same guy. As far as I knew, he was just some friend of hers who didn't show up when he was supposed to. Why would I think it had anything to do with the damn camping trip?" He didn't offer the absolution I was hoping for. "You're a cop, Sam. You look for information. I'm a shrink. People bring me information."

"That's your excuse?" he said, laughing. "Nobody brought you the right information? You're blaming your ignorance on the help?"

"What can you tell me about Jack?"

"Nick Paulson said that Jack called him earlier in the week to find out what he remembered about the search for Jaana. From reading the file, I can tell you that no one had any suspicion about Jack at the time of the search. I'll look into him some more when I get to L.A. I'll get back to you—you know, bring you some information on a silver platter. Just the way you like."

"You learn anything from Paulson that's going to help Merideth, Sam? To find Lisa?"

"Not yet. But if it turns out this Jack guy is really missing, he makes three. That should get some attention from law enforcement."

"What was your impression of Nick Paulson?"

"He acts like somebody with nothing to hide. Which either makes him innocent and naïve, or guilty and good."

"You're vote is?"

"Pending. Headline? Jaana was pregnant. She wasn't happy about it. Had an appointment set up for an abortion a couple, three days after she disappeared. He said a girlfriend of hers—somebody else from Estonia, the girls partied together in Vegas—was going to take her to get it done."

"Was Nick the father?"

"He admits it's possible, but he doubts it. Called Jaana a 'party girl,' implied she slept around. Remember, Ranger Ramona thought Nick Paulson considered Jaana one of the disposable girls."

The news was interesting, but sounded irrelevant. I said what I was thinking. "Don't see how it helps Merideth, Sam."

"Hard to say. Paulson says he told the Park Service ranger all of this in his original interview. The pregnancy. The abortion. The girlfriend. But none of it's in the file. Ranger Ramona doesn't know anything know about it either. She would have said something to me."

"You're sure?"

"I read the file cover-to-cover. Somebody is lying. Or misremembering. Can't see the advantage for Paulson to lie about possibly getting Jaana pregnant. I tend to believe that part."

"Still don't see how it helps Merideth find Lisa."

"One foot in front of the other. Tomorrow I'm going to drop in on the ranger who was in charge of the original investigation, the one who interviewed all these people, including Paulson. Name is Oden. He's living near L.A. He's a Good Hands guy now."

"What?"

"Sells insurance for Allstate. What do you think? Should I try that? When I get off suspension, tell my captain I'm starting a new career selling insurance?"

He didn't expect a reply. I said, "Oden say anything interesting on the phone?"

"He thinks Jaana's in the river. Makes the search sound like the highlight of his ranger career. Has no memory of Lisa, other than that her name is familiar from the file."

"His version of events make sense?"

"What do I know?"

"He say anything about those shoes?"

"The sneaks or the hiking boots?"

"Whichever."

"I'll ask him tomorrow when I ask him if Jaana was pregnant. Those are look-him-in-the-eyes questions. I also left a message for Ranger Ramona, asking her if she could get any follow-up information on Jaana's girlfriend. The one who was going to take her for the abortion." Sam burped. "I'm coming up on the cutoff to San Bernardino. You like the way I let that roll off my fat tongue like I have a damn clue who the hell little Bernard was and why he was worthy of saintification? I should be in L.A. before long. Maybe we can connect later, go to a club."

I laughed at the thought of Sam clubbing. Or me clubbing. "I think that's where the first McDonald's was, Sam. San Bernardino."

"No shit?"

"No shit."

"It's sad," he said, pausing wistfully, "but there was a time in my life that I would've found that fact worthy of a detour."

I was tempted to encourage Sam's earlier diversion and hear his fantasy about us clubbing in L.A. But I was more tempted to ask Sam if he ever took the same route he was on right then on any of his road-trip visits to see Carmen in Laguna Beach. His pointed counsel about not prying into sensitive areas caused me to hesitate.

He didn't give me a chance to reconsider. "I'm on Merideth's dime. I'm thinking I should live a little. Know a nice place in Beverly Hills? Someplace trendy? I'd like to maybe have a cocktail or two, sitting a couple stools away from a star."

Sam wouldn't cross the street to meet a celebrity unless he had a reason to interrogate him. I considered how Sam and Hector would get along. Couldn't predict it, but decided it would be fun to watch. Then I tried to guess how Merideth would feel about Sam staying at her condo. Once Sam spotted my ex-wife's empty bed, he would not share my reservations about inhaling the aromas embedded in her zillion-thread-count sheets.

Merideth would not be thrilled with the idea of Papa Bear sleeping in her bed. She'd be much happier springing for a room for Sam at the Comfort Inn on La Cienega.

"Let me think about it," I said.

In a voice laden with sarcasm, he said, "Call me back when you're done with that. I'll stay close to the phone."

He hung up.

Thirty-seven

I watched an immense translucent pillow of mist creep inland from the Pacific. The slippery mass seemed to be losing forward momentum on the far side of the 405.

I replayed the conversation with Sam. His initial openness about Ranger Ramona left me regretting that I might have done something to poison the interlude of intimacy I'd been enjoying with him. I called him back.

He said, "You decide to be my wingman after all?"

I took a leap of faith. I said, "I was out with a . . . woman tonight," trying not to sound as though I'd just dropped to my knees in a confessional. When Sam didn't reply instantly to my disclosure, I added, "She didn't say as much as a word about suspecting that I was an unreliable lover."

A few seconds of silence preceded Sam's next comment, which was delivered in a slightly sardonic timbre. "They usually don't, is my experience. Ranger Ramona was unique in that fashion," he said. "Was this part of that favor you're doing for your friend in Boulder? Or was it . . . something else?"

He was offering me an out, a rationalization for my indiscretion—if it indeed constituted an indiscretion—with Amy. It felt like a small gift, but nevertheless one I was disinclined to accept. "Seeing this woman was tangentially related to Wallace. She's his daughter's roommate. I had a good reason to talk with her, but it didn't have to include us having dinner in some place in West L.A. that's so trendy it doesn't have a name, only initials. But that's what we ended up doing."

"Good food?" he asked.

I laughed. Was he offering me another exit? I weighed the possibility that he wasn't eager to hear what I had to say. I said, "Nothing you couldn't get in Boulder. The people were very L.A."

"I wouldn't have been happy?" he said with a laugh.

"Probably not. Earlier in the day I drove out to the San Fernando Valley looking for Wallace Poteet's kid. She and I were supposed to meet, but she was with her boyfriend because she was upset about this guy Jack not showing up. Once I was in the Valley, I ended up not being too far from . . . the town where I was raised. Lots of memories."

Sam knew about the family tragedy in Thousand Oaks in my youth. He understood that my prodigal visit to Southern California wouldn't be uncomplicated.

"You wanted some company?" he said, offering me a cushion. "Went out with a pretty girl?"

"Yeah."

"Anything happen?" he said. "You now an official member of the axis of evil?"

I laughed. It felt good, considering the complicated emotions of the day.

"She's fun. She's pretty. She's smart." I pictured the freckles by her nose. "Cute. People her age are different from us, Sam."

The cop that Sam had been involved with in Boulder—the friend with benefits, the one who had helped him earn his suspension—was young too.

"Yeah?" he said. "I've already been across that bridge. Warning for a friend? It's dangerous over there. People on the other side don't view things the way we do."

Sam's sexual fling with the young cop in Boulder had cost him dearly. "Coming back to L.A. can't be uncomplicated for you, either," I said. "You spent a lot of time here with Carmen."

Silence at first. Then, "I was doing pretty well ignoring that aspect of this trip. Until you brought it up. Thanks for that."

"Sorry," I said. "I was trying to be sensitive. In case you were having some . . . feelings about being so close to—"

"Save it for someone who likes backrubs, Alan. You know damn well that's not me."

The edge in his tone convinced me of the wisdom of a tactical retreat. "I hear you."

"This girl you were with got a name? The one nothing happened with?"

"Amy."

"No Amys on that canyon hike. I have the whole damn roster in my head. Like the seven dwarfs."

"Think there were only six, Sam."

"I'm counting the guy from Vegas."

"After we finished dinner, Amy invited me to invite her to come back here for a drink," I said.

"A 'drink'? Her word or yours?"

"I knew what she meant, Sam. I don't get out much, but I hear stories about stuff like this from my patients."

"And 'here' is where? Your hotel?"

"The motel was . . . full. Merideth offered to let me stay at her condo."

"There's only one motel in L.A.? Damn, I didn't make reservations."

I laughed again. I could have embellished the earlier rationalization I'd concocted about my aborted plan to stay at the Holiday Inn Express, but even with extra buffing, the tale wasn't going to pass Sam's bullshit sensor.

"I'm staying at Merideth's condo, Sam. Let's leave it there."

"Well," he said. "Let me see if I have this right. You went out for a spontaneous L.A. on-the-town dinner with a woman, a young woman, someone you just met. It turns out that she finds you so . . . What? Charming? Yeah, so charming that she was dying to join you for late-night cocktails and . . . whatever might come next. And you suspect that whatever might come next was going to take place on the clean sheets of your ex-wife's Beverly Hills condo while your current wife is off with your child looking for her long-lost daughter in Denmark."

I swallowed a sigh at his synopsis. "Amy is . . . beguiling, Sam."

"Did you just say 'beguiling'?" Sam said. "I think you're a fucking idiot."

Thirty-eight

I opened my mouth. Nothing came out.

Sam waited an additional ten seconds before he said, "Was I right-on with my little summary?"

It was as though he'd forgotten that he'd just called me a fucking idiot. "When you put it that way, I admit it makes my evening sound kind of sleazy."

"Hey . . . no criticism intended. Not from me. Despite all my recent scar tissue from tangling with women I had no business tangling with, it took all my willpower to decline Ranger Ramona's invitation of midnight recreation and a hot breakfast. Mostly I was trying to highlight the complication factor you're attempting. My assessment? The degree of difficulty you're considering for this dive may be well beyond your demonstrated ability."

I didn't want him to be right, but suspected he was. I said, "For what it's worth, Merideth's place is in West Hollywood, not Beverly Hills. And Lauren and Grace are in Holland, not Denmark." As soon as the words were out of my mouth, I regretted them.

Sam wasn't about to let me get away with having uttered them. He said, "As though the first part is consequential to anyone who doesn't work for FedEx, and the last part matters to anybody but the Dutch—or on a slow news day, maybe the frigging Danes. I got two questions. Why didn't Merideth tell me she had a damn condo? That's one. Two is, did you have that drink?"

"I came close to saying yes."

"That's not an answer."

"I'm telling you what was going on in my head."

"The part of your anatomy we're discussing is not your head. You either did or you did not have that drink."

We were officially talking sex, not beverages. "We didn't."

"You were tempted?" Sam asked.

I hadn't allowed myself to explore the temptation equation—I found comfort in the illusion that deeds and desires were the most distant of relatives. I said, "I was tempted, Sam."

Confessions, I knew from years of listening to them in psychotherapy, often come in bunches. The first is only the initial splash that springs from a siphon as the vacuum gets sealed. From then on, new admissions of guilt tend to keep cascading until the source vessel is empty. Sam, no doubt, had learned the same lesson in his years of interrogating perps.

He waited. Once I'd finished spitting out the first mea culpa I went on to the next. I said, "Not for the first time lately. I was tempted with Kirsten, too. Last spring."

My avowed sexual attraction to a woman who had been my patient in the distant past and whose most recent role in my life was as my defense attorney caused Sam to go silent for a protracted moment. Then he said, "Can't relate to that. Kirsten. Don't get me wrong—she's . . . a lovely girl. But I've never found myself attracted to a defense lawyer. Not even once, not even a little. It's almost like a cross-species thing for me. Has to be something God never intended. Don't ever recall actually seeing one naked, but I'm not even a hundred percent sure the parts would fit."

Sam was giving me room, making it clear that any confession by me was not going to be coerced by him. "There was a woman in New York. Couple weeks ago. I sublet her apartment. She let me know she was . . . available . . . the night before she left on vacation. I kind of asked her out."

"You did?" No judgment in his question. Maybe a little wonder, but no judgment.

"We didn't go."

"She turned you down?"

"She said yes. I could tell what was on the dessert menu."

He went quiet again. I could hear him breathing until he said, "Lemon meringue pie?"

I laughed. "Something like that," I said.

"So you stood her up?" When I didn't answer immediately, he added, "You can make me ask a ton of questions here, Alan, or you can just tell me what the hell happened. I got nothing but time. My tank's half full, you're on speaker, and there's paved highway in front of me as far as I can see."

"I canceled. But I wanted to see her. I'm trying to be honest."

"Can I interject a thought? Maybe I've been missing something, hanging with you all these years, but it certainly seems to me that you're suddenly much more willing to walk up to the roulette wheel and bet your marital future on red/black than you used to be. You aware of that?"

I recalled his Grand Canyon metaphor. The drip-drip of erosion versus the drama of cataclysm. The last year of my life had taught me about erosion. I was toying with lessons about cataclysm. I said, "At some level I was tempted."

"You're focusing on what's tempting, not why you're tempted. That's the trap. Been there. Doesn't work out."

"Go on."

"You might be the relationship expert, but I'm the fucking-up-relationships expert. Tempted's a lesson," he said. "With women, I mean. And lessons are what they are. God, they are. But it sounds to me like you're looking for solutions in places where you ain't got no problems."

Country song? I thought. "Which means what?"

"From where I sit, your problem is at home. If that's the case, you can't solve it in New York or L.A. by letting the WMD out of the bunker with some hottie. That's when things go south. For tonight at least, you avoided that. You did? Alan?" Without offering me much latitude for a timely response, he added, "Right?"

"I did."

"Got to feel good about that, yes?"

Any initial reticence that Sam might have felt about having this kind of conversation with me had evaporated. He was officially into it. I was aware the conversation felt a little like psychotherapy. I was not in the role of doctor.

I said, "I guess."

He pressed, "You said she's young? Tonight's woman. Amy."

"Kirsten's almost my age, Sam. So was the woman in New York. Ottavia. The temptation isn't about age."

"Ottavia? Oooh, her name sings. Has to be a story there. If it's not about age, what it is about?"

It was a good question. Sam's spinning roulette wheel image hadn't exited my consciousness. I wished it would. Was I really intent on gambling my marriage on red/black? I said, "I don't know."

Sam knew. "Tonight wasn't about Amy," he said. "You barely know her. What did you say, that she's cute? You're fucking beguiled?"

I didn't bite. I was proud of myself. "She is cute. But no, it wasn't about Amy."

"New York wasn't about Ottavia?"

I wanted to tell Sam about Ottavia's scent, and how it made me catatonic in the hallway of her flat. I said, "It wasn't."

"Quick answer," Sam said. "Too quick." I thought he tried to make the question that he tacked on next sound more casual than it really was. "Other than Ottavia—what is that by the way, Greek? Italian?—any other temptations? I'm thinking Merideth. She press any of your buttons?"

"Not one, Sam."

"No urge to jump in the sack with her? Déjà vu? Old time's sake?"

"No."

"That would be significant."

"Nothing."

He digested my denial. "Sometimes something happens even when nothing happens. Other times nothing happening is exactly what it sounds like. I have a friend in the mental-health field who would tell me that at times it can be difficult to tell those two things apart."

I was that friend. Sam was good at this. I might have been surprised. But I wasn't.

He said. "Forget everything I just said if you'd like. Really. I'm no genius about this shit. I've screwed up everything that matters in the past couple of years."

"Except Simon."

"Except Simon."

I said, "Maybe you're wiser than you know."

"This is easy. Listening to your problems. Doing color commentary on your situation." He paused. "I ever tell you how I think about psychotherapy, what you do every day?"

"I don't think so. Not in so many words. Do I want to hear this?"

He didn't care whether I wanted to hear it. "Seems to me doing psychotherapy is like looking over somebody's shoulder while they play solitaire. You point out shit that they miss, simple shit, stuff they can't see for some funny reason even though they're staring right at it. 'You need to put the black ten on the red jack.' Like that."

"Okay."

"Solitaire's always easier when it's somebody else's game. Ever notice that? It's not hard to see what card somebody else isn't playing."

"Is that what we're doing now? You're looking over my shoulder, spotting the card I'm not playing, pointing out my mistakes?"

"Hope not. Nobody likes the wiseass looking over their shoulder while they're playing solitaire. I'm no therapist. I'm a schlub."

Sam turned up the sound on his radio. The twang of a country ballad—female, contemporary, and completely indistinguishable from fifty other laments I'd heard involuntarily in recent years, often in his company—blared in my ear.

For the first month after Adrienne's death my personal musical tastes were stuck in an Edith Piaf rut. If malaise had a soundtrack, at least one or two tunes would be from Ms. Piaf's opus. I was relieved when I'd emerged from the extended Edith Piaf runnel. But I still wasn't ready for Sam's country tastes.

"I like this song," Sam said, apparently entertaining the delusion that I had devolved musically to share his dubious fondness for contemporary country. "Know what? I need to pee. Maybe I'll top off the tank. Get some ethanol, or whatever the hell they sell in this state. Know what else?"

With that prelude, I didn't want to know what else.

"I'm craving a patty melt. You like patty melts?"

I was having trouble keeping up with him. The truth was that my mind was still stuck on Kirsten and Amy—okay, both Amys—and Ottavia and Thousand Oaks and erosion and cataclysm and WMDs and roulette and temptations and solitaire and whoever the hell it was singing the song that was playing on Sam's radio that I wished would just stop.

"Rye bread, fried onions, good old American cheese, and a cheap hamburger—all smashed together and toasted up golden brown on a griddle that tastes a little bit like this morning's pancakes. I like it best if the rye has seeds in it. Know what I'm talking about? Is there a better meal to have on the road? I mean, if you're not in the South. If you're in the South, then . . ." His voice turned wistful at some gustatory memory of a Dixie roadtrip. "Turns out there's a truck stop ahead that seems like it's just what the doctor ordered. As long as the doctor in question is neither my internist nor my cardiologist. We'll talk tomorrow, Alan. Oh shit, gotta go."

"What?"

"I have another call. You take care. Don't do anything I wouldn't do."

I could hear him laughing before the call went dead.

Behind me, on the other side of the screen door, Merideth's phone started ringing.

Thirty-nine

It rang anew every few minutes.

I kept my butt planted on the terrace. The fixed-ass solution was proving an effective strategy for hobbling the urge to chug chilled vodka. That night the process took about ten minutes, and more willpower than I considered ideal.

I spent most of that interlude musing on Sam's provocative suggestion that I needed to be more honest with myself about what I had been risking with Ottavia and Amy. The whole time, some primeval part of my brain kept insisting that the introspection could be better accomplished with increased levels of ethyl alcohol circulating in my blood.

I covered a lot of ground during my muse, but I reached no conclusion other than that Lauren and I had a lot of work to do when she got home from Europe. In the meantime, I had to find a way to deal with my temptations. All of them.

When I finally felt it was safe to go back inside the condo, I switched off the ringer on Merideth's landline.

I indulged in one more long shower. It was a sybaritic, not a hygienic, act. All those heads. I was aware it was a less-than-ideal substitution for the cocktail—in its broadest denotation—that I had not had earlier in the evening with Amy. And for the vodka I hadn't had alone afterward.

I found some spare bedding in the linen closet and got ready to convert the long part of the sleek sectional sofa in the living room into a makeshift bed. I knew exactly how the bed in Merideth's bedroom would feel—the perfect mattress would be encased in linens so soft I would swear the threads had been spun from clouds. But I was determined not to spend a night with any of Merideth's pheromones banging around like pinballs in my brain.

A light rapping sound distracted me from the bedmaking. I paused and listened. The sound was repeated five seconds later. I threw down the sheets and checked the peephole.

A young woman. Red eyes.

Carmel.

It turned out I did recognize her.

Forty

I asked her to wait. After I threw on some clothes—the Spicy Pickle T-shirt and pair of jeans I'd stripped off before the shower—I invited her inside.

"Mel?" I said.

"Dr. Gregory."

"Alan, remember?" I offered my arms for a hug. She leaned into me, I thought gratefully.

She took a step back, nodded, kicked off her shoes, and glided across the room. She perched cross-legged on the sofa right beside the pile of linens, immediately pulling the pillow to her chest. "Nice," she said, looking around.

"I'm a guest," I said.

"That's what I hear. Guy downstairs."

She had a fleck of a diamond stud impaled through the otherwise pristine skin of her left nostril. The wavy brown hair she'd had as long as I'd known her was streaked with maroon highlights in unexpected places. Her wardrobe seemed designed to feature her surprising—to me, at least; I hadn't seen Carmel in many years—curves in ways that I had no doubt would make my old friend Wallace lose sleep at night.

"Should I call you 'Mel'? 'Cara'? What works?"

"Mel. I guess."

I sat across from her. "Something to drink?" She shook her head.

I asked, "How did you get past Hector downstairs? I find him kind of intimidating."

She grinned. "He called you about letting us come up here. You didn't answer the phone. We tried you on your cell, but you didn't answer that, either."

I heard the "we"—if Cara knew where I was staying in L.A., she had learned it from Amy, her roommate. I looked across the room and saw the missed-call indicator light flashing on my mobile. I had indeed received a recent call.

"I was in the shower. Long shower."

She shrugged. "Amy kind of distracted the doorman. That's Hector? I slipped by him. Rode up the elevator with a guy who lives on fifteen. He said he works at CAA." She rolled her eyes. "I told him I was surprising my boyfriend on our six-month anniversary. Hector's probably pissed."

I agreed that Hector was probably pissed. I didn't know what CAA was.

Mel shrugged again. Her attitude? Hector would just have to get over it.

I pointed to Merideth's phone. "Should I call downstairs and tell Hector to send Amy up? Or do you want to talk in private?"

"No, invite her up," Mel said. "She's cool."

I called Hector. He pretended he wasn't annoyed. I was becoming more enamored of doormen all the time.

Merideth would learn the whole story from Hector before breakfast. What would she make of it? Only God knew. Merideth had more important things to worry about. Neither Sam nor I were getting any closer to finding out what had happened to Lisa or to the baby she was carrying.

Once Amy made it upstairs, the three of us sat around in the living room. The girls talked shop—a curious mix of industry-speak and bitching that was probably no different from the kind of unwinding that two nurses might do after a day in the OR. Since the inside-Hollywood gossip was meaningless to me, I sat back and observed.

After fifteen minutes I suggested to Mel that we retreat to the balcony. She excused herself to the bathroom. Amy asked if it was okay with me if she made herself a drink.

"Whatever you find in there is yours," I said. "There's some vodka. A few beers. Nothing fresh."

I sat on a Plexiglas stool at the island while I watched her assemble the components for a martini. She was wearing the outfit she'd worn to dinner.

The top still popped. The roulette wheel was still spinning. I remained beguiled.

Jesus.

Amy filled one martini stem with ice to chill the glass and held up a second toward me. She said, "Happy to make you one too."

"No, thank you," I said.

It was my night for temptations. Amy had great intuition about the best bait to use.

She had made cocktails once or twice before. The refrigerator door was stocked with condiments, including a jar of olives of indeterminate age. Even tempered by the antiseptic properties of the vodka I could not think of any circumstances under which I would have imbibed the juice in that jar, but Amy seemed fine dribbling some of it into her vodka and vermouth. She winked at me as she carried her drink to the living room, where she curled up on the sofa and grabbed the remote control to Merideth's big flat-screen television.

"That drink," she said without looking at me. She raised her glass. "From earlier? Didn't think I'd be having it alone, watching TV."

With a quick flick of her thumb she found *SportsCenter.*

I moved outside onto the terrace.

Yes, Sam, fucking beguiled.

* * *

I stood at the railing. The bank of diluted fog I'd watched earlier had breached the 405 and was threatening West Hollywood. The leading edge of the mist was infused with an aroma suggestive of petroleum by-products.

The evening was cool, a welcome change to the day. Mel joined me outside. She said, "My God, it's gotten cold." She shivered once, retreated inside, returning seconds later with a throw that she wrapped around her shoulders like a shawl. She lay down on the solitary chaise, propping herself on her side with her knees curled up to her waist. I selected one of a pair of hard teak chairs and faced it in roughly the same direction as the chaise. Though I was confident that Merideth had tasteful cushions for the chairs stashed some-where inside her condo, I didn't know where to look. The naked wood wasn't comfortable. Not even close.

"You didn't need to come out here," Mel said after about a min-ute of silence.

She meant California, not the balcony. I'd anticipated that she would say something like that at some point in our conversation.

"Probably not," I admitted. "But your dad thought it was impor-tant. He's worried about you. The Grand Canyon thing." I caught myself just before I added a comment about how much I respected her father, or how much I owed him. I hesitated because I didn't want my feelings about Wallace to determine the tone of the talk I was having with Carmel. The therapist in me knew that as soon as I inserted my transference about her father into the equation, I would be limiting Mel's freedom to express her transference about him with me.

Psychotherapy 101.

Amy opened the sliding door. "Sorry. Mel, I left my bag in the car. I'm going to leave this door open while I'm gone. It's getting hot in here."

She slid the screen shut.

I thought I spotted Mel tightening her jaw. "My father says you know . . . something about what happened?"

"At the Grand Canyon?" I asked.

She nodded.

I wanted to cut to the chase, hear what she had to say, pack my bag, and go back to Boulder. I wanted to say, "Okay, Mel, What the hell happened in the Grand Canyon?" But I was cognizant that Wallace considered his daughter fragile, and I forced myself to take the measured steps of a patient therapist. I said, "Was it a good trip?"

"Life-changing, in good ways, until the end."

I said, "I know what was in the newspaper back then. That's it."

I was being disingenuous. I not only knew what was in the news accounts, but I also knew what Sam had told me earlier that evening after his visit to Arizona—all that he had learned from his dinner with Ranger Ramona, from reading the search-and-rescue file she'd made available, and his interview with Nick Paulson in Las Vegas.

"There's more to it," she said. "From our point of view."

"Our"? Not "my"? I waited. Waiting was my psychotherapeutic specialty, as well as my all-purpose conversational safety net.

"Jack was there. My friend? The one I told you about this afternoon? He was with us." She nodded her head once in a single long motion as she spoke. Her voice cracked a tiny bit as she said Jack's name.

I deflected yet another instinct—to provide comfort to Mel about Jack. From an information-gathering perspective, my compassion would be counterproductive.

"You've remained friends?" I asked. I was consciously aware of not wanting to sound like her therapist father.

"Jack's my buddy. He is everybody's buddy. That kind of guy. People like him. He can laugh at himself. He has a big heart. He's funny." She stopped speaking in a way that let me know she wasn't done. I waited. "Jack was one of the reasons we went back down the canyon looking for Jaana. He couldn't leave her alone down there. He knew something was wrong."

"Wrong?"

"Wrong."

I hoped for more. I didn't get it. "Was it just you and Jack who went back down?"

"It was shortly after dawn, we were trying to get an early start to beat some of the heat. God, it was hot. Broke records the whole time we were there.

"We knew that Jaana was missing from her camp—the guy she was with came by—but we started to hike out anyway. All of us. It was just beginning to get light—we were making good progress up the trail—when Jack and Jules and I decided to go back down to help find Jaana. A couple of others didn't, went with Eric. It was a big deal. Us splitting up. We'd been tight." As she was speaking she was looking past me.

Jules was a new player to me. "You and Jack and . . ."

"Jules. We're the ones who went back down. Jules was . . . with Eric back then. Four of us—me and Kanyn and Jack, and one of Jack's friends from high school, Lisa—were together, and we ended up sharing a cabin with Jules and her . . . boyfriend. Eric. The six of us spent almost all of our time together. It was a great week, mostly." She smiled. I assumed at some memory. "It was like a hundred and twenty-something degrees. The heat didn't bother Jack much, or Kanyn. Kanyn's immune, I swear. The girl likes Palm Springs in August."

The "mostly" caught my attention. I prodded, gently, for clarification. "Everyone had a good time?"

Come on, Mel, I was thinking. *Help me out, here.*

"I had never been on . . . a trip like that before," she said. "It was so . . . *intense* down there. The people, the place, the history. It was . . . transformative for me. Is that a word?"

The emphasis she'd placed on the word "intense" gave me pause. I didn't know what kind of intense Mel was talking about, but I was no longer convinced she was talking merely about the scenery or the ambient temperature. "Intense?" I said, still hoping she'd become more forthcoming.

She smiled, glanced at me sideways, and quickly looked away. "Yeah," she said. "Intense."

Mel was skilled at parrying the simple thrusts of conversation. I said, "Jack was the one who was most determined to look for Jaana?" I asked. "Or was it Jules? Or you?"

"I wanted . . . So did Jules. But I'm not . . . Jack is a stronger person than me. Doesn't care so much what people think. I tried to get people interested in what was going on with Jaana, tried to get everybody to agree to do it together—it's what I do—but people don't always take me seriously. Jack and Jules, they just did it. Said they were going back down. Turned around, hiked back down."

"But Kanyn continued up to the rim."

"That surprised me. She feels bad about it still. She's not sure why she did it. It's not like her. She has a big heart. She can seem flaky, but she has a big heart."

I said, "No luck when you got back to the river?"

"Nothing. Somebody found a bracelet—a woven thing—that Jaana had been wearing. But that's it. After a few hours the rangers took over. The three of us hiked out at the end of the day. It was miserable on the climb up. Unbelievably hot. Jack kept our spirits up. Jules was okay. I was a wimp."

"You've all stayed friends?"

"With Jules and Jack? Yeah, absolutely. Jack lives in San Diego. . . He's in the Chargers' public relations office. We go down to San Diego sometimes. He gets us seats for the games. We—my boyfriend and I—are going down for the home opener in a few weeks. Jack is so . . ."

She opened her eyes as wide as she could open them, trying to evaporate her tears before they could flee down her cheeks. A solitary escapee meandered from her left eye and tracked toward her ear.

"I haven't decided if I'm going to tell you . . . any more about what happened," she said. "At the canyon. Not now."

I gave her a chance to continue. She didn't. I wasn't surprised. But I was getting frustrated. "I hope I can get you to change your mind." I was thinking, *You could have told me all this before I flew out here. Your father said you wanted to talk with me.*

"Nothing makes any of us look like . . . heroes."

"Is that important? Being heroes?"

She snorted, shook her head. My question had been a therapist thing to say. Mel wasn't about to fall for it.

I took the bat off my shoulder and swung again. "Going back down to help search for her? In that heat? That sounds altruistic."

"All of us—every one of us who went back down to help search for Jaana—lied about not seeing her the night before. We lied to the guy she was with. We lied to each other. We ended up lying to the rangers who interviewed us. When the guy Jaana was with came to our cabin looking for her in the morning as we were getting ready to climb out, we all denied seeing her anytime after dark."

"You did see her?"

"Some of us saw her, most of us. Maybe all of us. Not all to-gether. But we saw her. I didn't find out about all the others that morning, but it's come out since."

She stopped herself.

"So Jack saw her that night?"

"Yes, definitely."

"And Kanyn?"

"I can't say."

Can't, or won't? "And—what did you say that Eric's girlfriend's name is—Jules? She saw Jaana too?"

"Jules was with me . . . when we saw her. It was a dark night. The canyon was in moonshadow. We weren't sure what we were see-ing at the time. But we saw the same thing. Later, Jack convinced us it was Jaana."

"But at the time you didn't know you saw her?"

"We saw someone. We could have said something about it, but we didn't. Okay?"

I'd sensed a hitch in Mel's delivery of the information about what she and Jules saw. "What did you and Jules see?"

"We weren't sure. That's why . . . we didn't say anything. At the time we thought the woman we saw might be . . . someone else. Lisa. From a distance, Lisa looks like Jaana. Especially in the dark. We thought it might have been Lisa."

"Are you certain now?"

She hesitated before she said, "Certain? No."

"Tell me a little about Jules," I said.

"No," she said again, without hesitation.

"Maybe later?"

"Don't hold your breath."

She attached just the tiniest bit of levity to the last pronouncement, just enough that I couldn't easily list it in the column marked "overt hostility."

Ten more minutes of this, I said to myself. *Then I'm out of here.*

"Eric and Lisa continued up to the rim," I said. "Did either—"

"And Kanyn."

"And Kanyn. Did Eric or Lisa see Jaana the night before?"

"One did. I know that for sure. Maybe the other one did too. Lisa . . . keeps strange hours at night."

I decided to postpone following up on the issue of Lisa's sleeping behavior. I said, "But you know one did? Either Eric or Lisa. Did you see that person . . . with Jaana?"

"That's the part I'm not sure I'm going to tell you."

That, and the part about Jules, I thought.

Forty-one

Reading between the lines is part of what therapists do. I like to think I'm better at it than most people, but most of the time I'm objective enough to admit that being better at it than most didn't make me good.

The dots that needed connecting were becoming more obvious to me while Mel talked, like stars appearing in the night sky as layers of clouds cleared. I could draw lines between the dots, but the clarity of a constellation eluded me. I said, "You saw Eric with either Lisa or Jaana the night before? That's what you're saying?"

I intentionally left a couple of things out of my conclusion. One was that the mysterious Jules likely saw whatever Mel saw that night. And the second was that whomever the two women saw with Jaana after dark had to be considered a possible witness—or worse— to whatever ultimately happened to her.

I wasn't at all clear where Jack fit into the equation. Mel said he'd seen Jaana too. And that he'd helped clarify what she and Jules had seen.

"I didn't say that," Mel said, in reply to my question.

I was on familiar ground. I was lost.

It was apparent that Mel was choosing her words with the care of a White House spokesperson. She was interested in appearing cooperative; she wasn't interested in being illuminating. "I didn't say that" wasn't exactly a denial of what I had proposed.

As she circled the narrative wagons, Mel pulled the throw tighter around her. It wasn't that cold on the balcony. I was nearing a conclusion that whatever Mel had seen that night in the Grand Canyon was part of what had had left her so uncomfortable upon her return to California. What had she seen? I didn't have a clue.

When I find myself lost in a psychotherapy session, it is because I find myself out in the lead. Aware of that tendency, I tried to allow Mel to step back in front of the story where she belonged. I had no business guiding this expedition.

I got quiet. We kept eye contact. Mel was my match. Or my better.

"So Jack knows what you and Jules saw?" I said finally. As I asked that innocuous question, I recognized that our conversation had devolved into a game of twenty questions. It's not an effective interviewing technique. If I hoped to learn anything useful from this meeting, I had to find some way to get Mel talking freely.

My self-imposed deadline was five minutes away.

She shook her head in reply to my question in a manner that I couldn't interpret. I had no way to know if the headshake was the simple answer to my question or whether it was an indication of her refusal to tell me what I wanted to know.

"Mel, do you know what Jack saw that night?"

She nodded. "You too," she said. She punctuated the thought with a girlish giggle. "The world does."

Me too? The world does? Huh? What does that mean?

On a busy therapy day—one with eight, nine, ten patients—I could count on having at least one moment during the course of the day when a patient would say something that feels like a complete non sequitur. As though I'd somehow missed an essential segue. That was how I felt after hearing Mel's "You too"—"the world does."

Too many facts, not enough context. "I didn't get that," I said. "I'm sorry."

She didn't repeat it.

I said, "I'm getting the impression that what actually happened that night in the canyon is different than I might be thinking. Is that what you're telling me, Mel?"

It was a hanging curve. Mel hit it out of the park. She said, "And what exactly do you think happened in the canyon, Alan?"

I chuckled at her reply. She joined in. She knew I had begun reaching. She was also feeling increasingly confident that she was up to the task of hitting my best pitches. Wallace had trained her well. Probably inadvertently, but still . . .

She said, "Your turn to tell me something. How does your wife know about all of this? What's her connection to the trip? My father told me that Merideth knows somebody who was down there. Is she—"

"Merideth's my *ex*-wife, Mel. We were divorced a long time ago, when you were still in Boulder. Probably when you were still in junior high, hanging out on the Pearl Street Mall." Saying that made me feel old. "And yes—she knows someone who was on the trip. She's engaged to a guy who was down there. At the canyon, at the river. Part of this . . . thing. I don't know where he fits in.

"Merideth has become involved and asked for my help because . . . They've been— Mel, will you agree to keep this next part to yourself? Merideth doesn't want it to become public. It's important to her. You'll understand why when I tell you what it is."

She shrugged. "Goes both ways. You don't tell my parents anything unless I tell you it's okay?"

It was territory that I anticipated visiting with Mel during our conversation. "Fair," I said.

She seemed surprised at my easy abdication about keeping her confidence. She'd expected a fight. I had already decided that the best I could do with Wallace and Cassandra would be to share my conclusions about their daughter's well-being. I didn't need to betray confidences to do that.

"My friends and I didn't hang out on the Mall. We hung out on The Hill." The Hill was the student neighborhood close to the university in Boulder. Things happened on The Hill that most parents of junior high school students wouldn't want their progeny exposed to on a daily basis. "That . . . made my parents crazy, especially my dad," she said. "So who is Merideth's fiancé? Eric or Nick? I know it's not Jack. It's Eric, isn't it?"

I said, "Yes. It's Eric."

"Figures." She shook her head. "It's funny. Jack was sure that Nick was in the closet. I never found out if he was right or not." Her next question: "There's something I don't get, Alan. Why are you helping your ex-wife? That's kind of . . . weird, isn't it?"

Good question. "I suppose it is. Eric is still friends with someone from back then, and—"

"Lisa. She's the only one who would still be talking to him. Eric was the biggest asshole about not going back down to help. He didn't slow down while he was climbing out, didn't even consider it might be the right thing to do, he just kept marching up the trail. Lisa went along like she was leashed to him. She'd been throwing herself at him all week." Mel shrugged, shook her head. "There were times when we were all together down at the cabins that I thought Jules was going to kill her. All the attention Lisa was paying to Eric was . . ."

"Attention?"

"She was all over him."

Shit. I'd just officially heard something from Mel that I didn't want to have to tell Merideth: Lisa had once been romantically, or at least sexually, interested in Eric. I assumed that for Merideth it would be a disconcerting piece of news about the woman she had chosen to be the couple's surrogate. I recalled, of course, that both "sex" and "Lisa" had been part of a recent conversation I'd had with Merideth.

I asked Mel, "You mentioned Lisa had odd sleeping patterns . . . on the trip? Does she have problems sleeping?"

Mel narrowed her eyes. "How do you know that? Did Eric tell you?"

"I've never spoken to Eric. Lisa has been staying in an apartment hotel recently in Manhattan. I went there with Merideth. It looked to me like Lisa hadn't used the bed. It's an . . . anomaly, that's all."

Mel rolled her eyes. I winced. I'd apparently just managed to sound like her father. In an attempt to recover I said, "I don't like pieces that don't fit."

"Lisa can't sleep in beds. Don't ask me—something from her childhood. I don't know. The cabins in the canyon have bunks. She never slept in hers. She slept on the floor the whole time, I think."

Lisa can't sleep in beds.

I recalled the unused bed in Morningside Heights. The clutter by the sofa in the living room. Mel was providing an alternative explanation to the one Merideth and I had jumped to: that Lisa had been sleeping, or screwing, somewhere else.

I could tell that Mel's patience with the conversation was diminishing. I decided to try to lower the temperature a little. I said, "Jules and Eric were a couple?"

"When the trip started. By the time we'd been down there for a day I really think Lisa was . . . " She didn't finish the sentence. "No," she said to emphasize her change of heart about completing the thought about Lisa. She tightened her hands into fists. "No. Sorry."

Rather than try to scale the wall she completed with the brick of the final *no*, I instead replied to her earlier question. I said, "Okay. Back to my story and why I'm helping Merideth. As you guessed, the woman from your trip who is involved with Merideth and Eric is Lisa. Lisa—this is the confidential part—has agreed to help them have a baby. Merideth has a long history of fertility problems—miscarriages—and Lisa agreed to act as their surrogate. She apparently did it once before, for a relative. Eric knew about that. They all came to an arrangement. Did an in-vitro procedure. As of a few weeks ago Lisa became pregnant with Eric and Merideth's baby."

Mel sat up and her mouth flew open. "No shit! No way! Lisa is having Eric's baby? That's perfect. Kanyn is not going to believe this. I wonder if she's off work. I have to call Kanyn."

"Our deal? Mel? You can't tell Kanyn."

She looked at me like I was nuts. "Kanyn can't be part of the deal," she said. "I tell Kanyn everything."

I swallowed a sigh. I had no leverage. I said, "Just you and Kanyn?"

"Wait. Whose egg did they use? Is it Lisa's?"

"No, it's Merideth's."

"Ohhhh, too bad. It'd be so much a better story if it was Lisa's."

I reminded myself that Mel worked on the set of a soap opera. The over-the-top was everyday drama for her.

I said, "Does Eric know that you and Jules think you saw Jaana that night?" When she didn't respond right away, I added another thought: "Maybe more importantly, did he know it then?"

"Eric's an ass. He knows he's smart, he knows he's hot, he expects everyone to . . . whatever. I didn't find it easy to be with him during the trip. He wasn't kind to Jules. He plays it so cool. I mean, he's gorgeous, but there're lots of pretty boys in L.A. So what? That night? He said he didn't see Jaana."

"You don't believe him?"

"He said he didn't see her. It's either true or it's not. Just go to the video."

What? "I'm trying to understand this," I said, forcing patience into my voice.

"Welcome to the club."

"What about Lisa?" I asked. "Do you know if she saw Jaana that night? Where does she fit into the story?"

Mel looked off into the night. "I'm sorry, Alan. Answering your questions won't help you. I don't want to talk about it anymore."

She actually sounded sorry. I looked away from her into the fog. I could barely make out the time on an electronic clock atop a building a few blocks away. In one more minute I would excuse myself so I could call the airlines and see if there was a red-eye back to Denver. Before I did, I played one of the few cards remaining in my hand.

"The reason I'm in Los Angeles? I mean, other than to check on you for your parents? This is my reason, not your parents'. Okay? About a week ago, Lisa disappeared with Merideth and Eric's baby. They are desper—"

"We are desperate," said a voice from behind us, "to find Lisa."

Mel and I spun simultaneously.

A man stood silhouetted behind the screen in the open doorway. He was wearing a dark suit over a white shirt. No tie.

"Hello, Carmel," he said. "Long time." He looked at me. "You must be Alan. I'm Eric Leffler." To establish his bona fides, he held up a condo key and electronic fob on a ring. "Hector pointed out your friend when I was downstairs. Amy? She was kind enough to explain what's been going on up here.

"Merideth forgot to tell me you would be using the condo, Alan. I bet she doesn't know you're having a party. I don't think she'd be happy."

Forty-two

Amy was standing a few feet behind Eric. She had an I'm-sorry-what-could-I-do expression on her face.

Mel said, "Oh my God. Oh my God."

Eric asked, "Carmel, do you know where I can find Lisa?"

"How much did you hear?" she asked him. "Just now."

"Simple question, Carmel. Do you know where Lisa is?" he repeated.

Eric's tone with Mel was stern and condescending. My first impression was that although he was superficially gracious, he had some latent bully in him. I reminded myself that there was a lot of history between him and Mel that I didn't know.

Mel was shrinking into her chair. She said, "What did you just hear?"

"Nothing. Not a thing. I just got here. Do you know where Lisa is? Yes or no?"

"I don't believe you, Eric."

"I don't care what you believe, Carmel. Does Jules know where Lisa is?"

"I don't know what . . . Jules knows."

Eric slid open the screen door and stepped outside. He walked between us and leaned against the railing, facing back indoors, looking down on Mel. "Is Kanyn here? Has she heard from Lisa?"

"She's at work."

He said, "I know about you and Jules. And I don't . . . care. Just tell me if either of you knows where I can find Lisa."

Mel and Jules? I thought. *What about Mel and Jules?*

Mel said, "I know all about you and Lisa, Eric."

Mel's reply to Eric sounded to me like immature retaliation—pure playground in tone.

"What?" he scoffed. "There is no *me* and Lisa, Carmel."

"And I know about— No."

"About what, Carmel? You think you know about what?"

"Never mind."

"Carmel . . ." he said. "Come on."

She said, "I know about you and Lisa. Okay?"

"Jaana? Were you just talking about Jaana? What do you think you know about Jaana?"

"Nothing." Mel pulled up her knees and wrapped her arms around them.

"Tell me all about Jaana, Carmel. Come on. Tell me your delusions. You were a silly kid back then. It appears that hasn't changed."

Mel turned her head away from him.

Eric spoke to me. "Alan, would you please leave us alone for a moment? We need to discuss some things in private."

Mel seemed to be at a significant disadvantage. I thought about Wallace, what he might like me to do in that situation. "Mel?" I asked. "Would you like me to leave?"

"No. Please stay."

"I think I'll stay," I said to Eric.

"I could ask you all to leave."

As Merideth's fiancé, not her husband, he really didn't have any authority to ask us to vacate the condo. I could phone Merideth and ask her to referee. But that wasn't a fight I wanted to start. I said, "If you want us to go, Eric, we will leave."

A yell from inside intervened before he could cast his vote.

Forty-three

"Mel! Mel!" The clarion call was from inside, from Amy. "Come here, come in here! Quick. Mel! Get in here. Oh my God. That's our house! That's our damn house. Right there. Look!"

I stood to see what was going on. Amy was standing in the middle of the living room, pointing at the television with one hand, urging Mel to come back inside with the other.

I followed Mel to the living room. It took me a moment to orient myself to what was on the screen. The camera view was from a helicopter. The shot was focused on what looked like a residential street on a hillside. A small fleet of stationary vehicles with flashing lights was clustered nearby. After a couple of seconds I was able recognize that the home the searchlight was illuminating was the charming duplex that Amy and Kanyn and Mel were renting in Mt. Washington.

The sky seemed clear. The misty fog that was hovering over West L.A. apparently hadn't drifted inland that far across the basin.

A brilliant floodlight highlighted the street-side façade of the duplex. One side of the building was dark and curtained. One side had large urns by the front door. In those urns, I knew, were birds of paradise.

The television screen split. On the left side was the aerial shot. A police chopper—the one with the floodlight—passed quickly into and out of the frame, entering on the lower left corner, exiting on the upper right. The camera choreography was becoming clearer—the shot we were watching had to be from a news chopper that was tracking the movements of an L.A. police helicopter from a higher altitude. The right half of the split screen was a live, street-level view of heavily armed officers moving away from large police vans. I guessed SWAT.

Shit. I wondered if it was some kind of hostage situation.

Mel said, "Oh my God, that's our—" Her tone had an odd hollowness to it that caused my clinical antennae to perk.

"Yeah, it is," Amy said. She sat on the edge of the coffee table, gripping the remote in both hands, the same way she'd grasped the spent flower bud earlier that day on the steps in front of the house.

"What is—" Mel stepped closer to the screen. "Why are they . . . Is that the police that's—"

The same hollow affect continued to invade her voice. Shrinks call the tone "flat." I suspected that her recognition of the crisis at her home wasn't the only precipitant for her sudden affective vacuum. Eric's presence was certainly a contributing factor.

Amy stood, then she sat again. "Some kind of shooting—that's what they said when it first came on. They broke into *Jimmy Kimmel*. Then there was . . . Another woman came on and called it a home intrusion, not a shooting. I don't think they really know."

The ground-level side of the split screen refocused to become a grainy shot of the front of the duplex. The heads of the two anchors in the studio popped up in a box in the lower left corner of the busy screen.

"It couldn't be our house, could it? It must be the Addams Family. Right? Don't you think?" Amy said. "I wonder what they did. Wait, are they back in town, Mel?" Mel didn't respond. Amy said, "We have to call Kanyn. See if she's okay. She could be home from work."

In seconds, Amy had her cell phone on speaker, the call to Kanyn placed, and the phone was ringing. "Pick up, baby. Pick up," Amy pleaded.

The center of the left side of the television screen flashed brilliant white.

The reporter at the scene screamed, "Oh shit!" as she ducked out of the frame. The person holding the camera at ground level lost his balance. The shot jumped to the sky before it resettled on the front of the duplex.

Dark gray smoke billowed out and up, obscuring the view of the porch.

One of the anchors in the TV studio, a taciturn woman whose manner reminded me of an assistant principal, said, "Was that an . . . explosion? Jennifer? Jennifer Itou is our reporter on the scene, live. Do we have Jennifer? Jennifer?"

I found myself hoping we still had Jennifer. And that she was still live on the scene.

Amy said, "That was a bomb. My God."

I looked at Mel. Her lips were parted. She wasn't blinking.

I turned to find Eric. He was standing on the far side of the room, near the entry hall. His arms were crossed.

A second explosion rattled the front of the duplex.

Jennifer Itou had one hand covering her earpiece in a way that was almost a parody of a reporter at a scene full of chaos. She said. "Brett and Carl? My cameraman, Tony, is telling me the second explosion was a flash-bang. Repeat, we think the explosion was a flash-bang. Tony was a Marine."

Kanyn hadn't picked up her phone. The ringing finally stopped. Voice mail kicked in. "Hey, it's me," her recorded voice announced. "Leave a message, or even better send me a text. A nice one. Adi."

"Adi?" I said.

Amy said, "Adios. Oh my Jesus."

Mel lowered herself to the floor in a single, languid, motion that was as fluid as a dancer's. It was as though she felt the long bones in her legs dissolving at a measured pace and she was determined to get her torso to the ground before the bones disintegrated.

Amy said, "We have to go home, Mel. Get up. Come on, now. We have to check on Kanyn."

My eyes returned to the television screen. As the smoke from the explosions drifted away from the front of the building, it wasn't apparent to me which side of the duplex was the focus of all the law-enforcement attention.

Eric said, "Does anyone know what is going on?"

Amy said, "That's our house."

He turned and walked out the door.

Forty-four

The plan was for me to follow Mel and Amy to Mt. Washington.

Execution turned out to be a problem. Amy was more inclined to obliterate L.A.'s speed limits than I was. Her speed, or my lack thereof, caused me to lose track of the solitary working taillight of her car—she drove an aging Honda CR-V—before I was five blocks from Merideth's condo. I wasted a few minutes weaving through traffic trying to once again spot her car before I pulled to the curb on Beverly Boulevard. I pushed tiny buttons until I had communicated my pathetic situation to Chloe, the GPS lady.

Chloe was cool.

I'd elaborated on Chloe's avatar life. She was a work-at-home single mom sitting in a pleasant, quirky room lined with north-facing windows. She was mildly agoraphobic. When she wasn't busy responding to my electronic queries about road life in Los Angeles, she did watercolors.

Chloe said, "Turn left in . . . three . . . blocks." I was grateful that she delivered her geographical counsel without either irony or sarcasm. She was the perfect shotgun.

I speed-dialed Sam while I was stopped at the next red light.

"Hey," I said. "Where are you?"

"I'm on the 10 heading into L.A.," he said. His voice was bright. "That's California talk, by the way. They don't say 'I-10,' or 'Interstate 10, or even plain old '10' like we do. Here it's got to be the damn article *and* the damn freeway number. You need to remember that if you don't want to sound like a tourist. Sometimes the locals trip me up and use the name of the freeway instead. The San Diego. The Pasadena. I haven't figured out why they do that. Any-*hoo*, I am on 'the 10' somewhere in the vast suburban wasteland between Pomona and L.A. I can already see the glow of the big city on the horizon."

Sam blew through his entire speech without an audible inhale. I was pretty sure he had topped off his personal tank with a few cups of nasty truck-stop coffee to wash down his sublime truck-stop patty melt.

Before I had a chance to tell him why I was calling, he started up again. "You make a decision whether I'm going to be allowed to bunk with you in Merideth's palace? I should be in your general vicinity before too long. Be nice to know where I'm sleeping. My butt is, like, numb."

Sam was still listening to contemporary country on the radio. The volume was still loud. I still didn't like it. I paused to be certain he was done before I said, "Have an emergency here, Sam. Need to run something serious by you."

"Okay." His tone lost all its playfulness.

"Something's going on with all these people. The Grand Canyon people. Eric showed up in town. I don't think Merideth knows he's here. And there's a police emergency at the place where Mel lives with her friends."

"What kind of emergency? What kind of serious?"

I explained to Sam what I knew about the events taking place at the duplex, starting with the fact that the two girls had stopped by Merideth's condo so I could finally have a chance to talk to Mel. I stressed the part about the live TV coverage, the hovering helicopters, the apparently determined SWAT response, and the possibility of dual explosions.

I added, "I'm on my way there now. The girls are in Amy's car, heading home—I'm following them. Or I was. . . . I couldn't keep up. You know anyone in the LAPD? Can you find out what's going on? It's a big deal, Sam." I reconsidered, and added, "Maybe not for L.A., but it would be a big deal in Boulder."

The girlfriend Sam had broken up with in the wake of the disclosure of his sexual affair with the young Boulder cop was a detective with the Laguna Beach police. Laguna was in Orange County, not L.A. County. I didn't think Sam and Carmen were on speaking terms anyway. I held out hope that Sam had met someone through Carmen who might be able to shed some light on all that was going on, but I wasn't counting my chickens.

"Maybe," he said. The intimate timbre I'd been enjoying during our last few phone calls had evaporated. "Carmen has a friend who's LAPD. Another Raiders fan. I can try her. You've thought this through, Alan? You think it's wise? For those girls to go home? Given what might be going on?"

I hadn't considered that it might not be wise. My instinct would have been the same as theirs was when they saw the televised live shots of the explosions at their house: get home as fast I possibly could to check on my roommate.

I said, "There are a lot of cops there, Sam. Your colleagues will keep the girls at a safe distance from trouble. I'm sure they'll be fine." I didn't bother to tell him that I didn't think the girls really cared what I thought was wise.

"That conclusion," he said evenly, "is based on an assumption that my colleagues recognize that they may need . . . some attention. And that the girls aren't mixed up in . . . whatever this is."

"You mean Jaana?" I said.

"I mean Jaana going missing when all of these people were together. The girls were there. That's means and it's opportunity. And now there's Jack. Where the hell's Jack?"

"You're right. I have been assuming that the girls had nothing to do with any of that. For right now, they're worried about Kanyn. Their roommate."

"Kanyn—K-a-n-y-n—was on that damn trip too," Sam said. It wasn't a question. He had read the file. "What's their address?"

The street and number in Mt. Washington remained on the screen of the GPS. *Thank you, Chloe.* I read them to him.

"I'll meet you there," he said. "Wait, what are you driving?"

"I got upgraded to a Camry. It's a hybrid."

"Shit. Figures. What color?"

Sam arrived in Mt. Washington before I did. I spotted him almost immediately—he was the only person on the scene wearing a Colorado Avalanche sweater. The old-school kind. Sam didn't tilt toward svelte. The sleeves were pushed up to his biceps. His forehead—as prominent as the grill on an old Buick—was mottled with sweat. He was overdressed for a summer evening in L.A.

Sam was behind the taped-off perimeter almost a block away from the duplex. He was chatting with a woman cop. His hands were in his pockets. The fleet of SWAT vehicles that I'd seen on the news less than a half an hour earlier had departed. I couldn't hear any helicopters overhead. Only one ambulance remained nearby. The paramedics were killing time. Uniformed cops were doing sentry duty, feet apart, arms crossed over their chests. The firefighters were more industrious. They had hoses to retrieve. Equipment to pack up.

I tried to spot Mel and Amy. They weren't in the crowd that had gathered at my end of the street. Before I approached Sam, I hiked the long block that ran parallel to the one the duplex was on so that I could search for the girls behind the perimeter tape at the other end of the street. They weren't part of that group either.

I called Mel's cell phone. No answer. I left a message.

I called Amy's cell phone. No answer. I left another message.

I retraced my steps to the other end of the block. I tapped Sam on the shoulder.

"Took you long enough to get here," he said. He barely glanced my way.

I had an urge to give him a hug, something I wasn't sure I'd ever done with him as a greeting. Sam's reluctance inhibited my spontaneity.

The penalty for crossing the line? I didn't want to know.

"I've been looking for the girls," I said. "Can't find them. Are they inside with the police?"

Sam shrugged. He repeated my question to the patrolwoman standing on the other side of him. She shook her head, raised herself on her toes, and whispered a couple of words toward his ear. *Damn,* I thought, *she's flirting with him.*

"Don't know," Sam said to me.

I said, "What's going on inside the house? You learn anything?"

He put a hand on my back and led me a few steps away from the patrol officer. "That friend of Carmen's? She had an LAPD detective call me with a status report on this. RP—older lady next door on the left—saw an intruder at the back door. That's how it started—she thought she saw a man go in a window in the back. The first explosion was from a gas wall heater near the front of the house. Could have been deliberate—somebody may have screwed around with it. The second explosion was a flash-bang from SWAT. The uniforms who responded to the initial call thought they might have a hostage situation and went in after the first explosion." He shrugged. "They're no longer sure about the intruder theory, but they're thinking a woman inside may have tried to kill herself. She was taken away by ambulance. She's okay. Some minor burns, that's it."

"That might be Kanyn, Sam. The Grand Canyon alumnus. She has a history of dysthymia."

He glared at me. "That's like a secret shrink code word for depression? How do you know that?"

"Her roommates." If the word "dysthymia" bothered him, I wasn't about to tell him about the trichotillomania.

His jaw tensed. "Something's up," he said. "That's what I think."

I gestured toward the cop. "Would your new friend know where they took Kanyn?"

He walked over and said something to the officer in a voice low enough that I couldn't hear him. After a brief exchange, they both ended up laughing. He came back over to me. "Kanyn's probably at County." He glanced back at the patrolwoman.

She smiled at him in a way that made me grin, partly in disbelief, partly in admiration. She was indeed flirting with him.

Sam was the most unlikely of sex machines. *They've all been cops,* I thought. Even Ramona.

"Well, I can't find the girls," I said. "They haven't called back."

"You said that."

Sam's rejoinder took me back to sitting on the front steps of the duplex with Amy—script supervisor Amy—earlier that day as I watched her dissect the bird-of-paradise blossom she'd deadheaded. I said, "I've been repeating myself a lot lately."

"You're getting old. What's next?"

"I was hoping you would tell me."

Before Sam had a chance to scoff at whatever I suggested, my phone buzzed. Sam took the opportunity to saunter back over to the patrol cop. I looked at the screen, where I saw an unfamiliar icon. I guessed it meant I had a new text message. Or maybe an attachment to something. If I did nothing, I figured whatever it was would find a good temporary home—digital foster care—alongside the map to A.O.C. that Amy had sent me before dinner.

I didn't know how to open attachments. The instructions for the phone were in Boulder. Jonas, my teacher, was asleep—I hoped—in White Plains.

Texts and attachments would have to wait until our next chat.

I longed for my old phone. The one I knew how to use. The one that the taxi had obliterated. During our electronics shopping trip in Times Square, Jonas had explained to me that if I paid the monthly fee I could even watch TV on the phone he'd picked out for me. He thought that was a pretty cool feature. At the time, I'd been dubious about the usefulness of watching television on my phone. Standing behind the police line in Mt. Washington, I must admit I had begun wondering if it might be a good time for an episode of *CSI*.

Cell TV would be an advanced lesson. For me, mobile telephone graduate school. I returned the phone to my pocket.

I was thinking how much I liked Sam Purdy. I couldn't think of anyone I would rather be loitering with at that hour on that street corner in Los Angeles. When I looked up, I caught his eye. He took a step my way.

I said, "You're a good friend, Sam. Thank you."

He looked at me as though I were something he'd just stepped in that he wished he hadn't just stepped in. He said, "We're only visiting SoCal, Alan. Don't go all Left Coast on me. Deal?"

I could tell that he was trying to keep from smiling while he said it.

Forty-five

Sam asked me how to get to Merideth's condo. I explained about the peculiar gifts of Chloe the watercolorist—my GPS avatar. He was amused. He agreed to follow Chloe and me back to West Hollywood.

Chloe knew the way, of course. Hector was gone for the night. His replacement at the first-floor desk was a guy in his fifties who'd recently lost a lot of weight. The man's clothes didn't fit. His skin barely fit. Unlike Hector, he was looking for neither drama nor trouble. I told him I was the guest who was staying in Merideth's unit.

He said, "Fred. Nice to meet ya." The man glanced at Sam, but didn't give him an apparent second thought.

The on-duty sign on the Carrera marble counter read FREDRIC. Fred was a Fredric like I was a doctor. The tag was all part of L.A.'s alternate reality.

What was surprising to me was how okay I was with it.

Sam was impressed with his boss's condo.

He did a quick self-guided tour, returned to the kitchen, grabbed two Asahis from the fridge, and joined me out on the balcony. More fog had infiltrated the atmospheric mix. I could still smell refinery fart.

"Never seen a shower like that," Sam said, handing me a beer. "Looks like a car wash. I might need directions from you on how to operate it."

"Keep turning knobs. You won't want to get out," I said.

Sam wasn't done with his design critique. "Place is kind of modern for my taste. But that's better than girly. Nice TV. Big flat screen covers a lot of sins. Bet they don't teach that in decorator school. Maybe they should. Is that plasma or LCD? You know? In case you hadn't noticed, there's only one bed here."

I sipped the beer, wondering when Sam's caffeine overdose would wear off. "The bed's yours, Sam."

"I wouldn't want to sleep in Sherry's bed either." He shivered. I couldn't tell whether the shiver was real or a dramatization. Sherry was Sam's ex. Either way, it was clear he understood the whole ex-wife pheromone thing.

He said, "That was Ranger Ramona who called me earlier, just before I stopped for the patty melt."

"Yeah? Just staying in touch? Women love you, Sam. That cop at the duplex? She was all over you. I admit I don't get it. Just for the record."

He drove over my opinion as though it were an inconsequential speed bump. He said, "I'd asked Ramona to check a few things for me. The Park Service keeps a log of who goes down what trail in the Grand Canyon when. So the rangers know if someone's overdue. Missing. Whatever. What supplies they have with 'em, like that."

I wasn't surprised by what Sam was saying. The Forest Service used the same voluntary procedure to track hikers in Colorado's mountain parks and national forests. But Sam didn't have my full attention. I remained preoccupied with what had happened in Mt. Washington. I was increasingly worried that I hadn't heard back from Amy and Mel. I'd called them again while on the way back to the condo.

Sam didn't notice my distraction. "Specifically, I'd asked Ramona to check the logs for the days before Jaana's hiking boots were found. And for a while before that sneaker showed up downriver. I had a theory that the Nick guy from Vegas, Jaana's companion, might have gone back down to cover his tracks somehow when he realized the shoes were a problem."

I looked at Sam. "Yeah? Cover his tracks for what?"

"If he was involved."

"If he hurt her while they were down there? That's your theory?"

"Hurt her. Killed her. But Nick's name wasn't on Ramona's list. Doesn't mean he didn't go back down. Just means he was smart enough to send somebody else or to use a pseudonym if he did it himself. But you know who did go down on one of the South Rim trails six days before Jaana's boots were found under that brush? A one-night trip, rim-to-rim?"

"Eric?" I guessed. *Poor Merideth.* Despite the rotten first impression Eric had made earlier in the evening, I didn't want it to be true.

"Good guess. But no. This Lincoln Oden guy. The ranger who coordinated the search. He went down."

I didn't see the significance. "So? You think he was following a lead?"

"Maybe. Maybe he had a hunch. But it was his day off. Ramona checked. If he had a lead, he could've grabbed a seat in a chopper, saved himself a long, hot walk."

Sam's "maybe" sounded suspicious, but I didn't see the relevance of Oden's presence on the canyon floor. "Oden wasn't down there the night Jaana went missing, was he? You don't think he—"

"No, he wasn't. He was up at the North Rim. Coordinating."

Sam actually said *cord'natin'*—an Iron Range linguistic cousin of *c'n-oo-in.*

"What then? If he was up to something, he could have used a fake name."

"Too many people knew him. Don't know what I think. Just talking it out. It's one of those things that doesn't line up right. Been thinking about it since I got back on the road with my belly full of grease. Could be a coincidence, of course. That happens . . . sometimes." Sam said "that happens" grudgingly, the way he reluctantly admitted to me one night on the roof of the West End that the president had mishandled certain aspects of the Iraq War. "Could be Oden knows what really happened to Jaana down there and has reason to want it to stay secret. Or could be that Oden knows she made it back out of the canyon, and he has reason to want that fact to stay secret." He took a long slug of beer. "Just about covers all the possibilities I'm considering. Got anything to add?"

"Why would he go back down?" I asked. "Does Ramona have a theory?"

"Ranger Ramona doesn't like Nick Paulson. She recognizes the timing of Oden's rim-to-rim as peculiar. But she says rangers explore the canyon all the time on their days off. Once they fall in love with the canyon—and almost all of them do—they can't get enough of the place. Did say that the fact that he went down that section of canyon, and that he did it from the South Rim, was surprising. Guy worked on the North Rim. That section of the canyon is heavily trafficked by visitors and tends not to be terribly interesting to the rangers. Usually they go to more remote parts of the canyon."

He was being tantalizing. I'd seen him do it before. "You got more, Sam. I can tell."

He made a face. "I had to press her, but Ranger Ramona admitted she always thought Oden was kind of creepy. She'd heard stories about his trips to Vegas. Gambling, whoring." He shrugged. "And he used to hit on park visitors. There had been some complaints. She thought he had the recessive stalker gene."

"Her words?"

"My words."

I asked, "Men or women?"

"Good question. I didn't think to ask," Sam said. "I assumed women. Ramona would've said something if it was men."

I had a feeling Sam's theorizing was more advanced than he was letting on. He wanted me to be patient. I wasn't feeling patient. "What are you thinking, Sam?"

"I'm thinking that if I were a real cop"—he turned his head and smiled an ironic smile—"and if this were my case, I'd want to take a peek at Lincoln Oden's finances back then. See if he had a rich aunt die or something. Won the lottery. Came into some cash."

"You think he was paid off?"

"Nick Paulson's family has money," he said. "A lot. Oden quit the Park Service a few months after all this came down. That surprised everyone, Ramona says. None of his colleagues saw his resignation coming. Guy ran the investigation. Have to think it's possible Oden figured out what happened down there with Jaana. Let's say he had something, confronted Nick with it. Maybe they cut some kind of deal. Crazier things have happened."

"Oden interviewed Nick back up at the rim? You're sure?" I said.

"I read his report. Remember, he left out the parts about Jaana being pregnant. Oops."

I said, "And that's the part that might have given Nick Paulson a motive."

"Yeah."

I thought about Sam's theory. "If you're right about this, Sam, and if they were smart about how they did it, it could be very hard to trace. We're talking Vegas. Oden could have been paid in chips, cash . . ."

"Drugs," Sam added. "Some of those around too."

"Ranger Ramona share your suspicion about Oden being involved?"

"Hard to tell. She's had her money on Nick for a long time. If Oden cut a deal with him, it'll turn out she was right. Indirectly."

I took a deep breath. I was tired. I was thinking I wanted to call Lauren. I asked, "See any way this is going to help Merideth find Lisa? Or Wallace feel any better about how his daughter is doing?"

"My philosophy is this," he said. He finished his beer with a flourish, standing the bottle straight up above his tongue to catch the final drops. For a moment, I thought I was going to have to guess how finishing a beer amounted to a philosophy. My brain, I knew, wasn't up to the task. Sam bailed me out with a more easily digestible explanation. "You solve the big puzzle, the little ones tend to fall into place. Nicely."

"You're still working on the big puzzle?"

"I am." He pointed the beer label my way. "My first Japanese beer, ever. I like it."

"You don't eat sushi."

"So?"

"That's when most Americans drink Japanese beer. At sushi bars."

"Is that a dig?"

"Just saying," I said. "I could take you to one."

"No, thanks. I think I'll just pick up a six-pack of these"—he displayed the empty—"at Liquor Mart."

"It's from Canada," I said. "It's not really from Japan."

He sighed a you-can't-trust-anyone sigh. "One other bit of news from Ranger Ramona—Jaana's girlfriend from Estonia, the one that Nick said was going to go with her when she had that abortion?"

"Yeah?" Sam was finally about to tell me what he'd been tantalizing me with earlier.

"Her info is in the original file—she was Jaana's emergency contact for work. After I asked about her, Ramona ran her. The girl went missing six, seven months after Jaana did. Circumstances were kind of like Lisa. Clothes gone. Suitcases gone. Her friends were clueless, her boss had no idea."

He had my attention. "She didn't go back to Estonia?"

"State Department said no. Passport wasn't used, at least not in the old U.S. of A. Lease on her place was almost up when she left. Local cops decided she left on her own."

"Where was she living?"

"Bullhead City? Is that right? Near Laughlin. She'd been dealing blackjack at one of the casinos. Maybe I should go to Laughlin. Bet they have five-buck blackjack tables there."

"You think this is all one puzzle?"

Sam stood up. "I do. I told Ramona about Jack falling off the radar yesterday. She agrees there's way too much disappearing going on for coincidence. We figure out any one of the puzzles, we'll get all the others." He paused. "Time, I think, is the kicker. You going to drink that beer?"

"Enjoy." I handed the almost-full bottle to him. "You like L.A., Sam? Seriously."

He drank a third of the beer before he responded. "You know, I do. I don't like what that might say about me, but I do like L.A. Against all odds, the place just . . . kind of works."

"Me too," I said. "I like the sun. I like the people. I like that the Pacific is right there. I like the . . . optimism. Think the traffic would make me psychotic."

"Maybe," Sam mused, "I'll sell my North Boulder house and buy—I don't know—I might be able to afford a four-hundred-square-foot studio above somebody's garage in Venice. I could be out in the sun every day. Live close to the ocean. Walk everywhere. Learn to surf. Lift some weights. Play beach volleyball. Get a good attitude."

"Cute," I said.

Sam took a step toward the door. "I'm on my way to defile Merideth's fancy shower. Then I'm going to fall asleep in her poofy bed. Got me a feeling I'm going to solve me a puzzle tomorrow. Earn my bonus."

"Merideth's paying you a bonus?"

"She is."

I said, "I'm not as confident about all this as you are. It's morning in Holland. I think I'll call Lauren. Then I'll try to get some sleep too."

* * *

I waited for noises that indicated that Sam had figured out Merideth's shower before I phoned Europe. I got Lauren's voice mail. I told her I loved her and that I would try again later.

I spread out some of the linens from earlier in the evening and sacked out on Merideth's sofa. I expected to find sleep elusive. Just after midnight my ex-wife proved me wrong.

When my cell rang I was sound asleep.

Forty-six

His Ex

Eric and I kept two club chairs in front of the only window in our apartment that had a partial view of the park. My butt was on one of the chairs. My feet were on the windowsill.

My mobile came alive.

I thought Eric was calling from wherever he was. Portland? Sacramento? He would know that I might still be up that late. No one else would guess. Okay, maybe some of my girlfriends would know what I was going through.

It wasn't Eric, or my girlfriends. It was Stevie.

"I'm so sorry," she said. "Are you up? This is Stevie." She didn't wait for me to reply. "I haven't been . . . kind . . . to you about all this. And I'm so sorry."

I tried to imagine what Alan would say right then. For many years I had used him as an internalized model for how to act with compassion, especially at those moments when I wasn't feeling much compassion. I ended up channeling that side of him more frequently than I would like to admit.

The Bitch was of no help; she was no better at compassion than I was. And she wasn't her sharpest in the wee hours anyway.

I lifted the Alan halo into place. I used a soft voice with Stevie. A nonconfrontational voice. Yes, an Alan voice. "What's going on, Stevie?"

Nice, the Bitch whispered.

Stevie was in determined mea-culpa mode. "I want you to know I'm sorry. Okay?"

"Thank you, I appreciate it. That was a stressful night for both of us." I rewinded and went back to the start. "What's going on?"

Stevie said, "I may have heard from Lisa."

Holy effing—I inhaled so that I could scream in relief that Lisa was alive. And if she was alive, that my baby was alive too. But I stifled the scream as I spotted the caution clouding Stevie's words. She'd said "may."

I had questions for her. *Where? When? With whom? Why? Why did she run away?* I locked them up. I blurted, "She's okay? The baby is—"

"I got an e-mail. It must be her. I don't know who else could have sent it."

"Go on," I said without inflection. I wanted to hear what else. I dreaded hearing what else.

"It was just an e-mail. That's all. The e-mail says that Eric might have killed that girl. I'm guessing that's why Lisa ran, why she can't let him have the baby."

"The baby." My baby. My baby must be okay.

I mouthed *Thank you* to the sky. If Eric's God heard me, so be it. I said, "The e-mail is from Lisa?"

"That's what's confusing. I don't recognize the address. It's not Lisa's e-mail address."

Can't . . . have the baby? What? Wait. *Eric might have killed that girl?*

What?

I paused to allow Stevie to say more. Maybe two seconds, that's all. Alan would have allowed the silence to last much longer. I couldn't do it. "That's it?" I asked. The impatience in my voice was, by then, undisguised. My Alan-esque calm had deserted me. I could wear the halo for a while. But not indefinitely. I waited for the Bitch to chime in. Even wanted her to. She had nothing.

"Do you know what girl they're talking about, Merideth? I don't know about any dead girl."

Stevie didn't know about Jaana. "Lisa never talked to you about the Grand Canyon?" I said.

"The Grand Canyon?" She repeated my words with hushed amazement, as though I were about to tell her details of her sister's secret sojourn in the Foreign Service in Katmandu. "We aren't close," Stevie said. She delivered the concluding line as a seamless combination of accusation and apology.

I could see myself in a similar situation offering the same confusing contraction to someone else. Stevie and I had some things in common. I made a mental note to tell my shrink what I'd just realized.

"The girl Lisa is talking about, her name is Jaana Peet. I don't think anyone knows if she's dead," I said. "Jaana . . . disappeared on a camping trip in the Grand Canyon a few years ago. Lisa and Eric were both there—in Arizona—when it happened. That's how Eric knows your sister. From that trip."

Stevie digested the new information. "And now Lisa thinks your fiancé . . . what, killed her?"

Eric? Not a chance. It's that simple, I thought. *Not a chance. I know the man.*

"I haven't seen the e-mail. I've seen the news reports from back then. They all describe her as . . . missing. There was never any evidence that she was dead. Fear, sure. Presumption, yes. But that was all."

"There's an attachment of some kind with Lisa's e-mail. I can't open it on my laptop—I have all this anti-virus, anti-spyware, anti-everything protection on it. I can't open half the stuff that's sent to me anymore. I think it's a video file—only because Media Player is trying to open it. My husband's asleep. He'll be able to get it going for me in the morning."

"Please send it to me," I said. "I can open it."

"Now?"

"Now." I dictated my e-mail address. "I'll take a look at it and call you in the morning. Okay? You can get some sleep."

Stevie forwarded the e-mail. The note was written from a gibberish Gmail account. Could've been Lisa's. Could've been anybody's.

Before I opened the attachment, I forwarded a copy of the e-mail to my IT guy at work, along with a note, asking him—okay, telling him—to track the message's electronic origins as well as he could. I didn't expect much—the Gmail account was probably defunct already—but in my business a dead end wasn't a dead end until a few days after you got to the part with no place to go. I would press until I got there.

I was able to open the attached video file on my laptop without a problem.

The first time I played the video on my Mac, I learned little. The clip was twenty-two seconds long, taken in the dark by an amateur with bad equipment. Grainy as a piece of cheap oak. I thought the clip had been shot outside, but the resolution was so poor I couldn't be certain.

There was audio on the clip too. The background noise was loud, a rustling sound almost crushing out all other sounds. Almost.

I could hear voices.

Six seconds in: "Is that? Who is that?" Voice one, hushed, female.

Eight seconds in: indecipherable. Voice two, female.

Nine seconds in: "Oh, no. No. No," From farther away. Voice three, male.

Eleven seconds in: indecipherable. Voice two again? Or a new voice? I wasn't sure. Female.

Fourteen seconds in: "Please, please, please. Oh . . . please. You—" A new voice, or the same one as at eleven seconds. Distant. Female. Maybe. Intense.

Twenty-one seconds in: "Shhhh." Voice four. Gender? I couldn't say.

* * *

I called one of the video guys on my staff. My ace editor. I woke him up, which surprised me. I'd pegged Dru as a man who saw the light of dawn more often on the back end of a night than on the front end of a morning.

He wasn't happy I woke him. I didn't care. Dru knew I didn't care. We had a good relationship. He didn't pretend with me. I didn't pretend with him.

"I need to lighten up a video clip on my Mac," I said. "It's dark. How do I do it?"

Dru—his full name was Druid Lebeq—was a cornrowed thirty-something man who finessed video signals the same miraculous way Stevie Wonder juggled melodies. Dru was the brightest gem on my fine production team. I say that even though he was late for work as often as he was on time, and even though he took more suspicious sick days than the rest of my staff combined.

I cut him slack for his indiscretions at work. If the latitude I granted wasn't sufficient to cover his ass, he knew I would cut him more. He could get away with twice as much shit as he actually did and still not get fired. He knew that, too. I actually granted him bonus points for not taking advantage of me.

Alan had once explained to me about the concept of idiosyncrasy credits—the fact that certain individuals in systems are so valuable that they aren't required to adhere to the same norms as everyone else.

If idiosyncrasy credits were real money, Dru would live sixty floors above Columbus Circle and drive a Bentley coupe to work.

Suffice it to say that waking Dru to clean up this crappy twenty-two-second clip was like calling Thomas Keller at five a.m. to make a peanut-butter-and-jelly sandwich for your kid's school lunch.

" 'Chu got?" Dru asked.

He kept all the annoyance out of his voice. I noted the effort and doled out more idiosyncrasy drachmas.

"Low res, probably night, probably outside, amateur, available light. YouTube-ish at its worst."

Pause. "Now?"

He was somehow able to ask the question with no you-got-to-be-kidding frosting. I was impressed. More bonus points.

"Dru," I said, "would I call you now if I needed it tomorrow?"

I'd bumped into him once in the corridor at work when my head was turned. It felt like I'd walked into a walnut tree. I bounced off of him. The man was grounded in every possible good sense of the word. I didn't know if he was gay or straight. Attached or single. I didn't want to know. Dru's significant other could be the source of some considerable relationship envy for me.

" 'Bout you jus' send it t'me?" he said. The next sound in my ear told me he was fighting either a sigh or a yawn. "Jus' . . . do it my-self."

He made "myself" into two words, the accent hard on the first. I asked, "How long?"

" 'Bout a tent' of the time it'll take if I try to s'plain t'you how t'do it. No 'fense, Boss."

I said, "None taken. It's on the way."

Nobody else called me Boss. No one else had figured out that I liked it.

I'd been avoiding alcohol since Lisa's in-vitro because I wanted to feel at least a little pregnant while she was a whole lot pregnant. My vow slipped from my grasp as I waited to hear back from Dru about the clip. I did two shots of Drambuie, back-to-back. I only drank Drambuie when I was alone and upset.

It wasn't party booze for me. I don't think I had ever had a sip of the stuff in a restaurant or a bar. Maybe once in a crappy hotel bar while I was on a trip to Kansas City to produce a piece. I may have resorted to Drambuie after I'd been hit on by two different members of the New York Jets on the same night. The second of the two play-ers had bloodstains on the sleeve of his shirt.

* * *

My in-box dinged after fifteen minutes. I had an e-mail. The subject line read nhncd aud 2. Dru figured I couldn't translate the text-talk. *Ha.* I loved beating expectations.

I opened the *nhncd* file and adjusted the volume to listen to the *nhncd* audio, 2.

I played the clip once. My lips were together when it started. My mouth was wide open at the end.

I played it again. And again.

I pecked out an e-mail to my favorite video doctor. "You're off until one tomorrow, Dru. Sleep in, or whatever. Thx."

Then I started crying.

I fell asleep, I thought, just before two o'clock, the images from the clip frescoed on my dura. My fiancé was getting a—okay, okay, I'll clean it up—my fiancé was being fellated by a long-haired woman only yards from the banks of the Colorado River on the floor of the Grand Canyon.

Lisa, or Jaana? Jaana, or Lisa?

I awoke covered with sweat. The clock beside the bed read 2:42. The same images, of my fiancé getting a blow—sorry—of my fiancé being fellated by a long-haired woman, instantly resumed its Technicolor assault on my consciousness. I didn't need to play Dru's *nhncd* clip any more; I apparently had the damn thing committed to involuntary memory.

My brain had added Stevie's voiceover, too: *"The e-mail says that Eric might have killed that girl."* Eric might have killed that girl.

Jaana. That girl.

Not a chance. But until I knew more, I wasn't about to call Eric to hear his side of the story.

I was having a difficult time deciding which was worse: Eric and my surrogate together or Eric and a dead girl together.

I called Alan.

* * *

Though it was three hours earlier in L.A., Alan didn't sound any happier to hear from me than Dru had been. Unlike Dru, Alan didn't try to hide his displeasure. Unlike Dru, Alan had no desire to accumulate any credits I might be doling out.

After Alan's predictable "It must be late there, Meri"—as though I didn't know that—I said, "Lisa and my baby may be alive. Stevie got an e-mail. It might be from her."

"That's terrific. Do you know where she is?"

"No," I said. "And it's not all terrific. The e-mail says that Eric may have had something to do with . . . what happened to that girl, Alan."

Alan's voice grew soft. "I'm sorry," he said. I could tell he meant it. The man had a good heart. It was one of the things that had attracted me to him.

At the beginning of our relationship he loved to put me first. Why it became such a problem later on, I still don't understand. I didn't surprise Alan with my myopia. My self-focus was there from the beginning. He's the one who changed. Not me.

"Thank you," I said.

"That's it? That he may have been involved? No details?"

"It actually says he may have killed her."

"Jaana was killed?"

"I don't know. It's cryptic. You learn anything at the Olive Garden?"

"We ate at A.O.C. Nothing that will help you with Lisa. Carmel doesn't seem to know much, or isn't eager to share what she knows. I did learn some things later. Lisa had—"

I stopped him. "Alan, have you seen the clip?"

"What clip?" he asked.

"There's a piece of short video from the Grand Canyon. It was attached to the e-mail Stevie sent."

"No," he said. "I don't think so anyway. I got something in my e-mail earlier, but I'm not real good with my phone."

"Check it," I said to him. I knew what was coming next.

"While we're talking?"

Exactly what I expected. Alan is a tech moron. "Do you need help?" I asked.

My ex-husband said, "I do."

Forty-seven

Her Ex

I explained to Merideth that I preferred to call her back on the landline while I tried to figure out if the clip she was talking about was already on my cell.

I also needed to decide whether to tell her that Eric was in L.A., and that he had stopped by the condo. I had hoped to postpone sharing that news until the next morning. I had also hoped that by then I would have learned something helpful.

I phoned her from her condo phone and began to explain my mobile telephone challenges. I would ease into the Eric news later in the call. "I have this brand-new phone. There are some messages and . . . things . . . on it, but I don't know how to open them. Jonas was going to teach me, but . . . he's— Can you . . . walk me through it?"

With the practiced frustration of an ex-wife who was way too familiar with her ex-husband's technological impairments, she asked me what kind of messages. "Texts, or e-mails?" she said.

I told her I didn't know. "I think one's a map to A.O.C."

She asked what kind of phone I had.

I told her the brand. "Do you have the same one?" I asked hopefully.

"Doesn't matter," she said. "Remember 'schema,' Alan? Piaget?

He was a psychologist? Ring a bell? This is all schema." She asked two simple questions about the configuration of buttons on my phone. I was able to answer one of them. At my failure regarding the second one, she said, "Never mind."

It took her about ten seconds to explain the process of opening the attachments to me. I felt stupid when I hit the final button and a video file began to load.

"Got it," I said.

"It's going to be dark," she said. "The clip."

"I think I can handle it," I said.

"Not that kind of dark," she muttered, almost under her breath. Almost. Merideth was careful with knives. When she didn't wish to draw blood, she didn't draw blood. With me, however, she always seemed to make sure the tip of the blade scraped some flesh so that I would be reminded how good she was with the weapon.

The clip started playing. I was watching a short film of Jonas boogie-boarding at the Atlantic shore. I could spot his smile from three thousand miles.

I said, "That was from Jonas. He's at the shore with his cousins. He's boogie-boarding."

"That's it?" Merideth asked.

"There're more attachments. Hold on." I pecked at the phone. I got the map to A.O.C. "Wait, there's another one."

I repeated the steps with the final attachment. A second video started to load, then began to play. Twenty-two seconds later—my cell did the timing, I didn't—I said, "I'm not sure what I just saw. It was dark. Some movement. Some voices, maybe. There's lots of noise on the audio. Crackles. White noise."

"Was it clear enough that you could make any of it out?"

"No. I'll play it again, but I don't think it will help. It's very dark."

"Told you."

"What is it, Merideth?"

"I don't want to put any ideas in your head. I want you to see it yourself. Do you have a computer with you? I'll send an enhanced version. My video guy cleaned it up."

"I don't have a laptop with me." I didn't tell her I didn't own a laptop. "You'll have to send the enhanced version to my phone."

I couldn't believe I just said that.

"Okay." I heard her typing. She said, "Who sent you the clip first? The dark version you just saw?"

"Don't know." My suspicion was that Mel had sent it, only because I couldn't imagine any else doing it. "Just a second. It's from a . . . Yahoo account—I don't recognize the name. Oh . . . there's a YouTube link too. In the subject line. Lot of numbers."

As the words left my mouth, I recalled the doodles on the cover of the bound book of Sudoku puzzles in Lisa's limited-stay apartment in Morningside Heights.

One of the scribbles had been YOUTUBE.

"Really? What's the YouTube link? Never mind, just forward the clip you have to me," Merideth said. "I can capture the link that way."

I hesitated while I stared at my phone. Forwarding wasn't an intuitive process. While I tried to apply the schema schema, Merideth recognized my digital dyslexia. With surprising patience, she walked me through the simple process of forwarding the clip to her so she could capture the YouTube URL.

I waited to receive the enhanced version of the clip from her while she waited to receive the YouTube address from me. She won. I wasn't surprised. I was operating with a pretty high handicap.

After about thirty seconds she said, "Okay, I have the YouTube version on my Mac. It's playing now. It's not enhanced. But the effing thing is really posted on effing YouTube. Forty-seven views so far. It's been up for, let's see . . . almost a month."

"I'm not . . . YouTube conversant, Meri. Could you translate?"

"Somebody uploaded—you know what that means, yes?—the clip to YouTube about a month ago. It's called 'Grand Canyon Floor:

HEAD and shoulders, KNEES and toes.' 'Head' and 'knees' are in caps. Cute. It's been viewed forty-seven different times. Forty-seven views is nothing in YouTube land. Nothing. There're only a couple of viewer ratings. They suck. Given the quality, that's not too surprising. There are three comments . . . not kind. One complains about the resolution and the light. A couple more ask what it's supposed to be."

"Who posted it? Is there a name?"

"The user name is 'g-g-i-f-t-t-m.' " Lowercase, all one word. I'll get one of my people on it, see if we can find the originating ISP or maybe even track down a locator for the machine that uploaded the file. That might lead us to Lisa."

I wasn't sure what any of that meant, but I could guess. Merideth was looking for electronic evidence of the original source of the clip.

"We can talk in the morning after your people do their checking," I said.

"It's not just this one, Alan. There is a series on YouTube from the same user name. A lot."

"Can you play them?" I asked.

She grew quiet. I stayed quiet.

"This will take some time," she said finally.

My mobile phone was in my lap. It buzzed. I read the screen. Amy.

Merideth said, "It's—"

"Hold on, Meri. Just a second." I covered the microphone on the landline, and flipped open my cell. "Hi," I said to Amy.

"We need your help. Did you go to the house? Do you know what happened?"

"I went. I couldn't find you. I heard some things, but I don't know if—"

"We're with Kanyn. They said she'd tried to . . . hurt herself. They took her to the hospital for evaluation. Then they released her from the ER. Just like that. She told them what happened at the house was an accident and they let her out, Alan. We asked them to keep her overnight. They wouldn't. We don't think she's in great shape."

I recalled my earlier discussion with Amy about Kanyn's apparent mood disorder. "Has she tried to hurt herself before tonight?" I asked.

"Sure. Yes. A few times. Not serious. Mel said to tell you she's a cutter."

Shit. Cutting could mean a few different things that ranged from concerning to awful. Added to the dysthymia and trichotillomania, though, it was an alarming sign. From my view as a psychologist the only reliable data for predicting future behavior is past behavior. A history of recent suicidal ideation plus a legacy of previous self-mutilating acts equals nothing but trouble.

"The ER discharged her?"

"They thought she'd be okay with me and Mel. That's what they said."

I said, "I assume she doesn't have insurance."

"Of course not."

The bar for inpatient admission for mental health problems—especially for patients without insurance—had risen higher and higher during the years I'd been in practice. The bar had become so high that friends and family members were often required to do a terrifying job—suicide watch—that should only ever be handled by clinical professionals in controlled settings.

"Where are you right now?" I asked.

"Mel's car, on the 101. We're going to Tarzana. We can't go home. The fire department says it's not safe. With the gas thing."

"Is Kanyn . . . stable right now?"

"Yes, that's right, she's with us in the car. I think she just woke up."

"You're telling me that you can't talk freely in front of her?"

"That's probably right."

"But you're worried she might be a danger to herself?"

"That's a good description. Not too much traffic."

"Does Kanyn have family close by? Anyone you can call?"

"Chicago. We talked to her dad. Didn't go well. They don't get along."

I heard another voice through the phone.

Amy said, "That was Mel. She thinks it would be great for you to come to Tarzana. We could really use your help, Alan."

My phone buzzed in my hand. I looked at the screen. OUT OF AREA. *Lauren*, I thought. I considered trying to use call waiting. I rejected the option immediately. I knew I couldn't juggle three phone calls. Reluctantly, I let Lauren slide to voice mail.

"Now?" I said to Amy. I knew the answer.

Amy said, "I'll send you a map to the house, okay? In Tarzana. To your phone."

"Why don't you just give me an address? I do better with GPS. I'll find it. Can you hold a second?" I switched phones. "Merideth?"

"Where have you been?"

"I have an emergency here. I need to go."

"I have one here, Alan."

I could hear the offense in her voice. "This may be part of yours. Can we continue this in the morning? Then you can tell me what's on those clips. What your people were able to learn . . . about that stuff they're checking for you."

I didn't wait for her to begin her counterargument. I hung up the landline and grabbed a pen. "I'm ready for that address," I said to Amy.

She gave me the address in Tarzana and added some details.

I said, "I'll be there as soon as I can."

I closed my cell.

I hadn't told Merideth about Eric.

I retrieved Lauren's voice mail. It was sweet and warm. She was hopeful she would meet her daughter soon. She said she was almost ready to come home.

* * *

I sat in the empty room, trying to find some energy. If I were in Ottavia's apartment, I would have strolled to Times Square for an infusion. I wondered if there was an L.A. counterpart. If there was such a place, I didn't know it.

I played the enhanced version of the clip on my phone. *Oh God,* I thought. *Oh God.* I had to guess who was who.

The building creaked. I held my breath. *Earthquake.*

The sound repeated itself.

I exhaled in a little laugh. It turned out that Sam snored. Loudly. I hadn't known that.

I scribbled out a note so he would know what I was up to and left it on the counter.

Forty-eight

Traffic cooperated. Chloe knew the way to Tarzana. She was so confident in her directions that I began adding some backstory to her bio: She had a brother who was living in Tarzana. He'd lost a leg to an IED north of Baghdad. She visited him all the time. He suffered from PTSD, but he was doing the best he could.

My final turn was from Ventura Boulevard to Topeka Drive.

Without Chloe's help, my unfinished adolescent business might have drawn me to the other side of the Valley, and left me prowling the dark lanes of Hidden Hills for the first Amy, the one on the white horse.

The Tarzana landmarks were pedestrian. I was disappointed. I'd expected some Edgar Rice Burroughs influence in the burg's street names. Cheetah Lane. Jane Way. Or better still, Jane Lane. Instead I was going to end up on a street—Topeka Drive—apparently honoring the capital of Kansas, an appellation that would have been acceptable for a town commemorating L. Frank Baum for *The Wizard of Oz*, but not for recognizing the Edgar Rice Burroughs for *Tarzan of the Apes*.

Tarzana, I thought, deserved better.

My short drive down Topeka Drive started beside a large LDS center—I guessed it was a stake; it looked too big to be a ward, but a tad too modest to be a temple. Just beyond the Mormon edifice, the neighborhood transitioned into a lush residential lane lined with houses that were large enough to garrison troops if we were planning to invade Mexico. Amy had warned me on the phone that the street address I was looking for was set far back from the road, was unmarked, and that it was difficult to spot the driveway if you didn't know where to look. She instructed me to park my car on a wide part of the shoulder not too far past the building on the corner and then call her on her cell. She would find me and lead me in.

Although it was out of character, I did what I was told. Must have been Chloe's influence.

The tree canopy on Topeka Drive was lush, and the landscaping near where I parked the Camry was more thicket than manicure. The houses sat on big lots and were set back from the road. The façades mostly disappeared behind greenery.

Moments after I called, Amy appeared out of nowhere. Mel was with her. I wondered whom that left inside with Kanyn.

Both girls looked as tired as I felt. "Long night," I said. I knew from experience what it was like to be in the immediate vicinity of someone whose suicidal risk was high. Minutes passed slowly, like time spent waiting for an ambulance. Once fatigue set in, the only thing that kept the caretakers awake was terror about what might happen if they slept.

Mel waved, stuffed her hands into the pockets of her shorts—they were short indeed—and sighed.

Amy said, "Kanyn's a mess. She sounds paranoid. She said there was someone in the house. She says that she didn't touch the gas line in the wall heater, that he did—whoever it was. I've never seen her paranoid before."

Delusions? I thought. *I'm out of my league.*

Mel wasn't quite as surprised by Kanyn's mental state. Mel's voice was weary with physical fatigue and something more fundamental. She said, "She's been like this before. And there might have been someone in the house. We don't know."

"Is she alone?" I asked, praying the answer was negative.

Amy started to speak, but Mel interrupted. "Jules is with her."

So, I was about to meet Jules. "I'm sorry you guys have to go through this. Is Kanyn awake?"

Mel nodded.

"Did they medicate her?"

"No."

I asked, "She's okay physically?"

Amy said, "Has some burns on her legs. Not serious."

"After I spend some time around her I'll tell you what I think," I said. "But I can't do much. I'm not her therapist. I'm not licensed to practice in California. You understand?"

They both nodded.

I knew they didn't understand. "If she's still a danger to herself, you'll have to take her to another ER. I can tell you what to say when you get there, but that's about it."

"Then what?" Mel asked.

"Pray, if you're so inclined," I said. I stuffed my hands in my pockets. The night air had a little chill. "Let's go do it."

Neither of them moved. Mel said, "I need to tell you something first." Amy moved from the glow of the streetlight into the shadows. If I were on my game, I would have recognized that Amy knew what was coming. But I was so tired that I missed the poignancy of Mel's overture—my pulse didn't register the slightest blip at her words. I said, "Sure, I'm ready."

"This is my . . . boyfriend's house. The one I was at this afternoon when we were supposed to meet?"

I glanced toward Amy. She wasn't looking at me. I said, "Yeah? So?"

Mel's eyes were pointed at my feet. She said, "No one actually lives here. It's a . . . vacant house—the old barn from the Edgar Rice Burroughs ranch." She looked up and—accurately—read confusion in my face. But she mistakenly guessed I was confused about Burroughs and Tarzan and the apparent barn/house continuum problem.

"Burroughs is the guy who wrote the original Tarzan book," she explained. I nodded to let her know I was still with her. I was hoping she would skip to the good part. "His old barn was converted into a house in the forties. The grandparents moved to a nursing home. They held on to the barn hoping, you know . . . Anyway, when they finally died they left it to their grandkids. The kids can't agree what to do with it. One wants to keep it, the others want to sell it. But it's been empty for, like, ever. Since the fifties, maybe. Or sixties. Inside, it's . . . like a museum from back then."

"Okay," I said. I was hearing much more house history than I wanted.

Whatever Mel was saying through her anxiety was lost on me. I forced myself to adopt therapy ears, which meant assuming there was a point to the story. I couldn't find the point. I wasn't processing well.

I said, "No judgments about the house. The barn. Whatever. I promise." I raised my right hand to cement the oath. "It's just a barn to me. Everything else is gravy. Let's go in."

I took a step. Neither of the girls moved to join me. I turned to Mel.

Mel said, "I haven't been honest with you."

Who is? I thought. Then: *Sam. Sam is honest with me.*

I suspected that some more barn/house history was coming from Mel. If that was the direction we were heading, I was hoping for some facts related to the jungle. Without some fascinating Cheetah or Jane anecdotes to prime my neural pump, I knew would have to take some notes if I were going to remember any of this in the morning.

"I wasn't here before. This afternoon. That was a lie. I was with Jules."

"Jules?" I asked.

Mel said, "I'm a lesbian, Alan."

My first thought was, *Well, then what the hell are you doing with a boyfriend in Tarzana?*

It took me a couple of additional moments to recognize that I'd just been granted the gift of a profound revelation. I was too tired to choose the right words. I said, "You've known . . . for a while?"

She grinned. "Yes. A few years."

"Okay," I said as I continued to gather my wits. "So Jules is your . . . girlfriend?"

Mel nodded.

"This is her place?"

"With her brothers. Jules lives in Westwood. The part about her brothers and what to do with the house, that's all true."

I considered saying something quasi-therapeutic and profound, or at least profound-sounding. But I recalled how fine-tuned Mel's radar was for therapy-speak. I said, "I'm looking forward to meeting Jules. Can we go in now?"

She shook her head. She wasn't done with her revelations. Mel said, "My dad doesn't like gay . . . people."

Ah, so that's why I'm here, I thought. *Because Wallace doesn't like gay people.*

The way Mel said that her father didn't like gay people carried all the presumed disappointment—of children about themselves, and of sons and daughters about their parents—that children are able to stuff into simple-sounding but explosive-laden parental appraisals like, "My parents really wanted a son." Or "My dad wanted me to play football."

I said, "I'm sorry to hear that, Mel." I hadn't been aware of Wallace's bias against homosexuals. I got lost for a moment wondering how a therapist in Boulder could be as successful as Wallace with that particular prejudice. I also wondered whether everyone else in town knew. Was I the last?

Is that why Wallace didn't come to Adrienne's service?

"Does he know you're gay?" I asked.

"I don't think so. He'd say something. You know my dad."

The crossword finally began to take form—16 Down was a seven-letter word for "uncomfortable." *Awkward.* "That must make things hard for you. With your family."

"I don't go home much. I don't like him to visit here. It's pretty weird."

"You keep that boyfriend handy in the Valley just in case?"

"I do." She smiled. "For a long time my dad thought I was seeing Jack. Jack's gay, but he can do straight."

I stepped forward into the light of the streetlamp and made my eyes as warm as I could. I didn't want to pretend to Mel that I was in any position to repair whatever damage had already taken place between her and Wallace. "Can we go in now?"

She nodded, but she didn't take a step.

I thought she had been expecting some additional drama from her disclosure. What kind? I didn't know. It had taken a monumental effort for her to tell me she was lesbian. I thought it was important for her to know that for me it wasn't monumental news.

"Dr. A—Adrienne—your friend? The one who was killed? She's the first person I ever told how I was feeling."

"Adrienne was a sweetheart," I said. "Good choice on your part."

She kicked at the dirt. "Are you going to tell him?" she asked.

The wrinkle. "Your father? God no. No more than I would tell him that I came to L.A. and discovered that you're straight. My friends' kids' sex lives don't come up in conversation very often." I thought about it for a moment to make certain that exhaustion wasn't poisoning my appraisal. "Nope, doesn't usually happen."

My babbling hadn't convinced her. She said, "That means no?"

"That means no." I paused until she seemed to notice I was pausing. Then I said, "Would you like me to tell him?"

She inhaled quickly. She said, "Therapist question." Then she laughed.

I laughed, too. She was right—it had been a therapist question.

She said, "I'm not ready."

"Your mom knows?"

"She's cool."

"I'm glad. For you. That Cassandra's cool. That's something."

Mel had been prepared for a reaction from me that was apocalyptic. That was transference. Once she finally accepted the fact that her sexual orientation wasn't monumental news to me—that was reality—she was ready to move on.

She took Amy's hand and led the way to the barn/house.

Forty-nine

The barn was on the downhill edge of what had been the Burroughs Family's grand estate. In the part of the twentieth century before L.A. required suburbs, the ranch must have enjoyed a spectacular vista over the undeveloped valley below.

A narrow asphalt driveway led back thirty or forty yards from the road, opening onto a rectangular lot of more than half an acre. A contemporary house adjacent to the driveway screened the barn from the street. The shell of the barn had not been rebuilt during its transformation to accommodate human occupants. Other than the addition of midcentury windows and doors, the old building was an anachronism. I couldn't decide if the nearby Mormon edifice and the neighboring mini-mansions mocked the barn, or vice versa.

I consciously forced one foot in front of the other as I followed Mel around to the front door, which was down a narrow path on the opposite side of the house from the driveway. The groundcover along the way was ivy and ice plant.

I was aware that my errand had changed. I'd driven to Tarzana to be in a position to help Wallace's daughter deal with her roommate's apparent emotional meltdown. I had just been invited to become a silent partner in a family subterfuge about an adult child's sexual orientation. And I was steps away from engaging with a group of people that Merideth hoped held clues to the location of her missing surrogate and child.

I was at least as wary about becoming part of the Grand Canyon group's reunion as I was about doing an unofficial assessment of Kanyn's emotional condition.

Mostly, I feared I was too drained to adjust my footwork to the complexities of all the fresh choreography.

Amy came up behind me and whispered, "I'm sorry for lying to you about the boyfriend thing. Mel wants us to do that with anyone from . . . back home."

"I understand," I said.

Jules greeted us at the door.

The décor didn't match the rustic architecture of the barn. Jules's grandparents had been a couple with modern tastes. The living room was decorated like the showroom of a cutting-edge contemporary furniture retailer from the late forties.

Kanyn was curled into a ball at one end of a well-preserved mid-century sofa. Her face was turned away from me. I wasn't convinced she was awake. Amy was sitting on the scratched floor, leaning against a wall that separated the living room from the dining room.

Mel seemed to have been energized by her skip, however abbreviated, from the closet, and was in the mood for continued revelations. She took a deep breath before she announced, "I have something to say." Everyone but Kanyn looked at her. "I'm the one who called Lisa in New York," she said. "Jack had told me what she was doing for Eric and . . . his fiancée. He gave me her phone number."

A couple of hours earlier, Mel had led me to believe that my story about Lisa's surrogacy for Eric and Merideth was news to her. It was increasingly apparent to me that the kid did a lot of dissembling.

Mel's pronouncement piqued Amy's interest. She stood, walked across the room, and sat on the sloping arm of the upholstered chair where I was sitting. Almost immediately she slid toward me. I scooted over to give her some space.

With Amy almost in my lap I was officially more uncomfortable than I'd already been—something I hadn't considered possible.

I waited for someone else to ask the obvious question. No one did. I said, "Why? Why did you feel a need to call Lisa?"

Mel seemed to think her answer was obvious. "After I saw the clip that Jack's partner had posted on YouTube, I felt Lisa should know"—Mel flicked a glance at Jules—"exactly whose baby she was carrying. I would want to know."

Jules's face remained serene as her partner revealed her role in the recent events. Mel's story about calling Lisa wasn't news to Jules.

I didn't know Eric's story. Or Lisa's. I didn't even know all of Merideth's. I didn't know what was best for any of them. When I was Mel's age, though, I'd felt some certainty about other people's lives. Looking back, it turned out that I'd been wrong a lot. Someday Mel would discover that she was wrong a lot too.

It had been only hours earlier that Sam was explaining to me that people are complicated, but usually in uncomplicated ways. For even more uncomplicated reasons. Getting to the point where I accepted my ignorance about people and their complications had taken a lot of experience. Mel was still young. She had plenty of time to get there.

"What's on YouTube?" Amy asked.

I was wondering the same thing. I suspected that I was about to hear a version of the story that Merideth was so eager to tell me concerning the dark video I'd seen before I'd been summoned to the Valley.

Mel explained the story of how the video vignette from the Grand Canyon ended up on YouTube. The tale wasn't nefarious. Jack had recently been seeing a guy who was fascinated by an old collection of video clips from what Jack called his "brief, tortured docudrama phase." Jack's romantic partner had thought the world should have a chance to see the archive of nearly a year of his lover's life. He called them "Jack's short films." The guy had uploaded almost twenty clips to YouTube from half a dozen different old SmartDisks he'd discovered in the cabinet in Jack's condo where he kept his DVDs.

The boyfriend had dumped Jack about a week after the uploads.

When Jack saw the clips from the Grand Canyon, he asked Kanyn and Mel to look at them too. Mel had called Lisa.

Before Mel got any further along in her story, we heard crisp footsteps coming from down the hall. The person was not trying to sneak up on us.

Mel flashed a look at Jules. She whispered, "Who else is here?"

Jules shook her head. Her eyes got big.

The footsteps grew louder until Eric appeared at the near end of the hallway that led back toward the bedrooms. The suit jacket was gone. His sleeves were rolled up.

He did a little dance step. "Hello," he said. "Jules, hi." He smiled warmly at her. "Long time. You look great. I like your hair. Sorry about the intrusion. I remembered where you keep the key to the back door."

"You could have knocked," Jules said. She wasn't angry. "I would have let you in."

It was evident there was a whole lot of backstory between Jules and Eric that I didn't know. From the vibe in the room, I suspected that much of what had happened in the past was good.

Eric said, "I'm looking for Lisa. If she's here, I didn't want to give her time to hide. I want to know where my baby is. I want to know that Lisa is okay. That's it." His demeanor impressed me. His voice was level. He'd bullied Amy and Mel earlier. He'd just broken into Jules's house. He had to be aware that among this group he was the designated bad guy. All in all, the man was playing well to a hostile crowd.

Mel said, "I don't know where Lisa is, Eric. But I bet Jack knows. Help us find Jack, then maybe you'll find Lisa."

"I wish I knew where he was," Eric said. "I'm as worried about Jack as you are."

Mel rolled her eyes.

Jules said, "How do you know what's going on with Jack, Eric? Are you in touch with him?"

"No," he said. "I'm not."

Mel hooked a thumb to point at Kanyn and raised her eyebrows. Mel's message was clear—she was wondering if Kanyn had told Eric that Jack was missing. Kanyn didn't budge.

Has Kanyn been in touch with Eric? I didn't know where to slot that data.

"You mind if I take a quick look around, Jules?"

"Knock yourself out," she said. "Nothing's changed since the last time you were here. Oh—the toilet doesn't work upstairs. Don't know what's up with that."

Eric said, "You're gay, Jules. That's a change."

Eric had been hoping for a retort, but Jules's expression remained serene. He shrugged before he began to climb the stairs, two at a time. We heard the footfall of every step he took on the second floor. In less than a minute, he came back down to the living room. He pulled a chrome-and-vinyl kitchen chair away from the dinette set and spun it around. He straddled the chair, facing us.

"I just came from your place in Mt. Washington, Carmel. Cops said someone had been hurt. I thought it might be Lisa. I went to the hospital. Wild goose chase."

"You thought Lisa was staying with us?" Mel said.

I was still waiting to see some emotion from Jules. Earlier, when she had greeted me graciously at the front door, she'd demonstrated a self-possessed quality and tranquility that I'd found soothing. I wondered if the presence of her old male lover, Eric, and her current female lover, Mel, in the same room was causing her to withdraw.

I said, "Would someone please tell me what is going on with Jack? Why everyone is so worried about him?"

Eric turned to me. In a slightly affected tone, he said, "Dr. Gregory. You get around, don't you? You hang with my fiancée in New York. Make yourself at home at our condo. And now you're slumming with my old friends in the Valley."

Mel said, "I invited him. Do you have a problem with that?"

It was clear that Mel had a chip on her shoulder about something with Eric. Was it merely the fact that he was her girlfriend's old boy-friend? I didn't know.

She turned to me. "Jack was coming up here from San Diego," Mel said. "Was that just last night? He wanted us to talk this out, as a group. The clip. Jaana. Lisa. The bad feelings. He wanted to clear the air. That's Jack." Mel looked around the room. "I think he's the only one of us Lisa's been in touch with. After he found out she left New York, he felt he had to do something to settle all this. He thought he might have come up with something that might convince her to . . . come out of hiding. Some solution. That's why he was coming to L.A."

I recalled that Sam had said that Nick Paulson had spoken with Jack sometime during the past few days. I wondered if that's when Jack had learned the something that might convince Lisa to come out of hiding. But I still didn't understand what had happened to Jack. I said, "What exactly happened? Jack didn't show up for a meeting? Is that it?"

Mel said, "There wasn't a set time for him to come. He called or texted Kanyn from the road—he was someplace near San Juan Cap-istrano, on his way to meet with Lisa. After he saw her he was going to come here, to Tarzana. That's the last anybody's heard. He stopped answering his phone. Hasn't called any of us. Isn't respond-ing to texts."

"The meeting with Lisa was going to be where?" I asked.

Mel said, "Lisa didn't want him to say. L.A. someplace."

Eric said, "Lisa is in L.A., then?"

I waited to see if anyone would respond. No one did. I suspected that Jack had not told his friends that he'd been in touch with Nick Paulson. I wondered what that meant, and I wondered whether Jack had discovered something that someone in the group might not want him to know.

"Does anyone know if Jack ever met with Lisa?" I asked.

No one knew. Or at least no one was saying.

"When was the call or text to Kanyn? What time?" I asked.

Mel looked at her wrist, seemed surprised to discover that she wasn't wearing a watch. "Last night. Two nights ago." She shook her head. "Day before yesterday. God, I need some sleep."

I understood completely. I said, "So . . . about thirty-six hours ago?"

"Less," Mel said.

"That's not much time to be out of touch," I said. I'd had a version of this conversation with Merideth about Lisa's disappearance. I reminded myself how wrong I'd turned out to be about that. "Jack could still be with Lisa, right?"

Mel wasn't buying it. "That's not like him. He would have been in touch."

Jules said, "You don't know that. She may have told him not to call anyone. She can be pretty . . . controlling."

Eric's said, "You should know about that, Jules."

She fluttered her eyes at him like an ingénue.

There was a little murder in the air, after all.

"I haven't seen this clip you're all talking about," Eric said. "What's so special?"

If Eric was bluffing about the video—either lying about not having seen it or pretending there couldn't possibly be anything damning involving him in it—I didn't want to play poker with him. The man could act.

In a hell-I'll-call-your-bluff tone, Mel said, "Jules? You have your computer? Is there a network here?"

Jules sighed. She said, "It's in my bag. The neighbor kid's network isn't secure. You can log onto it."

Mel looked at Eric. "I'll show you what Jack took." She retrieved Jules's laptop, booted it up. In a couple of minutes we were staring at YouTube.

Mel searched for "grand canyon floor" and selected the "HEAD and shoulders" clip from the choices that popped up. It was the same clip that Merideth had sent to my phone hours before.

Eric leaned forward as the clip began to load. He read the name of the person who had posted it. He said, "Who is ggifttm?" He pronounced it *"g-gift-t-m."* "Anyone know?"

"God's gift to men. Jack's old boyfriend, Reginald." Mel said.

Jules said, "Before you play that—before everybody sees it—I want to know what everyone thinks happened to Jaana. Mel?"

Mel said, "I thought she was lost in the Canyon. Now I think she ended up in the river."

"You think she's dead?" Jules asked.

"Yes."

"Eric?"

"After we left the canyon I didn't follow the story. I don't know."

Jules didn't ask Kanyn her opinion. Lisa wasn't around. Neither was Jack. I said, "Jules? What about you? You have a theory?"

"I think somebody . . . hurt her. I thought it that morning. I still think it."

Mel started the clip. It was the dark version.

Five seconds in, Eric said, "I don't get it. What is this supposed to be?"

"Wait," Mel said.

At nine seconds, a male voice—Eric's?—said, "Oh no. No. No."

Mel paused the clip. She said, "Remember now? Ring any bells?"

Eric said, "Who is that?"

Mel restarted the video.

I didn't know if Eric wasn't recognizing himself, or if he wasn't recognizing the animated Rorschach that, to me, was a woman on her knees in front of him. A woman whose head was moving fore and aft.

"Please, please, please. Oh, please," cried the female voice.

Mel said, "Does that help?"

Eric didn't speak. He scooted to the front of his chair to get closer to the screen. "Shhh," he said to the room.

Seconds later the clip ended with another male voice saying, "Shush." It wasn't Eric's voice.

"That was Jack," Kanyn said. "At the end. That was Jack's 'shush.'"

Well, hello Kanyn.

Amy said, "Hey, babe. How you doing?" She moved to Kanyn's side.

"I'm okay," Kanyn said.

She scanned the room. She skipped over Eric. When her eyes got to me she seemed stumped.

I said, "I'm Alan. We met tonight at the restaurant. You were kind enough to find us a table. Thank you."

She nodded. I noted that her left hand was hooked in the waistband of her shorts. Four fingers in, her thumb out. Kanyn was fighting an urge—maybe an intense urge—to track down an errant pubic hair, give it a good tug, and pluck it. *You can pick your friends, but you can't pick your . . .* I was curious to see how long she could postpone the craving. I expected that at the point her anxiety became intolerable to her, she would excuse herself to the bathroom.

Eric said, "Jack took that? On that damn camera of his?"

Jules said, "It took video clips."

"Not very well," Eric said.

Eric either didn't understand what he had just seen, or he did understand and was unconcerned about the fact that it was public. I had trouble imagining the second option could be true.

Mel said, "That's you, Eric. Jules and I were with Jack when he took it. You were off the trail. Almost down to the river. Near the boat beach. Hiding."

Jules said, "Eric? Do you still maintain you didn't see Jaana that night?"

I thought her tone was tender. I found the tenderness surprising.

"What? That clip doesn't show anything," he said. "It's just darkness. Voices. I'm not even sure who's in it."

I was disappointed. I was hoping for some progress. And then some sleep. I was hoping for some sleep even if there wasn't any progress.

"I wasn't hiding. It doesn't matter if I saw her that evening," Eric said.

He looked around the room, searching faces. He skipped over Kanyn.

Why won't they look at each other?

"Why did you lie?" Jules asked. "To all of us? To the shirtless guy that morning? About not seeing her?"

Eric said, "Apparently Jack saw her. Why did Jack lie? Apparently you saw her, Jules. And you too, Mel. Why did you lie?"

Mel said, "Jules lied because I asked her to. Jaana had seen us . . . knew we were . . . I wasn't ready for anyone to know . . . then."

Jules said, "I wasn't ready either, Eric. I was confused."

Eric wasn't buying. He said, "So you threw Jaana in the river to shut her up?"

I hoped he intended it as a joke.

Eric hadn't answered Jules's question about why he had lied. With a that's-all-you-got tone, he said, "Is that it?" He asked Mel, "Any more videos to show me?"

He wanted to see all the evidence they had against him.

Before Mel answered, I said, "I have a better version of the first one. It's on my phone. The video and audio are . . . much clearer. I think I can forward it to Jules's computer." I held up my phone.

I thought I sounded like a techie. My wives, ex and current, would laugh. Jonas would be proud of me.

Jules tightened her jaw before she recited her e-mail address.

I acted like I knew what I was doing while I tried to recall the details of Merideth's recent mobile-phone tutorial. I was pretty impressed with myself when I hit Send and the phone appeared to spring into action.

Half a minute later, Jules's laptop pinged. She leaned forward and opened the file. A media player popped open. "Excuse me," she said. She stood and moved away from the computer. "Anyone need anything? I have . . . let's see . . . water. Would anyone like some water? If I'd known we were having a party . . ."

Eric said, "Alan, how did you get this?"

I didn't want to tell him that his fiancée had sent it to me. I thought that Merideth should be the one to reveal her role to him. But I didn't want to lie. I said, "I don't know who sent it originally." That was a fact, even though it wasn't the truth. I was still thinking the first version I had received had been from Mel.

Jules stood in the doorway to the kitchen while we watched the enhanced version of the twenty-two second clip. As the seconds passed, doubt vanished.

The man was Eric. Clearly. I ached on Merideth's behalf as soon as I recognized him.

I didn't know who the woman was until Jules said, "Well, that's not Lisa." Her voice carried the spice of something. Surprise? Relief? Both?

"Lisa?" Eric sighed. "You thought Lisa and I were— Jules? Come on. Lisa?"

Mel said, "That's Jaana, Eric. You were with her. She was—"

Eric stopped her. "Enough. You don't know anything, Mel. Don't embarrass yourself."

At the conclusion of the video, Eric put his elbows on top of the chair and locked his fingers behind his neck. In turn he looked hard at each of the women he'd been with on that camping trip in Arizona. He looked at Mel. He finally looked at Kanyn.

Jules continued to stand in the kitchen doorway. He looked at her last. His eyes lingered.

He said, "Did you know you were . . . gay? Back then?"

Her expression remained tender. "Before I met Mel? No," she

said. "If I'd wanted to know, I might have known. But I wasn't ready to know. I was still fighting it. I was in love with you, Eric." Her smile was bittersweet. "I was."

Mel said, "I knew." Whether she was claiming to have known that she was gay or claiming to have known that Jules was gay, I couldn't tell. Either revelation could have waited. The delicate poignancy of Jules's moment with Eric was fractured. That was probably Mel's intent.

Eric held his eyes on Jules. He pointed at the laptop. "You think that's Jaana giving me head? Do you really think that?"

Was he defensive? Or offended? I wasn't sure.

Jules was a litigator. She smelled a trap. "The first time I saw that clip a couple of weeks ago? I didn't know who the woman was, but that's something I was considering. Tonight? It is what it is, Eric. That's not Lisa. You lied to us about Jaana. It was a long time ago."

Good answer, I thought.

Mel didn't have Jules's gift for nuance, or for forgiveness. She was still young in so many ways. She said, "That's what I think it is, Eric. It's Jaana giving you a—"

"Kanyn?" Eric said. "What do you think? Tell everyone what you think."

Eric's tone had changed. He was challenging Kanyn. I was curious.

Kanyn's face remained buried in Amy's bosom. Amy was caressing her friend's back, touching her hair.

"Kanyn?" Eric said again, still challenging her.

"She's had a tough day," Amy said. "Maybe it's not the best time to—"

"Kanyn?" Eric said one more time.

The room went quiet. Thirty seconds stretched into a minute.

Kanyn lifted her head. She sat straight, pulled her knees to her chest and wrapped her arms around her legs. Tears were running down her face, but her crying wasn't audible.

"It's not sex," she said. "On the video. Jaana's not . . ." She shook her head. "That's not sex."

Kanyn looked at the ceiling for a couple of seconds before she lowered her gaze to the floor. She said, "I told Jaana to go see Eric. I pointed him out to her. . . around sundown. She'd asked me for help. She was afraid . . . The guy she was with . . . He threatened to . . . The guy—the shirtless guy—was going to turn her in to Immigration if . . . She didn't know what to do." Kanyn glanced at Jules. "I thought it was a legal problem of some kind. I told her Eric was a lawyer—that he'd know what she should do. I told her to talk to Eric. That's what's on the video. Her talking to Eric."

Mel said, "That's talking? She shouldn't talk with her mouth full."

Kanyn ignored Mel. She looked at Eric. She said, "You always—always—seemed to know what to do, Eric. Jaana didn't want to go back to . . . her family. Where she lived, where she was from. She said she . . . couldn't. She'd been . . . abused when she was younger. By her family. If she told you that, I was sure"—she swiped at her streaming tears with her fingers—"you would help her."

Mel queued up the clip again. Started it. I'm sure she was trying to make a point. The point eluded me.

"Did she tell you, Eric? About Estonia? Her family?" Kanyn asked when the clip was done. "What they did to her?"

Eric's eyes turned moist. "She was begging for my help," Eric said. His voice was a hair above a whisper. "At the end, anyway—that's what you all just saw. At the end she went down on her knees. . . . She was begging for my help."

The room grew silent to accommodate his lowered voice. Everyone had been expecting the worst. They just hadn't been sufficiently imaginative about guessing what the worst might be.

Eric went on. "I told her I couldn't help. I had a new job starting in a few days. I offered to get her the name of someone in Las Vegas who did immigration law. That's when she started begging."

Jules lifted her fingers in front of her mouth. She started to cry quietly.

Eric said, "Jaana wanted to climb out with us. All of us, the next morning. She thought she had to get away from him right then. She said she would get him drunk and he would sleep through us leaving. She wanted me to take her to California. To be her lawyer. To help her get her visa problem straightened out.

"I told her that wasn't possible." He let his eyes wander among the group. "I didn't think her situation was all that desperate. Lots of people overstay student visas. Things get worked out. She was pretty hysterical. I didn't get it. I thought she was overreacting. I didn't want to get involved."

Kanyn said, "She'd didn't have any money. Her car was dead. Her job in the cafeteria was ending on Labor Day." The tears, from some pressured spring deep in Kanyn's marrow, continued to flow down her cheeks. "The shirtless guy lived in Vegas. She wouldn't go there. She was afraid of him. She was sure he would turn her in if she didn't do what he wanted.

"I thought Eric would know what to do. When she wasn't around the next morning, I thought Eric had helped her, had taken care of her problem. That's why I went back up to the rim with him and Lisa. I thought it was okay. Eric didn't say anything, so I didn't say anything. I thought it was a secret. I was confused."

Fifty

"You have kind eyes," Jaana said to Kanyn. "I choose you because . . . you have kind eyes."

The Grand Canyon floor was in shadows, the rim world still in sunlight. It was late afternoon.

The Eastern European inflection in Jaana's words was pronounced.

Kanyn asked, "Choose me for what?"

"I am Jaana. We met before?"

"Yes. I'm Kanyn."

"It is so hot, yes?"

"I don't mind," Kanyn said. "I like it."

Kanyn was on a final solo stroll before the day's light disappeared on her last night in the canyon. Jaana had come up on her from behind.

"Where's your friend?" Kanyn asked. "He's cute."

"Blisters," she said. Bliss-tares. *"Big ones." She made her thumbs and index fingers into orbs the size of robins eggs.*

"Ouch. Sorry," Kanyn said.

Jaana stepped in front of Kanyn, blocking her path.

"Can you help? Please? I'm sorry."

"With the blisters? We have some stuff. Come by the cabins later. At the ranch? I'll give it to you."

"No, please. Can you help me? I need help. Nicholas, he is, uh,

*he is making me— No, no, he is going to . . . I don't know how to
say. Visa. I broke my visa. If I— He will . . ."*

Kanyn leaned her head onto Amy's shoulder. She said, "It's funny,
but at first, I thought Jaana was talking about a credit-card problem.
That kind of Visa." Amy stroked Kanyn's hair. "But that was only
part of it. That's not all she was dealing with. Jaana was pregnant.
She didn't want to get an abortion. Shirtless Guy wanted her to. She
needed to get away from him, or . . ."

Jules and Mel each looked at Eric.

Eric said, "She didn't tell me that." With his denial, everyone
looked at him, even Kanyn. "She didn't. I didn't know she was pregnant. I swear. What she told me—she made it sound like a visa problem. That's all."

Kanyn said, "She didn't want me to tell anyone. If she ended up
having to have the abortion, she didn't want anyone to know. She
was ashamed."

The irony slapped me. Jaana was shamed by the prospect of ending a pregnancy. Eric was shamed by the prospect of people discovering how far he was willing to go to ensure one.

"Was it Shirtless Guy's baby?" Jules asked.

Kanyn said, "She thought so. She wasn't certain."

Mel said, "My God. She was pregnant when she disappeared.
That's horrible."

Mel was jumping to the end of the story, looking for tragic conclusions. Everyone else, I thought, was still turning pages, looking
for motivations that might make sense of the tragic conclusions.

*When Jaana told him she was pregnant, the shirtless man insisted
she have an abortion. He would pay. Jaana had initially agreed,
made plans to go to a clinic with a girlfriend from Estonia. But she
changed her mind. She told him on the hike down she would keep
the baby.*

He didn't say anything for an hour after that.

The heat was relentless. Shade, where the temperature was a mere one hundred and eight, felt like a bad joke.

Just before they reached the river he said, "You either get the abortion or I'll turn you in to Immigration. They'll send you back to Estonia. The baby will stay here."

Kanyn said, "She asked me if I'd ever had an abortion. What it was like. Did I know? She wondered if it would hurt. Would she forget?"

Oh shit, I thought. *Here it comes.* Years of doing therapy had taught me what the monumental looks like in the instant before it explodes from unremarkable clouds.

Jules drew in a breath and held it. She sensed something incoming too.

Kanyn said, "I was young. Fourteen." She tried to take a deep breath. The air seemed to catch in her throat. She coughed. "Four . . . teen."

Amy stroked Kanyn's hair. She felt what was coming too. She said, "You were so young. Too young."

"The baby I aborted was my daughter, or my son." Kanyn pressed her lips together tight, as though that would be sufficient to keep the next words inside. It didn't work. She barely opened her mouth to say, "The baby was also my sister, or my brother." Her face contorted into agony. "Okay? Okay?"

Amy said, "It's okay. It is okay."

It wasn't okay.

Fifty-one

It had been a long night.

Kanyn whispered something to Amy. Amy took her hand. They went off by themselves to talk. I decided to allow myself the luxurious pretense that Kanyn would be safe until morning.

Mel rooted around in the kitchen until she discovered a half-full thirty-something-year-old bottle of Wild Turkey stashed in a dark corner of the pantry. The price on the red tag on the top of the quart bottle read $5.79. Mel and Eric and Jules started downing whiskey shots in juice glasses that memorialized Looney Tunes characters. After the second round Mel mused aloud about selling the glasses on eBay.

The Tweety Bird/Wild Turkey combo was sufficient cause for me to leave, but I eventually manufactured the energy to get up because I didn't want to listen to them argue the unarguable any longer. There was no point in debating what had happened. Thanks to Jack's old boyfriend and the infinite reach of YouTube, we had the video. We had Jack's story, and we had Kanyn's.

The rest, to me, was rationalization.

Eric had his reason for keeping quiet. Mel and Jules had theirs.

Kanyn's demons were the most compelling.

The unknown parts of the story—the fiasco earlier that evening at the duplex, the whereabouts of Jack and Lisa, the elusive truth about what ultimately happened to Jaana—would all keep until morning. When I left the room, Jules and Eric had just begun to discuss going to the police for help in finding Jack and Lisa. They also seemed to recognize they had to come clean with the authorities about what had happened that last night in the Grand Canyon. Those moves were long overdue.

The reconfiguration of the old barn into a dwelling had left the house with three almost identical bedrooms on the main floor and two larger ones upstairs, in what had been the hayloft. Like everything else in the home, the bedrooms appeared to have been unused for decades. Without saying good night, or anything else, to anyone in the group congregated below the hayloft door, I stood and wandered down the solitary hallway. The midcentury modern touches were absent from the bedrooms. Each bed I found was neatly made with a pastel knotty-chenille bedspread that screamed "grandma." I did a quick survey of my options and picked the room farthest from the Grand Canyon group.

I wanted to get a little sleep and go home. My job was done. Even though I hadn't found Lisa, I'd solved some of Merideth's Grand Canyon riddle. I had the keys to Wallace's concerns about his daughter. When I was less mentally exhausted, I would ponder what to do with what I had learned.

Would I tell Merideth the truth about Eric? Would I tell Wallace anything at all?

Before I flicked off the light, I glanced at the decades-old clock beside the bed. It slapped me with the news that it was a few minutes before five a.m. I judged it unlikely that the clock had earned anyone's attention after random power outages or during the past few decades of annual changeovers to daylight saving time and back. I checked my phone for confirmation of the hour before I believed what I was seeing. The cell screen let me know it was actually twenty-two minutes before five in Colorado.

In California, it was an hour earlier. Twenty to four, give or take. For some reason, that news cheered me. I wouldn't get a night's sleep—not even close—but at least I might get a decent nap before morning.

I stripped off my filthy clothes, pulled back the musty sheets, and fell into bed. I said a silent prayer for sleep. My prayer was not addressed to any particular god—whichever one was on call that night for inconsequential requests, like mine, was fine.

In the transitional minutes before my mind yielded to my exhaustion and headed toward REM, I did two familiar things. The first was to try to clear my thoughts about what I had just learned. Recent experience with insomnia had taught me that cogitating on the day's conundrums usually served only to postpone or prohibit my rest.

It was on nights that I was unsuccessful in warding off the temptations of smoldering rumination that I had fallen into the unfortunate habit of trying to douse the incipient flames with vodka.

As a strategy, that had proven to be about as prudent as it sounds.

The other familiar thing I did after my head hit the lumpy, Bee Gees–era polyester pillow was to allow my conscious mind to wander across open items on my life agenda. The scan was a closing-the-day's-books exercise for me.

I will be picking up Jonas in three days . . . Lauren and Grace will be coming home from Holland in four. Maybe I can find a flight from the Burbank airport into Denver the next day and avoid the drive back to LAX. No . . . won't work. All my shit is still at Merideth's condo. I wonder if Hector will let me in.

It will be good to see the dogs.

I need to call Sam, catch him up, see if he learns anything from the Good Hands guy. And Merideth and Wallace. Oh yes.

The dream started in the middle of a blind narrative, as my dreams tend to do. The part where I picked up the thread felt like a near suburb of reality. The line of demarcation was invisible to me.

Lauren put a hand on my shoulder for a moment to let me know she was there. I felt the movement of another body on the mattress and the coolness of her flesh as she pressed up behind me, her knees bent against mine, the firm front of her thighs caressing the soft backs of my legs, her pliant chest mashed to my back, her hair tickling my neck and my shoulders. I wiggled my ass against her abdomen in greeting. Her closeness was comfort. I returned to sleep. Or I never left it.

I woke again when she reached over my naked hip and rested her hand flat below my navel. Her fingers spread, her pinky exploring the upper border of my pubic hair.

I stirred.

She lifted her leg over me at the same moment that I reached behind me, over her, and found the curve of her ass to be a good fit for my open hand. Her ass felt . . .

"Thought you'd never wake up," she said.

. . . Different.

There was an unfamiliar melody in the words.

Dreams have their own rules. I've pondered the question plenty, for both personal and professional reasons, over the years. But I've never discovered the rules of dreams. I have never even come close.

My patients would ask me frequently what a particular dream might mean. I never shared the confidence that many of my colleagues professed about the interpretation of dreams. I always told my patients that all the sages who think they know the rules of dreams are either wishful or they are full of hubris. Dreams are poetry about your life, I would tell them. You are the author, but the poems your unconscious writes at night are in a language you don't speak and in a dimension you can't visit when you're awake. Interpret slumber poetry any way you like—you will discover marvelous things about how your waking mind assesses the primitive concoctions your sleeping mind constructs.

But all that the humble—where dreams are concerned, I include myself in their ranks—know for certain is that dreams don't play by the rules of ordinary.

I was hard and in her hand before I was awake enough to recognize that the woman I was about to have sex with wasn't Lauren.

And that it hadn't been a dream. Not completely.

"Hi, Cowboy," the woman said when I opened my eyes. She smelled of sweet sweat and flowers. I liked the bouquet. Her voice was husky and playful and more purely lustful than anything I'd experienced since I'd inhaled Ottavia's perfume in the confines of the narrow hallway of her flat.

My first thought? I wanted the dream back. I so much wanted the dream back.

My second thought? *Holy shit. Amy.*

Neurochemistry began doing its thing. A jolt of adrenaline agitated my post-REM haze. The mix wasn't salutary. For a prolonged moment my mind couldn't decide which Amy was gripping me in her hand.

Was it the silver-blond-haired equestrian Amy of my youth?

Or the cute, beguiling Amy of the previous day?

My brain took over—went all graduate school on me. The theory of dream work—that the manifest content of a dream should come from the most recent waking period—argued that either Amy could be the stuff of my dream. I'd spent the previous day hanging with one, musing about the other.

My eyes, adjusting to the dim light in the room, confirmed that the Amy in the bed had short hair that wasn't silver-blond. I decided I would go with that reality.

It was script supervisor Amy, not equestrian Amy.

She moved her fingers. I gasped, a little.

Intentionally or not, she was re-reminding me that it wasn't a dream.

Fifty-two

A ramshackle garage sat at the end of the driveway, farther from the road than the back of the barn. One of the original swinging doors on the garage was open almost ninety degrees. The other door was gone. The bottom hinge was still attached to the jamb. The top hinge was history. I didn't think the building had originally been built to store cars. The pitted concrete on the floor was poured in sections—some recessed—that didn't correspond to the size of four-wheeled vehicles. I guessed that the structure had once been a milking parlor, or something else.

My barn outbuilding knowledge was limited.

In other circumstances I might have been sufficiently curious to explore the space for historical clues about its utilitarian origins. Not in that predawn. I was looking for a quiet place to elude a cute naked woman and to make some calls.

I sat on the open tailgate of the only vehicle in the garage—a rusty Ford pickup. The truck was one that I would have considered ancient when I was a child up the road in Thousand Oaks. The rear window was tiny, maybe eight inches by twenty-four. I couldn't see anything through the film and muck that age and neglect had caked onto the glass. Was the truck from the forties? Early fifties? I didn't know. It was old. From the exterior appearance of the red Ford, I didn't think the vehicle had been outside the Burroughs family barn since Johnny Weissmuller was at RKO.

Right behind my perch on the tailgate a stack of old license plates had tipped over and spread out like a hand of cards. The one on top was from Iowa. Nearer the cab, the truck bed was littered with the contents of a fifties-era toolbox. Rusty iron pipe wrenches were scattered around close to the box. The toolbox—I guessed it had belonged to a plumber—was standing on its end, top open. It was from Sears.

A persistent sough in the distance announced that rush-hour traffic was beginning to assemble on nearby Ventura Boulevard.

I opened my phone.

Before my fingers hit the keypad, I heard a sliding sound from the rear of the garage, then a *crack/pop*. I translated the sliding sound and decided it might have been a scurrying sound. *Critters,* I thought. Rats? Raccoons? Skunks? I had no idea what varmints inhabited decrepit buildings in the urbanized foothills of the San Fernando Valley.

My brain registered the fact that the garage reeked. I was pretty sure I didn't want to meet up with whatever animals were living there. I stood and followed an overgrown stone path that led into the jumble of thigh-high vegetation in the yard behind the barn.

I stopped in a spot where the weeds reached only to my knees, exhaled softly to settle myself, and held down the 2 key on my phone. Thanks to Jonas's programming, that solitary, simple motion would connect me with Lauren half a world away.

For real. No dreams.

And no sex. That would, no doubt, be an option in next year's version of the cell phone. For the present, with current-generation phones and wives on European holiday, the rules of ordinary applied.

Time-zone arithmetic said that it was midafternoon in Holland. In the seconds that passed while the fiber optics and the satellites and the computers between Tarzana and Amsterdam were doing their things, I recalled Lauren's tease to me a long time before about being number two on my old phone's speed dial.

*   *   *

"I'm number two," she'd said with faux disappointment in her tone. "Does that mean Merideth is number one?"

"It's not about wife numbers," I'd replied. "Home is number one. Always. You're next. Merideth doesn't get a number. Is that okay?"

She'd kissed me. It had been a sweet moment.

Lauren didn't answer. I desperately didn't want to get kicked to voice mail.

The yard behind the barn was dotted with holes. Beside the holes were mounds of dirt. The neglected space behind the barn had become a resort village for gophers. Gophers didn't worry me, but I continued to keep my eyes peeled for other varmints. For some reason, I was particularly concerned about porcupines.

And skunks. I didn't want to run into a skunk. I was confident I smelled bad enough.

I got kicked to voice mail. *Maybe Lauren didn't hear it ring*, I thought. I hung up and tried again. It took a minute, but I got booted to voice mail again.

"Here's the thing," I said. "I love you. That's first." I paused. I hadn't prepared anything to say. "I . . . um . . . have made some mistakes. I've been distant. And I'm sorry. We have some work to do. I have no doubt we can do it. I'm ready to begin to do that the moment you get home. I can't wait to see you. I love you guys. Call me. Okay?"

I closed the phone and retraced my steps toward the garage. I had sufficient observing ego to recognize that I was walking in the footfalls of my doing and my undoing. I looked up when I heard a sound in front of me.

I expected a porcupine. But I found Amy standing near the open door. She was about ten feet away from the pickup. Her purse was hanging from her shoulder. She was wearing big sunglasses, carrying a clunky ring of keys.

"Wondered where you went," she said. "So . . . all-of-a-sudden."

"Out here," I said. "It felt like a good idea to . . . get away. I was in there at first." I pointed toward the back of the garage. "But I think there's something creepy living in that junk, so I went out back. I'm kind of a wuss. I don't want to meet whatever is camping in the garage. It stinks."

I was babbling. She didn't reply. She sniffed the air. She could smell the stench too.

"You were terrific last night with Kanyn," I said. "It was special to watch how tender you were with her."

"Kanyn's a good person. She's in a lot of pain. I didn't know about the awful stuff with her family before last night. It's . . . unbelievable what she's been through. But thanks." She looked at her feet for a moment. "Don't know if I should tell you this, but I need to tell someone. Kanyn opened up to me last night. It was almost like a confession. Lisa's been living in the Addams Family apartment for the last few days. Kanyn let her in. Jack knew, but they weren't supposed to tell anyone else. Kanyn doesn't know if she did the right thing by helping Lisa hide. After what she thought happened to Jaana after she sent her to Eric, she didn't think she could say no to Lisa this time."

"Okay," I said. I was beyond judgment.

"Kanyn thought all the commotion last night was someone coming to get Lisa. At first she thought it might be Jack, and it was okay. But then she smelled gas from the wall heater. When she went to check on it, it exploded."

"Who knew Lisa was there?" I asked.

Amy said, "Other than Kanyn and Jack? I don't know."

I shook my head. "Someone else had to know. Whoever was sneaking in the back of the duplex. Has Kanyn told this to the police?"

Amy shook her head. "No, she wasn't honest with them last night. She's a mess about not helping Jaana back in the Grand Canyon. She feels so responsible for whatever happened back then that she's almost paralyzed now. She doesn't know if she did the right thing by agreeing to help Jack with Lisa. She doesn't know if Lisa is okay. She's worried about Jack. She's afraid everybody is going to blame her no matter what she does now." Amy pursed her lips for a few seconds. "I don't know what I'm going to do with this information. I need to get some sleep before I decide. I guess I've just given you the same dilemma. Sorry." She shrugged.

"The police need to know," I said. I didn't need sleep to come to that conclusion.

"Yeah," she said. "I'll take Kanyn down to talk to them."

"Jules, too," I said. "I think there should be a lawyer present."

Amy took half a step back down the long driveway. Her CR-V was parked twenty yards away, halfway to the street, directly across from a fat eucalyptus. Stringy bark was peeling from the trunk like old scabs. She stopped her retreat and set her feet. "I'm not Glenn Close, Alan," she said. "It was only going to be sex."

She made the carnal act sound as uncomplicated as a visit to Starbucks.

One of us was misinformed. I was not at all certain it was she. Sex was among the things I'd expected to get less complicated as I aged.

Ha.

I thought about her words for a moment, fought a temptation to get further detoured by the generational and gender irony of it all. I considered explaining that I wasn't Michael Douglas and my decision to hightail it from the bed wasn't about whether I could get away with a tryst without entanglements or discovery. Instead I said, "You're young. Unattached. For me it's not only about sex, as tempting as the sex might be. Not anymore."

She pulled her sunglasses down to the tip of her nose and narrowed her eyes in genuine, or mock, consternation. I found it disorienting that I didn't know which she intended.

She said, "Despite what I said at dinner, I . . . I don't do this . . . often. When I do, I'm not used to . . . ." She shrugged, perhaps too modest to finish the sentence that had formed in her head.

"Having men jump out of your bed?" I guessed. "I bet you're

not. You're . . . gorgeous, Amy. Smart, funny, kind. I'm beyond flat-tered. You . . . I think you know that the reason I ran isn't because I'm not attracted to you."

"Most men would have stayed," she said in acknowledgment. She did that smile-with-only-one-side-of-her-mouth thing that I'd first seen the previous afternoon in Mt. Washington. It was part of what had beguiled me. I was wishing she'd stop doing it.

"Yes," I admitted. *Most men would have stayed. Definitely.* "It's been an uphill battle, but I'm trying not to be most men."

"I'm not looking for . . . a relationship, Alan. I know you're leav-ing. Going back to Colorado. You leaving is part of the plan."

I said, "I have a family. Kids." Plural. "A wife." Singular.

"I don't know what that means," she said. "Right now, this min-ute."

How can you not know what that means? "At dinner you said that you don't hook up with men who make your heart go flip-flop. Maybe I didn't know it for sure last night, but . . . I don't think I want to sleep with women who *don't* make my heart go flip-flop."

She put on a face that was all acting-workshop pouty. She said, "And I don't make your heart go flip-flop?"

The over-the-top frown made me smile. "You make a lot of my bits go flip-flop. But not my heart. Not yet, anyway." I considered, then rejected, trying to explain the beguiled thing. She gave me a puzzled look as she ran her upper teeth front to back over her lower lip. When I spoke again, my voice was soft. I was talking to myself as much as I was to her. "I want to wake up every morning and adore the person sleeping beside me. I want to go to bed every night and feel adored by the person sleeping beside me. This—hooking up with you—would have been nice. Better than nice. Maybe great. But it might have poisoned the . . . whole adored thing."

"You have that? The adored thing?"

"Did once. I'm trying to find it again."

"Really? You had it?"

She was skeptical. I understood that. I said, "I did."

"Who had to know about last night?" she asked.

"I'd know. My truth doesn't change because I'm out of town."

"You're hopeless, aren't you?"

"Maybe."

She pulled the sunglasses from her face with her left hand and crossed her arms over her chest "I know this script. This is where I'm supposed to say your wife is a lucky woman. Yes?"

"But?" I asked.

She put her glasses back on her nose. "Is she, Alan?"

I stuffed my hands into the back pockets of my jeans. I looked at her. She lowered her chin so I could spy her eyes over the top of her shades.

"She wasn't yesterday," I said. "Or last week. She may be tomorrow. There's still a chance I can do something about tomorrow."

Fifty-three

Amy took two steps forward. I mistook her move as evidence of carnal persistence. I'm sure I looked befuddled.

She shook her head, dismissing my interpretation of her movement with another of those half smiles of hers. She pulled the glasses from her face and walked to the side of the truck. "What is that?" she asked, pointing in front of her with the eyepiece of the shades. "There. Is that . . ." I turned. "Could that be . . . ?"

Morning light was infiltrating the garage.

A dark stain about the size and shape of one of Grace's soccer shin guards interrupted the dust near the front wheel of the truck. The dust around the dried pool was disturbed by dozens of footprints and scuffmarks. Beyond the stain, a wash of teardrop shapes the same deep color had pebbled the dust in a pattern that extended along the floor until the droplets got lost amidst the tall jumble of junk where I feared the critter was living.

The clear outline of the toe of a shoe was preserved in the large stain.

My eyes settled immediately on the door handle on the driver's side of the truck. On the dirty chrome lever was another stain. The color was redder, more bronze.

"I think it might be blood," I said. My pulse accelerated from the implication. *God, don't let it be Lisa. Please, please.*

Amy moved up next to me and leaned in for a closer look at the door handle.

"The stain is dry," I said. "Whatever it is, it's not an emergency. We should be careful about what we touch."

She moved within an inch of the door glass. "I can't see. It's too filthy. Yuck."

I cupped my hand above my eye to peer into the cab. "Me neither."

I lifted the door handle, using the hem of my T-shirt as a barrier. I didn't want to leave my fingerprints. Nor did I want to disturb the stain. "It's locked," I said. "We should call someone."

She had her phone in her hand before I finished the sentence. I held up mine. "I have a friend in town. With me. He's a cop," I said. "He'll know what to do."

"So call him," she said. "I only know people who play cops on TV."

I speed-dialed Sam. He wasn't going to be happy to be woken.

Before he picked up, someone behind us said, "Oh heck, don't do that."

Fifty-four

The voice—it was a man's voice—came from the back of the garage. From the general direction of all the junk. Amy and I would have had to turn around to see him.

I froze. Amy did too.

"Close that. Both of you put your phones on the floor. Kick them this way." At that point he added—I thought reluctantly—"I have a gun. If I have to use it to shut one of you up, I will."

I closed my phone.

Amy and I followed his directions, scooting our cells behind us on the concrete. I could hear him collect the two phones. It sounded as though he turned them both off before he dropped them into the same pocket. They clacked together.

"Now your keys."

We skidded our rings of keys toward him. They clinked as he lifted them, clattered as he examined them. He said, "Girly? That old Honda is yours?"

"Yes," Amy said.

"You. The rental car, what kind is it?"

I said, "A Camry. It's on the street."

"We're going to leave," he said. "All of us." He tossed some keys to the floor of the garage.

Leave? I don't think so. I wasn't planning to go anywhere.

I couldn't guess who the man was. I could tell from a quick glance at Amy's face that she didn't know who he was either.

I wondered if he was part of the family dispute that Jules was having with her brothers about the future of the barn. I said, "We're guests, we're here at the invitation of the . . . of one of the owners . . . of that barn. The house. They'll tell you."

"Jules," Amy said. "She's inside. She's my friend. She'll—"

The man said, "Shut up. I don't care."

He moved behind me. I could hear him come close. His shoes made a distinctive clicking sound on the concrete. I told myself it was an important sound. I tried to remember it. After he took three steps, he emitted a satisfied sigh. I could feel his breath on my neck. He was that close to me. I waited for him to grab one of my wrists.

I wasn't planning to cooperate if he tried to bind my hands.

The rules of abduction are much more predictable than the rules of dreams. Abduction rule number one is: Good things never happen when the bad guy takes you someplace else. I wasn't willingly going anyplace else. Having my hands bound would be the first step toward going someplace else.

He reached around me and stuck a roll of duct tape into my gut. He said, "Take this. Wrap her mouth, all the way around her head. Do it good, a few times."

I took the tape from his gloved hand. I did what I was told. Amy's eyes were pleading with me the whole time to do anything but what I was doing.

He stuck another roll of tape in front of me. Filament tape. He'd come prepared. "Now her hands," he said. "Use this. Figure eights around her wrists."

I had already begun contemplating a plan. My strategy was to spin hard toward Amy—that way if I managed to hit the guy's gun hand with my raised wrist as I turned, the barrel of the weapon would rotate away from her. If my fancy spin move failed, I would try to get my elbow elevated high so I could land a sharp blow someplace important, like the guy's face. My first thought had been to use a simple backward kick with my heel into the man's nuts. If I missed and hit his knee or his thigh, though, I'd probably not be alive long enough to apologize for my bad aim.

I would scream my head off the entire time.

I refined my strategy while I finished binding Amy's wrists. It was at that point in my planning process that the man either shot me or pounded me on side of the head once with something hard.

Unconsciousness prevented me from knowing which option he'd selected.

Fifty-five

The first thing I did when I regained consciousness was puke on my shoes.

The man said, "Oh, Lord in heaven. Was that necessary? Open a window. Darn it, what did you eat?"

I fumbled for the window switch. Before I found it, he opened all four windows using the driver's controls.

I didn't remember what I'd eaten. I didn't remember the man beside me. I didn't recall why my wrists and ankles were bound together with what seemed like bushels of tape or how I'd gotten into the front seat of the car I was in.

The left side of my head felt like someone had whacked it with a mallet. Although I didn't recall any blow to my head that might have left me amnesic and nauseous, I was assuming a connection between my headache and some unrecalled closed-head trauma.

I sat up straight so I could look around.

A man I didn't know was driving. He looked like a younger version of Sam. His hair was cut short. He was big and strong—taller and heavier than me, I was guessing six-two, two hundred-plus pounds. His waist was protruding over his belt more, I was sure, than he liked. He wore dark sunglasses and an L.A. Angels cap that was stained from plenty of use.

Traffic was thin. At that moment, nonexistent. The car we were in was on a two-lane rural road in one of those geographical transitional areas where sparse chaparral has given way to desert.

I'm in California, I remembered. I felt like I deserved a gold star.

My bound wrists and ankles were a reliable clue that I was in an unfortunate predicament of some kind. I said, "Where am I?"

Suddenly, I recalled spooning naked with Amy. The context escaped me. But the image focused me, as naked memories with pretty girls do, and I discovered fragmentary recollections of the old Ford pickup and a rusty Iowa license tag. Gophers, too—I remembered gophers.

The pieces felt like remnants of some strange psychological scavenger hunt. I couldn't fit any of the items into a context that would have allowed a naked encounter with a young woman.

I remembered I was married. "Where's Amy?" I asked.

A muted roar from the backseat—"ellllllllll eeeeeeee"—offered a clue. I turned to look behind me. An electric pain—a mini lightning bolt—shot from my injured head into my neck and shoulder. Amy was curled up on the floor behind my seat. She had tape winding over her mouth and behind her head. The roar I heard had been her attempted scream for help.

Newspaper pages were taped to the side windows of the back doors.

As I came back around I noticed the GPS device near my left knee. Another clue. I remembered Chloe, the watercolorist. *The Camry.* We were in my rented Camry. I so much wanted to turn the screen of the GPS my way so Chloe could whisper a clue about where the hell I was. Chloe would know. The woman was a mensch.

The man pulled the car to a gradual stop on the side of the road beside a wide field that seemed to have been most recently cultivated with a cash crop of tumbleweeds. "Throw the floor mat out the window. Can't stand that smell. Just do it."

It wasn't easy with my wrists taped, but I managed to toss the floor mat out the window without spilling any vomit. I didn't think I would like what the man would do if I spilled the vomit.

The carpet mat was almost the same shade of brown as the dirt on the shoulder beside the road.

Every movement I made caused my head to ache more. I figured

I had a concussion. Any notion of the precipitant continued to elude me.

The man shifted the car back into Drive and hesitated. Before he took off he said, "Are you going to be quiet, or do I need to tape your mouth? You get difficult, I'll truss you up like I did her. You know how small the trunk is in this thing? Because of the darn hybrid batteries?"

I said, "No. I don't think I ever looked." If I had looked, I didn't remember.

"If it was any bigger, you'd be in it. So would she."

If I survived this, I'd try to remember to send the Toyota designers a thank-you note. I didn't like the idea of vomiting into a barrier of duct tape, or of getting hogtied and dumped on the floor of the backseat. "I'll be quiet," I said. "One question? Please?"

"Sure."

I asked, "Are you taking us someplace?"

He looked at me for a second and chuckled. It wasn't a mocking or denigrating laugh. He was simply amused. He pulled back onto the road. He said, "I am indeed."

Fifty-six

"What do you do?" he asked me ten or so miles down the road.

The topography indicated we'd completed the transitioning into the desert. I had no idea which one, but I guessed that we were east of L.A. I guessed that only because that's where the closest deserts were. I hadn't seen a road sign. I couldn't see Chloe's video screen from where I was sitting.

"I'm a psychologist," I said.

"Seriously?"

"Yes."

"Her? What does she do? I don't recognize her, either."

The man said he didn't recognize us. In the context, I assumed that meant there might have been someone around that he thought he would have recognized. That simple insight led nowhere. I had nothing. Blanks.

"She works in Hollywood. A script . . . coordinator. Supervisor. I don't know." I couldn't remember. "She keeps track of . . . dialogue."

Amy roared into the tape again. "Eeeeeeeeeeeaaaaaaaaa." I was trying to treat her outbursts like sound effects—I hoped the man was doing the same. I didn't want his focus to be on her. I feared her continued screams were going to make him angry and attract his attention.

"Eeeeeeeeeeeaaaaaaaaa."

"What's she like?" he asked. He glanced toward the backseat. At Amy. "She's kind of hot."

Oh God. What's the right answer to that question? That she's a saint? That she's a bitch? That she's not that attractive? How do I keep this man from mistaking his dominance over her for lust?

"I just met her today," I said.

"Yesterday," he corrected me. "That's more likely."

"Yeah, yesterday."

He dropped it. "You're a shrink, tell me something—how is it that a thing can go so well for so long and then all of a sudden turn to crud?"

In my office with a patient, I would have sat silently, waiting for more. At most, I might have said, "Tell me." I was so not in my office. I decided to be a little bit more assertive. "Your life?" I guessed.

He contemplated for a moment. "I got into a thing. Maybe shouldn't have—it was impulsive like—but I did it. I convinced myself I had a fall guy, you know, the guy I'd pin it on if things got tight. Things got tight. I should have seen it coming. Didn't, whatever. I got out of the thing. Getting out wasn't easy, wasn't pretty, but I did it. Still had my fall guy, like an ace up my sleeve. Life was okay then. Life, you know?" He made a dismissive sound with his lips. "It's always some kind of mess. Now the darn thing has crawled back out of the grave and won't leave me alone. I don't think I'm going to get away from it this time. I just don't think I am."

"Your fall guy?"

"My fall guy didn't work out the way I expected."

There were wise things that someone with my training might have said right then. I didn't say any of them. I said, "You could let us go. That might help."

He chuckled. "Nice try. See, I think I could get lucky again. Doing this same exact thing earned me a few years last time I was here. Maybe it will work this time too. Though this one has more variables. The variables get you. They do."

Following the ripped threads of his story was an excruciating task for my concussed brain. "Doing what exact thing?"

"What we're doing."

"Doing this earned you . . . what . . . a few years in prison?"

He chuckled. "Nope. Never been. Don't plan to ever go. No . . . way. Earned me freedom, bought me time, peace. Doing this, that's what I'm talking about. You take some risks, you cross your fingers. I had to protect what I had then. I did it. I have a family, got to do it again. I need more time." He sighed. "So here I am again, taking some risks, crossing my fingers."

I responded to the only piece of his speech that I understood. "Me too," I said. "I have a family."

He said, "I'm not worried about your family. I don't want to know. I don't care."

He said it in a way that left me no doubt it was true.

"Why us?" I said.

"You found the darn body before I could dump it. I was waiting for all of you to leave so I could take the body and be on my way."

The body? Suddenly I remembered the blood in the garage in Tarzana. *Tarzana, damn. Merideth and Mel and Lisa.* Jules. Eric. Kanyn. YouTube.

I said, "In the truck? The red pickup?"

"That one. You're having trouble with your memory, aren't you? I might have hit you too hard back there. Bad luck for you. Wasn't sure you were going to wake up at all. You were knocked out for a long stretch."

I wondered about the "bad luck" I had suffered. *The too-hard head hit? Or finding the body?* Maybe both. Or maybe something that hadn't happened to me yet.

The body has to be either Lisa or Jack. I recalled Amy telling me that Kanyn had been hiding Lisa in the other half of the duplex. Did this guy learn she was there? How?

I said, "We didn't see a body. Just . . . stains."

"Still," he said. "That's enough. One thing leads to another. Always has for me. Always. Somebody learns one little thing. They take advantage. Pretty soon . . . You know? Ever tried to keep everything quiet, you know, to cover your tracks? Hardest darn thing. Damn computers. I hate 'em. Hate 'em. Swear my next job won't have any computers." He exhaled audibly. "Need a lot of luck. A lot."

I replayed the sequence of events I could recall in Tarzana and wondered how desperate my captor might be. He hadn't seemed too worried about being discovered by anyone when he ambushed us in the converted barn. Were the people who were still in the house the ones he would have recognized? Had he killed them all before he confronted Amy and me? My mind manufactured an image of a massacre in the midcentury living room.

I spotted the grip of a handgun flat on the seat between his legs. The barrel was under his left thigh. Odds were he was right-handed. To shoot me he'd have to grab the gun and get it turned toward me in the narrow air space above the console. That awkward motion might prove to be a minor advantage for me.

In my head, I began to choreograph some moves. The fact that I was bound at my wrists and ankles was a major complication. The moves I was considering were fine—grabbing, kicking, biting. The fast-forwarded outcomes of the ensuing close-quarter combat always involved me getting shot, which wasn't the ending I was hoping for.

The handgun caused me to reflect on the first rule of abduction. The reflection reminded me that I had already allowed the rule to be broken. "You're taking us someplace to kill us, aren't you?" I said, naïve surprise in my voice.

"Most people wouldn't say it out loud," he said. "You just did. Give you credit for that. The other two, they just whimpered the whole time." He chuckled. "I ended up putting them both in the darn trunk."

He got quiet. After a moment, he lowered his voice a little and said, "So you know, do something stupid, I'll kill you right here and then take you someplace to dump you. The order doesn't make any difference to me. This ain't my car. I don't care."

"I don't care" was beginning to sound like his trademark phrase.

I'd known at some level he was taking us someplace to kill us. At that moment I knew it at the conscious, here-and-now level. I felt a chill spread across my back.

I wondered about the "last time" the man had referred to. He'd done this errand—killing and dumping—before. With two people— "the other two." Which two people?

Jaana was only one.

Lisa was one.

Jack was one.

The Grand Canyon story I'd been learning over the past week didn't have any parts where two people went missing.

"Does this have to do with the Grand Canyon?" I asked. I figured I had nothing to lose by exposing the fact that I knew about what happened back then—there was no sense dying with cards left to turn over.

He turned his head toward me, his eyebrows jumping up from under his shades. "You know about that?"

"Just what was in the papers."

"I do my best to stay out of the darn papers."

My head was finally clear enough that I thought I knew who had abducted us. *You're Lincoln Oden,* I thought. I recalled Sam's theory that Oden had cut a deal with the kid in Las Vegas, Nick Paulson.

Why would Oden's deal with Paulson require him to kill people and dump bodies in the desert? I was hoping a multiple choice would appear in my brain and that I could choose an answer from a list. But nothing.

Was I with Oden right then because Sam had visited Paulson's office in Las Vegas? The connections weren't apparent. I didn't know why I was about to die at the hands of Lincoln Oden.

But I was thinking that I was about to die and was wondering how it would happen. Without seriously considering any alternatives, I had already decided to do my best to go down fighting.

I was trying not to think about my family. My children did not need any more losses.

"You hear that?" the man said. "Dag . . . nabbit."

I didn't hear anything. I listened more intently.

After five seconds, I did hear it. The sound was far away. But it was a siren.

I had an insight right then: *If I had been praying, I would be thinking that my prayers had just been answered.*

But since I hadn't been praying, it was all just chance.

Fifty-seven

Oden lifted the gun from below his thigh. The gun was a revolver. Big, but not too big. Sam had once shown me a .38. Oden's pistol looked like a .38. Oden raised the handgun with a fluid motion of his left hand. He was comfortable with it in his hand.

Had I ended up playing the odds about his hand dominance, the house would have won. I would already be dead.

He pointed the gun at me. A dowel stuck in the hollow in the barrel would have run straight to my neck, low, below my Adam's apple. He said, "Don't be a hero."

I hadn't yet figured out how to be a hero, but I was working on it. I'd reached a sobering conclusion that where I got shot—here in the car, or someplace in a forsaken part of the California desert—was inconsequential to me. I was intent on either finding a way not to get shot at all or finding a way to get shot that might increase Amy's odds of escaping.

Helping Amy survive wasn't purely magnanimous. It was a product of my simple acknowledgment that as bad as my predicament was, hers was worse. She was gagged and trussed—her bound wrists were taped to her bound ankles behind her back—on the floor of the car. She was in no position to be magnanimous or chivalrous and maneuver to take a bullet that might save me.

I felt my adrenaline spike as the siren's wail approached. The hormonal surge—my primitive limbic system read the siren's screeching as hopeful—only underlined how weary I was. I was so tired that I had to remind myself to exhale. Except for the period when I'd been unconscious, I'd been awake for well over a day.

Oden dropped the car's speed to just over the posted limit. He kept the gun leveled at me with a casualness that was disconcerting. Of all the variables he was concerned about at that moment, he was least concerned with me.

I had to find a way to take advantage of that fact.

His eyes were flicking back and forth between the rearview mirror and the ribbon of road in front of us. "There he is. He's coming. He's coming," he said. "He's . . . flying."

His tone was a paste of anticipation, awe, and dread. And just a little excitement, too. The excitement component worried me: Oden wasn't totally averse to a confrontation. I didn't turn to look back. The changing pitch of the squeal of the siren indicated a rapid approach.

Oden's index finger pulsed into and out of the trigger guard. *Ambivalence? Nervousness?* I wished I knew.

I had to act. I didn't know when my last chance to act would come. But I suspected there was a decent chance my opportunity would expire in the next few seconds.

"Oh, darn, I think he's slowing down," Oden said. He waggled the gun. "Don't you even . . ."

He left the final caution unfinished. I was back on his radar.

I was about to reach out with my bound hands and grab the wheel. My hastily assembled plan was to try to force the cop's attention by swinging the Camry hard so it would weave into the other lane just before the cop's arrival on our section of road.

A split second before I lunged for the steering wheel Oden tapped the brakes and slowed the Camry onto the shoulder. We rolled to a stop.

Shit!

He returned his eyes to the mirror. He said, "Holy heck . . . It's an ambulance. Not a cop. It's stopping . . . It's stopping . . . It's . . . not stopping. Heck, heck, heck, and hell."

The siren's squeal changed to a strident *whoop, whoop, whoop.*

Five seconds later, the boxy shape of a rescue van rolled past us. It seemed to accelerate as it flew down the road.

"Didn't stop," Oden said, in obvious relief as he stared at the departing truck. A moment later, he added, "Thing must be going ninety by now. You think?"

"At least." I watched my hope being consumed in the vortex of its wake.

Amy moaned, "Noooooooooooooo." It wasn't a scream. It was a plaintive moan that made my protoplasm quiver.

Amy, too, had heard opportunity come, and go.

Fifty-eight

Oden climbed out of the car and stepped in front of the hood. He pulled my cell from the side pocket of his cargo pants, did an exaggerated big-league windup, and tossed the phone fifty yards into the scrub. He repeated the motion with another phone. I assumed it was Amy's. He'd wanted me to see the phones were gone.

He got back in the car. "Hate cell phones, too," he said. We waited there, parked by the side of the dusty road, for a good two minutes.

Oden, I thought, was deciding when to shoot us. He hated computers and cell phones but had demonstrated some disconcerting comfort with guns.

Amy was loud the whole time. Her gag was limiting her to vowels.

"Eeeeeeaaaaaaeeeeeeeaaaaa. Eeeeeeaaaaaa, eeeeeeeaaaaa."

"Shut her up," Oden said. "Or I will."

For the first time I heard irritation infiltrate his tone. I had to shut her up.

"Eeeeeeeaaaaaaa."

"Hey," I said as I turned to Amy. I didn't want to use her name in front of him. She was struggling, writhing against the tape. Her eyes were frantic. She kept rolling them to the tops of their sockets. The position she was in left her contorted in the worst possible way. It would have been a painful pose for a rag doll to maintain.

I tried to imagine her agony.

"Hey," I repeated softly. I waited until her eyes locked on mine. I fought to keep from blinking, fearing I could lose her again with a single blink. "It's not helping," I said in a monotone. "The yelling. The writhing. I know what's going on is awful for you. The alternatives"—I paused so that she could fill in the blanks—"are worse."

She glared at me. In a tone that was almost conversational, she repeated her cry, "Eeeeeeaaaaaa."

"Do you ever do yoga? Meditate?"

She glared some more. Then she dry swallowed. Narrowed her eyes. Nodded.

I nodded back. I began to blink in a steady rhythm, every few seconds, adding a tiny head nod of a centimeter or so with each blink. I did it ten times, fifteen. When she started to mimic my movements, I did it twenty more times. I counted. In my mind, I did an inventory of the few things I knew about Amy's loves. I would need them to guide the imagery.

In my softest office voice, I said, "Look at me. My eyes. In your mind, go someplace you would love to do yoga. Imagine it all. Look at me. Good. A secluded beach. Yes? The salt air. A warm breeze. Birds are singing a melody that soothes you. The hillside is covered with flowers. Every last one is a bird-of-paradise. . . . The colors are deep green and that lovely orange. . . . The smells are heavenly. . . . Now imagine what you're wearing . . . The texture of the sand on your bare feet. Pick a starting pose. . . . Perfect it. . . . Hold it. . . . Go ahead, pick one, your favorite." She was staring at me with heavy, unblinking eyes. Reluctant eyes. "Your eyes are heavy. . . . They want to close. . . . So heavy." Her breathing was slowing.

Her eyes closed. "Find your center. Good. Ease into it. Now breathe . . . from your gut. You know how. Work your diaphragm. Listen to your body. . . . Imagine . . . Lead . . . Follow. Breathe . . . Good. Stay there . . . Hold the position. Breathe. In, out. In, out. In . . . out. In . . . out."

I timed my words to her breaths so she didn't have to adjust her breathing to my words.

I waited about ten seconds for my desperate soporifics to do their thing before I said, "Good. Relax. Breathe . . . stay right there. In that peaceful place."

I lifted my hands in front of my face and raised a solitary index finger to my mouth. I whispered "Shhhh" to Oden. I hooked a thumb in the direction of the road, and mouthed the words "Let's go."

"Thank God in heaven," he mumbled. "Some quiet. You just hypnotize her?"

"Something like that."

"Try it on me and I'll shoot you in the face. I don't care." A white twin-cab pickup riding on oversized tires flashed by us at a healthy clip. Oden said, "Nice truck." He pulled the Camry onto the road behind it. In no time the truck was swallowed by the horizon.

Our speed leveled off at the legal limit. Oden said. "Something you should know? I used to care. More than most people."

Another chill skittered across the wide flesh on my back. It felt like a terrified cluster of semi-frozen bugs running for their lives.

"Since she left, I don't care. I went all-in on her."

The gambling analogy gave me yet another chill. "She?" I asked.

"She," he said.

I found my therapist voice. "Part of that thing," I asked, "that crawled back out of the grave?"

"Yeah. Part of the thing. Since then, I don't care. I . . . just . . . don't . . . care."

I'm already dead, I thought. *Why not?* I said, "You talking about Jaana?"

I listened for the gunshot.

"Whew," he said. "What the heck do you know?"

In the next ten minutes I twice returned my attention to Amy, trying to help her maintain her trance. I had her change poses, find her balance, readjust her breathing. She was hungry for my suggestions—desperate to be almost anywhere other than where she was.

In between, I began to parcel out the Grand Canyon story to Oden, hoping to keep him calm, and buy us time.

"Accident," he said suddenly. "That's what it was. That ambulance. See?" He pointed down the highway.

Oden had eagle eyes. Above the thermal waves radiating off the road on the distant horizon I could spot the pickup that had passed us—its white paint was reflecting in the sun. Beyond it I could barely make out the blue and red pulses of the rescue vehicle's flashing lights. From our distance, I couldn't have identified it as an ambulance if my life had depended on it.

It was possible that my life did depend on it. *How odd is that?* I thought.

Oden slowed the Camry. We closed in on the accident at forty miles an hour. Then thirty. A quarter mile away we were going ten.

The ambulance had stopped on the near side of a narrow bridge at a forty-five degree angle, intentionally blocking our lane. An old Chevy Blazer was spun out in the other lane, completing the barricade. The old SUV was beat up—I wondered if it had rolled before returning to its wheels. A body seemed to be lying in the shade on the near side of the SUV, almost straddling the centerline of the road. One of the EMTs was squatting beside the injured person. Another EMT was standing in the open rear hatch of the Blazer. He or she was leaning in. I couldn't tell if there was a second victim inside the Chevy.

The white pickup rolled to a stop a few feet from the scene. The driver leaned across the cab and spoke to the paramedic who was working in the back of the Blazer. The paramedic poked his head out for just a second, said something back to the driver. The pickup driver straightened up behind the wheel, waved, and steered his truck off the road onto the dirt shoulder and then over the edge. The twin cab completely disappeared into a gully for five seconds before it popped up on the other side of the accident, climbed a steep embankment, and hopped back onto the road. The truck gained speed until it crested the hill behind the accident, vanishing from view.

"No cops there yet," Oden said. "That's lucky. I'm going to go around too. Like that truck did. Before the cops get here."

I turned to Amy. "Breathe . . . Breathe."

She growled. Coughed. So much for her trance.

When I turned back, the pistol was pointed at my head. "Don't be a hero," Oden said.

"Don't kill her," I said.

He seemed surprised. "I'm not going to kill her. Not yet."

My heart hiccupped at the thought of the alternative he had planned.

He lowered the gun to my belly. "You don't want to be gut-shot and left to die in the desert," he said. "That's my offer. Not if you die. How. You don't want to be alive when the scavengers come. So be good. I don't care."

We approached the ambulance at a crawl.

The accident had taken place where the two-lane road crossed an arroyo at the base of a small hill. I could tell that the Camry sedan was going to have a difficult time doing what the twin cab pickup had just done—circling around the scene by dropping down onto the soft sand of the dry streambed before climbing the steep bank back to the highway on the other side.

Oden recognized the predicament. With stunning understatement he said, "Darn."

He couldn't risk the three of us getting stuck in the arroyo within sight of the paramedics. I was certain he'd turn around before he'd risk that. He checked the opposite side of the road. But it fell off too steeply to even consider using it as an alternative bypass. Someone was going to have to move the ambulance if we were going to get past the accident.

Oden apparently reached the same conclusion. He stopped the Camry thirty yards from the ambulance. He ripped a long piece of duct tape from a roll he had on the floor in front of him. "Wrap your mouth," he said. "All the way around your head."

I did. He ripped another piece. "Again."

I did. I immediately felt like I couldn't get sufficient air through my nose.

The paramedic tending the person on the road was preparing a backboard and neck brace. I couldn't tell what the other paramedic was doing in the back of the Blazer. I assumed there was someone hurt inside the car.

The man said, "You get out, hit the horn, do *anything,* everybody dies. Everybody. Got it?"

I nodded. *You don't care.*

He ripped off another, longer piece of tape. He yanked my wrists over the GPS monitor and taped me to it. "Should hold you for a minute or two. Be right back."

He killed the engine but left the keys in place, prepared for a rapid getaway. When he got out of the car, he tugged at his shirt, reached into the front pocket of his jeans, and pulled out a handful of bullets. He dropped the ammunition into his shirt pocket. Then he stuck the revolver into his pants at the small of his back and started walking toward the accident.

In my head, I sprinted through all the heroic scenarios I could imagine. Hit the horn. Roll out of the car. Try to remove Amy's tape. Pull a David Blaine and escape my own binding. Try to drive the car with my hands and feet bound. Pull out the keys and toss them into the desert.

The outcomes of all the fantasies were the same: Bleeding bodies all around. Mine, Amy's. All the people at the accident scene.

He doesn't care. I believed him. The binding, the gag, the circumstances felt paralyzing. I felt certain I would die if I did nothing.

I decided to die doing something. But what?

The man walked only a few yards in front of the Camry before he stopped. He called out to the paramedics. I could hear him speak, but he was facing away from me and was speaking into a dry, hot wind. I wasn't sure what he said.

The paramedic on the ground was facing me. The wind was at his back. He replied, "No, thank you. We have it covered."

I lifted my bound ankles over the console. I strained and reached to get the toes of my left foot on the brake pedal. I felt the pedal give. With my wrists taped to Chloe I had to devise a way to push the button on the gearshift knob while pulling the knob toward me at the same time. I lowered my forehead to the knob and twisted my left elbow to the gearshift.

Oden spoke again. Again, I couldn't hear. The EMT couldn't either. "Come closer, man. I can't hear you. Don't want to yell. My patient."

My kidnapper spoke again, louder. I froze at his voice. I still couldn't understand him.

The paramedic could. He said, "Don't know. Few minutes, maybe more. Not now. Can't leave her."

Oden said something else I couldn't hear. I pushed down with my head, felt the button yield to the pressure. I pulled my elbow toward me. The shifter popped into neutral. I sat up and removed the pressure from the brake.

The horizon offered no clues. I had no idea if the Camry would stay still, roll forward, or roll back. I prayed for back. I wanted to roll away.

The EMT said, "Few minutes, sir. At least. Got our hands full. Help is coming."

The EMT's tone had changed. He was losing patience. I leaned back as though I could goad the car into moving.

Oden raised his voice even more. He said, "Maybe I'll just move the darn thing myself." He meant the ambulance. He hadn't appreciated the "help is coming" admonition.

The EMT said, "Come closer. I have a patient in shock here. I don't want to yell. We'll work something out. Don't make this difficult, sir."

Oden clenched his fists. I had a bad feeling about how this was developing. I lowered my face down to my hands and used my fingers to peel the tape from my upper lip.

When I looked up again, Oden was taking a solitary step back.

He scratched at his neck below his ear with his left hand. I got hopeful for a second that he was going to find a way around a confrontation.

He'd be furious to find the car in neutral. I thought, *What the hell, I'm already dead.*

But Oden's next step was deliberately forward. As he lowered his left hand from his neck, I watched with alarm as he curled the middle finger over the index finger.

He had crossed his fingers. He was about to take his chances. *Damn. He's going to kill them all.*

He shifted his weight. He was up on his toes. One step, two, three.

He's all-in.

By the third step Oden was solidly into the rhythm of his march. At step five he uncrossed his fingers and reached toward the small of his back.

I saw a massacre coming. I yelled, "He has a gun!"

Fifty-nine

All at once, everything in the set piece in front of me changed.

The EMT leaning over the person on the ground lifted the backboard off the asphalt. But it wasn't a backboard. It was a riot shield. He raised it into position.

The patient on the ground sat up as fluidly as if she were doing a crunch at the gym. Her back was fine. She came up wearing body armor, a pistol in a two-handed grip. In a blink, she had the weapon leveled at Oden from behind the shield.

She immediately rolled behind the cab of the ambulance. The EMT followed her.

The twin back doors at the rear of the ambulance flew open. Two more shields filled that space. Gun barrels protruded from above and below.

The paramedic from the back of the Blazer disappeared from view, reappearing behind the hood, a rifle steady.

Everyone was yelling. Someone screamed, "Highway Patrol! Drop it!"

The guy behind the Blazer yelled, "Police! Drop your weapon!"

Oden stopped his march. He had the .38 in his hand behind his back, out of view of the cops.

I screamed, "He has a gun! Left hand. Left . . . hand!"

Oden's head moved slowly side to side. He had to be assessing the massive firepower that was assembled in front of him. He had to realize he was too far from the Camry to regain control of his hostages.

He had to realize he'd been set up.

He had to feel the déjà vu of looking at the embodiment of the thing—the one that wouldn't leave him alone—crawling back out of the grave. He had to know he wasn't going to get away from it again.

He had to be wondering what the hell had gone so wrong.

He held the pistol so that it hovered just above the crack of his ass, its barrel pointed at the glistening macadam ten feet behind him.

"Drop it!" three or four people continued to scream.

I barely heard them. For me this had become all about the guns. The ones pointed at him. And the one in his hand. I realized that from their vantage, the cops couldn't see his weapon. They had only my word for it.

They wouldn't make a move until Oden did.

Time stopped. My adrenals were squirting hormones like my glands were fire hoses and my damn toes were ablaze.

The yelling stopped. Standoff. Seconds passed.

Without looking back, Oden rotated his left wrist. He slowly raised the barrel of the revolver until the gun was pointed at the Camry. He squeezed off two quick shots.

I couldn't have been more surprised.

The fuck was shooting at us just to be vindictive. He had no chance to survive what he just did. Not that it would have done any good, but I was so flabbergasted I didn't even have the presence of mind to duck.

Oden may have squeezed off more than two shots at Amy and me. If he did, the fusillade that followed the first two shots prevented me from hearing any subsequent rounds.

Oden's body jerked as though he'd been shocked. Dark dots appeared on his lower back and on his upper back and high on his left buttock. Blood flowed down his neck on the right side. It came in pulses. Red splotches formed around the dark dots.

He swung his left hand and the .38 forward, but the motion was more about balance than it was about threat. His arm stopped when it was parallel to his leg, the barrel pointed toward his feet. It was as though the revolver suddenly weighed too much. He couldn't lift it any higher.

The cops had stopped firing. They were waiting for Oden either to die or to channel Rasputin and refuse to die. All the cops' weapons stayed trained on the man standing wounded, stunned, and defiant in the road.

Five seconds became ten before he dropped to his knees.

The .38 slipped from his fingers and clattered to the ground. I didn't hear it clatter. I did see it bounce.

Blood was streaming from the end of the pinky of Oden's right hand in a dark rivulet, like a shot of espresso dripping into a cup.

He swayed for a few seconds before he fell onto his face with a *splat* that I heard clearly. He didn't thrust out either hand to break his fall.

The cops swarmed forward, guns ready. They were barking commands to a dead man, still wary about Rasputin.

My eyes caught motion on the near horizon. On the rise beyond the bridge, a half-dozen vehicles stormed over the ridgeline in formation, three abreast. Reinforcements for the ambush.

I tried to turn my head back far enough to check on Amy. I saw a bullet hole in the windshield. Low, passenger side. Right where I would have been had I not crossed the console to find the brake pedal.

I said, "Amy, it's over."

She didn't reply.

"Amy, wake up. It's over. Come out of it."

She didn't say a word.

Despite popular misconceptions, hypnotic trances are typically not hard to break. My normal speaking voice could have done it.

The screaming and gunfire should have done it.

I resorted to cliché. Even though I hadn't given her any suggestions on exiting the trance, I said, "On the count of three, open your eyes. One . . . two . . . three. Now say something. Amy?"

She didn't say anything.

Come on, girl, give me a good eeeeeeeeeeaaaaaaaaaa. It's safe now.

I used my teeth to rip at the duct tape that was tethering me to the GPS. When I finally ripped through the tape some of it stuck to my teeth and lips. I contorted my position so I could rotate my head and swing my bound hands to Amy's face.

I saw blue below her nostrils. I touched her neck with eight fingertips. I couldn't find a carotid pulse.

Amy wasn't breathing.

"Help here!" I screamed, spitting at the damn tape. "Help here! She's not breathing."

Help came in the next few seconds.

I hoped there was a real paramedic someplace in the phalanx of vehicles that had crested the hill behind the arroyo.

The Camry chose that moment to start rolling forward, not back. I strained to find the brake with my toe.

Sixty

Sam helped me onto the stretcher. He leaned over me so that his big head blotted out the radiance from the sun. From my perspective it was like looking up at a solar eclipse.

"You know who he is?" Sam asked.

I said, "Yeah. You do too. Lincoln Oden."

"He kidnapped you in Tarzana?"

"I think. He knocked me out."

"The girl?"

"That's Amy."

"Ah," Sam said. "The fucking beguiler. The paramedics have her—a chopper's on the way. I'll catch up to you again in a minute. Alan, you did good."

A few minutes later Sam joined me in the back of the ambulance that had been the primary prop in the ambush of Oden. He made himself at home beside me. At my request the ambulance doors were wide open despite the heat. I didn't want to feel confined again. Even a little. Sam took over the job of cutting and yanking the tape off my wrists and ankles. A paramedic—a real one, not a cop pretending to be one—was on the other side of me. She had a catheter prepped and ready, waiting for Sam to finish clearing my wrist of tape so she could start an IV.

I said, "Amy?"

Sam explained that she was being loaded into the medical evacuation helicopter some distance down the road, out of my sight, on the far side of the rise in the highway. I'd heard the chopper arrive moments before. Sam said that Amy was breathing. That's all he knew about her condition. He asked me to tell him what happened.

I gave him the highlights of what I recalled from the moment I first heard Oden's voice in the garage in Tarzana. He listened to my choppy tale without any questions. When I was all done he said, "Wait. You're telling me you hypnotized the poor girl and then she stopped breathing? I don't know whether that makes you the second coming of Franz Mesmer or a complete quack."

I was shocked that Sam knew anything about Franz Mesmer— Mesmer was an nineteenth-century German physician whom many consider the father of hypnosis. But, I also had enough of my wits to know that I lacked sufficient brainpower to engage in any repartee with Sam about nineteenth-century mental-health practitioners.

"Where are we?" I asked him.

"Couldn't tell you exactly. The cop I've been hanging with is from Randsburg."

"Never heard of it," I said, as though it were important that I had.

Sam turned to the paramedic. "Where you from?" he asked her.

"California City," she said.

I'd never heard of California City, either.

Sam said, "This piece of paradise you're looking at"—he gestured outside—"is the Mojave Desert. Not too far from Death Valley. You might have noticed it's a little warm." He paused. "But at least it's a dry heat."

What a friend I have, I thought.

"How the hell did you find us, Sam?"

"The girls. Chloe and Ramona."

The paramedic from California City was finally content that my wrist was antiseptic. She gripped a needle and leaned over my arm. "Little stick coming," she said. I winced as the point pierced my skin.

A blast of *thwop-thwop-thwop-thwop-thwop* from the revving blades of the departing helicopter intruded, providing cover for the involuntary "ouch" I squealed as she adjusted the positioning of the catheter.

"It's in," she said. "We'll have you hydrated lickety-split."

"I didn't know you were such a wimp," Sam said.

I said, "I don't like needles. I don't understand what you're saying. Chloe and Ramona? Come on, tell me."

Sam opened his mouth and then closed it as the pulsating popping of the helicopter blades grew louder. I watched the chopper speed past us a hundred yards away at about ten o'clock. It was only fifty feet above the ground when it banked, climbed, and disappeared from view as though it had been yanked away by the gods.

"I wish I knew how to do that," Sam said.

The EMT from California City taped the catheter in place.

Sam opened his mouth again to tell me about Chloe and Ramona. Again, he closed it. The intrusion the second time was the roar of a Highway Patrol cruiser blasting past the ambulance. The cop car was demonstrating a show of speed worthy of a street racer on a Friday night. The howl of the car's big engine exploded in my ears for only a second before the driver jammed hard on his brakes and squealed the car to a stop five feet from the Camry.

Sam was on the move before I could make any sense of what I was seeing.

The Camry was baking in the sun right where it had stopped rolling. It looked like a wounded animal dying slowly in the desert heat. All four doors were open. The right front tire was deflated.

I sat up. "What's going on?" I said.

Sam was jumping down from the ambulance. He hit the ground running toward the Camry.

I yelled at his back, "What is it?"

Two Highway Patrol troopers hopped out of the cruiser. One ran to the back of the Camry, the other to the driver's door.

"Pop it! Pop it! Pop it!" the cop at the trunk yelled.

"Where the hell is the— Got it! Got it! Go, go!"

The trunk flew open. Both cops disappeared from my view.

One yelled, "Medic! Now! Oh Jesus. Now!"

A second paramedic appeared in the open doorway of the ambulance. He said, "The other rig's gone. We're it. Is he stable?"

He was asking about me.

The woman who had started my IV looked at him, then back at me. I could tell she was as baffled as I was. The male paramedic didn't get agitated. In a calm voice he said, "Kathy? We have a critical. Is he stable?"

"I'm stable," I said. I slid onto the jump seat Sam had vacated. "Take the stretcher."

Kathy got with the plan. Together the two paramedics yanked the stretcher from the rig, piled equipment onto the sheets, and sprinted toward the half dozen law enforcement people clustered behind the Camry.

I unhooked the saline bag from above me and climbed down from the back of the ambulance, suspending the bag above my head with my left hand. The asphalt felt soft beneath my feet, as though it were padded. The heat radiating up from the black macadam was, literally, breathtaking.

I started to jog toward the Camry.

Sam had backed away from the car to give the local cops and the paramedics room to work. He saw me approaching. He held up a hand to keep me from edging any closer.

"There's another woman," he said. "In the trunk."

I blinked. *Another woman?* My mind settled on Jaana. My heart sank.

"Alive?" I said.

He swallowed. "Maybe. Not very."

I heard the distant *thwop-thwop-thwop* of the evacuation chopper.

This time the helicopter was getting closer. Coming back.

"Eeeeeeeeeaaaaaaaaaa."

Oh no, I thought as recognition landed on me softly, like a mosquito alighting on my nose. *Oh no.*

L—*eeeeeeeeeeee* S—*aaaaaaaaaaaa.*

Li—sa.

Amy's screams from the backseat of the Camry had been her way of trying to tell me that Lisa was in the damn trunk. I'd missed it.

Over and over again, I'd missed it.

"It's Lisa?" I asked Sam.

"When Amy regained consciousness in the chopper, the first thing she wanted to know was if we got Lisa out of the trunk."

Sixty-one

The Canyon

Lincoln Oden knew Jaana Peet. During the time they both worked on the North Rim, Oden had talked with Jaana whenever he could manufacture a reason to do so. He had invited her out on dates three different times. Each invitation was more awkward than the one before.

She had turned him down all three times.

Oden fantasized that his assignment to coordinate the search left him an opportunity to be heroic. He would find Jaana. Save her. She would be grateful. They would go out. They would fall in love. They would marry. In his fantasy, Oden didn't seriously consider the possibility that Jaana wouldn't be grateful to him.

But once he finished interviewing Nicholas Paulson, Oden began to consider the possibility that Jaana hadn't disappeared into the Colorado River at all, but rather that she had chosen to disappear, period.

Two additional facts helped confirm his suspicion. Jaana's hiking boots had not been recovered along with her other belongings. And the amount of water that could have been carried in the containers found at her campsite was barely sufficient to accommodate two people making a rim-to-floor journey in the August heat.

He concluded that Jaana had worn the boots and carried the

missing water bottles, probably in a daypack she'd stashed inside her backpack. She had hiked out, probably on the Bright Angel Trail, the route to the South Rim, in the dark.

Based on his investigation, Oden thought he had a pretty good idea where Jaana had gone.

On his first day off after the search was called off because of the flash flood, Oden staked out Jaana's Estonian friend's rented home on the outskirts of Bullhead City. He watched Jaana's friend leave for work. Less than an hour later, he spotted Jaana. She was hanging laundry in the fenced backyard.

Another day and a half of observation convinced him that Jaana was in hiding. For Oden, that was good news.

He returned and watched her on his days off during the next two weeks. She never left the property.

The third week, he waited for her friend to leave for work and for Jaana to step outside. Late morning she rolled a trash can to the street. She didn't raise her eyes as he stepped out of his car, but she spun to get back inside the house as fast as she could.

"I can help," he said to her back from thirty feet away. "I can help you."

She took two more steps before she turned to see who had spoken. Her hand flew to her mouth to cover her gasp. She recognized him.

The fact that she had recognized him felt like a gift to Oden.

"I can help," he said. "I'd like to help. I know what he tried to do to you. I understand what you did. Why you did it."

She invited him in. She didn't feel she had a choice.

To Oden, the little house where she was living looked like it was begging to be scraped from the earth. In its thirty-five years of existence, too much maintenance had been deferred. The desert hadn't been kind.

"You can't stay here," Oden said to Jaana. "Your friend is already in trouble. If you're discovered here with her . . . you'll both be deported."

"She has a green card."

"It won't protect her if she's helping you hide."

"I stay inside," she said.

"I found you. Someone else will find you too. You can't stay here with her."

"I have no money."

"I can help."

Jaana couldn't resist the urge to place a hand on her belly.

"You have a baby to consider," Lincoln Oden said, his eyes following her hand. Oden had calculated that he had about five months to get Jaana Peet to fall in love with him. "If I can keep you hidden until the baby bis born, your child will be a U.S. citizen. That changes everything."

She asked, "Why should I trust you?"

He flipped open his badge wallet. "Because I could take you into custody. I should take you into custody." He put the wallet away. "The question is, can I trust you? If I don't put you in the car right now and take you in, I will be as vulnerable as you are. Maybe even more."

"Why would you help me?"

"I think what he did was wrong. The baby deserves a chance. So do you."

Three days later, Oden found the little ranch outside Kingman, Arizona. Two days after that, he moved Jaana from Bullhead City. He helped her write a good-bye note to her friend. In the note, she said she'd met someone who would help. She would be in touch.

The arrangement in Kingman worked fine for a few months. Jaana was relieved that she could go outside—the closest neighbors lived a quarter of a mile away. Oden arranged for Jaana to receive prenatal checkups at a free clinic for migrants. Her pregnancy was uncomplicated. He visited the ranch on his days off. When he was there, he doted on her, but he slept in the second bedroom.

Jaana enjoyed her new home. She was as wary of seeing strangers as Oden was. Unlike her friend's decrepit shack, the ranch house was relatively modern, and air-conditioned. She had a television. Other than the isolation—Oden refused to let her have a phone or a computer—she convinced herself that she was better off in Kingman than she had been in Bullhead City.

Her baby would be a citizen.

A month before Jaana was due, Oden quit his job with the Park Service so he could be with her. He moved into the house in Kingman. He convinced himself that she was warming to him. He used his free time to take courses to become an insurance agent.

Jaana give birth to a son with the aid of a midwife.

Almost immediately after the child was born, Lincoln Oden knew that everything had changed for Jaana.

He had conversations with himself. They all ended with him telling himself he should walk away. That his plan hadn't worked.

He didn't walk away.

The day that Jaana's friend arrived to rescue her from her captivity in Kingman, Oden was parked out of sight, waiting. Jaana thought he was in town, on errands. He'd parked in the same spot down the road every time he'd left the ranch for five days, expecting that the Estonian girlfriend would come.

When Oden drove away from the little ranch an hour later, the baby was asleep in his infant carrier in the middle of the backseat of the car.

Jaana and her friend were in the trunk.

Sixty-two

Her Ex

The ambulance transported me to an ER in Tehachapi, another town I hadn't heard of. After a local cop finished interviewing me, Sam loaned me his phone. I tried Lauren in Holland. She didn't answer. I left a message letting her know I'd lost my new cell phone, and that I would try to reach her again soon. Sam had already tried to reach Merideth to update her about Lisa.

He'd gotten her voice mail. Told her to call him immediately.

He couldn't get any medical updates about Lisa or Amy.

While we were waiting for my turn with the ER doc, Sam finally began to answer my question about Chloe and Ranger Ramona. He was in a storytelling mood.

"Okay," he said, "I get a call at some awful hour. I'm sound asleep in the comfiest bed I think I've ever slept in my entire life. All I know is, it's too early. That was this morning. I manage to get the phone to my ear and before I can even curse at whoever's calling, I hear some guy I don't know saying, 'Kick them this way,' then 'I got a gun.' Then nothing.

"From my perspective, not necessarily a good thing to wake up to. 'Kick them this way, I got a gun.' I check caller ID. It says it was you, but I was ninety-nine percent sure it hadn't been you talking. I admit I'm confused—it's early, I'm foggy, and I'd been thinking you should be asleep in the other room. But if it's really you calling me that early in the morning I'm guessing the 'kick them this way, I got a gun' is something important. That, or you're feeling suicidal and you're hoping I'll put you out of your misery.

"I stumble out to the living room for a reality check and sure enough you're gone. The note you left out on the counter said there was a psych emergency with Mel's friend. You remember that much?" I told him I did. "And that you're heading to Tarzana. You leave nice notes, Alan. Lots of detail. Lauren's trained you well.

"I called you back, of course, but you're not answering. Not a good sign.

"My options are kind of limited. I wake up that LAPD detective I talked to last night—the friend of the friend of Carmen's—and I tell her about the emergency you have in Tarzana involving the women whose house almost exploded the night before, all the missing people from the Grand Canyon, and the 'kick them this way, I got a gun' phone call that woke me up, and she agrees to have a patrol car sent to the Tarzana address to look around. Two cops get there within a few minutes. They find a bunch of sleeping people. A suicidal girl—"

"Kanyn."

"Yeah, Kanyn—"

"Still suicidal? Or by history?"

"All I know is 'suicidal'—what the—"

"Did she make an attempt last night? After I left?"

"Suicidal, that's it. And—"

I said, "The body. Oh shit, Sam. I haven't told anybody about the body. Did they find the body?"

"The one in the garage? That's Jack. Somebody whacked him on the head with a wrench. Timing? Not sure, the forensics guys will get all that—"

"Oden?"

Sam took my face in both of his fat hands like a grandmother about to plant a wet one on her favorite grandkid. "How 'bout you stop interrupting me so I can tell you what the hell happened?"

I nodded. I was relieved he didn't actually kiss me.

He released his grip on my cheeks. "At that point we still don't know who said he had a gun into your phone.

"The patrol guys find lots of interesting stuff when they look around. First, they spotted blood in the garage—Jack's body came later. A stolen pickup on the street out front. Your beguiling friend Amy's car on the driveway, and her keys on the floor of the garage—but no Amy. We think you were there, too, of course, but your rental's no place to be found. One theory getting a lot of immediate attention is that you and Amy have been abducted, probably in your car. That's when I tell the LAPD detective about Chloe."

I almost said, "You remembered Chloe?" I didn't say it.

"I remember how enamored you are with the GPS in the car. It's worth a shot, is what I'm thinking. Sure enough, Hertz tracks your car in like no time. They find it heading northbound on the 15, not too far from San Bernardino.

"We scramble to put our little operation in place. The resources they got here? In L.A.? Helicopters. Highway Patrol. Rescue rigs. Bang, bang, bang. Like being in the damn Army."

Sam hadn't been in the Army. In other circumstances, I would've mentioned that just to aggravate him.

"Anyway, by the time the Camry gets to the other side of Barstow and cuts off the 15 onto some little road that heads toward The Mojave, we were mobilized."

I said, "Can I ask a question?"

He said, "Yes."

"Why did you drive past us in the ambulance? That must have been one of the most depressing things I ever saw in my life."

"Had to know what we were dealing with. Drove by, we saw him, saw you, saw the gun. We didn't see Amy, though. That worried us. We didn't know how much time we had. We also had to come up with a way to lure him away from the car without you. If he heard us tracking him with a chopper or saw us pass by in a marked car, we knew there was a good chance he'd get suspicious and we'd end up in a standoff. If we tried to stop him or approached the car, we knew we might get into a chase, or he might kill anybody in the car before we were able to kill him. One of the local guys suggested using the ambulance for surveillance. Brilliant.

"We were mobilizing down the road for whatever might come next. Once we knew what we were dealing with, we faked the accident to block the road. Had to get the guy out of the car. Had to. We guessed he wouldn't drive up next to the accident with a bound hostage in the car."

"You knew it was Oden?"

"Not at first," Sam said. "That's where Ranger Ramona comes in."

I could tell from the way he said it that Sam was proud of Ranger Ramona's contribution. I understood. I was proud of Chloe.

Ramona had been thinking. Two things had gotten her going. One was her discovery that Jaana's Estonian girlfriend had walked away from her life only months after Jaana disappeared in the canyon. The other was Sam's curiosity about Lincoln Oden.

Ramona had done some quick checking and discovered yet another coincidence—Oden had moved from Kingman, Arizona, to L.A. exactly five days after Jaana's girlfriend was reported missing by her boss in Las Vegas.

Ramona went to the Internet looking for signs of Oden. She located a recent photo from an online community newspaper of Oden and his son—Ramona didn't know Oden had a son—and another Allstate agent and that guy's son after the foursome had won a charity father-son team sandcastle-building contest over the previous Father's Day weekend. The team had built a giant serpent of some kind, using plastic buckets for teeth. In the photo, they were all sweaty and happy and covered with sand.

Ramona had immediately called Sam. She didn't know that at

that moment he was in an LAPD patrol car being escorted to catch a helicopter for the short hop to the edge of the Mojave Desert.

She told him about the timing of Oden's move from Arizona to California. Sam told her he found that interesting. She'd said, "There's more," and told Sam about the sandcastle photo. "His son's Asian, Sam. Not all Asian, but part. Japanese, be my guess. You can tell clearly from the picture the kid's got Asian features."

Ramona explained to Sam that she had been in the Navy. She'd been stationed on Okinawa for a while. She knew the Japanese.

Sam had understood the relevance of Oden's son's Asian features immediately.

"Oden got a wife? Girlfriend?" Sam had asked. "She Asian?"

Ramona had wondered the same thing. So she had called Oden's house just minutes before she phoned Sam in the back of the LAPD patrol car.

Ramona told Sam that when a woman had answered at Oden's house, she'd said, "Mrs. Oden?"

The woman had said, "Sí."

Ramona told Sam, "I speak some Spanish. We talked a little. I told her I was an old colleague of her husband's. She said he was out of town on business, he'd be back that evening. She's from Oaxaca. I don't think that lady is the kid's natural mom."

Sam didn't either.

"The kid's the right age, Sam," Ramona told him.

"The right age for what?" I asked at that point in his story.

I blamed it on the concussion, of course, but I didn't add things up right away. Sam was able to recognize that some of my neurons weren't firing on command. He encouraged me to lie back on the gurney in the exam room.

In a kind voice, he said, "Oden's kid has Asian blood, Alan. The only Asian on the roster we've developed from that week in the Grand Canyon is Jaana's old flame in Vegas. That rich guy I talked to, Nick Paulson. He's definitely part Japanese. I saw him. Sure, there are other explanations for the kid having Asian features—Oden could've married an Asian woman that no one knew about, that's one—but the most obvious explanation is that Oden somehow ended up with the baby that Jaana was pregnant with when she disappeared from the canyon."

I said, "There're lots of Asian adoptions these days. Lots of mixed-race kids. L.A.'s diverse, Sam."

"You playing devil's advocate, or are you injured worse than I think? China? Yeah, there're adoptions. Korea? Sure. Other places? Yeah. But not too many from Japan," Sam said. "Bet you the kid isn't adopted."

"Then where's Jaana?" I asked. As soon as I said her name aloud, the pieces fell together in my head. I said, "Oh shit, that's the two."

"What?" Sam said. "What's the two?"

"Jaana and her friend from Estonia?" I said. I was frustrated that my memory was returning in burps. "They're the two people that Oden said he dumped in the desert. Oh my God, Oden told me that he had dumped two people once before. He left their bodies in the desert. Two people, Sam. I couldn't figure it out. But it had to be Jaana and her friend, right?"

Sam's shoulders dropped. "If my theory is correct about Oden, it has to be Jaana and her friend," he said.

"Nick Paulson?" I asked.

Sam thought about it. "Asshole? He's guilty of that. Everything else? My guess is the guy skates."

The ER doc was a moonlighting resident from UCLA. She was a tall, thin black woman with a wry wit. She checked me for other things— a fractured skull and a subdural hematoma—but settled on the diagnosis of a concussion. "Common things happen commonly," she explained. She told Sam and me what to watch for, and she sent us on our way.

The Camry had been wounded. It had taken three slugs during the Mojave shootout. I was trying not to think about what amount of additional brain damage I would suffer making Hertz happy with me again.

I couldn't remember if I'd opted for the extra insurance.

I hoped Chloe hadn't been hit.

Sam finagled a ride for us back to L.A. with the brother-in-law of the cop who lived in Randsburg. The guy's mom was coming back from a holiday in China. He was picking her up at LAX.

I slept the whole way to West Hollywood.

Southern California was having one of those days that makes L.A. magic. When L.A. is stunning, the hills come closer, the basin shrinks, the Pacific sparkles, and the air is as clear as the melt from an icicle. A billion fanciful dreams have been born on days when L.A. is stunning. Most of the dreamers have stayed behind.

I woke up to the L.A. brilliance thinking that I didn't want it to be the day that Lisa and Amy died.

Hector was on duty when Sam and I walked into the lobby of Merideth's condo. Hector greeted me with the news that Merideth had been trying to reach me. Sam told Hector he'd already left her a couple of messages. I told Hector I'd lost my cell phone.

Hector's face said, "Yeah, right."

Sam sensed some attitude. His tone morphed into cop. He said, "You can watch it on the news tonight if you want. Any channel."

Hector thought Sam was blowing smoke up his ass. He lifted his chin before he spoke to me. "She's on her way here. To L.A. You have to leave. Got somebody coming to clean the place"—he looked at his watch—"in an hour."

Hector was infusing a little more street into his accent. It was an interesting metamorphosis.

"No problem, Hector." I turned to Sam, "God, I hope that means she's talked to Eric. And knows about Lisa. I'd rather not be the one to have to tell her."

Sam kept his eyes on Hector. "I got it covered. Don't worry."

Each of them was stiffening. I put a hand on Sam's back and led him to the elevator.

Sam still hadn't learned anything about Amy or Lisa. We weren't family, and he hadn't been able to bluff his way around the HIPAA privacy restrictions at the hospital. Merideth might have better luck—she and Lisa certainly had family ties, even if theirs were the kind of postmodern relationships that tend to give institutions fits.

The first thing I did inside the condo was to use the landline to again call Lauren. Again she didn't answer. I left her a message that I was heading home to Boulder and would call her from the airport. I didn't tell her about the concussion or the shootout. There was no reason to alarm her at that point. I prayed she was staying away from the day's news.

The second thing I did was shower in Merideth's splendid shower.

The concussion was evolving. My head felt as though it was being propped up on my neck by a couple of swollen spikes. I couldn't wait to get home.

Sam drove me to LAX. On the congested drive from Hollywood to the airport, Sam's phone buzzed with updated information about the aftermath of the confrontation with Oden in the desert. Oden's wife was being interviewed by authorities. His son was indeed of mixed race, with Asian features. A photograph—suspected to be of his son as an infant—had been discovered in his wallet. The baby in the picture was being held by a white woman. The photo was scanned and sent to the Grand Canyon. Ranger Ramona phoned Sam. She was ninety-nine percent sure the woman was Jaana Peet.

Oden's oxidized Mazda hatchback had been located a block and a half from the Mt. Washington duplex.

After getting that last piece of news from his contact at LAPD, Sam said to me, "I bet Oden followed Jack there. That's how he found Lisa. He must have stolen that truck to follow Jack to Tarzana."

"But how did he find Jack? Why was he looking for him?" I asked.

"Still working on that," he said. "Must have something to do with Jack's call to Paulson."

Sam still couldn't get any information about Lisa or Amy.

I gave Sam a big hug at the curb at LAX. He played along.

He was undecided about what he was going to do next. He wanted to hang around L.A. long enough to learn the final pieces of the Grand Canyon puzzle. After that, he thought he might head north on Highway 1—he'd never been to Big Sur—before crossing the wide expanses of the desolate west on I-70.

He was determined to have one last Animal Style burger at In-N-Out, and to find a Trader Joe's before he returned to Colorado. He admitted that he'd become addicted to some of the market's peculiar victuals on his visits to see Carmen. He wanted to get a few months' supply of his favorites. I asked him to pick me up a mixed case of Two-Buck Chuck. I wondered how the wine would taste after spending a week in the desert in the back of his Cherokee.

I bought a phone card and tried unsuccessfully to connect with Lauren before I boarded the plane to Denver.

I was having a hard time understanding why she hadn't answered her phone all day. It had been midafternoon in Holland when I'd phoned her from the bed of the old Ford pickup. As I stood at a public phone near the gate at LAX, it was well past Grace's bedtime in Amsterdam. Lauren should have noted my missed calls. I had checked our home voice mail to see if she'd left a message there. She had not.

My wife got along fine with technology. She was adept at every esoteric feature of her mobile phone. She should have heard my messages. After listening to them, she should have been ready for my next call.

The landing at DIA was crappy. The captain had warned during the approach that there were microbursts in the vicinity of DIA. We bounced twice and had a hold-your-breath moment as the left wing took a dive in the instant after the second bounce. My pulse barely registered the jeopardy. I was running out of adrenaline.

I checked my cell voice mail from the nearest pay phone in the concourse. I had no messages from Lauren. I had one from Merideth: "I just heard the details. Oh my God. Call me. I'm in L.A."

And I did have one from Marty.

Oh, God. I hadn't worried about Marty in at least a day.

Sixty-three

"Marty? Alan."

I started a silent mantra. *I will be at LaGuardia in two days to retrieve my son. I will be at La . . .*

"Alan," Marty said. His tone of voice was like a warning flare in front of my eyes. He had spoken my name softly, and without any of the usual nasal qualities that made me wince. "We have a . . . problem with Jonas."

Don't. Don't tell me he wants to stay in White Plains. Fucking don't. I don't want to fight you, but I will fight you with every last watt of energy in my body.

"Is he okay?" I said in my best therapist voice.

"Umm . . ."

"Tell me," I said, fighting to feign composure.

"It's been going so well here," Marty said.

No. He is not staying. I will be at LaGuardia in—

"But . . . it's like he hit a wall. He didn't want to get out of bed yesterday morning, said his stomach hurt. We almost had to drag him out for breakfast. Kim made pancakes. All of a sudden he's barely eating. He never eats much—you saw how skinny he is—but he likes Kim's pancakes. Everybody does. And now he's started crying at nothing. When we ask him what's wrong, he just says that he misses Callie."

I held an imaginary level to my demeanor to be certain I could make my voice appear calm. The bubble floated to the middle and stayed. *Good*. My act would have to suffice—I did not want to alienate Marty. "That's what Jonas said?" I asked. "He said he misses Callie?"

"Callie" was the emergency code word Jonas had chosen to use with me.

"We have a dog," Marty said, misinterpreting the problem as canine in nature, and misinterpreting the solution to be generic. Marty believed his dog should have been enough for Jonas.

"The puppy was a gift from his mother," I said, offering a fresh perspective.

Marty paused a beat before he responded. *He's getting it*, I thought, hoping I was wrong about him.

Marty said, "So? Everything he has is a gift from his mother, isn't it? I mean, think about it."

Were I not so intent on not alienating Marty, it would have been a fine time to ask if he'd ever taken Introductory Psych. Or ever watched *Oprah*.

"Is he there, Marty? Can I speak with him?"

"Hi," my son said a few seconds later. His voice was completely devoid of the confidence I'd heard from him as he kicked the stone during our walk in White Plains not too many days before. I imagined Marty hovering behind Jonas as he spoke to me on the phone that hung from the wall next to the refrigerator in Kim's cluttered kitchen. I needed to find a way to give the kid a cushion.

"Hi," I said. "Hey, can you grab your cell and head out to the swing? There are some important phone lessons I need, and this may take a while. Will you do that for me? I will call you there in two minutes."

My impulse was to go straight to New York from the Denver airport, but a compassionate gate agent at DIA quickly helped me comprehend that such a trip wasn't in the cards. The last two flights from Denver to LaGuardia that day were overbooked. I'd be at the end of long stand-by lists. Other than the red-eye into JFK—I really didn't want to make Kim schlep Jonas all the way to JFK from White Plains at the crack of dawn—the first chance I had to get out of Denver to New York was on the earliest United flight the next morning.

I phoned Jonas and told him the plans. He seemed relieved that I was on my way. He assured me he would be fine until the next day. I was tempted to believe him. What choice did I have?

I phoned Lauren again before I left the airport. Again, she didn't answer.

I left Lauren yet another message when I got to Boulder. I let her know I was getting concerned at her silence. I wondered if she, too, had lost her phone.

In my life I was learning to always leave room for irony.

Sam had left me a voice mail on the home line. Lisa was alive. She was at Cedars-Sinai. The hospital, at the patient's request, was not releasing information about her condition. He hadn't heard anything about the baby. Or Amy. He said he thought that was good news— that he hadn't heard anything about Amy.

He also thought his L.A. law enforcement colleagues had pieced together a pretty good scenario to explain what had come down.

Jack's cell phone memory contained evidence of a call to Oden two days before I flew to California. The cops' theory was that Jack had inadvertently started the final ball rolling when he made a decision to confront Oden with the news Jack had learned from Nicholas Paulson about Jaana's pregnancy.

Oden instantly began to sense that his house of cards was crumbling. LAPD detectives found a receipt from a gas station in the Marina district in San Diego in Oden's car. The receipt was dated the same day that Jack was planning to drive to L.A. to see Lisa. Oden had apparently arrived in San Diego just in time to follow Jack north for his rendezvous with Lisa in Mt. Washington. Jack's next stop was Tarzana. Oden followed him there. The cops figured that it was at that point that Jack must have told Oden what Lisa knew. Oden killed Jack in the garage of the old barn and stashed his body in the decrepit pickup until he could decide what to do about Lisa. He returned to Mt. Washington the next day to get her. With Lisa bound and gagged in the cab of the truck he'd stolen, Oden drove to the Valley to retrieve Jack's body.

He probably thought he was one trip to the desert away from dodging a second bullet.

But that's when I ran from Amy's naked overture to the bed of the old Ford.

Sam ended his message with a laugh as he shared the fact that the local media had identified me as Gregory Alan.

I thanked the copywriting gods for that small favor.

I'd appreciated my time in New York City. I'd been surprised at how much I enjoyed being in L.A. But I felt consummate relief being back in Boulder. The gestalt of the place—the city against the mountains, the mountains against the sky—provided a much-needed anchor for my soul. It was one of those days that I found the Front Range so lovely that the tableau seemed preposterous. On one side of the valley, my home sits near the crest of pedestrian hills. On the opposing side of the valley, mountains soar from fifty-five hundred feet to fourteen-thousand feet in the blink of a geological eye. Above the Rockies is western sky. Above that is possibility.

Tucked into the western edge of the valley is a town that is so full of contradictions that it is hard to believe it is the work of so much planning. Prescient leadership has left the city of Boulder as the hole in one of the most appetizing geographical urban doughnuts anywhere. The town, peculiar in so many amusing ways, is surrounded by pristine greenbelts stretching as far as my eyes can see. I marvel at the splendid economic wastefulness of the undeveloped acreage whenever I slow down long enough to be grateful for it. Developers, I imagine, want to fall on their bejeweled subdivision swords whenever they view the immense swaths of prime mountain and valley real estate that Boulder taxpayers have cordoned off from bulldozers. Forever.

Once I get my family back here, I was thinking, *I might never leave.*

I gave Mona a brief respite from her dog-sitting chores but explained that I'd be flying out the next morning to retrieve Jonas. The three dogs and I went on a late-afternoon walk on the familiar trails of Spanish Hills. Huge thunderheads were building along the Front Range. One reached toward the stratosphere in Jefferson County to the south, and another one did the same in Weld County to the north.

For that moment Boulder was dry. During monsoon season that could change in an instant.

A female voice stunned me when I walked back into the house with the dogs. I was disoriented enough to blink a few times and consider the possibility that I was hallucinating. I finally realized that someone was leaving a message on the answering machine. I charged for it. The dogs charged after me, barking. Just before I reached the phone, the voice said, "Adi."

Adi. Amy.

I hit Play.

"Alan? I got this number from Mel's mom. Hope it's okay to call. I'm kind of glad you didn't answer, that I got your machine. It's easier, maybe. Listen . . . I'm fine, still shaky and sore, but okay. I'm staying with some friends from the show for a couple of days. Thanks for all your calls. Someday—not too soon—maybe we can talk about what happened. Something. Wow." She sighed. "Okay . . . Last part. I want you to know that—when the whole adored thing ends up not working out for you and your wife—feel free to give me a call. I think you know what I mean. You take care. Adi."

Yes, the whole adored thing.

A second message began to play. "Hey." It was Sam. "No more news about Lisa. Can't get anyone to talk about the baby. Merideth's here, but I haven't seen her yet. Amy's been discharged from the hospital.

"Jack had contacted Oden after he talked to Paulson. Oden knew Jack had learned about Jaana's pregnancy. Oden panicked—he started following Jack as soon as he left San Diego to come up to meet with Lisa. Jack was Oden's initial target. It looks like Jack just told Lisa too much. I'll keep you posted if I learn more. I . . . uh, I'm leaving L.A. Something came up." *Beep.*

The phone rang. Caller ID read OUT OF AREA.

Amy's calling back, I thought. My pulse raced.

I said, "Hello."

A crisp, clear, male voice said, "Hello."

The man had the type of generic accent that caused me to think that I might be getting an unwelcome robo-call from a politician or a charity. Before I could respond to his greeting, he continued, "This is Joost Holkenen. I am calling from Hilversum, in Holland. It's not far from Amsterdam. Is this Alan Gregory?"

Why do I care where Hilversum is? I thought. Then I felt my legs begin to buckle.

I was no longer enjoying the afterglow of a pre-dusk walk with the dogs on the dusty trails of Spanish Hills in late summer. Suddenly it was the previous April all over again and it was three o'clock in the morning and I was trying to decipher the shocking news from Israel that my friend Adrienne was dead.

Oh, God. Joost Holkenen was in Holland. *Hilversum is in Holland.*

"Yes. Are Lauren and Grace okay?" I said. *Please, please.*

"Your daughter is well. Good. She is a fine child. Lauren is . . . ill, I'm afraid. Suddenly. This afternoon . . . early evening, really. She is in hospital here, in Hilversum. She has suffered some . . . paralysis. She is resting right now."

Lauren is paralyzed. Holy shit. "Lauren? Her MS?"

"Yes, the doctors say. The MS, in her legs."

I tried to recall the neurological anatomy. I thought "legs" likely meant a spinal-cord lesion. "Leg"—singular—was more indicative of a lesion in the brain. "Both legs?"

"Yes."

"Where is Grace? My daughter? Is she with Lauren?"

"Of course, of course. She is with my daughter, Sofie, and her family. In Amsterdam. She is fine. By now asleep, I'm sure. It is late here."

The situation he was describing made no sense to me. Why would Grace be with this man's daughter and her family? Why wasn't Grace with Lauren?

I swallowed down more panic. "I'm sorry. I'm not thinking clearly. Are you Lauren's doctor. You said your name is . . .?"

"Holkenen. Joost Holkenen. No. Please, do not apologize. I am . . . Sofie's father." He paused. "Grace's . . . sister's . . . father."

Grace's . . . sister. Grace's sister's . . . father.

Gibberish. *Who are you?* I wondered.

An old relational brain-twister I had stumbled over since I'd first heard it as a child invaded my brain, uninvited: *Brothers and sisters I have none, but this man's father is my father's son . . .*

I could never figure the damn puzzle out.

I forced myself back to the suburb of reality that included Joost Holkenen and a town in the Netherlands called Hilversum. *Could the concussion be causing my brain to misfire this badly?*

"My daughter Sofie, and her family." That's what Holkenen had said. He hadn't said "my daughter Sofie, and my family."

My daughter Grace was with Holkenen's daughter Sofie, who was with *her* family. Sofie's family was not her father's family.

How does this work? My brain felt incapable of determining how many quarters were in a dollar, let alone solving this intercontinental relationship riddle.

Grace was with Sofie, and Sofie's family. Okay. But was Grace also with Sofie, and Grace's family? Did Grace's family now include Sofie, and Sofie's family?

I gasped. *Does Grace's family include Joost Holkenen?*

When that last question formed in my head, I suddenly understood everything.

By the time my comprehension had endured for the duration of two eye blinks, I tried to shake it away with a silent, plaintive, *No*. I tried to pretend that I understood nothing.

It was too late. I did understand. I attempted to take a deep breath. I couldn't. My lungs had shrunk to the size of walnuts. I coughed, then choked down vomit. I almost gagged as I swallowed it back into place.

I said, "Sofie is the daughter that Lauren gave up for adoption . . . when she was in college? She has been trying to arrange to meet her."

None of what I said was news to Joost Holkenen. "That is correct," he said. "Sofie is Grace's sister—her half sister."

His delivery was unremarkable. He could have been reciting the Hilversum–Amsterdam train schedule. His matter-of-fact tone made it clear to me that Joost didn't have a bike in this peloton.

What did his neutrality mean for me? I wasn't sure.

I steeled myself to ask the Powerball question, the one that could change our futures. Mine and Joost's. Lauren's and Grace's. Maybe Sofie's.

I said, "And you are . . . Sofie's birth father?"

"I am," said Joost Holkenen.

With surprising equanimity, I reviewed the facts in my head: *My wife's long-ago, year-abroad college lover is on the phone telling me all these years later that my wife is paralyzed in Hilversum in the Netherlands. That same man is my daughter's half sister's father.*

The particulars, I recognized, were not good news for me on so many levels.

"Mr. Holkenen?" I said. "You live in Hilversum?"

He hesitated. Not for long—it was hardly a pause at all—but I noted the delay, perhaps because of how badly I feared it. Holkenen had been expecting me to connect some dots—and my question about where he lived provided all the evidence he needed that I had accomplished some important dot-connecting. His hesitation before he answered informed me that he hadn't looked forward to witnessing the advent of my awareness.

I appreciated that the anticipation of my anguish made him uncomfortable. I liked that about him.

He finally said, "I do. I produce television here. News."

The irony, finally.

I could feel cell walls imploding in my soul.

Sixty-four

I met Jonas and Kim in the terminal of LaGuardia the next day just before noon. Jonas gave Kim a protracted, poignant hug when the time came for her to go back home. They each had tears in their eyes as they said good-bye. I thanked Kim and promised her we would stay in touch. I felt good that Jonas had connected with his family, and especially good that Kim was part of it.

I could feel Jonas's fragility as he watched her turn to walk away.

While we waited to clear security, I distracted him with a question about the Rockies' chances of meeting the Mets in the playoffs. He reacted with a pronounced exhale that almost reached the threshold for a chuckle. He told me he'd done the math and that the Rocks would have to win almost all their remaining games just to be a wild card. I told him that I thought I remembered the Yankees winning something like fifteen in a row once to end their season. With more heartbreak in his voice than someone his age should have been able to muster, he said, "The Rockies just lost three of their starting pitchers for the season, Alan. And anyway, the Rockies aren't the Yankees."

He was right, of course. The Cubs may have written the book on futility and heartbreak, but in their brief history the Rockies had been doing a fine job of polishing the abridged version of the same tale.

We made it down the concourse only as far as Auntie Anne's before I heard a telltale quiver radiating in Jonas's voice. He'd just started describing a double-play in the previous night's Mets game, but he couldn't remember the name of the Mets' second baseman. His frustration threatened to engulf him. With a hand on his shoulder I led him over to the side of the narrow concourse. I sat down with my back against a wall below a bank of pay phones and pulled him onto my lap.

He didn't resist. He leaned into me, resting his head against my shoulder. He shook—quaked, really—before he started to cry. Once he began to sob, he continued for at least five minutes.

My own emotional balance remained sketchy. I was logy from the concussion, and ragged from everything else, but I felt strong enough to be Jonas's dad at that moment.

Between sobs, he said, "I—I—I—"

I said, "I know. I miss her too, Jonas. I miss her too. I'm so sorry."

Healing is not an event, it's a process. Despite the hiccups of The Mojave, Holkenen, Hilversum, and Lauren's paralysis, the process of healing was proceeding for me. I was getting better, stronger. I could feel it.

Despite his premature visit to connect with his mother's family, the process would proceed for Jonas. He would heal too.

When I was pretty sure Jonas was done with this round of tears, I said, "Want to go home, buddy?"

"Yeah," he said.

"I think I can do that. Brownie?" I asked. I was thinking Au Bon Pain.

He said, "Maybe a pretzel." He had his eye on Auntie Anne's.

"Or both," I said. "A brownie and a pretzel. I can do that, too."

We stood up.

Grief visited, comfort food on the way, Jonas turned the page back to baseball. "You think the Rockies could do it?" he asked, all cynicism suddenly absent from his voice, hope's pendulum swinging far into the realm of fantasy. "Win the rest of their games? Maybe win the division or get the wild card?"

I wanted to be an optimist, but believing the Rockies could win-out sounded borderline psychotic to me. "No," I said. "Have they even won five in a row since the break? You think it will be the Mets in the East?"

The Mets would be a good consolation prize for Jonas.

"Gotta be. No way they can lose this lead," Jonas said. We stepped into line for the pretzel. He added, "Yankees will fold. Mets–Sox World Series, Mets in six, that's what I think. Can I get a Coke, too? Please."

"It's yours," I said. "You know what—I didn't tell you what your dog can do to a piece of paper, did I?"

"No. What?" His red eyes brightened.

"She makes confetti," I said. "Perfect confetti. Times-Square-on-New-Year's-Eve confetti. So be careful where you leave your home-work. She'll shred it in seconds. She's a machine."

He laughed.

It gave me hope.

The Rockies winning out? *Ha, no chance.*

It was okay with me. I already had my great news—a son who liked to talk baseball.

Sixty-five

Jonas and I were back in Boulder by dinnertime. I was suffering a bad case of airplane-seat ass. I'd get over it.

I did something I'd been putting off. I called Wallace. He wasn't home. Cassandra answered. I said, "This is Alan."

Without prelude, she said, "I have to tell Wallace, don't I?"

She wanted me to disagree with her. I said, "Or Mel could tell Wallace."

"She's a wreck. That girl broke up with her. Jules. She told Cara she needs to do some growing up."

"Maybe," I said, "she does."

Cassandra pondered that simple reality for a moment. "There are worse things," she said.

"A million," I replied. I was tempted to offer a few examples. I didn't. Cassandra neither thanked me nor apologized to me.

I hadn't decided if I deserved either.

I called Sam just to talk. He was, I guessed, on some desert road—north or south, highway or not—in the immense emptiness that fills most of the map between California and Boulder. I got his voice mail. I let him know I was back in town with Jonas. I didn't tell him about Lauren. That wasn't voice mail fare. I gave him Jonas's cell number and asked him to call me as soon as he got a chance.

My working hypothesis was that Sam had retraced his route through Las Vegas—maybe he'd stopped for a while and resumed his search for a five-buck blackjack table—and was someplace on 15 or already heading east on I-70. I allowed there was a chance that he'd reconsidered his earlier decision and strayed south to rendezvous with Ramona on the North Rim of the Grand Canyon. If that appetite had prevailed, Sam would be coming up I-25 a few days later than I expected.

Not up "the 25." Up I-25.

Back in graduate school I'd had a psych professor who used axioms to teach important psychological principles. One that had stuck with me was: You can go broke buying insurance.

Over the many years since I'd been exposed to his wisdom, the reach of that particular rule kept expanding. Experience had taught me that it contained a wealth of truth about many things. Even, it turned out, about insurance.

Before she and Grace had left for Europe Lauren had suggested that we buy a travel policy that would pay to fly her or Grace home by air ambulance if either of them got sick in the Netherlands. The cost of the plan was a few hundred bucks.

I'd scoffed, reciting my professor's dictum about going broke buying insurance. She'd insisted that the coverage would give her peace of mind. I'd relented of course—not because I thought we'd ever use the insurance, but because I felt that a few hundred dollars was a reasonable price for Lauren's peace of mind.

My professor would have laughed at our gullibility. He'd once told the class that it was because of gullible people—like me and Lauren—that he kept a good chunk of his retirement-plan assets invested in insurance companies.

I bought the coverage and paid the premium. In return the company promised to fly my girls home on an air ambulance if either of them became ill enough to be admitted to a hospital while they were away. A couple of hundred bucks for many tens of thousands of dollars of coverage.

The company kept its promise. I made a solitary phone call to get the process started. Less than twenty-four hours later, Lauren and Grace were in an air ambulance crossing the North Atlantic with a doctor and nurse at Lauren's side. The small jet refueled on the East Coast on the way to the airport in Jefferson County, not far from Boulder.

I went back and forth. Had I had been too naïve, or too trusting? Maybe both, maybe neither. I couldn't decide.

The reality was that the possibility of Lauren reconnecting with her old lover during her trip to Holland had never crossed my mind.

If Lauren had gotten sick in Amsterdam and not in Hilversum, I'm not sure I would have ever found out that she was getting together with her old boyfriend. But the fact that she was hospitalized in Hilversum when she suffered the MS exacerbation told me all I needed to be convinced that her rendezvous with Joost had taken some planning.

My girls' European adventure's original goal had come to fruition during those last two days in Holland. Lauren and Grace had finally arranged to meet Lauren's daughter—Grace's half sister—Sofie.

After the two families met for lunch in a restaurant, Grace received an invitation to do a sleepover with Sofie's adoptive family in Amsterdam. That was wonderful. Gracie had fresh family. She would have memories of meeting Sofie that she would treasure for years.

Lauren took advantage of her surprise night off from parental responsibility to do a sleepover of her own. Lauren's sleepover was with Grace's half sister's birth father, Joost Holkenen. Joost lived in Hilversum.

The logistics protected Grace's innocence. Our daughter would be spending that night with Sofie's family in Amsterdam—they lived on a canal within walking distance of the Van Gogh Museum—and in a perfect world Grace would never know that her mother wasn't sleeping in their hotel room.

In that same perfect world I would never learn that Lauren wasn't sleeping in their hotel room, either.

Lauren's was an almost perfect plan in a world that I was grow-ing ever certain was tilted much more toward irony than it was to-ward perfection.

What had Sam said as we finished our beers on the roof of the West End Tavern before we'd left on our trips west? He'd said, "Fate abhors planning."

Got that right, Sammy.

My friend Diane drove Jonas and me to meet the air ambulance.

We watched the jet land. Jonas got a chance to spend a few min-utes with Lauren. Grace and I had a brief chance to reconnect. She gave her brother a present—a T-shirt she'd picked out for him from a board store called TOMS Skateboardwinkel in Amsterdam. " '*Win-kel*' means shop in Dutch," she explained to him with a giggle. " 'Skateboard' means skateboard."

He loved the shirt. He was also a mature enough kid to recognize that what Grace had said about skateboards was pretty darn cute.

Diane drove away from the airport with the kids strapped into the backseat of her convertible. The top was down. The kids were waving. White cumulus clouds were billowing like cartoon balloons above the Rockies, highlighted against a sky the blue of blind hope. Diane would take the kids back to Spanish Hills and turn them over to Mona. Mona would keep an eye on them until I got home.

As the fog of crisis cleared, Lauren's medical condition was com-ing into sharper focus. She wasn't actually paralyzed. She was suffer-ing acute bilateral paraparesis—sudden profound weakness in both her legs—as the result of a new MS lesion on her spinal cord be-tween the second and third cervical vertebrae. The news was far from good, but it was better than the awful report I'd heard from Joost Holkenen.

I climbed into the ambulance after my wife's stretcher was secure. I could smell fear seeping from her pores.

"I'm relieved to see Jonas," she said. "I was so worried. Marty didn't put up a fight?"

"Even Marty could see that Jonas needed to come home. He has a lot of grieving to do."

"Yes," she said.

The EMT was young. She wore a lot of makeup. She was busy getting everything ready for the road.

"You must be scared," I said to Lauren.

"This is the worst yet for me," Lauren said.

I reminded myself that Lauren was talking about her illness. The worst exacerbation of her MS yet.

The EMT closed the ambulance doors. I was flooded with memories of The Mojave. I could feel my jawbones clench as I tried to corral my panic.

She fussed with the monitors. The ambulance started rolling.

I hadn't told Lauren about Tarzana or The Mojave.

"What does Larry think?" I asked as the ambulance turned onto Wadsworth. Larry Arbuthnot was Lauren's longtime neurologist.

Lauren said, "He says it's too soon to tell. We have to give the steroids a chance. He'll stop by tonight at the hospital. We'll talk about starting Tysabri."

Tysabri would be high-tech prophylaxis against the next exacerbation of MS. Solumedrol was treatment for this exacerbation of MS. If the steroids succeeded in reducing the inflammation on her spinal cord, Lauren's paraparesis might wane, maybe even disappear. If it didn't?

Holy shit. "You've had one day of Solumedrol so far?" I asked.

"Two. Two more to go," she said.

I held her hand. We were quiet. It was not the natural silence of a couple that had been married for years, comforting each other during a time of crisis. It was dead time.

We were dropping into the Boulder Valley. Out the back window of the ambulance I could see the blunt southwest corner of Adrienne's house in Spanish Hills. While we were married, Merideth had often maintained that the original architect wanted to use that spot on the house for a dramatic turret and covered porch, but that the homesteaders had been too timid to build it. I'd always assumed that the unspoken point of Merideth's story was that I, too, would have been too timid to build the turret.

A quarter-mile flew by while I tried to find a contemporary parable there. Failed.

As the ambulance neared the crest of the scenic overlook south of our Spanish Hills home, Lauren said, "I'm sorry."

The EMT flashed a glance at me. When she caught my eye, she looked away. I wondered what version of the truth she'd heard.

I tasted Lauren's words. Was she sorry? About her exacerbation? Certainly. About hurting me? Maybe. I would give her that one. But about what she'd done with Joost?

Was I sorry about what had happened with Ottavia and Amy? Not really. Was I in any frame of mind to make a judgment about the nature of Lauren's regret? I wasn't. Whatever had happened between Lauren and Joost in Hilversum wasn't the worst thing that had happened lately. Not even close.

I chose to cast away my doubts about the veracity of Lauren's sorrow. "I don't think now is the time to talk about it," I said to her. *Not in front of this stranger.* "Later."

"I didn't plan it this way," she said, reeling the damn issue back in. Lauren seemed inured to the presence of the EMT inches from her side. I reminded myself that she'd spent more than two days in the constant company of caretaking strangers. She had grown accustomed.

I pondered what it was she didn't plan. *The getting caught part? The getting paralyzed part? Or the screwing Joost in Hilversum part?*

I was pretty sure she had planned the getting from Amsterdam to Hilversum part.

I said nothing, assuming whatever I'd say would be the wrong thing. I cast the problem away, again. Hoped an upslope would catch it, carry it even farther into the distance. Perhaps all the way across the Divide.

Lauren's throat was dry. Her voice cracked as she said, "I didn't know I would see Joost when I was there. It was a complete surprise when he called me. Sofie's family told him we were in Holland. He wasn't part of this. I didn't reach out . . . to him. I hadn't talked to him in . . . forever."

Joost wasn't the issue for me. On the phone he hadn't sounded like a man who was in love with my wife. He had sounded like a decent enough guy trapped smack in the middle of one of the most complicated one-night stands in Dutch history. I thought he had performed the last act of his unsavory role with surprising dignity.

"I can't wait to hear about Sofie," I said. I meant it. I had a stepdaughter. That was a revelation. My daughter had a half sister. I thought that was wonderful for her. Grace had gained two new siblings in less than half a year. "I hope I can meet her someday," I said, squeezing Lauren's hand.

Lauren finally got the message. She didn't reel Joost back in that time. "Sofie wants to come and visit," Lauren said. "Maybe in a year or two, she thought. When she's a little older. She's great, Alan. A terrific kid. She speaks four languages."

"I'd love for her to visit," I said.

"She's taller than me already. Her hair is dark," Lauren said. "She has my eyes."

My imagination sketched a picture of her while my eyes locked on the Foothills park-and-ride through the back window.

Lauren said, "I don't want you to stay with me because I'm sick. I couldn't stand that."

Was the staying or the going up to me? I didn't know. I did know that I was so far from approaching that particular intersection that I would have to go rent a car from Hertz and power up the GPS so I could ask Chloe for directions on how to locate it.

I was in no hurry to get there. I turned toward Lauren. "I'm not with you because you're sick today," I said. "I won't be with you because you're sick tomorrow. Let's talk about it later. For now, just focus on getting better."

I had already been pondering and re-pondering how much difference there was—really—between what I had done with Ottavia and Amy and what Lauren had done with Joost.

Did it matter that I didn't sleep with either the alluring Ottavia or the beguiling Amy? Did it matter whether Lauren did sleep with Joost?

She hadn't said what happened with him before the exacerbation felled her. I hadn't asked. One moment, I thought it made all the difference in the world.

The next moment, I thought it made no difference at all.

If someone posted clips of the events on YouTube, I could ask Merideth to get her tech guy to clean up the video and enhance the audio so we could all have a clearer version of the past.

A version that contained some hints about our future.

Maybe that would help.

Or maybe not.

I was feeling hopeful, either way.

Sixty-six

Once she was settled into her room at Community Hospital—her bed had a view of a corner of North Boulder Park and of one of the curious hogbacks that form the first vault of the foothills of the Rockies—I told Lauren about L.A.

Tarzana, The Mojave. The Camry, the ambulance, the helicopter. The concussion.

I left out little. But I left out some.

It was the first time I'd told the story in a single sitting.

It exhausted me.

Her, too.

Lauren and I had talked about her, and about me, and about the kids—all three of the kids. The time had come to talk about us.

She started. "What now, Alan?" she asked.

I didn't know.

After only a few seconds of silence Lauren said something about letting the dust settle. I agreed that was probably wise.

I left her flat on her back in her hospital bed. I headed home to be with Grace and Jonas and the dogs.

The cab driver took Valmont east. I would've taken Broadway south and then picked up South Boulder Road. I thought of Chloe. Wondered what route she would have chosen. It didn't matter. We would all end up in the same place.

Sam called as the cab veered onto Foothills.

His "Hey" soothed me.

"You back in town?" I asked.

"Not exactly," he said.

I heard something buried in his words. "That detour?" I asked.

"You could say that."

"Too bad. I was hoping I could buy you a beer at the West End. I have a lot to tell you," I said.

"Won't be happening. I'm staying in California for . . . now."

He paused. I said, "Yeah?" yearning for more. He didn't respond right away. I added, "The Grand Canyon thing? Something new?"

"No. That's all done." He gave me a concise update about Lisa and the baby. Oden and Jaana. The dead girlfriend from Estonia. Kanyn.

I asked a couple of questions. He answered them.

Two seconds of silence. Then he said, "Carmen's pregnant."

"What?"

In a tone as flat as a groomed run below an overcast sky, he said, "You heard me."

His admonition was spot-on. My question had been reflexive.

He inhaled and exhaled. I did the arithmetic. Yes, it was possible.

"Are you—" I said. "Is it—"

"It's my baby."

More cleavage. I thought of my molecular biology teacher in college. *The other kind.* "Cleavage is division," she'd said during that first lecture. "A split from one into two."

From a couple to two singles.

From parent/child together, to father-daughter apart.

From an ancient grand mesa, to two plateaus separated by a canyon.

From a zygote to a blastocyst.

Sam had said that separation wasn't always about cataclysm, that sometimes it was about erosion.

It isn't always about ending, either, I thought. Sometimes it's about evolving. Other times, it's about beginning.

Conversationally, it was my move. I took a stab at guessing Sam's feelings about the current cleavage. I said, "Congratulations, Sam. You're going to be a daddy again."

His voice brightened. He said, "Thank you."

"You and Carmen? You're . . . ?"

"We're going to work at it. Yeah, we're working at it." He paused. "How about you? How're you doing?"

"Good," I said. "It's good to be home."

Sam's question hadn't been merely polite. My reply hadn't been merely banal.

Despite the cyclones spinning on my flanks, I'd meant what I said. I was doing good. It was great to be home.

I was wondering where to start with Sam. Lauren's illness? Jonas's meltdown? Amy number two? Joost?

For some insane reason I felt confident I could deal with all of those.

I started elsewhere. I said, "I have a new kid too, Sam. A teenage stepdaughter. In Holland. Her name is Sofie."

He laughed. "Hot damn," he said. "There you go."

Sixty-seven

Epilogue

His Ex

Eric didn't get that job he coveted. The next election cycle would somehow go on without his guidance. He returned to Columbia to teach.

It turned out I liked having him around more often. I was so relieved.

After the rescue in The Mojave, the Grand Canyon episode finally became news. A true-life tale of guns blazing in the desert sun proved titillating enough to give my colleagues in the media, especially those on cable, a reason to discover they actually did care about what had happened to Jaana Peet. Before the first week was out, the events in The Mojave were being hyped in a promo titled "High Noon in Death Valley." Every newsmagazine but mine did a long segment on some aspect of the story.

Truth, of course, got transplanted along with the saguaro cacti the graphics departments felt compelled to include in the art. Joshua trees just didn't cut it. The confrontation hadn't been quite at noon, and it hadn't been quite in Death Valley. But the details were close enough to the truth for today's fourth estate. I'm not pointing fingers. If I had produced a story on the shootout, I would have committed some—hopefully more imaginative—version of the same sins.

The exhaustive coverage meant notoriety for my new husband. Notoriety, as he suspected it would be, was toxic for him.

All the attention meant notoriety for my ex-husband, too. Alan refused to cooperate with the media. He gave interviews to no one.

I didn't ask. He would have turned me down too.

I knew from experience that Alan was a tough get.

Lincoln Oden had covered his tracks well. Despite an army of investigators, the details about his crimes developed slowly. It took a few weeks for the authorities and the media to sketch out a timeline of what Oden had done.

Some things became clear before others. The son Oden had been raising as his own was in fact the child of Jaana Peet and Nicholas Paulson. Social Services took custody of the boy days after Oden's death. Paulson's attorneys in Las Vegas had weighed in since, as had Jaana Peet's family in Estonia. The ultimate determination of the boy's future promised to look something like the scrums that follow a hundred-dollar bill dropped into a crowd.

A solitary neighbor identified Oden and Jaana as the couple who had been living together on an isolated ranch outside Kingman, Arizona, during the final months of her pregnancy. The landlord confirmed he'd rented the place to Oden, but he knew nothing about any woman who lived there. Oden had terminated his month-to-month lease just around the time the child was born.

Jaana Peet had not been seen since the move. Jaana's friend from Estonia—the blackjack dealer from Laughlin—walked away from her seemingly settled life the same week that Oden moved from the Kingman home.

Based on what Alan had heard from Oden's lips, the police suspected that years earlier Oden had driven the two young women—Jaana and her friend—to some desert wasteland in Arizona or California. Oden had killed the women and left their bodies for the scavengers and buzzards. The dry desert climate is kind to skeletons, and experts hired by the networks weren't ruling out the possibility that someone would stumble across the girls' bones.

Oden's next stop after leaving Kingman, Arizona, with Jaana's baby was California. His neighbors in Fontana, outside of L.A., said he was a single father when he arrived in town with his infant son. He was an insurance agent. A Good-Hands guy. A devoted father.

He'd married a woman from Mexico a couple of years after moving to town.

Everyone who knew Oden in Fontana was surprised that he had ended up facedown on that two-lane desert road in The Mojave.

Everyone who knew him in Fontana was surprised that he had ended up on the evening news.

The neighbors are always surprised.

Except when they knew it all along.

Lisa lost the baby. My baby. Our baby. The dehydration she'd suffered in the desert in the trunk of the car was too much for my fragile fetus.

But Lisa survived.

Eric and I reached out to her every way we could, but she wouldn't speak to us. Neither would Stevie. Eric prays about it a lot.

I wish Lisa well.

Eric and I canceled our big fall wedding in the renovated ballroom at the Plaza.

We took that week off from work, flew to Molokai, and were married in a traditional Hawaiian ceremony overlooking the vastness of the Pacific. Our witnesses were Eric's God, three Molokai natives, and the tropical sky.

We repeated our vows two weeks later in front of a dozen people at Eric's church.

I didn't invite Alan. I didn't invite my shrink. And I didn't invite the Bitch.

* * *

We had some frozen embryos left.

We were close to deciding whether to adopt or try to find another surrogate.

To me, each option felt fraught with peril.

Eric was more sanguine. He was praying on it. I was cool with that.

No matter what we decided, I was one hundred percent sure I was ready to be a mom.

Acknowledgments

Among the ways I've been fortunate in this business—since fate, with an assist from Patricia Limerick, initially led me to Al Silverman's door—is that I've been blessed with the wisdom and guidance of old-school editors. For the past few books, including this one, I've been in the skilled editorial hands of Brian Tart. My admiration for him became even greater as his patience, focus, and determination helped me maintain my vision on this project. Brian, I'm most grateful.

Kelly Mills nurtured the inspiration for this story, answered many questions, and pointed me toward an important reference. I gratefully acknowledge the background information I learned from *Over the Edge: Death in Grand Canyon*, by Michael P. Ghiglieri and Thomas M. Myers. Their book is a fascinating compendium of the myriad ways visitors to the canyon have ended their visits without ever leaving.

I would also like to acknowledge the memory of Peter Ossorio. Over thirty years after I sat in his classroom I find myself surprised by how many of his lessons have stayed with me. I can only imagine what his impact would have been had I been capable of understanding more than ten percent of what he was trying to teach me.

Jane Davis and Elyse Morgan were, again, invaluable in helping to sharpen early drafts. I thank them. I also thank my anonymous copy editor. No other role in the process of turning a manuscript into a book is less heralded than that of the copy editor, but few people have more of an impact on the ultimate pleasure of the reading experience.

My gratitude goes out to Robert Barnett for his calm, astute guidance and counsel.

And to my family, my most profound thanks.

About the Author

Stephen White is a clinical psychologist and *New York Times* best-selling author of fifteen previous suspense novels, including *Kill Me* and *Dry Ice*. He lives in Colorado.

For more information, please visit www.authorstephenwhite.com